BELOW THE DECK

NIKKI ALLEN

PAN BOOKS

First published 2026 by Pan Books
an imprint of Pan Macmillan
The Smithson, 6 Briset Street, London EC1M 5NR
EU representative: Macmillan Publishers Ireland Ltd, 1st Floor,
The Liffey Trust Centre, 117–126 Sheriff Street Upper,
Dublin 1 D01 YC43
Associated companies throughout the world

ISBN 978-1-0350-7200-2

1 3 5 7 9 8 6 4 2

A CIP catalogue record for this book is available from the British Library.

Illustrations © perfectart99/Shutterstock

Typeset in Sabon MT Std by Palimpsest Book Production Limited, Falkirk, Stirlingshire
Printed and bound in the UK using 100% Renewable Electricity by CPI Group (UK) Ltd

Visit **www.panmacmillan.com** to read more
about all our books and to buy them.

Praise for Nikki Allen

'A brilliant, twisty thriller that makes you want to shout warnings out aloud to the characters! I was gripped'
Peter James, author of the bestselling Roy Grace series

'A tense, atmospheric thriller packed with dark secrets, simmering desires and bitter grudges . . . I couldn't put it down!'
T. J. Emerson, bestselling author of *The Last Mrs Sinclair*

'A cleverly written journey into the dark reaches of deception and misogyny. It's a trip that you won't forget'
Chris Bridges, McDermid Debut Award-shortlisted author of *Sick to Death*

'I couldn't wait to keep reading this . . . A destination thriller with something to say!'
Kingsley Pearson, prize-winning author of *Flat 401*

'An accomplished white-knuckle ride from start to finish'
Kate Riordan, author of Richard and Judy Book Club pick *The Heatwave*

'I gobbled this up in two days . . . An absolute must-read for your summer – Nikki Allen is one to watch'
Sarah Goodwin, bestselling author of *The Yacht*

'Captivating . . . The perfect destination thriller to lose yourself in this summer'
Natasha Boydell, bestselling author of *The Fortune Teller*

'Exhilarating'
Prima magazine

ABOUT THE AUTHOR

Nikki is a former journalist and copywriter, and a qualified therapist. A voracious reader, Nikki was inspired to write her debut novel *The Hideaway* after reading true stories of people disappearing in the Costa Rican rainforest. Nikki was born in Holland, grew up the only Jewish kid in her Worcestershire village, and now lives in North London with her family. *Below The Deck* is her second novel.

For my sister, who would murder for me.

(After carefully weighing up the options and deciding this and only this course of action was appropriate under the circumstances.)

PROLOGUE

10 JUNE

It is dark and quiet on the spiral staircase leading her towards the yacht's underbelly. There are no bright lights from above to guide her down the steps below deck: only low, muted beams from the emergency floor panels guide her path. No peals of laughter or quieter chatter reach her ears from the decks above.

This feels wrong.

The urge to flee the boat and everyone on it rises, hot and desperate. She needs to get back to the safety of her cabin.

She is halfway down the staircase when she hears it. A thud; then, as she reaches the bottom of the steps and begins to creep along the dim passageway, a low, strangled moan.

It is coming from somewhere close by. It's reaching her through the door in front of her with its rectangular gold nameplate that reads: *Master Stateroom.*

She switches on the torch on her phone and holds it up as she steps towards the door and touches the handle. The door opens without effort. She walks inside to this, the largest of the cabins: a luxurious suite with thick carpet, a king-sized bed, a sofa adorned with fat cushions.

Everything is as it should be.

Everything except for that godawful noise.

It's coming from the en-suite bathroom. And it's louder now, the sound, as her feet walk her closer.

She reaches the bathroom door, pushes it open, looks inside, and . . .

There he is. The man she both despises and is desperate for.

His back is facing her; he doesn't know she's there. He hasn't heard her yet, and he can't see her in the gloom. She hides the torch behind her back and stands frozen for a heart-beat, then her mind leaps into action: she has to do something, she needs to stop him – *now*. She creeps back into the cabin to grab at something – anything – she can use to arm herself; then she moves back towards the bathroom, raises her weapon high.

She falters. Now that she is here, so near him, she is full of dread that his gaze might fix her one last time – that he might catch sight of her at this exact moment, saying *you'll never be free of me, never* – that he might reach for her, try to clasp thick fingers around her neck and drag her with him to hell, to wherever she hopes he will soon be going.

Please don't let him see me, please don't let him see me, please don't let him—

She breathes too loudly.

He swivels to face her.

ELENI

7 JUNE

Eleni pushed her shades back onto the crown of her head and waited for her eyes to adjust to the fierce South Pacific sun. The *Lusso di Mare* shimmered in front of her, glints of sunlight reflecting from its gleaming hull, its dazzling white a striking contrast to the vivid turquoise-blue of the ocean's surface.

'Holy shit!' she blurted, then clamped a hand to her mouth. *Remember where you are – and who you're with.*

This superyacht was the location of Ashworth Property Partners' famous incentive scheme for 2026. It was one of her favourite things about the firm she'd worked at for more than eight years now: instead of handing out annual bonuses, the three top performers across the company won a luxury trip to a glamorous destination. She could recall the words in the email they'd received six months ago from their CEO, Rory, like she'd read them yesterday: *I am thrilled to announce that the three top performers from across the business will come sailing with me on a stunning superyacht around French Polynesia next June . . .*

'Meets your standards, does it?' said Rory, giving her a wink.

Eleni grimaced. 'Of course,' she replied. 'Sorry, I can't help myself sometimes. This is just . . . incredible!'

'Glad to hear it. Nothing's too good for our top land-buying lady, isn't that right?' he said, reaching over to give Eleni a pat on the shoulder.

Eleni dug out her phone and, giggling like a schoolgirl, started snapping photos. Running along the superyacht's pearl white hull was a sleek, champagne-gold strip at the waterline, which tapered off at the front – the *bow*. It had four decks – the lower one sitting below the ocean's surface, then three above it, all the same pure white with gold trim.

She glanced at her five companions for the next few days – the people she'd be casually *hanging out on a superyacht* with – in addition to her husband, Nick. With just under two hundred employees at Ashworth, she didn't know the others – except Rory – that well. Eleni barely socialized with her colleagues – she hardly saw her *actual* friends these days, not for lack of trying. There was just never a good time.

Rory wiped the sweat from his balding temples and waved the collar of his salmon pink polo shirt back and forth in the fierce heat. He was smiling from ear to ear and trying to catch everyone else's eyes, bursting with pride. His company had paid for this – he'd made this happen. *The hero of the day.*

Talia, his wife, stood next to him, right hand resting in the crook of Rory's elbow, Gucci sunglasses covering half her face, long black hair set in bouncy curls that settled around her shoulders. She wore an elegant cream jumpsuit that Eleni couldn't believe had just survived a twenty-hour journey, even in business class. At Eleni's murmur of profanity, Talia had lifted her shades and raised her eyebrows in her direction; there was a slight scrunch to her nose.

Inwardly, Eleni reprimanded herself. She really didn't want to get on the wrong side of Talia; her plans for this week involved getting as close to both her boss and his wife as she possibly could. Champagne-infused evenings, relaxed chit-chat, the opportunity to all get to know each other better – she couldn't botch things up by allowing her messy internal monologue to reach Rory's and Talia's ears.

Eleni's colleague Sam, who'd also won a place, stood a little way from the others, one hand stroking his neat brown beard, the other shoved into the pocket of his combat shorts. Turning to face her, his bright blue eyes caught Eleni's and he grinned: 'Well, I'm with you, Eleni,' he said. 'This yacht is deadly.'

Eleni laughed. Sam seemed all right, from what she knew of him – they usually had a chat when they were in the office on the same days, catching up about clients over coffee. He was a considerate guy – always taking an interest in how Eleni was, how work was going. Sam and Nick had a laugh on the flight over, too – mainly sports related. He was alone: the only colleague from Ashworth here without a plus one. Eleni was curious as to whether there was a backstory to that, but hadn't found the right time to ask.

Then there was their third winner, Lucy – quiet, socially awkward, mousey-haired Lucy, here with her equally quiet and awkward-seeming partner Mark, who stood about a foot taller than his girlfriend. 'Yes, it's very nice,' she said flatly. *Jesus, could she sound any less enthusiastic?*

Eleni had to be honest: she was baffled when she learned

Lucy had won a place – she'd only started at Ashworth that year, and she worked in the finance department, in *data analysis*. Usually, it was the people like them – Sam in residential sales, Eleni in land acquisitions – who got the visible success it took to win the bonus. But Lucy was a whizz with numbers: apparently her scrutiny was quietly making – and saving – the company millions.

Eleni watched as Lucy twiddled with her wavy brown hair, bobbing up and down on her heels. *Does she even want to be here?* Then she started as a hand landed on her shoulder – she'd almost forgotten Nick was standing next to her. As she looked up at his chiselled, handsome face, his olive skin glowing in the sun, and into his deep-set, dark eyes, she felt the familiar rush of breathless adrenaline.

'This is something else, Els. Can't believe we're about to get on that boat,' he murmured. 'Some proper time, me and you – it'll be just like the old days, before the kids.'

Eleni could only nod in reply. If it *was* just like the old days – a return to the time before her children, and her demanding career, and the daily grind of her life – she could be her old self again, maybe. She wondered whether the old Eleni was waiting there patiently, ready to rise up from under the surface – bubbly, enthusiastic, full of wonder. *I like that idea.*

From the yacht, a tall, muscular woman in her fifties with chin-length blonde hair waved to the group, beckoning them up the sleek white and gold ramp leading to the boat's main deck. Perhaps this was a stewardess, ready to greet them. They strolled towards the yacht, Nick's hand in Eleni's. Rory and Talia headed up the gangway first, then Sam; Nick and Eleni followed, with Lucy and Mark at the rear. A crew of seven people – three men and four women – was lined up under the awning covering the outside space, waiting for them in neatly pressed white shirts and trousers with golden stripes pinned to the shoulders.

'Good morning, everyone,' said the woman who'd waved to them; she was standing at the front of the line. 'I'm Captain Sophie Taylor.'

Captain? Eleni caught herself before she let her snap judgement form any further – she hadn't been expecting a female captain, but then – why on earth not? There were plenty of women in male-dominated industries – she was one of them herself; the property development field remained robustly led by straight white men, even now. She chuckled – if anything, having a female captain made sense. Rory had probably sought her out intentionally as part of his focus on equality and diversity. She could just imagine him: *Equal opportunities are at the heart of the business. Inclusion is our top value here at Ashworth . . .*

'Welcome to the *Lusso di Mare*,' said Captain Taylor. Her accent was Australian – or maybe New Zealand, Eleni wasn't quite sure. 'I'm delighted that you're here to join me for our cruise of the Society Islands. Are you all happy to remove your shoes before you step onto the deck, please?' The group did as she asked, placing their shoes in a tidy row next to the entrance ramp. 'Thank you. We stay barefoot on the yacht to protect the floor out here, and the interior,' explained the captain. 'Now, let me introduce you to the crew who'll be taking care of you and keeping you all safe for the next few days.'

The guests turned towards the crew, Rory making his way down the line first – *naturally* – introducing himself, with Talia behind him. Eleni went next.

'I'm Brett, the first officer on board,' said the broad, smooth-looking man standing first in line next to the captain, holding out a hand for her to shake. He was in his late twenties, clean-shaven, with a crew cut, the whitest teeth Eleni had ever seen, and an American accent.

Next in the row was a woman who looked younger than Eleni – late twenties, maybe – very pretty, with a freckled button nose and reddish-brown hair in a tight ponytail – who shook her hand warmly as she reached her along the line of crew.

'Welcome aboard, Eleni!' she said. *She already knows my name . . . how cool is that? We're all VIPs for the week.* 'I'm Michaela, your chief stewardess on board the *Lusso di Mare*.' Eleni detected a hint of Essex in her inflection.

'Here, these are for you.' Michaela placed a *lei* of white flowers around Eleni's neck, then reached to the tray that the woman standing next to her was holding, and pressed a cool glass of champagne into her hands.

'Thank you so much,' Eleni beamed. 'I'm so excited to be here.' She took a long sip, savouring the fizz of bubbles on her tongue. Next came Michaela's second stewardess – a young, petite, olive-skinned brunette who introduced herself as Johanna; then their chef, a Polynesian woman in her forties who said her name was Leilani. Finally, they met their bosun – a stocky, bearded Australian guy called Noah, and a slight but muscular Tahitian deckhand, Kai.

Captain Taylor raised her glass to the group. 'Now, I'm going to make my final preparations before we cast off. I'll leave you in Michaela's capable hands for a tour of the *Lusso*.'

As the captain headed up the stairs, Eleni took another sip of champagne and marvelled at the main deck. She wanted to tattoo this image on her retinas. She'd never board a superyacht or go somewhere like French Polynesia again, would she? Their annual holidays were to the same house in Paphos, visiting their extended Greek Cypriot family. And she'd only seen yachts like this in gossip magazines – actors and models lounging on sun decks next to infinity pools, or diving off platforms into crystal clear seas. When she got back, her boys, Theo and Lucas, would want to know *exactly* what she'd done each day.

My boys. Eleni's throat tightened. She'd never been away from them before – not once in nine years, not even overnight, let alone for a week. *They'll be fine. They're with the world's best auntie and yiayia*. She'd be fine too – better than fine: four days on a superyacht, right now anchored at the marina in Papeete on the island of Tahiti. And her plans for while she was here were going to make life so much better – for Eleni, and her family too.

As her eyes roamed the walls and floor, something caught her attention on the gleaming oak surface of the bow's deck beneath her feet: a hairline crack in one of the boards, running along the edge of the dining table underneath the awning. Someone had done a hasty fix-up job on it, smoothing on another coat of glossy brown varnish rather than filling it properly. She could still see the fracture underneath; the surface looked slightly sticky. She noticed too as she stood there, mixed with the scent of the briny sea air, the faint smell of varnish.

They must have literally just painted over it. Eleni smiled. *It might look perfect, but even superyachts have cracks under the surface.*

It was comforting, somehow. She knew what that was like: to seem as though she had everything together, but to be quietly fracturing beneath the facade. If anyone looked at her life on paper, they'd think she had everything: the handsome husband, the two gorgeous kids, the career success, the beautiful suburban home, the expensive haircut . . .

She scanned her fellow passengers: Rory, the mega-rich CEO of a thriving business and his poised, elegant wife. Sam, the charming sales superstar from Dublin, liked by everyone. Lucy, the young financial prodigy and her keen-eyed journalist boyfriend.

Appearances could be so deceiving. Perhaps that was the case for them all.

LUCY

'Let's take the grand tour, shall we?'

Maybe it was the jet lag, but Lucy felt exhausted just listening to Michaela trill every word with the energy of a children's TV presenter. *Surely no one's always this enthusiastic?*

The stewardess picked up a pile of cream envelopes from the dining table underneath the awning and handed them out. Lucy's name was written in immaculate gold handwriting; she stifled a smirk at the thought of trying to pen something so neatly herself. Her own attempt would look like it'd been written by a pre-schooler.

'First, here are your welcome packs, with your cabin key cards inside as well as lots of useful information about the *Lusso* and your charter,' Michaela chirruped. 'As I mentioned, I'm your chief stewardess, so if there's anything you need – any request, big or small – please do ask away!' Without meaning to, Lucy met her eyes; Michaela beamed at her and Lucy felt the usual flush of ineptitude that crept over her whenever she made eye contact with someone she didn't know.

'Thanks,' she said, then stared intently at the floor.

'Of course! Now, let's get to know your new home! At thirty-four metres long, with four decks and living space for eight guests, the *Lusso di Mare* is a classic ship built to a modern Italian design. We'll explore the outer decks first, then head inside.' The group followed her through a central passageway to the rear – *no, the stern*, Lucy corrected herself – of the main deck.

'Here we have the first of our two hot tubs and relaxation areas,' said Michaela, sweeping her hand across the space.

Mark leaned down to whisper in her ear: 'Two hot tubs? This boat is mad, Luce.' She nodded, looking up and into his face – the edges of his grey eyes crinkling as he grinned; the ginger flecks in his beard that appeared more orange under the blazing sun – and gave him a smile that she knew didn't reach her eyes. Yes, it was incredible here – and my God, she needed the break. But she couldn't help it: she felt awkward. All this attention on them, all the fuss. The VIP treatment.

Most people seemed to love that stuff. But then again, Lucy wasn't most people.

'On the extendable swim platform,' Michaela pointed to a flat area of the deck, 'you can jump right into the sea. And in the garage here, we've got jet skis, paddleboards and inflatables to keep you all entertained when we're at anchor.'

'Oh my God, this is going to be so much fun!' Eleni squealed, jumping up and down and clapping – before she seemed to catch herself abruptly and clear her throat, replacing her excited expression with a more muted look of pleasure. Nick laughed next to her, then reached over and wrapped an arm around his wife's shoulder.

Eleni was right to be thrilled, though: the yacht *was* incredible. Lucy looked up at Mark again. He looked happy, if a bit overwhelmed. The fanciest place they'd ever been together was a four-star hotel in Hertfordshire that Mark's parents had paid for after a family wedding. On his newspaper salary, and with all Lucy's money going straight out of her account before she could plan things like holidays, they could never afford a trip like this themselves. She started to reach for his hand, mirroring the affection of Eleni's husband – then pulled it back before he noticed.

They followed Michaela up a black spiral staircase with a polished gold handrail, and continued the tour: the upper deck with the bridge – the command centre for the captain – then one more level up, the sun deck, with another hot tub, a bar and reclining, double bed-sized loungers.

Then it was time to head back down to see the yacht's interior: the upper deck's 'sky lounge', with its L-shaped sofa and an enormous flat-screen TV in the centre of the wall. Down the spiral staircase to the salon on the main deck, with floor to ceiling windows on each side, two curved cream leather sofas dotted with blue and gold cushions set at one end of the room, the polished oak dining table at the other. It was all so . . . *pristine.*

'I'll be too worried about making a mess to ever sit down anywhere,' she whispered to Mark, who grinned in response.

Michaela pointed to one more staircase at the aft end of the salon, leading downwards. 'Below the deck, you'll find your cabins, including the master stateroom – your suitcases are already in your rooms. All the cabins have their own en-suite. You'll find the names of each of your rooms in your welcome packs, and you can explore them at your leisure.'

She paused as the first officer – Brett, Lucy remembered from that whirlwind of introductions – strode into the salon. 'Sorry to interrupt your tour,' he said. 'We're ready to cast off for the first stop on our charter, Opunohu Bay on Moorea. We'll be sailing for around two hours this morning to reach the island.'

Michaela nodded. 'During the sail, you'll enjoy a light lunch on board, prepared by the wonderful Leilani,' she said. 'Then when we're anchored at Moorea, you can go snorkelling and explore the stunning coral reef and marine life around the island. We'll come back to the yacht for games, dinner and cocktails under the stars on the main deck this evening.'

'Well, that all sounds perfect,' said Rory, beaming. The others nodded and murmured their thanks. Brett disappeared back up the stairs to the bridge; a moment later, the yacht's engine purred to life and they began to reverse slowly out of the marina.

Champagne glasses refilled by Johanna – though Lucy's was untouched; the bubbles made her queasy – the group headed back to the upper deck's outdoor lounge. They settled onto the soft cushioned benches lining the bow, their welcome packs resting on their knees, and watched as the vessel eased gently away from the marina, turned and began to sail out to sea.

'This is *so* amazing,' sighed Eleni, pouffing up her hair with her free hand. 'Still can't believe we're here – we're so lucky!'

'Indeed, it's marvellous. And it's quite right that you're here – you earned it, fair and square,' said Rory. 'And you, Lucy, of course – you girls are my right-hand women. Now, here's to a wonderful week.'

Lucy nodded. 'It's wonderful. Very pleased to be here too.' And she was, for the most part – she'd never imagined she'd win a place, even with her extraordinary skill as an analyst. That she'd been picked had come as a shock – though, of course, a welcome one. It meant she'd be well placed to do some digging this week – to shed some light on her burning questions.

Rory held his glass high, then leaned over to pat first Eleni and then Lucy on the thigh. Lucy moved her leg out of his reach, and sneaked a glance at Sam. Odd that he wasn't mentioned in Rory's little congratulatory speech; Lucy thought of *him* as Rory's right-hand man. And clearly Sam had noticed it too: his expression was gloomy as he stared out to sea. He usually looked so cheerful – a permanent grin on his face every day at work. It made Lucy suspicious, when people always seemed that happy. She could practically guarantee they'd be the ones with the most skeletons in their closets. At least Sam had just shown emotion that wasn't unabashed joy; that was reassuring.

'Now, who's joining me in the hot tub?' Rory was back on his feet, already stripping down to his trunks – bright blue Speedos that clung embarrassingly snugly. 'Come on, Talia – let's start this holiday as we mean to go on.'

His wife smiled her agreement. 'I'll just go down and get changed,' she said.

'Ooh, I'll be right in too,' said Eleni, then, along with her husband and Sam, she disappeared inside to find her cabin. By the time they'd gone, Rory had already jumped in the tub, champagne glass in hand.

'This is the life, eh? Come on in, Lucy – Mark! The water's lovely.'

'Ah, we'll be there in a bit,' said Lucy. The yacht had begun to pick up speed as it left the harbour, and a wave of nausea bubbled up her throat. *Oh no, am I going to throw up?* She got up and clutched at the smooth metal railing at the bow, leaned down and inhaled gulps of briny air.

A few seconds later, a hand – Mark's – touched the small of her back. She edged away. She hated people coddling her when she felt poorly – the only person's touch she'd been able to put up with was her mum's when Lucy was a kid. It was bad enough dealing with the nausea, knowing her skin had roughly the pallor of an elephant's arse, fighting against the rising tide of vomit, without someone else getting involved. Mark's hand moved away: *Message received.*

'Sorry, Luce,' he said. 'Just trying to help.'

'I know.' Lucy had suspected she might get seasick; she'd had to ask Mark to pull the car over so she could throw up more than once. But she'd never been on a boat before, except a flamingo-shaped pedalo at a London park one summer. She'd had no idea it would hit so fast: they'd barely left the marina. *Not a good start.* She searched for the horizon, trained her eyes to focus on it – that was supposed to help, wasn't it?

'Oh God, you're not seasick, are you?' It was Eleni, back on the deck and looking like a *Love Island* contestant, her honed figure on display in a bright green, halter-neck bikini, pink lip gloss freshly applied. Lucy's cheeks flushed under the withering gaze of her glowing, fresh-faced colleague. Everything about Eleni was so shiny: her honey-coloured highlights, her glossy pout, the shimmer of her contoured cheeks. *How does she still look so lovely after such a long journey?*

Lucy opened her mouth to reply, but Eleni had already strutted off towards the hot tub, giggling.

Michaela approached Lucy then, with a sympathetic tilt of her head.

'I'm sorry you're feeling unwell,' the stewardess said. She pressed a glass into Lucy's hand. 'It's tonic water – the quinine should help.'

'Thanks,' Lucy said weakly, accepting the drink and taking a small sip. Talia and Nick had now joined Eleni, Sam and Rory in the tub. Lucy caught the five of them glancing over at her – Rory's sharp hazel eyes hidden by faintly ridiculous aviator shades, but still she could feel them on her – then returning to their laugh-filled conversation.

'No problem,' Michaela said. 'Happens to the best of us.' Lucy smiled politely and took another sip. It was helping a little; the bubbles were giving her the satisfying urge to belch, and each time she did, the queasiness ebbed a notch at a time. She sighed with relief.

'We've got some anti-nausea tablets on board too, would you like one?' Michaela asked.

Lucy was about to say yes, when she caught Mark's eye; the note of warning in his expression. She leaned towards Michaela. 'Ah – thank you, but I can't. I'm on other medication. I'm not supposed to take anything else.'

'Of course,' Michaela replied. 'I'll let the captain know the situation. We can see if she's got any other ideas.'

'Shall we sit down?' suggested Mark as Michaela walked away. 'I wonder if we'll see any dolphins on our sail . . .'

'Actually,' Lucy cut him off, 'I think I'll go and have a look at our cabin. Unpack our stuff.' She did want to check out their room, but also the nausea was rising again – if she was going to throw up, she'd rather be on her own to do it.

'Good idea,' Mark said. 'I'll join you.'

Lucy chewed her lip. Considering her partner was an investigative journalist – that his entire career required him to be able to follow subtle clues and read between the lines – it amused her how often Mark failed to get the hint. 'I'll go on my own. You know I'm no company when I feel sick.'

A trace of disappointment passed across his features, but – to his credit – he didn't push her. He nodded. 'Hope you feel better in a bit,' he said.

Lucy picked up her welcome pack, then turned and took slow, careful steps along the upper deck towards the door, worried if she moved too fast the nausea would peak again. She opened the envelope and scanned to find the name of their cabin: *Sirena*. She snorted. Lucy couldn't feel less like a siren if she tried. She walked downstairs and through the salon to the stairs leading below deck: they were lined with plush cream carpet, but narrow, and she held on to the banister as she descended.

The passageway at the bottom of the stairs was cooler, and dark with all the cabin doors closed and the receding daylight from the salon above. She was about to reach for a switch, but motion sensors detected her movement and the corridor flooded with sudden brightness. She exhaled – it had only been a second in darkness, but down here, far from the others – was enough to make her spine tingle.

Lucy checked the names on the cabin doors: Sirena was the first one on the right. It was directly opposite the master stateroom – Rory and Talia's cabin. She made a mental note of that information for later, then dug a key card from the envelope in her hand, held it to the door, and it unlocked with a soft click. She pushed the door open – even the *swish* it made sounded expensive – and gasped with delight at the room inside. It was a million times posher than that hotel in Hertfordshire. Thick cream carpet that bounced under her feet; a large double bed with fat cushions arranged on top of the pillows; a proper dressing table with little lights around the mirror, like in the movies.

She strolled to the bed, pressed down on the mattress – the perfect amount of firmness – then climbed on and lay back on the pillows. Her mind wandered; she replayed the tour of the yacht, the stunning view of the ocean. *This is going to be a good week.* She deserved this trip and she meant to enjoy it, even if she'd brought more baggage with her than the world's biggest suitcase could fit in.

Because just look where she was – a luxurious superyacht in one of the most beautiful places on the planet. Lucy – shy, scared-of-everything Lucy – sailing around the South Pacific, when all her life she'd never been further than France. And everyday life was an unrelenting slog. This was a chance to escape it all, on a trip that couldn't feel more different to back home: squeezing onto packed Tube trains, staring at numbers from nine to five, picking up ready meals in Tesco on the way home . . .

The boat bobbed gently on the water; Lucy's eyelids drooped, heavy. She forced them open; it was a bad idea to fall asleep now, wasn't it? She'd never get to sleep tonight if she did, and the advice she'd read online said she should try to shift her body clock to Tahiti time as soon as she arrived, even if she was shattered.

But it was overwhelming, the tug towards sleep. *Maybe if*

I set an alarm, I could just nap for ten minutes. She barely managed to set the timer on her phone before her eyes drifted closed . . .

She floats, disembodied, towards the kitchen door. She doesn't want to go in there – something is hideously wrong in that room and she can't bear to be reminded of it. She feels crippling guilt about what's happening on the other side of this door; it never should have got to this point. The door creaks open, and she sees them: the people she loves most in the world – and then she sees the blood; so much blood. A desperate cry lodges deep in her throat. She tries to scream, but she can't. She can only watch them in paralysed silence, knowing that she's to blame for this; that this is her fault . . .

Beep-beep. Beep-beep.

Lucy lurched upright, yanked violently from her nightmare, her nausea now cloying with the horror of what she'd just relived in sleep. She ran to the bathroom, lifted the toilet seat and threw up until there was nothing left. She pushed the button to flush, washed her hands and splashed some water on her face, then sat on the edge of the bed and cried into her palms.

It's happening again.

If only the images from her dream could be flushed away as easily. But here they were, always with her, her own subconscious stalker. She'd travelled nearly ten thousand miles, but there was no distance between Lucy and her nightmares.

Even here – *especially* here – there would be no escape.

GENDARMERIE MARITIME DE POLYNÉSIE FRANÇAISE

CASE NUMBER: 247849

POLICE EXHIBIT ONE

Transcript of emergency call to Maritime Rescue Coordination Centre, Papeete, via VHF radio distress channel

10/06/2026 18:16

Operator: Tahiti Maritime Rescue. Please state your vessel and the nature of your emergency.

Caller: Mayday, mayday. This is Captain Sophie Taylor of the *Lusso di Mare*, charter vessel TPF-773. Current coordinates 16.54 degrees south, 151.25 degrees west, sailing towards Raiatea, approximately three nautical miles east of the island. <raised voices in background> We need immediate help! Police – air ambulance – coastguard . . . whoever can get to us most quickly. I think— oh God, I think it's too late.

Operator: Coordinates received. Please confirm, Captain: you are stating you have a serious injury on board? Is this correct?

Caller: Yes – one of the guests on this charter – I was just alerted to a commotion in the cabins. He's suffered a major stab wound to the neck area – quick, Brett, get the defibrillator . . . <shouting and audible sobbing in background>

Operator: Captain, has medical assistance been attempted?

Caller: Yes. Hold on one moment. We've tried to stem the bleeding, and I carried out CPR straight away. My first officer just got the defibrillator and we've . . . stand clear! <long pause, background shouting; words inaudible> No . . . he's – I think he's lost too much blood. He's stopped breathing. It's too late. The passenger is . . . deceased. <audible sobbing>

Operator: Your passenger is deceased? Hold on, I'm dispatching immediate aid. <pause> Captain, did you say this was a stabbing? Have you managed to restrain the person responsible?

Caller: Yes – yes, of course. We will restrain the suspect in my quarters immediately.

Operator: Understood. Captain, please stay on the line. <brief pause> Captain, can I confirm the name of your vessel? Did you say the *Lusso di Mare*?

Caller: <brief pause> I . . . yes. I did.

Operator: Ah . . . I see the air ambulance has already been called out to you in relation to—

Caller: Yes, they have – I know, I know they have! But we still need the police – we need help, urgently. This is a separate matter. I'm trying to follow protocol here, but these are exceptional circumstances . . . <heavy breathing>

Operator: Try to stay calm, Captain. I understand. We've already dispatched an air ambulance to your coordinates, and the Gendarmerie Maritime will arrive at the vessel by tender shortly. In the meantime, please ensure the safety of all guests and crew aboard. And please keep this channel open until we can reach you. Help is on the way.

[TRANSCRIPT ENDS]

SAM

Sam took a swig from his bottle of icy beer. *That's more like it.*

'*Sláinte*,' he said, raising the bottle to Johanna. He turned back to lean on the railing of the yacht's uppermost deck – the sun deck, where a few of them had headed after that dip in the heavenly hot tub – and gave a deep, satisfied sigh as he took in the view. Aquamarine blue sky, crystal-clear ocean as far as he could see, a smattering of similarly luxurious super-yachts sailing in nearby waters.

I could get used to this. He had to get some decent pics for his socials; his mates back home would lose their shit when they saw this. And Claire – she still followed him on Instagram, didn't she? She'd be bound to see them.

Looking down into the moving water, he felt light-headed. Or was it the thought of Claire? It couldn't be vertigo – he wasn't *that* high up.

The boat was impressive, though – somehow, on the drive to Papeete from the airport, as they'd spotted the *Lusso* at the marina from the darkened windows of their chauffeured Merc, the yacht hadn't looked all that big. Sleek and smooth with its white and gold exterior, it had looked neat; compact, somehow. If he was honest, he'd wondered how it could house eight people plus a crew comfortably for several days.

Seven people – not eight. His chest tightened at his mistake – he'd forgotten, for a second, that he was supposed to be here with his girlfriend, and wasn't. *And meanwhile, the man who's to blame for Claire dumping me – he's here, isn't he?* He gave his head a shake and necked the rest of his beer; maybe he just needed another drink.

Sam turned to look around at his companions on the sun deck. Rory and Talia were down in their cabin unpacking – Sam hadn't bothered; he'd just shoved his suitcase under his bed and come outside – but the other four were up here with him. Lazing on a double sun lounger were Eleni and her husband, Nick. She'd tucked her legs up underneath her and was resting her head on Nick's shoulder; his hand rested protectively on her upper thigh. They were an unreasonably good-looking pair – probably in their early thirties, a couple of years younger than him. Eleni was all highlights and toned upper arms; Nick had the physique of a man who got to the gym at least five times a week.

Don't they have young kids? And isn't he a sergeant in the Met? How does he even have time for a daily workout?

He'd made some small talk with Nick as they waited in the lounge at Heathrow to board their first flight – decent fella, and an Arsenal supporter too – Sam's adopted team in England, though nothing compared to his beloved Bohemian FC back home in Dublin. Sam remembered now that Nick had said he actually *played* football – maybe that helped with the six-pack. Watching them now, curled into each other, Sam felt a flash of envy, and the hot sucker punch of hurt and anger: *he* should be soaking up this trip of a lifetime with someone else. Instead, he was here alone.

He tried to brush the thought away again. Maybe this trip would distract Sam from his heartbreak and help him get to know his workmates properly, without the distractions of meetings and calls. He'd sat next to Eleni enough times in their open-plan office near Great Portland Street since she'd joined Ashworth, but he'd barely had a conversation with her that wasn't to do with clients. Hopefully, this week would change that.

Then there was Lucy. She'd just come up to the sun deck and sat on a lounger, looking ashen, sipping a drink and twiddling with her hair. Her bloke Mark – who Sam had learned was an investigative journalist on a decent-sized paper; he'd have to chat to him, he'd always been fascinated by how they got their scoops – was lying next to her, snoozing. Lucy seemed nice enough, but it confused Sam that she'd got a place on this trip.

With Sam and Eleni, it was a no-brainer: they'd earned their places. Sam had worked his arse off to win a spot this year – his effort on the Rosenberg account; those late nights schmoozing with buy-to-let investors; the emails back and forth with commercial occupiers and the fecking local councils. Sure, there was some fortunate timing involved that he couldn't have anticipated – but nothing else about it was luck. It was hard graft, and dedication, and *relationship management* and learning the right things to say to people to win them over.

As for Eleni – well, he knew she'd managed to beat off a

bunch of top developer rivals to acquire a prime London heritage site. Lucy, though – Sam couldn't work it out. She'd only joined a few months back, and she worked in *data analysis*, for fuck's sake. She was smart, no doubt, and she'd impressed Rory. She could work out wildly complicated growth ratios instantly in her head, sums that most people would never manage without a calculator.

But clever didn't always translate to capable, did it? And it worked the other way around: you didn't have to be book smart, or get a first-class degree – or even a degree at all – to do well in life. *I'm living proof of that.*

Sam looked up as Michaela appeared at the top of the stairwell. 'We're ready to serve lunch,' she said. 'Would you all like to come down?'

'Yes! I'm starving,' said Nick.

'Me too – I'm dying to try Leilani's food,' Eleni replied, as the five of them followed the chef down two flights of steps to the main deck, and to the table under the awning, where Rory and Talia were already sitting.

'Leilani has made you a crab and lobster salad to start, then fresh monkfish in a creamy coconut sauce,' said Michaela. 'She's also prepared some crusty bread and crackers for anyone who'd prefer something simpler.' Sam saw Lucy smile gratefully. 'More champagne, anyone?'

Sam's mouth watered. He took the empty seat next to Talia – Rory had taken the spot at the head of the table, naturally – and tucked into his food, which was every bit as delicious as Michaela had made it sound. Between mouthfuls, he turned to Talia. 'What do you think of the *Lusso* so far, then?'

Talia was wearing a wide-brimmed hat that hid almost her

entire face; Sam couldn't make out much of her expression. But she seemed distracted, that much he could tell: she was picking at her food and her long, French-manicured nails had chips around the edges, with some of the white at the tips peeling off.

'It's wonderful,' she said. 'Although,' she lowered her voice to add, 'I'm not a huge fan of crab, to be honest.'

Sam grinned. 'I won't tell our chef. I promise.' He mimed zipping his lips closed, and that, at least, got a more genuine look of pleasure. *Wow, I forgot how stunning Talia is when she smiles.*

'But you're enjoying it so far?' Sam persisted. 'Your husband puts on the most amazing bonus trips.' He nodded in Rory's direction.

Talia nodded. 'He's quite literally pushed the boat out this year.' She smiled, reached a hand towards her husband and patted his arm; Rory stopped his conversation with Nick and turned to listen. 'It's marvellous,' Talia went on. Then she gave Sam a wry look. 'You did extremely well to get a place. You should be very proud.'

Sam felt a flicker of unease. *Why did she say it like that? Doesn't she think I deserve to be here?* He swallowed. *Best to get off the subject of Ashworth.*

'Ah, thanks – we all should be,' he said smoothly, gesturing to Lucy and Eleni. 'But yeah, I put a lot of effort in this year. And it's so good to have a breather from work for a few days, honestly.'

'Oh goodness, yes. I was ready for some time off myself.'

'Time off?' Lucy said. 'From *what*?'

Sam's eyebrows shot upwards. Was Lucy making a dig at

Talia – here, in front of everyone, on day one of the trip? It was a bold move, if so. Surprisingly bold.

Talia cocked her head to one side. 'From work,' she said flatly. 'Why – did you assume I don't have a job?'

Lucy shook her head; she looked genuinely baffled. 'No – not at all. I'm sorry. I wasn't assuming anything. I didn't mean it to sound like that.'

'Ha!' Rory guffawed. 'Lucy thought you were one of those bored, desperate housewives putting on luncheon for the ladies, I expect. What do you make of that, Talia?'

'No – no, I didn't,' said Lucy, flushing slightly. 'That's not what I meant. I just . . . I didn't *know* that. I've only met you once before, Talia, at that awards night a few months ago. I'm not sure if you remember. But it was so loud, and I didn't get the chance to speak to you much . . .'

Talia paused for a beat, then smiled – the first truly genuine one Sam thought he'd seen since they got on the plane in London. 'I see. Well, yes. I work for a children's charity, as a legal adviser,' she said. 'It's only part time, but the people – the impact they have – it's quite wonderful.'

'That's *so* amazing,' said Eleni, sounding almost breathless. 'Truly. Working for a charity that does such good things, when you wouldn't actually have to work if you chose not to . . . it's really admirable.'

Talia grimaced. 'There's really no need for all the flattery – praise is certainly not why I do it,' she said snippily. Clearly Talia didn't want compliments, but Sam had thought the same thing when he'd first learned what she chose to do with her time. It had warmed him to her; she was so much more than an uber-rich, uber-privileged housewife swanning around at home or going shopping every day. *She deserves so much better than Rory.*

'It must be good to feel like you're making a difference,' Lucy said. 'A lot more of a difference than moving around tabs in a spreadsheet all day, anyway.'

Talia laughed. 'Well, anyone who can put my husband in as good a mood as your work has done over these last few months is making plenty of difference, I can assure you.'

'Hear, hear!' boomed Rory.

From across the table, Eleni snorted, then tried to disguise the sound with a cough.

'You all right there, Eleni?' Sam asked with a grin. 'Something go down the wrong way?'

'Ha, no – I'm fine. Maybe it's just me, but I didn't realize *financial analysis* was something that gave Rory such a buzz. It's literally just a bunch of numbers, isn't it? Or am I missing something?'

Lucy's face fell. 'Well, I . . . er . . .'

'Now, now, Eleni,' Rory interrupted. 'It's far more than just a *bunch of numbers* when Lucy's saving me ten times your annual salary in a thirty-minute meeting.'

Eleni flushed pink. 'Of course,' she said, her voice small. 'Sorry, Lucy – Rory – I was only teasing.'

'Well,' said Talia coldly, 'I think we can all do without that kind of *teasing* over lunch. Everyone is here because they've made a valuable contribution to Ashworth – no matter what their role is.'

Eleni stared at the table, shame-faced. Sam cringed. *Oh, shit. Looks like she's got on the wrong side of the boss's wife already.*

In an ill-disguised attempt to dissolve the tension, Rory stood up with a satisfied groan, and stretched. 'Well, that was bloody marvellous. Michaela, please tell Leilani how much we all enjoyed it. And look – we were so busy concentrating on our lunch, we didn't even notice, but – *land ahoy*!'

Rory was gesturing wildly, almost leaping up and down now, as the yacht sailed into a bay then began to slow, the revs of its motor dying down. The deck crew jumped into action, radios crackling with instructions from Captain Taylor: '*Deck team, I need your eyes on the reef . . . make sure we're clear . . .*'

The bosun released a chain in stages to let down the anchor, and then the boat steadied and became still.

Here they were: Opunohu Bay on Moorea. They'd arrived at their first stop.

The lagoon where they'd anchored was, no contest, the most stunning place Sam had ever laid eyes on: a pristine beach with pinkish sand lined the nearby shore; the coral reef shone with hues of vibrant pink and orange; the water was so clear that he could see the detail of each tiny pebble and the patterns on every shell. And it was peaceful – there were only a couple of other yachts moored close by, a smattering of tourists roaming the beach. It was paradise – and it was nearly all theirs.

After a safety briefing from Noah, the bosun, on the stern of the main deck, everyone stripped down to their swimsuits and put on snorkelling masks. They were also offered flippers – Sam didn't bother; he found them cumbersome, he could swim better without them. They made their way to the swim platform and splashed into the sea, following Noah's instructions to head towards an area of bright orange-pink coral. 'Remember – don't touch or step on the reef, and keep a safe distance from marine animals,' he called after them.

Sam ducked his face under the water. The ocean was cool and quiet; as he swam and took in the rainbow of colour in the water – orange clownfish and white butterflyfish and patterned bannerfish – he felt like he was in his own protective undersea bubble. A stingray swam so close to the underneath of his .stomach, it almost brushed against him. He nearly laughed; he just stopped himself before he snorted out his mouthpiece.

Claire would bloody love this.

More fool her for dumping me less than two weeks before a trip to paradise.

Gazing around under the water's surface, he realized he'd lost track of the others. He should probably move closer to them, for safety – that was what Noah had said earlier.

Sam lifted his head above water, removed his mask and scanned the ocean. There they were – everyone else was about twenty metres closer to the shore. He tugged the goggles back down and swam smoothly underwater to reach the group.

He could see them through the crystal-clear waters. It was shallower here, so most people had a hand or a foot on the ground, taking care to avoid the patches of reef. He swam closer, until he was just a few feet away, his eyes moving between the stunning array of sea life underneath him and the legs of his travel companions.

He couldn't make out who was who as he approached them underwater; he surfaced just as Rory popped up right next to him, removing his mouthpiece.

'Ah, there you are, Sam,' he said, strings of saliva connecting his lips to the mouthpiece. 'Looked like you were drifting halfway out to sea, over there.' He lifted up his mask. 'Wouldn't want the current to drag you away now, would we?'

Sam narrowed his eyes behind his mask, then tried to move backwards and away from his boss, as fast as he could.

And then – *ouch, what the hell was that?* – his foot brushed against something sharp on the seabed. He'd been so busy trying to get some distance between himself and Rory, he'd put it down without thinking, not checking what was below.

A hot blast of pain shot across the sole of his right foot. As he lifted it, he saw a spiral of bright red clouding the clear water, and the pink formation underneath.

They even warned us about this.

He'd just done exactly what Noah said not to – in his haste to move, he'd dragged his foot across a patch of sharp coral. As he examined it, he saw a shallow but jagged cut slicing his sole horizontally. It was stinging like hell in the salt water.

He focused all his efforts and energy on swimming back to the yacht, trying to keep his injured foot above the water, attempting to wave for help from the deck crew.

I can't fucking believe this.

It was only day one, and Sam was already adding to his list of things to hate Rory for.

TALIA

'What are you still doing down here?'

Talia startled as Rory's voice reverberated through their sprawling cabin; she hadn't heard him open the door. She glanced up at the dressing table's mirror from her phone's screen – text message half-composed – as he closed the door and strode across the suite. She slipped the mobile into her Prada tote.

She sat up straight on the cushioned stool and fixed a smile, thinking how ill-suited the volume of noise that came out of her husband's mouth was to his body. He spoke with the depth of an operatic baritone, yet stood only five feet eight inches – barely as tall as she was. And despite eating nearly twice the amount she managed each day, he remained slight; neat. Even now in his mid-fifties, there was no sign of his metabolism slowing.

Probably because he never sits still. His boundless energy was part of the reason he'd risen so high over the years – from a graduate scheme with a bank, to founding and running

Ashworth Property Partners, a multinational developer; publicly listed on the London Stock Exchange since 2024.

Talia gestured to the phone tucked safely in her bag as she met his eyes in the mirror. 'I just wanted some privacy for a few minutes before dinner, darling, so I could try to call the girls.' She shrugged. 'No luck, unfortunately.'

Talia's gaze moved in the mirror from Rory back to her own reflection; she sighed. The fine lines around her dark eyes were prominent in the glaring light of the suite, its wall-to-wall windows ushering in a flood of unforgiving sun. She should have made time for her quarterly refresh of injectables before the trip – it wasn't like her to miss her appointments – but over the past few weeks, everything had run away from her.

And now . . . here we are. A jolt of panic sped from her stomach to her throat. She swallowed it down and fixed a broad smile on her lips. *Come on, now. I'm a very lucky woman.* Talia usually viewed Rory's annual bonus trip as the highlight of her year: no-expense-spared trips to exotic destinations. Luxury and fun and adventure. These were the holidays of a lifetime. She should be thrilled and excited – not a clammy ball of anxiety.

'Thought you might be,' he said, walking over to her, slightly unsteady on his feet. The yacht bobbed mildly on the sea beneath them, but as he approached, she caught the tang of whisky on his breath. A more likely cause of his wavering; the rest of them had started downing cocktails as soon as they'd got back from snorkelling.

He stood behind her at the dressing table, placed his hands on her shoulders, bent down to kiss the top of her head. Then he checked his watch and looked up suddenly, confusion on his face. 'But hang on a minute – we're eleven hours behind, aren't we? It's not even six in the morning over there – won't they both be fast asleep?'

Damn. The panic arose again; Talia took a sip of water and gulped it down. 'Of course we are – silly me,' she said from behind her glass. 'I completely forgot – no wonder neither of them answered.'

'Well, why don't you try them again in a few hours?' suggested Rory. 'Maybe wait until just before we go to bed tonight – you should give Chloe a chance to surface from whatever end of year bash she'll be recovering from.'

Talia smiled at the thought of her youngest child – still her baby, despite being nearly nineteen – getting home at goodness knows what time, passing out, starfished, on her bed, duvet crumpled at her feet, eye mask on, snoring with her mouth wide open. Alone, she hoped – though Talia was hardly one to judge; her own university days had been adventurous, to say the least. Her twenties and early thirties too – until she'd met Rory and decided to settle down.

Rory dipped his head down towards hers, buried his nose in her hair, inhaled. 'Let's go and have a drink and take in the view before dinner – you know, darling, these girls will make you any cocktail you can dream of . . .' He caught her eyes in the dressing table mirror, held her gaze for a long moment. Then he raised one eyebrow, began moving his hands lower down, stroking the curve of her breasts through her jade-green dress. 'Unless you'd rather spend some time alone down here first . . .'

'There'll be plenty of time for that,' Talia said, laughing and swatting his hands away. 'Anyway, you're right – let's go and mingle with your lucky winners. I'm sure they're all in the mood for celebrating.'

Rory nodded, then looked suddenly downcast, his shoulders hunching towards his ears. He was like that – changeable – his moods and thoughts and feelings shifting wildly in an instant, like the girls when they were toddlers. 'Do you – do you suppose it's going all right so far? Do you think they're all having fun? Shame about Lucy feeling sick, and Sam cutting his foot like that.'

Talia heard the note of anxiety in his voice. This was classic Rory: he could try to hide it, but he was just like her in that way. He worried about what other people were thinking. He wanted to make sure they were all right, and of course, that they approved of him. It was part of what made her fall in love with him two decades ago – that, and the fact he was clearly going somewhere in life.

With her gaze on her husband in the mirror, she felt hot tears begin to form. How had she lost sight of that man? Where had they gone – where had *she* gone? How had they disappeared through the decades, faded like the fresh glow of youth from Talia's skin? She blinked the tears back. *Now is not the time.* She stood, turned to face him, held his face in her hands and kissed him lightly on the lips.

'No,' she said. 'I don't think it's going all right.' Before Rory's expression could fall too far, Talia spread her lips into a wide smile. 'I think it's going wonderfully – despite any minor mishaps.'

His shoulders relaxed. 'Ha! My wife, the tease,' he said, laughing. 'Come on, then. Let's go and join the party.'

* * *

On the main deck, they found the rest of the group sitting and watching the sun set with ice-laden drinks at the outdoor dining table, their stewardesses both hovering nearby, looking chic in their fresh white linen and eager to please – as they should be. Rory would be expecting the top-notch service he'd paid through the nose for, and nothing less. Sam's foot was bandaged up now and resting on a stool next to him, and Lucy still looked a little peaky, but she gave Talia a smile as the couple came to join them.

'How are you feeling now?' Talia asked Lucy.

Lucy didn't quite meet her eyes as she replied: 'A lot better, thank you.'

Talia nodded, satisfied. She didn't want something as mundane as seasickness to get in the way of what should be a smooth trip aboard the *Lusso*. She sat next to Lucy, slinging her bag on the back of her chair, keeping her eyes focused on the ocean and the beginnings of the sunset on the horizon, then turned to Sam.

'And you, Sam? How's that cut to your foot?'

Sam shrugged. 'Ah, it's grand. Michaela bandaged it up for me.' He reddened a touch. 'Still can't believe I did that – after Noah warned us about the coral and everything.' He looked up at Michaela as he said it; she gave him a warm smile.

'That was your first mistake, Sam,' said Rory. 'Always listen to the people in charge – isn't that right, Chief Stewardess? Your crew know what they're talking about – much more than just a pretty face, aren't you, Michaela?'

Michaela flinched. 'Well, we're here to keep you all safe and happy,' she said smoothly. Apparently, this *particular* chief stewardess didn't enjoy Rory's sense of humour. Talia understood, but she hoped the crew would make sure they kept their opinions tightly under wraps. They were paying more than enough to warrant discretion, after all.

'The captain will be joining you at the table this evening,' Michaela added.

Talia nodded, pleased. She'd had a quick look at the statistics on female captains before the trip, and had to admit, she was impressed. Captain Taylor must have had to battle God knows how much misogyny over the course of her career to become one of the less than 2 per cent of female superyacht captains in the world. She was quite the trailblazer.

'Fantastic,' exclaimed Rory. 'I've got a lot to talk to her about. Sit the captain next to me, won't you, Michaela? Lucky lady!'

As Rory laughed at his own poor joke, Talia noticed Sam try to catch the eyes of both Lucy and Eleni across the table, though neither of them looked back. She frowned and made a mental note of it. She didn't want any tension creeping in among Rory's staff, certainly not this early in the trip – and there'd already been a strange atmosphere at lunch today, when Eleni had spoken so ungraciously about Lucy's efforts at Ashworth. But wasn't that so often the case with beautiful, glossy young women like Eleni? *They think they can say and do whatever they like, and get away with it*. Not on Talia's watch.

'Good evening, everyone,' said Captain Taylor, arriving on the deck and taking the remaining seat at the table, on the other side of Rory. 'I trust everything is going well so far?' Talia smiled.

'Yeah, the *Lusso* is perfect,' said Eleni. 'And the snorkelling today was incredible!'

'Can't even believe we're here, honestly,' added Mark, nodding.

'Absolutely marvellous – the best trip we've ever done for Ashworth, don't you think, darling?' agreed Rory.

Talia bit back the truth; the words she really wanted to say – *yes, it's luxurious and beautiful, but I'm afraid I'm quietly losing my mind – and you, my husband, can't even see it.*

Instead, she simply nodded.

As soon as they'd been served a mouth-watering main course of seared swordfish with tropical salad dressed with a pineapple glaze, Rory launched into a long-winded story about last year's trip to the Caribbean and an ill-fated rum tasting trip. Most people were laughing along, though Sam looked rather unimpressed, and Lucy sat in silence, eyes fixed on her plate. How out of place Lucy seemed here – not at all like the raucous, extroverted sales people Rory usually brought on these trips.

When her husband wound down, the captain gave him a polite smile. 'Now it's your turn,' said Rory. 'You must have one or two juicy stories you can share with us, Captain – just between us, naturally. What happens on the *Lusso* stays on the *Lusso*, eh?'

Talia stifled a groan. *Can't he stop trying to sound like a twenty-something on a stag do?*

'I'm afraid I try not to make a habit of gossiping about guests,' said Captain Taylor.

'Oh, come on, Captain! We won't breathe a word of it, will we?' Rory darted quick looks across the table; the group responded only with an embarrassed silence.

Captain Taylor sighed. 'Well, I suppose if I keep them

anonymous . . . I did have a supermodel on board once who demanded three hundred fresh roses in the salon every evening – the crew were run ragged. And then there was the tech mogul who insisted his Greek salad ingredients were cut into perfect twelve-millimetre squares – I'm not joking. Our poor chef quit halfway through the charter.'

The table burst into laughter. Talia was surprised that the captain was speaking so candidly; perhaps the wine was loosening her tongue.

'But I've been looking forward to this charter,' she went on. 'You're not the *Lusso*'s usual crowd. I get a lot of hedge fund types, footballers, the uber-rich. But a property development team on your bonus trip?' She smiled. 'You're a touch more down-to-earth.'

'We do try,' Sam said.

'And, Captain, have you ever had to deal with any tricky situations on board?' Talia asked, curious now. 'Any . . . I don't know, accidents, or things going wrong?'

Captain Taylor laughed. 'Well, there's never a dull moment on a superyacht.' She paused to take a sip of wine. 'Of course, there have been a few accidents among my crew over the years – nothing serious, thankfully – a few near misses from swinging fenders, things like that.'

'And what's it like to work in the industry?' asked Talia. 'You must be in the minority as a female captain, I assume?'

'Yes, we're a rare breed. And it's tough at times. There's still a lot of good old-fashioned sexism in the maritime world. It's my young female crew members who get the worst of it – from people in the industry, but also on board.' The captain stopped abruptly – perhaps she felt she'd said too much – and pushed back her chair. 'Anyway,' she said, 'this has been wonderful. I'll leave you all to your desserts and cocktails – enjoy the rest of your evening.'

Before the group could respond, Captain Taylor gave Michaela a brisk nod and strode off towards the stairs to the bridge.

After a sweet coconut mousse, it was time for so-called Polynesian Puzzles – a pub quiz-style game Rory had asked the crew to put together for their first night. Michaela handed out *Lusso di Mare* branded notepads and pens to everyone as they got ready to play.

Talia took a deep breath and tried not to keep glancing across the table. She'd stuck to one cocktail over dinner, but everyone else – except perhaps Lucy, who was still sipping tonic water – must have sunk three or four. It was getting louder, rowdier, by the minute. It was making her nervous. Who knew what people might say, after a few too many? Who knew what they'd do?

'I'm going for a bathroom break,' Talia excused herself. No one responded; leaving her bag hanging over the back of her chair, she turned and walked slowly to the nearest toilets, inside the salon. Alone in the privacy of the bathroom, she closed the lid to the loo, sat and let her head drop into her palms. She took deep, steadying breaths; she needed to halt her tears before they started.

How am I going to do this? It's only the first night and I'm breaking down . . . She blew her nose, dabbed at her eyes with the tissue, and took a few more deep breaths.

Come on. No one can see me like this. Appearances were

everything, after all; they were what mattered. She *knew* that; it had been drummed into her skull since she was a girl. Keep your emotions tucked inside; never let anyone know how you truly feel. As long as you *look* all right, you'll *be* all right.

Steeling herself, she flushed the loo, used a damp tissue to tidy her make-up in the mirror and headed back to the table. Hoots of laughter and groans of '*No one's going to know that except Rory!*' met her ears before she was halfway there. They'd started without her, then.

'Talia!' shouted Rory, as she took her seat back at the table. 'Oh Christ, I didn't think you were joining in, and now we've organized our teams – three on each side, with Michaela reading out the questions . . .'

Thank God. I can get away. 'Oh, that's a shame. But don't worry – I'm exhausted from the journey anyway. I'll leave you all to it and head to bed.'

'If you're sure, darling?' said Rory.

'Absolutely.'

Sensing eyes on her from across the table, and now keener than ever to make her escape, Talia picked her bag up from her chair, swung it over her shoulder and headed downstairs to the master stateroom.

With the door closed behind her, she was overcome with relief so strongly she almost wept again. One of the stewardesses must have been in here while she was at dinner: the bed was turned down ready for sleep, the pillows were plumped and the cabin's surfaces looked freshly polished. Even the slightly garish golden ornament on the desk near the window – a yacht-shaped sculpture with a long, pointed sail – had an extra sheen now.

She sighed and walked over to the dressing table, placed

her bag down next to her and rifled through the side pockets for her phone. There it was – untouched, safe and sound.

As she pulled it out, something white in the main compartment of her bag caught her eye. A scrap of paper, folded up. She was sure she'd taken all the rubbish out when she'd unpacked earlier – she didn't like any mess in her bag; it was always neat and tidy. Just a small pouch with her compact and a few pieces of make-up, her sunglasses and her phone. She must have missed a ticket or receipt or something.

She picked up the piece of paper, was about to throw it in the bin, when she noticed it wasn't a receipt or a ticket. It wasn't anything she had put in there herself. It was from the *Lusso di Mare* notepad – she could see the gold emblem through the fold.

Did someone drop one of their answers to the quiz in my bag by mistake?

Curious now, Talia unfolded the note, took in the sentence scribbled on it, and watched it fall to the floor as both her hands moved instinctively to cover her mouth.

This was nothing to do with the quiz.

This was no accident – the paper hadn't ended up in her bag by mistake.

This was a message addressed to her – it had the letter *T* at the top – and beneath it, in a hurried scrawl:

Get away from him before it's too late.

GENDARMERIE MARITIME DE POLYNÉSIE FRANÇAISE

CASE NUMBER: 247849

DATE: 11/06/2026

INTERVIEW EXCERPT ONE

Interview subject: Brett Marchant – First Officer on board *Lusso di Mare* charter

Interview conducted by Chief of Police Henri Robert

M Robert: Monsieur Marchant, can you tell me what your first impression was of the guests when they arrived on the *Lusso di Mare*?

M Marchant: Sure. I actually kinda liked them. It's not that often we get guests who are sort of . . . normal, everyday people. You know, not, like, super-rich? Most of our charters are for insanely wealthy power couples and tech moguls bringing along supermodels and shit. I knew the primary had a bit of cash, but everyone else was just, like, regular people. There for a party and a great holiday – a once-in-a-lifetime experience type thing.

M Robert: The primary? You mean Mr Ashworth?

M Marchant: Yeah, sorry, superyacht vocab – that's what we call the people who pay for the charter. He seemed okay too, at first. Friendly, didn't speak to the crew like sh— sorry, like dirt. He made some corny jokes here and there, but I didn't mind him.

M Robert: It's okay; you can curse. And what was the crew's general mental state that first day?

M Marchant: Our mental state? What, like, were we worried or something? <inaudible response from M Robert> I mean, no, that first day, everyone was fine – probably better than fine. We felt good – excited, well-rested. Everything was ready to go – the boat was clean and fully stocked, the skies were clear. Captain Taylor had all the anchoring spots booked and we'd had our briefings about the guests. All the guests seemed pretty happy and easy-going when they first arrived too.

M Robert: So you didn't pick up on any tensions between the guests – or among the crew – on day one? Nothing to raise alarm bells?

M Marchant: Well, I wasn't, like, hovering around the guests all day like the stews do. I'm on the bridge a lot of the time, with the captain. So maybe I missed something. But to me, they all seemed good. Sam had that cut to his foot, but it wasn't serious – Michaela cleaned it up for him. Lucy was a little sick, and we offered her some meds. But everyone perked up anyway when they had a few drinks in them.

M Robert: So there was nothing to suggest that events would unfold as they did?

M Marchant: <audible sigh> You're asking me, did I have any idea that we'd end up with a dead body . . . with a murderer on board? That these . . . these nice people would end up killing each other on their luxury freakin' holiday? No, man – fuck, no. No one, no one on this entire fucking planet, could have predicted that.

ELENI

8 JUNE

Eleni blinked and rubbed the sleep out of her eyes as the room came into focus. She was groggy, but something had stirred her from the depths of a heavy, still jet-lagged sleep.

She squinted and peered towards the window: soft pink and yellow tinges of daylight were creeping underneath the thick blackout curtains of their cabin and Nick was snoring softly next to her. She couldn't work out what had dragged her out of her dreams, but a voice in her head was insistent: *wake up.*

Her mind wandered back to last night. She'd headed below deck to bed around midnight, waited for Nick to come down – she'd hoped he'd stay on the main deck and chat to Rory for a while, but he'd wanted to catch the end of a football match up in the sky lounge. When he hadn't reappeared an hour later, she'd drifted off to sleep, tipsy, unsettled and frustrated that her attempts to get closer to both Rory and Talia had amounted to so little. *Never mind. I've still got plenty of time.*

Hushed voices reached her ears from the passageway outside the cabin. So that was what had woken her. She checked the time on her phone – *7.56 a.m.* – and rolled over to face her husband sleeping flat on his stomach, face buried in his pillow. She touched his shoulder.

'Nick?' she whispered into his ear. *Oh shit, that was probably a bad idea.* He *really* didn't like being woken up like that. She'd learned that after their first night together, ten years ago. She'd had too much Prosecco, but she'd known with sober precision that she wanted to go to bed with him more than she'd ever wanted anything. They'd only met a week before, in a bar – but she was intoxicated. The heat between them; the way his eyes moved across her body in her red dress as though he wanted to devour her; the soft parting of his lips as he watched her mouth; the weight of his forearms looped around her waist as he pulled her towards him . . .

When she'd woken the next morning in his flat in Oakwood, deliciously sore yet aching for more of him, she'd snuggled in close to his sleeping body and begun to plant gentle kisses on his cheek, his earlobes, his neck. He hadn't stirred. So she'd whispered his name in his ear – and that had done it. He'd bolted upright in bed with a shout, looking as if she'd just been holding a knife to his throat, rather than her lips.

'Jesus Christ,' he'd said. 'You just gave me the shock of my life.' She'd apologized, giggling – and as she started her kisses again, it was all quickly forgotten. A drawback of working in the police, he'd explained. His dreams were full of whatever unsettling incident he'd been called to that day, or whatever violence he'd witnessed on the streets during his patrol.

Ever since then, Eleni tried to avoid waking him abruptly. But it was too late now; Nick lifted his head up from the plush pillow and squinted at her. He was about to drop back down again when the sound of louder, more irritable mutters from the corridor dragged him, finally, from sleep. 'Who's out there? What time even is it?'

'I don't know. But whoever it is sounds . . . I'm not sure.' Eleni swallowed. 'Pissed off? Worried?'

Nick groaned as Eleni pulled back the covers and stepped out of bed. She reached for a T-shirt and wide-legged silk trousers from the wardrobe, threw them on over her silk vest, walked to the cabin door and opened it.

'Captain Taylor,' she said. The captain stood close to the entrance to the crew's quarters, talking to Johanna. 'Is everything okay?'

The captain's eyes flickered behind Eleni's shoulder, to where Nick was now standing, bare-chested and squinting. 'What's going on?' he asked.

Captain Taylor cleared her throat. 'Ah, nothing for you to worry about. Just – well, I'm afraid Michaela doesn't appear to be able to take on her usual duties this morning,' she said.

Is that all? Their smiling, bubbly, energetic chief stewardess was . . . what? Unwell? Off duty? It wasn't the end of the world, surely. They still had Johanna. Behind the captain, Sam, Rory and Talia had gathered in their doorways opposite, all half-dressed and groggy. She glanced to her left, to Lucy and Mark's cabin, just as the door opened and both of them poked their heads into the corridor.

'What's happened?' asked Mark, voice thick with sleep.

'Michaela's . . . indisposed, apparently. She'll be up and back to work soon, surely,' said Rory, making no attempt to hide his irritation. 'No need to make a fuss about it, eh?'

Eleni thought back to the last time she'd seen Michaela. It had been yesterday evening at dinner, hadn't it? She was as helpful and accommodating as she had been since they stepped on board the *Lusso*.

'Well, maybe she just needs a bit of a break,' said Talia irritably.

'I wouldn't be surprised,' added Rory. 'How many hours a day exactly are your crew expected to work, Captain? The poor girl could probably do with a rest.'

'In any case,' said Talia, with a quick glance at her husband, 'I expect our service to be maintained to the same standard.' Eleni made a show of nodding in agreement.

'Absolutely, Mrs Ashworth,' said Captain Taylor. 'I apologize for the disturbance this morning, and please don't be concerned. Michaela will be back on duty shortly. Please, do all head back to your cabins until you're ready for breakfast.'

After she'd dressed for the day, Eleni checked her reflection in the mirror of the en-suite; stared into the round brown eyes that always made her think of her beloved father. Her hair didn't look right, though she was using her usual products here, and she'd had fresh highlights last week. Maybe she'd slept funny. She frowned – she liked it to be *just so*.

'You ready yet?' Nick called out to her from their bedroom. 'I can hear everyone going upstairs. I'm starving – can you hurry up?'

Eleni smoothed down her bright pink maxi dress, turned away from the mirror and opened the bathroom door. 'I'm coming – look, I'm good to go,' she said, giving him a twirl, then taking in her handsome husband – the tiniest touches of grey that threaded his jet-black hair, the deep tan that had developed on his arms, his broad, muscular shoulders.

He let out a soft whistle as she moved towards him, then pulled her close and wound his arms around her waist. He leaned down to her ear. 'Mmm. You're wearing that perfume I like. And have I told you lately you're the most stunning woman I've ever met?' he whispered, between soft kisses on her neck.

Eleni shivered. 'I think you might have mentioned it once or twice,' she murmured. He pressed his firm stomach more deeply against her, began moving his hands up towards her breasts. She grabbed hold of them and moved them away. 'But now's not the time for getting distracted, no matter how stunning I am,' she said teasingly. 'As you just told me – you're starving, and it's time for breakfast.'

Nick pulled away from her with a sigh. 'Damn,' he said. 'Well, I'm looking forward to picking up from here in about, ohh' – he checked his watch – 'thirty minutes' time.'

Eleni gave him a long, deep kiss. 'That sounds like a recipe for indigestion,' she said. 'But if you insist . . .' Then – her heart finally starting to slow in her chest – she grabbed her beach bag and took Nick's hand as they walked upstairs and to the table under the awning on the main deck. They were the last to arrive; there were only two seats left – next to Lucy; that definitely wouldn't have been Eleni's first choice – so she sat down in one and patted the other for Nick. Mark, Sam, Rory and Talia were drinking coffee and chatting.

'Good morning,' said Johanna. Her voice didn't have quite the same buoyancy as yesterday; Eleni noticed light purple circles visible beneath the concealer under her eyes. 'Can I get you something to drink? We've got croissants, fruit and toast here.' She gestured to the table. 'And I can ask Leilani to make you a cooked breakfast too – anything you like.'

'Ooooh, yes! I'd love a cappuccino, please!' Eleni beamed. *Too much, Els. Tone it down in front of the others. Remember your banter at lunch yesterday went down like a lead balloon.* 'And, ah, some eggs Benedict would be simply divine.' Johanna nodded and turned next to Nick. As he placed his order, Lucy shifted in her chair. She was still looking peaky this morning, pushing some toast around her plate and taking the occasional nibble.

Eleni turned her back to Lucy and addressed Talia across the table. 'You look lovely today!' she said. 'That dress is so gorgeous – where's it from?'

Talia arched an eyebrow and placed her coffee cup delicately back on its saucer. 'It's Gucci,' she replied coldly. 'I picked up a few things in Harrods before the trip.'

'And I've got the credit card bill to prove it!' Rory bellowed.

Eleni smiled. 'Well, it's stunning.'

Talia stared coolly ahead. *Damn it; why isn't this working?* Despite her best efforts, Eleni was struggling to crack the surface of Talia's frosty exterior. She'd not expected them to become best friends overnight, of course, but she was trying here – *really* trying – and yet every attempt so far had been met with a snub. *I'll have to step it up a gear.*

'Talking about stunning, can you believe where we're eating breakfast this morning?' Sam said. 'Just check out that view.'

'It's *insane*,' agreed Eleni. Then she glanced quickly at Talia. 'I mean – it's just *wonderful*.'

Rumour had it, Rory splashed out over a hundred grand

on these holidays – and Eleni could believe it. This bonus scheme had been running a few years, and she thought she'd missed out when she didn't get on the last one: Ashworth had hired a luxury resort on a private Caribbean island for a week, and the winners had flown there and back first class. She'd chatted to them when they'd returned, their tales of private chefs and daily spa treatments leaving Eleni's jaw on the floor. *Unbelievable.*

But actually, thank God she'd not been picked. If she had, she'd never have got to come here – previous winners weren't eligible for the next trip. And this yacht made even the world's most glamorous resort look like a three-star motel. Shame she wasn't on social media these days, and that her girlfriends had drifted away. She'd love to share this with them – her best friend from uni, Bella, had a thing for sailing. She'd have been beside herself seeing pics of the *Lusso*.

'Yes, this is just about the most perfect start to the day any one of us could possibly imagine, isn't it?' Rory's voice was loud enough for people on the next island to hear as he went on: 'I hope you're all counting yourselves lucky to get a taste of how the super-rich live. Not something any of you will likely experience again, eh?'

Eleni cringed. She got on fine with Rory – she knew how to manage him: laughing along with his jokes, no matter their poor taste; allowing his patronizing comments to wash over her. She could handle it, if it meant she'd keep forging ahead in her career. But not everyone could; even Talia looked uncomfortable as he spoke.

Johanna returned then, placing coffee and a plate of delicious-looking eggs in front of her. Eleni started to dig in with gusto, then remembered where she was and who she was with. *Don't scoff the lot down in one big gulp like you're eating with the boys.* A few small, ladylike bites, then a delicate dab at the sides of her mouth with her napkin – and repeat.

As the table fell quiet, Eleni darted a sideways glance at Lucy: her expression was stony. She wondered if it was in response to Rory's cringey banter. *She looks so uncomfortable.* Not only was it odd that Lucy had managed to get a spot here, but now she didn't even look happy about it. *Why did she even bother coming, if she was going to be this miserable the whole time?*

She turned back to Nick; he was staring at the floor as he took mouthfuls of his eggs and bacon. He was probably hungover – he'd been walloping back the cocktails during the quiz last night, so this fry-up would be going down a treat. She took in his profile: the curl of his eyelashes; the curve of his lips. After a decade together, she still found him breathtaking.

'How's your breakfast?' she asked. 'Looks so good.'

He smiled at her. He had a way of looking intently at her – at *everyone* – as though no one else existed. He could make anyone feel special; he was known as the sergeant who could get even drug dealers and gang members to open up – for good reason.

'It's delicious,' Nick replied. Then he leaned close and said more quietly, 'But not as delicious as you.'

Eleni giggled – how did he still do that to her? 'Shh,' she said, flushing. As he pulled away, he dropped his napkin, then leaned down to the deck floor to pick it up and spread it back over his lap.

She was glad to see him happy here so far. She'd been worried how he'd react if she won the trip – before she knew she could bring a plus one. Nick would have been anxious about her going alone – they'd always travelled together, off on globe-trotting adventures before they got married and had the boys. In the ten years they'd been a couple, she'd never been away without him. And his job meant Nick was always on alert for danger – he worried about Eleni if she took too long in the corner shop.

So when she'd learned that winners could bring a plus one – well, that was it. She knew she'd do *anything* to be here. With Nick joining her, it solved the issues of leaving him alone with the kids and him worrying about her. And this was her chance to get closer to Rory and Talia. To spend some time together, the four of them – two successful, powerful couples getting to know each other, away from the distractions and pressures of life back home. Nothing to distract them – nothing to draw their attention elsewhere. When she won her place she'd told her mum and her sister why, in no uncertain terms, she and Nick both needed to be there. They'd fallen over themselves to help, as Eleni knew they would.

'Now, Johanna, remind us: what's on the agenda today?' asked Rory, through a mouthful of bacon.

'Of course,' she said. 'This morning, we've arranged for some local massage therapists to join us on board for a bit of pampering. Then we'll sail around the north-western tip of Moorea to Tiahura beach, where we'll anchor. After lunch, we'll take the tender to shore and you'll make a short jeep ride inland to see a Polynesian *marae*.'

'Super! I love the sound of all that,' said Rory.

'Then you'll have some free time to swim or relax on board before dinner.'

Free time? Eleni smiled: the phrase wasn't in her vocabulary any more. The boys, her full-on job, managing the household . . . the never-ending pressure of everything. She was constantly juggling a hundred balls – some made of plastic, some of delicate crystal, and she never knew which one was about to crash to the ground.

Excusing herself to freshen up after breakfast, Eleni headed back to her cabin alone, her brain ticking over her plans for the day. She was keen to get chatting to Rory and Talia and find a good time for Nick to join her – she was determined to engineer an opportunity for the four of them to get together today, ideally over some drinks.

Musing on the best way forward, she finished brushing her teeth and put on some sun cream. Then she left the bathroom, picked up her bag and was about to head up to the sun deck to enjoy the view as they sailed – when something stopped her in her tracks.

A sound. It had snagged at her awareness; it was such an odd noise, unlike the usual noises on the boat. It was a quick, soft whirring – something mechanical.

She studied the room, tried to work out where it had come from. It had a different edge to it than the consistent humming of the air-conditioning – and the extractor fan in the bathroom was still running, so it couldn't be that.

It's nothing. It probably came from the crew quarters.

She sighed and tried to shake off her disquiet.

Why is this bothering me? Everything's fine.

This was more than likely one of her 'Eleni being Eleni' moments that Nick ribbed her about: overthinking all the time, reading into things that weren't really there. But it was only by staying on alert, being tuned in to everything – everyone – that she could help life tick along smoothly. It was just what she *did*: at home, Eleni was the one who kept things running – Nick's shift patterns were unpredictable, and he often worked overnight. The only way to cope was for Eleni to stick to a strict routine, to run a tight ship.

She started to feel calmer, but then the unease came rushing back. Something else was nagging at her – her internal alarm bells were going haywire.

'Who's there?'

She whipped her eyes around the cabin, turned to check outside the windows, then went back into the bathroom to check.

Stop it. What the hell is wrong with you?

It made no sense, but the feeling wasn't going away. Standing there alone in her cabin, Eleni knew – and *yes*, it was more than just a feeling, it was absolute, rock-solid *knowing* . . .

. . . that someone was watching her.

GENDARMERIE MARITIME DE POLYNÉSIE FRANÇAISE

CASE NUMBER: 247849

POLICE EXHIBIT TWO

Transcript of audio from CCTV footage, *Lusso di Mare* camera 8 (Main Deck tender garage); conversation between Kai Tehau, Johanna Nebeker and Noah Bailey

08/06/2026, 10:04

Johanna: You know this is going to go down like a sack of shit with the guests, don't you? Maybe not for you guys on deck, but it's the first thing they'll mention to me. Their morning mimosas taking too long to come, slow breakfast service . . . never mind that something's wrong with Michaela.

Kai: Yeah, I know. It sucks. What's going on with Mic, anyway? Did you see her last night after dinner service?

Johanna: <audible sigh> Yeah. She was pretty upset. She even said she wants to quit the charter! In the end, she decided to just ask Captain for a morning off sick.

Noah: She was upset? Shit . . . What was wrong?

Johanna: Ah . . . I don't know if I should say. But honestly, I've never seen her like that before.

Noah: Fuck, man. Is it something to do with us? You don't think . . . I haven't pissed her off, have I?

Johanna: <heavy sigh> No, Noah. It's nothing to do with you, or any of us . . . Something happened with one of the guests. One of the men. That's all I should say . . . it's really not my place.

Noah: Fuck, man. Whatever it was, it must have been bad – she can handle anything usually. Poor Mic. She puts up with way too much shit, and she shouldn't have to. I'm always saying that to her.

Johanna: Yeah, well, we both do. They're all the fucking same . . . they seem nice on day one, and then you see their true colours. Aaaah, I really need Michaela, though. I'm getting so stressed already – I can't do everything on my own!

Noah: Come on, mate, don't get upset. Mic's going to be back up soon. She won't leave you in the shit. Not on a charter like this one. Hey, have either of you seen my key card? I've not had it since before breakfast – I must have dropped it somewhere earlier this morning . . .

Captain <audible over crew radio>: Please be mindful that our new CCTV system has an audio feed, and I can hear everything you're saying from the bridge. Noah and Kai, please return to your deck duties immediately. And Johanna, continue morning service as scheduled.

[TRANSCRIPT ENDS]

LUCY

Lucy's nausea made an unwelcome return during the morning sail to Tiahura. After the *Lusso* dropped anchor and Johanna came to the sun deck to let them know lunch was ready, Lucy realized her appetite had deserted her completely.

'I'll skip the food,' she told Mark. 'I'm feeling rough again. I think I'll just go and have a quick lie-down while everyone eats.'

His eyebrows knitted together. *Stop looking so bloody worried about me.* 'Do you want me to bring my lunch down – I could sit with you in the cabin?'

Lucy touched his arm. 'No. Honestly. Stay outside with everyone else, enjoy the views.'

Mark looked disgruntled, but didn't press things, to Lucy's relief. With everyone else gathered around the table, tucking into salads and some kind of weird savoury puffs, she made her way below deck. It was too much, being around people all the time; it was already getting to her, overwhelming her nervous system. Thank God she'd get some time alone now.

As she walked along the passageway towards their cabin,

something edged at the corner of her vision, something out of place.

One of the other cabin doors was ajar.

The master stateroom.

Lucy froze, her heartbeat picking up. Then, as softly as she could, she took one quiet pace towards Rory and Talia's room. *Rory and Talia are above deck. So why is the door open? Is Michaela back on duty and in there cleaning the cabin, maybe?*

She approached the door and listened; all was quiet, but she couldn't be sure none of the crew were in there. Safer to keep watch from a distance for a few minutes, to make sure the coast was clear.

She stepped softly back to her and Mark's cabin, unlocked the door and stepped into the room, wrapping her fingers around the door's edge to keep it open a crack. She stayed there, just behind the door, watching, for what felt like ages – but was probably only fifteen minutes – until she was completely certain that there was no one in Rory and Talia's cabin.

She crept out of the cabin and stepped carefully across the corridor to the master stateroom. Cautiously, she nudged the door open, inch by inch; when she had a clear view of the whole cabin – bed neatly made, water bottles refilled – she felt a rush of elation. There was no one in there. Johanna must have been in a hurry this morning – she was the only stewardess on housekeeping duties today, after all – and somehow forgot to properly close the door.

Now's my chance.

After a quick glance back into the passageway to quadruple check she was alone, Lucy darted into the cabin and pulled the door back to the position she'd found it in – almost closed, just a few inches open.

Her eyes scanned the enormous suite.

I need to be quick. Where should I start?

She paced to the desk at the opposite side of the room, in front of the vast floor-to-ceiling windows. There Rory's laptop sat, next to a gleaming golden sculpture shaped like a sailing yacht; she tapped on the touchpad and a request to enter his password popped up. She wouldn't have a clue what it was; she couldn't risk getting it wrong and locking the screen – that would be too much of a giveaway. She sighed. *What else?*

She looked around the desk. To the right of the computer was a small, leather-bound notebook. She opened it and saw Rory's scribbled handwriting on the first page.

She brought it closer and tried to make sense of the messy scrawl. Her heart sank as she realized it was just a to-do list with various client names and a few dates next to them. She recognized them all – there was nothing here that she didn't already know about.

She flicked to the next page and skimmed it; nothing of use. Same for the page after, and the one after that.

'What the hell are you doing in here?'

Shit. Lucy dropped the notebook and turned in the direction of Mark's voice. He stood in the doorway, his face a picture of confusion and shock.

'Mark! You made me jump.' *What am I going to say?* Her brain scrambled for something plausible. 'I was just looking for some sales figures that Rory was asking me about this morning – he mentioned it over breakfast. I was sure I gave them to him already, so I wanted to check. But I can't find them – they're not here.' She shrugged, then walked to the doorway to join him. 'What are you doing down here, anyway? Have you already finished lunch?'

He crossed his arms. 'Yeah – I ate fast so I could come and check on you. But how did you even get in here?'

Lucy smiled. 'Nothing sinister. The door was open. Come on, let's go up – I'm feeling better, and it must be about time for our trip to shore.'

Mark wouldn't even look at her as they climbed into the tender and Kai sailed them to Tiahura's tiny beach. *He doesn't believe me; he knows I'm up to something.* Once they'd docked, he walked on with the group – minus Sam, who was skipping the tour because of his injured foot – without so much as a backward glance in her direction.

Lucy drifted away from him and everyone else; away from the thatched beach huts, towards a thicket of palm trees lining the edge of the sand. She found a spot beneath the shade of a palm tree and sank to the ground.

Hot tears gathered in her eyes; she blinked them away and stared out to sea. She might not have planned things this way, but she'd wanted to make the best of this trip. She'd hoped it would make things better between them, this time together in a tropical paradise – but instead, she and Mark were drifting further apart.

And it's all my fault.

Lucy knew she was driving a wedge between them. She'd been so distracted, ever since she'd joined Ashworth. So hell-bent, focused on one thing only, there'd been no space for her relationship. Sometimes she wondered if she shouldn't have taken the job in the first place . . .

'Lucy?' She looked to her left and saw Eleni walking towards her. 'Come on – everyone's waiting for you.'

Lucy hesitated. She'd have liked another moment alone to enjoy the peace. But at the thought of holding everyone up, or causing a scene, she relented.

Eleni was perfectly made-up again today. Lucy was a few years younger – Eleni had said once in a meeting that she'd been working as a land buyer for more than a decade, which must put her in her early thirties, at least. But somehow, at twenty-eight, Lucy suspected she looked far older: pale and dry-skinned and tired in a way that felt more pronounced in the presence of someone as gorgeous as Eleni. Something about her carefully managed good looks irked Lucy – as if she were doing it on purpose to draw attention to Lucy's unglamorous appearance. It reminded her of the cool girls at school – the mean ones who whispered cruel jokes and turned their backs as she walked towards them. Those girls turned up every day, rain or shine, with lip gloss and lashings of mascara too.

But perhaps she was being unfair. Lucy wasn't at school any more, and Eleni wasn't either. *Besides, it's not her fault she's beautiful. I should give her a chance.*

'Yes,' she said, 'let's go.'

They began strolling to where everyone was gathered in awkward silence. Lucy's gaze was fixed on the sand beneath their feet when she noticed something strange.

'What's happened to your shoes?' she asked Eleni. The question came out in a more accusatory tone than she'd meant it to – but Lucy was baffled. It was one thing having to go shoeless on the yacht, but there were crabs and sharp stones and goodness only knew what else on the beach – it all looked like an overwhelming assault to the senses, never mind being dangerous.

Eleni frowned. 'I left them with Nick. I love it – the sand is so warm. I like feeling it in between my toes.' Lucy grimaced before she could stop herself. 'What's wrong with that?' Eleni asked, looking bewildered.

Lucy shook her head. 'Oh – nothing, really. I think *I'm* the weird one. I just hate it. Stepping on anything crunchy or squishy or sharp. And sand. I really, *really* hate sand.'

Eleni burst out laughing. 'You hate *sand*? Whoops – do you think you've come to the wrong place, maybe? Not much escape from it here.'

Lucy flushed. She wasn't sure whether Eleni was mocking her or trying to be friendly. Either way, this sort of banter wasn't one of Lucy's greatest skills. Eleni seemed a natural at it, though – it was probably part of how she'd ended up one of the top land buyers in the business.

After a few beats of awkward silence, Eleni asked, 'So, are you . . . having a nice time so far?' Eleni was smiling, though Lucy thought it didn't quite reach her eyes. Now *there* was something Lucy was good at: taking in the detail of people's facial expressions, picking up on subtle cues that others didn't. A skill she'd carefully honed since primary school.

'Of course – it's beautiful here,' said Lucy.

'But—' Eleni blurted, then clasped her hand to her mouth as Lucy looked at her sharply. 'Sorry,' she said, raising her hands. 'No bloody filter. I don't know why I said that. I just thought you . . . I'm not sure now. Forget it.'

Lucy was weighing up whether to reply, when she realized it was too late: they were in earshot of the other guests.

'Ah, here you are!' Rory waved at them as they approached

the palm trees that led away from the beach into the forest, where the others were standing, along with Kai and a man who Lucy assumed was their driver. 'We were just waiting for you before we get our instructions on how to sit in a jeep.' He gave Lucy a knowing wink, as if to say, *let's just indulge these over-cautious health and safety nerds, shall we?*

Lucy glanced at Mark: he was staring at her, his arms folded across his chest, his mouth turned down. *He's still angry.* He was too involved in her business, that was his problem. Perhaps it was understandable: he'd half carried her through these past couple of years. Stayed by her side on the nights she'd been unable to steady her breathing until the small hours. Spoon-fed her tomato soup when she couldn't stomach eating, let alone cooking.

But she didn't need that level of concern now – not from him; not from anyone. She was dealing with things her own way – and if that meant shutting him out, then that's what she had to do.

Lucy breathed in the smell of wet earth and swatted away the insects that buzzed close to her ears. They were a fifteen-minute jeep ride inland from Tiahura beach, on their way to see a *marae*, a set of ancient stone structures, now mostly ruined, but that had been a sacred site for the island's original people. Their guide Teva, a dark-haired man in surfing shorts, was leading them along a narrow uphill path, beneath a canopy of thick branches and drooping vines. Every few moments, the trees parted to show flashes of turquoise sea through the foliage.

The heat was intense, and she could feel her energy starting to fade twenty minutes into the walk, as the humid air settled in rivulets of sweat running down her back and the sides of her forehead. The atmosphere was thick with the scent of damp earth and something sweet: blooms she didn't know the name of, bursting in pink clusters between the gnarled roots of the surrounding trees.

Teva came to an abrupt stop a few metres ahead, as the path widened into a small clearing, surrounded by broad, waxy leaves, so dense they appeared to be swallowing the area whole. He pointed to the moss-covered stones at their feet. Lucy stared down for a moment, seeing only rocks – but then they came into sudden focus, like one of those Magic Eye pictures she'd used to love as a girl. These weren't random rocks, but blocks, stacked to form the outline of a structure – something that was once a building, but now lay in ruins.

'This is the *marae*,' Teva explained. 'A sacred place where the Maohi prayed to their gods. Come and take a closer look,' he said, gesturing to the group with his hands, urging them to examine the ground. Lucy crouched and brushed a hand over one of the stones; the moss was cool and soft beneath her fingertips.

'These temples were often built as symbols of power. Chiefs used to rule from exactly where you are standing now.' Teva smiled at Lucy as he said it. 'Some say they made sacrifices here – to the war god, Oro.'

Sacrifices. The word raised the hairs on Lucy's arms. She knew about those – more than most. She'd spent her whole life making them. She'd given up so much for those she loved – and though it had always been her choice, that didn't mean it was easy. *No. It's never been easy.*

After the tour, Teva led the group out of the trees. Rory and Talia followed behind their guide, with the other two couples at the rear. To Lucy's relief, Mark seemed to have softened during the trip; he was content, at least, to walk close to her.

Nick and Eleni fell into step alongside them as the track widened.

'I can't believe this heat,' said Eleni, through heavy breaths.

'Yeah, and it's so humid,' said Mark.

Lucy murmured in agreement. Absently, she stripped off her lightweight shirt down to her vest underneath, enjoying the air on her bare arms.

'What's that?' Eleni's tone was suddenly abrupt; Lucy stopped walking and turned to face her. Eleni was pointing at Lucy's right arm, peering at the fading purplish-grey bruise that sat close to her shoulder. Next to Eleni, Nick frowned, and tried to gently pull his wife away. 'Leave it,' he whispered. But his wife was standing her ground.

'Oh God. That,' said Lucy, pulling her shirt back on. *Damn. How much did she see?* 'It's the stupidest story . . .'

She fumbled for words, but Mark interjected before she could finish. 'Lucy got into a fight with the edge of a wardrobe before we left,' he said. 'And when I say a fight, I mean she walked into it in the middle of the night on her way back from the loo.' He caught Lucy's eye. 'I've never met anyone so clumsy in my life.'

Eleni eyed Mark for a beat, then looked back at Lucy. 'It's true.' Lucy shrugged, giving her best impression of nonchalance. 'I trip over thin air on a daily basis.'

'Uh-huh,' Eleni said. She nodded, but there was something meaningful in her expression – an intensity that made Lucy's skin crawl.

I should reassure her. She gave Eleni the widest smile she could: *everything's fine*.

After a long moment, Eleni offered her a tight smile back. 'Well, I know that feeling. I'm always doing stupid stuff and getting myself in a scrape.' They started walking again, picking up the pace to catch up with the others. 'The other week, I got my heel stuck in the Tube escalator on the way to work – had to take my foot out of my shoe then yank it out from between the steps. In bloody rush hour! You've never heard anyone scream so loud on an escalator at King's Cross, I swear to God.'

'Not that story again,' said Nick. 'She was on about that for days – you've not even put those shoes back on since then, have you?' Eleni shook her head, laughing. 'How many times have I told you not to wear five-inch heels to the office!'

Lucy was flooded with relief – Eleni's focus had shifted, and they were distracted now by Nick poking fun at her. It was a close call, though – too close. *I should be more careful.*

She tried to clear her mind, focus on her surroundings. But it was too late: the memory was back. It played on a reel behind her eyes: the day she got that bruise; what had really happened . . .

And then, in a violent rush, the rage and pain pummelled her, a storm of fury and sadness, snatching her breath, winding her. She gasped for air.

Come on, Luce. Just breathe. Try to stay in the present moment. Don't let it take you over. She forced herself to think about what her therapist would say: *You don't have to deal with all your feelings at once. Just take it a day at a time; an hour at a time; a minute at a time.*

She should make it shorter, while she was here: she should make it a second at a time. She could do one second at a time without losing the plot, couldn't she? Without bursting with rage, without unleashing her hurt and grief in an explosion of fury?

She'd have to – she couldn't risk losing control.

As much as she might want to, she couldn't risk leaving this trip as a murderer.

SAM

Sam hovered at the edge of the master stateroom's doorway, careful not to even breathe too loudly, as he watched Lucy rifling through the notebook on Rory and Talia's desk.

What the hell is she doing in there?

He'd only popped below deck during lunch to put his phone on charge before their afternoon trip. He was curious when he saw the door to Rory and Talia's cabin – the cabin next to his – was slightly open. And he was even more curious when he'd heard shuffling sounds coming from inside. He knew the stewardesses couldn't be in there – Johanna was clearing up after lunch, and Michaela was apparently still in the crew cabins, not well enough to work.

His intrigue had deepened a hundred times when he crept towards the crack in the doorway, and saw Lucy in there, scanning a notebook, then flipping the page and reading the next one, over and over again.

Sam was baffled. Lucy didn't strike him as bold enough to rifle through her boss's cabin; she seemed more like the kind of woman who wanted to apologize for merely existing. Yet here she was, scouring Rory's things, in the middle of the day, with the other guests and crew only metres away. *The gall of her.* Sam hated to admit it, but he was sort of impressed.

Before he could decide whether or not to announce himself, he heard footsteps on the spiral staircase; someone else was coming below deck. *Imagine if Rory catches her in the act.* Now, *that* would make for an interesting scene.

Quietly Sam backed away and slipped into his cabin, pulling the door almost closed. He listened as the footsteps reached the bottom of the stairs, and then heard Mark's voice from the corridor, loud and confused: 'What the hell are you doing in here?'

Busted. Clearly, whatever Lucy was up to, Mark knew nothing about it. Sam strained to hear the conversation between them that followed, but only made out a few words here and there: *sales figures . . . breakfast . . . can't find them.* So she was claiming this was just a bit of work admin. Careful not to make a sound, he watched as they slipped past his door, Lucy's head bowed, and walked along the corridor and up the stairs.

Sam stayed where he was for a few minutes. After their footsteps had faded, he sat quietly on his bed, trying to make sense of what he'd just seen. What was Lucy up to? He'd been wary enough already, mystified as he was by her presence here. Now, seeing her sneaking into the boss's cabin, clearly on the hunt for something, his confusion had become downright suspicion.

One thing's for sure: I'm not going to find out what she was doing by sitting in my cabin on my own.

He made his way back upstairs and across the main deck

to the stern. The group were gathered on the swim platform there, preparing for the visit to the *marae* – everyone was applying sun cream and checking their water bottles were filled. As he approached them, his foot stung uncomfortably – the cut on his sole had touched a small puddle of seawater. *Christ. It really fucking hurts.*

'Ah, shit. Listen, guys – I think I'm going to have to sit this one out. This foot's still giving me grief. Much as I'd love to join, I'll only slow everyone down.'

Disappointment tinged his voice. Noah tried to comfort him: 'Sorry you're not up to it, mate,' as Eleni flashed him a sympathetic smile.

Sam looked at the floor, embarrassed. He hated feeling like an invalid. He wanted to join in, hike to see the *marae*, swim in the sea. This was bucket list stuff he was missing out on – he was spending this trip of a lifetime holed up on a boat. But at least it was the *Lusso* – there were worse places he could be confined to hobble around.

Once they'd all climbed into the tender with Noah, Sam watched as the small boat made its way to shore. With them gone, the air seemed to abruptly change; he could breathe more deeply.

Maybe it'll be a relief to have some space from all the couples. Being around them all the time – it hurt. It made Sam miss Claire. And swirling among the sadness was the hot, eviscerating fury he felt towards the man who'd caused them to break up in the first place. The same man he was now sharing a living space with: *Rory.*

It was starting to do his head in, the rage and the pain and the injustice. He'd been all right back home, hanging out with his mates for the past couple of weeks every time he felt lonely, nursing his sorrows in too many pints of Guinness.

But here, he couldn't stop thinking about his ex and how they'd ended; he kept playing it over and over. The ultimatum she'd given him – telling him to stop pursuing his ambitions, asking him to potentially fuck up the career he'd been building for over a decade.

No. There's no coming back from that. No relationship was worth that, was it? She made the right choice ending it, if that's really what she'd wanted.

Sam caught sight of Johanna at the stern of the upper deck and called up to her for a cold beer. Once she'd brought it down to him, he wandered over to the edge of the swim platform, where Kai was hosing down the floor.

'You okay with me joining you here for a bit?' Sam asked, lifting his bottle.

Kai smiled. 'Of course. As long as you're not planning to try to help. I'm a bit too busy to train up a newbie.'

Sam made the sign of a cross on his chest. 'I swear I wouldn't dream of it, fella.' He settled himself on the edge of the swim platform and let his legs dangle over the side. 'So,' he said, 'how long have you been doing this – working on luxury yachts?'

'This is my third season now.'

Sam nodded. 'And you enjoy it?'

'I love it – it's my dream job, honestly.'

'I bet. You get to travel the world, sail the high seas . . . and you must see some pretty wild stuff sometimes too.'

Kai grinned. 'Define wild.'

'Ah, you know. Scandals. Secrets. Drama. It's got to be a bit like that reality TV show – you know the one?'

The deckhand snorted. 'Ah, I know it. But honestly, it's mostly drunk bankers vomiting in the hot tub. Though we do catch the occasional husband sneaking around behind his wife's back.'

Sam laughed, leaning back on his hands. 'Now, that's more like it. I bet you've got some good stories.'

'Oh, we do,' Kai said, nodding. 'We're just trained to keep them to ourselves.' He tapped a finger to his nose; Sam laughed. Then he tilted his head, studying the gleam of a dome camera mounted at the edge of the garage.

'You've got cameras everywhere on the boat, haven't you? For security?'

'Yeah,' said Kai. 'Well, except below deck. We had them upgraded recently, so now there's even sound on some of them.'

Sam raised his eyebrows. 'So technically you can see – and hear – pretty much anything that happens on board?'

Kai shrugged. 'Well, only the captain and first officer have the logins. We don't look unless something's gone pretty badly wrong. And that doesn't happen often.'

'Ah, sure,' Sam said. 'That makes sense.'

'Why do you ask?' said Kai curiously. 'Are you trying not to get caught on camera?'

Sam laughed in response, then looked away and back out at the water. Noah was approaching the swim platform now in the tender, having dropped his passengers at the beach. Sam watched as he steered the boat to a gentle stop at the side of the *Lusso* and, with Kai's help, attached it to the superyacht's stern with a towing line.

'You boys been all good?' Noah asked as he clambered on board, nodding at Sam.

'Ah, yeah,' said Sam. 'Kai's been keeping me company. Filling me in on all the crew gossip.'

'I should hope not,' said Noah, raising his eyebrows as he glanced at Kai.

'I'm just kidding,' said Sam quickly. 'I've actually been pestering him for the juicy details of what it's like working on the *Lusso*. He's been nothing but a total professional.'

'I see. Come on then, spill. Have you been pouring your heart out about Johanna again, mate?' Noah gave Kai a playful thump on the arm. Kai looked embarrassed for a second, then grinned.

'I hadn't said a word.'

'It's true,' said Sam, holding up his hands. 'We didn't even get onto the subject of women.'

'You didn't? Well, there's still time to change that. There's some stunners on this charter, all right,' said Noah. 'And I'm not just talking about the crew.'

Sam nodded. 'Yeah. Talia's something special, isn't she?'

Kai looked surprised. 'The primary's wife?'

'Uh-huh. I know she's older, but she's . . . you know, classy. A cut above.'

Noah laughed. 'A cut above her husband, you mean?'

Is it that obvious I can't stand Rory? Sam shrugged. 'I didn't say that, did I?'

Kai chuckled. 'Of course not.'

Sam took another swig of his beer. He was talking too much, he knew that. But the easy banter was comforting – it was like he was chatting to the lads back home. He missed that, needed it more than he'd realized. It was easy; he didn't have to think about everything he said before he said it. He didn't have to measure his words, like he did around his colleagues and his boss. 'I can't figure out why she's still with him, honestly,' he said.

'Maybe she likes the money,' offered Kai.

'Or maybe she just doesn't know she could do better,' said Noah, giving Sam a meaningful look.

Sam laughed off his words, but deep down he agreed. Talia *could* do better. So much better. 'Did you hear any of the stories he was telling last night?'

'Who?' asked Noah. 'Mr Ashworth?' Sam nodded. 'Nah. Dinner and drinks are the stews' domain. Why, what was he saying?'

Sam rolled his eyes, and repeated one of the embarrassing anecdotes Rory had taken it upon himself to share last night. He'd overheard his boss recounting to Nick a viral video about a woman on a London Underground platform. Rory had been making an animated gesture of grabbing something with his hands, and the anecdote ended with '*the woman with the tits stepped back, but the guy was talking about a passenger with actual juicy melons*', before Rory dissolved into laughter.

'Gross,' said Kai, when Sam finished. Sam nodded; his flesh had crawled when he heard it, and it crawled again now.

For the first few years he'd worked for him, Sam just accepted this was Rory: an embarrassing drunk with an outdated sense of humour, stuck in the days before MeToo was a thing. It irked him, but he didn't think about it too much.

These days, though, it was hitting differently.

That story was exactly the kind of thing Claire had complained to Sam about after she'd met Rory at the awards night a few months back. At the time, he'd not wanted to hear his girlfriend's point of view – he *couldn't*. He'd tried to explain that it was just harmless banter from an old-fashioned fella – a man of his time. That all the ways Rory supported women at work, all his generosity towards his colleagues, more than made up for the times he said stupid things. That his outdated chat merited an eye-roll, and nothing more.

But Claire hadn't agreed. She'd been convinced that if Rory behaved like that in public, he'd be doing far worse behind closed doors – in meeting rooms and during one-to-ones.

They'd fought about it. Sam thought it was a massive over-reaction; he couldn't understand why they were disagreeing about something so fucking trivial, something that had nothing to do with their relationship.

He'd changed his mind soon after, when he realized that she'd been right and he'd been wrong.

Because, it turned out, Claire wasn't the only woman to warn Sam about Rory.

GENDARMERIE MARITIME DE POLYNÉSIE FRANÇAISE

CASE NUMBER: 247849

POLICE EXHIBIT THREE

Text message exchange between crew members Noah Bailey and Michaela Stevens, 08/06/2026

16:37 Noah: Hey. You coming back on soon? Just went to pick up the guests, they're back on board now. But I've got a few minutes. Can I come see you?

16:39 Michaela: I'm still below deck. Coming up in a sec to help Johanna before dinner. Just needed some time out today – sorry, I feel bad for letting everyone down :(

16:39 Noah: Ah, no worries. We all need a break sometimes. Are you ok, though? Waiting on these rich arseholes getting to you? ;)

16:41 Michaela: Ha. Something like that

16:41 Noah: They're all the fucking same, Mic. Especially the blokes. Don't let em bother you

16.44 Noah: Mic?

16.46 Michaela: Sorry, got distracted. Thought I heard something. But yeah – I know. You're right. I thought these ones were going to be ok. But nope . . . just more entitled dickheads. Tbh, I think I might be done with it after this one

16:47 Noah: Done with charters? Ah man. Johanna said you were thinking something like that. But hasn't this been your entire life for the last five years? You're chief stew! I thought you lived and breathed superyachts

16:48 Michaela: I dunno. I'm tired. The travelling, the sea – the appeal wears off after a while. For me anyway. And I miss my mum and my little niece – I've not seen her since she was born and she's nearly one now!

16:48 Michaela: And you know what, these guests might be some of the worst. They seemed nice enough yesterday morning, but nope – it's always the same. They get hammered and it all comes out. Some of the guys on this charter . . . gross

16:49 Noah: I'm sorry. But I'll miss you if you quit. It's been cool getting to know you this season. Hey, want some goss to cheer you up? I reckon there's some shady shit going on with these guests . . .

16:50 Michaela: Hang on. Just heard it again. There's someone else down here. Didn't think anyone else was on break. Did you send Kai down early?

16:50 Noah: Nope. Kai's out in the tender, Leilani's prepping dinner in the galley, Brett's on the bridge. Must be Johanna?

16:50 Michaela: Weird! Didn't think she'd have time for a break. Whoever it is, they're checking all the crew cabins' doors. WTF? I'm going to check

16:51 Noah: Wait a sec! My key card . . . Hang on. I'll borrow Kai's and come down

16:52 Noah: Hello?

TALIA

The drumming began just as Talia swallowed the last mouthful of her syrupy pineapple pudding. One slow, steady beat sounded out to begin with, loud enough to attract everyone's attention. From their spot in the open-air dining terrace adjoining the five-star hotel where they'd eaten tonight, she couldn't yet see the source of the sound, but she knew what it was.

The sound, at least, might force her back into the present moment; she'd spent the entire day – into the early evening, now – scanning her companions. Who had left her that note last night, and what the hell did they mean by it?

Get away from him before it's too late.

She'd played the words over and over and deduced it could only be from one of Rory's colleagues; and that whoever had written it was referring to her husband. She'd since spent all day wondering what Rory could have possibly done to offend them; what it was about him they objected to? Why did they think they needed to warn her off?

Talia was well aware of her husband's flaws – the patronizing pats on the shoulder; the outdated jokes that usually related to women – though sometimes she pretended not to be. She also knew that Rory expected a lot from the people who worked for him, and that he'd do pretty much anything, within the bounds of the law, to keep his business on the up.

But none of that was a crime. She'd been with him long enough to know the difference between ego and actual malice, hadn't she? And she'd always observed him to be a fair, decent boss. More than that: he *fought* for his employees. He encouraged women to speak up for salary increases and promotions and to tell him if they'd been subjected to discrimination in an industry that remained male dominated, especially at senior levels.

He encouraged Talia too, and their daughters. She still remembered the day he'd lost the plot at their eldest daughter Nina's primary school. He'd seen a story in the weekly parents' newsletter about investing in facilities for a computing club. The article had the title '*Exciting news for our boys!*'

'How dare they insinuate that girls aren't going to be interested in a computing club? We're paying for one of the top prep schools in London, and they send us this rubbish!' She'd tried to calm him, suggested it was just a typo, but there was no talking him out of the blasting he gave the head teacher. *That* was who Rory was. So what could he have done to merit this?

How ungrateful they all are. Rory wanted to make this experience exceptional for his winners, to reward them for their hard work. He'd been so excited, showing her the photos of the superyacht before Christmas. And now here they were – one of them, anyway – trying to cause trouble between Rory and his wife. *As if there isn't enough trouble already.*

Since the morning, Talia noticed, Lucy had barely looked Rory in the eye. And just now, she'd caught Sam glaring at him across the table. The tension between the two men was palpable. Only Eleni seemed warm and friendly towards both her and Rory at all times – rather ingratiatingly so, if Talia were being honest.

Perhaps she should ask Rory about the note – see if he could think of anything he'd said or done to upset anyone. But she could picture his reaction: amusement verging on annoyance, telling her she was *fretting over nothing again.* And of course, drawing attention to the note might lead to more questions – more spotlight on *her* – and that was the last thing she needed.

'It's starting,' said Rory, gulping down the remnants of his fried dough fritters – *firi firi* – and jumping to his feet. 'Come on, Talia, get your lazy bottom off that chair – we don't want to miss this.' She stood, trying not to roll her eyes, and, in the seat next to her, caught Sam looking at her. A flash of something – *recognition? a shared frustration?* – passed between them briefly, and then was gone.

'We should all go and watch, shouldn't we?' said Mark, standing up. With Rory and Talia taking the lead, the group walked from the terrace down onto the sand.

The drum beat steadily – *tah-tum; tah-tum* – its rhythm vibrating to Talia's core. They waited a moment, then a young woman with long black hair, wearing a blood red dress, took her spot on the beach in front of her audience. A garland of white flowers was placed on her head. Behind her, four more women emerged from the shadows; then the same number of men, each wearing armbands made from coconut shells and wide, woven belts.

They danced together, slowly at first, their hips and shoulders rolling, their hands carving shapes in the air. Talia's breath caught in her throat. It was stunning, yes, but more than that – her body was responding; she was turned on. A hot pulse of desire rose from her hips, her pelvis. She resisted the urge to reach for her phone to send a text: to put down in words what she was seeing and feeling.

Mercifully, the urge passed and she brought her attention back to the mesmerizing display in front of her. A man stepped into the centre of the dancers' circle and raised a long staff, wrapped in cloth, its tip and base glistening with oil in the moonlight. Another man lit it with a torch, and the rod burst into orange flame, spitting tiny sparks in a halo of vibrant colour. Talia gasped, and Rory squeezed her shoulder; she cast a quick glance at him – he was beaming in boyish delight. From a little to her right, Eleni erupted: 'Oh my God – wow!'

The rest of the dancers came closer to him, holding shorter torches, bending their bodies gracefully in his direction to light their own, smaller flames. Then, the man with the largest staff began to spin it – first in slow arcs, then more quickly until it became a blur, a wheel of fire orbiting his body. The others swung their smaller flames in circles, weaving spirals around their bodies, some of them resembling flowers, or geometric symbols. Talia couldn't look away. The combination of the drumming and the hypnotic shapes created by the light from the fire had her enchanted.

Gradually the dancers slowed and the beats began to soften.

One by one, they extinguished their torches in the sand with a *hiss* and a plume of smoke.

The small crowd stood in stunned silence for a breath, before Rory erupted into applause and shouts of praise; everyone joined in. In unison, the dancers gave a low bow. Then they melted into the shadows, leaving behind thinning plumes of smoke and the smell of burning oil – and Talia with a deep, sensual heat between her thighs.

After Noah sailed them back to the *Lusso* in the tender, Talia walked to the railings at the front of the boat, leaned back and craned her neck towards the sky.

Her fingers itched to unlock her phone, to reread the messages that sent a thrill of desire through her body. *Don't even think about it*. There were too many people around – too many eyes on her. Everyone was bound to notice – if they hadn't already – that she was clutching her phone at all times, gripping it like a raft in a storm. No; she couldn't risk it.

Johanna stirred her from her thoughts, announcing the arrival of their cocktails. Talia picked hers up from the silver tray and took a long sip, then turned back to admire the sea and Tiahura beach beyond, enjoying the dip in temperature and the chill music mix playing from the speakers in the centre of the deck. She stared up at the sky: the night had created a clear, cloudless black canopy dotted with infinite stars. Talia gasped as a shooting star burst across the sky directly above her, the longest and brightest she'd ever seen.

Perhaps it's a good omen. It's telling me everything is going to be okay.

Or a bad one: it's warning me. It's all going to go wrong . . .

'Are you all right, Talia?' asked Lucy, eyeing her curiously from her seat on the sofa, a few feet away.

Talia hadn't meant to gasp so loudly. *How embarrassing.* She gave an awkward laugh. 'Yes – just . . . this sky. It's quite something. I just saw a shooting star.'

Lucy looked up at the stars for a second, gave Talia a quick smile, then turned back to her conversation with Nick, Sam and Eleni. Nick was entertaining them all with some funny stories about his young boys, by the sounds of it, though Lucy didn't look particularly amused. Elsewhere, Mark and Rory stood nursing their drinks at the bar. The two men seemed deep in conversation; Talia wondered what they could possibly have to chat about. Mark was a journalist, wasn't he? Rory usually had no time for the lot of them. All *useless hacks*. She decided to join the group on the sofa, but just as she sat down, Lucy stretched and stood up.

'I think I'm going to head to bed,' Lucy said, yawning. 'The sun today has tired me out.'

'Oh, was it a bit too hot for you?' said Eleni. There was a patronizing tilt to her head as she spoke, Talia noticed with distaste.

'I suppose so,' said Lucy. 'I'm just not used to it.'

'Well,' Eleni said lazily, turning to Nick, 'I think we should stay up for a while. You could have a proper chat with Rory – I'm sure he'd love that.'

Lucy nodded her goodbyes, then made her way towards the doors to the salon. Talia settled into the sofa and listened as Nick carried on his story, his wife giggling next to him.

'I don't know how she did it,' he continued, tears of laughter gathering in his eyes. 'How Eleni kept a straight face as the head teacher told her what a serious health and safety hazard it was for Lucas to lock the teaching assistant out of the classroom . . .'

But his voice was abruptly drowned out by the sound of raised voices from the bar. Talia looked over, alarmed, to see Mark squaring up to Rory, and Rory backing away – Mark was slurring as he spoke. He was trying to keep his voice low, but she made out the words: 'Whatever's going on, I'm going to find out about it.'

Talia froze. *What the hell is he talking about?*

Rory was blinking, his head shaking back and forth. He looked bewildered. 'I have no idea what you mean,' she heard him say.

Talia needed to do something; she should intervene. She got to her feet and marched over to the two men. 'What on earth is going on over here?' she demanded.

Now only inches apart – Mark had moved closer again – Rory's eyes didn't move from Mark's face as he said, 'Nothing to worry about, Talia, darling. Mark here's just had a few too many, that's all. Can't handle his drink – typical journo, biting off more than he can chew. Isn't that right, Mark, eh?'

Mark stumbled backwards; his eyes were slits, his lips curled into a snarl. He shook his head. 'No . . . no, that's not what—'

What in God's name . . . ? This didn't look like someone who'd just taken a bit of drunken banter too far. Mark was *raging*.

'Mark, what the hell has got into you?' It was Lucy; she must have heard the commotion and come back to the deck. She laid a hand on her partner's shoulder, ushering him backwards and away from Rory. 'I think we all need to call it a night, yeah?'

'Ah, come on, Luce,' slurred Mark, reaching a hand over to pat her on the shoulder and missing; waving at thin air. 'It's still early. One more for the road, yeah? We've all got a lot to talk about—'

'No,' she said firmly. 'It's time for bed. Let's go.'

Mark's eyes roamed the rest of the group. 'Who's staying for a nightcap with me? Anyone? Sam? Eleni, Nick – you'll have another with me, won't you?' He could barely focus on anyone's face as he spoke.

'I would, but . . . I think I've had enough to drink,' said Sam.

'We could stay for a while longer, couldn't we?' Eleni addressed her husband. 'Rory, Talia – you'll stay too – we could have one last drink, all together?'

Talia flinched. *Why is she so keen to get the four of us in close proximity?*

'I dunno,' said Nick, with a shrug. 'Let's head to bed too. I'll finish my drink on the sun deck and come down. Seems like . . . everyone could do with a bit of space?'

Perhaps I should get out of here too. Maybe Mark and Rory need to clear the air – alone.

But then Mark turned back to the bar and dumped his glass down on the counter. 'All right, all right. Bunch of party poopers. Fine, then, I'll go,' he said, allowing Lucy to guide him away inside.

When everyone else had gone, Talia turned to her husband. Rory was leaning against the bar, tight-lipped. 'What on earth was that about?'

He shook his head. 'Talia, I honestly have no idea.' He shrugged. 'I mean it – I can't imagine why he'd turn on me like that. And I didn't get it out of him – he just kept saying, *I know what you're doing*, and that it was *all going to come out*. But . . . I mean, what? What have I done? I barely know the man.'

Talia turned cold. She stared at Rory for a long moment; she knew when he was telling the truth, and he was telling the truth now. Whatever Mark's issue was, Rory was none the wiser.

She sighed. 'Well, there's no use trying to resolve it tonight. Let's go to bed, and try to make sense of it with clear heads in the morning.'

'You go,' said Rory. 'Get a good night's sleep. I think I'll stay out here for a while, enjoy the fresh air. I want to try to clear my thoughts.'

Talia nodded, gave him a brief kiss on the lips, then backed away and headed inside the salon. Despite the warmth of the evening, she shivered – the furious expression on Mark's face still haunting her.

Did he leave me that note? Did Mark have some kind of grudge against Rory? But no, surely not – the two men scarcely knew each other. They could only have met once before this trip – on that one fateful night she wished she could erase from her life altogether. This couldn't be about *that*, could it?

No; impossible. Then perhaps Mark's anger was to do with Lucy. That was the only way it could make sense. *But why?* Rory had no problems with her; he'd have mentioned it if he did, and he certainly wouldn't have invited her here. His personal preferences always influenced the winners of bonus holidays, much as he claimed to be an 'entirely impartial judge'.

Talia sighed; she wasn't getting anywhere with this. Best

just to sleep on it. She'd try to talk to Mark once he'd sobered up – alone, just the two of them. And Lucy too, if she could manage it.

As she approached the spiral staircase leading below deck, she paused, waiting. No one appeared; there was only silence pierced by the hum of the air-conditioning, the gentle purr from the engine room, and the sound of Talia's own heartbeat pulsing in her ears.

'Hello?' she whispered. 'Is anyone there?'

There was no reply, but . . . was that someone's soft footsteps behind her? Was that the rhythm of someone else's breath in time with hers?

Talia froze. She stayed unmoving at the top of the stairs – and waited.

SAM

9 JUNE

Sam lay in bed, willing his brain to switch off so he could finally get some sleep. It was gone two in the morning; he'd been tossing and turning for more than two hours, and now he'd missed the soporific, alcohol-fuelled point in time where he could pass out in a haze. To make matters worse, he'd actually started sobering up; he was vaguely nauseous, his tongue coated with fur despite two rounds of mouthwash, his heart juddering erratically in his chest. The cut on his foot was throbbing again too; it had felt better the previous morning, but he'd clearly overdone it during the day.

Sam winced as he brushed his injured foot against the mattress. It wasn't just the pain, though: his confusion about the evening was spinning around his brain, wiring him up. It had all ended so strangely tonight – Mark kicking off like that, Lucy having to drag him away, Rory so bewildered by it all. They were on a superyacht exploring some of the most beautiful places on earth – what did Mark have to get so pissed off about?

He'd only known him a couple of days, sure, but that behaviour seemed out of place. Mark didn't give off the vibe of someone who'd turn aggressive when drunk; he'd seemed sensible, quiet, a little awkward – a bit of a geek, honestly. He'd have been that boy at school who sat at the front, arm straight up with the answers before the teacher had finished speaking, covering his exam papers with his hands. The opposite of Sam, who spent his days messing about, sticking chewed-up bubblegum under his desk, scrapping with kids in the year above – popular; excellent at sports, but not much else.

Sam had his suspicions about what could have given Mark the rage, though. It was to do with Lucy – it had to be. Mark had caught Lucy snooping in Rory's room so maybe he thought there was something going on between them.

And maybe there is. Whether it was romantic – Sam was grossed out by the idea, but wouldn't rule it out; that was Rory's style, after all – or something else altogether, some kind of secret agreement between them might explain what she was doing here. It just didn't add up otherwise. Lucy wasn't Rory's usual pick for a bonus trip; it was basically unheard of, bringing along an *analyst*, for fuck's sake. Then rifling through his stuff, alone in his cabin, clearly up to something. Looking for something. Did Lucy have any idea what she might be getting herself into?

His brain felt scattered. Giving up on sleep now after so long trying, Sam decided he needed some fresh air. He swung his legs out of bed and got up, chucked on a T-shirt and shorts over his boxers, grabbed his key card and phone – smiling as he noted the new text from his little sister, Anna: *How's the superyacht, bro?* – then opened his cabin door, as quietly as he could.

The corridor outside was dark and silent – except for the

sound of some guttural snores coming from the master stateroom, next to his cabin. He crinkled his nose in mild disgust – of course Rory was a horrendous snorer. He'd expect nothing less.

As he stepped into the passageway, the sensor picked him up and the lights blazed on, blinding him for a few seconds. Squinting, he stumbled, hopping on his good foot towards the staircase.

When he reached the top, he felt something squelch as he placed his injured foot briefly on the ground. Peering down, he saw with horror that blood was seeping through the dressing – he must have opened the cut again somehow. *Shit*. He needed a new bandage, and for someone to clean up the smears of blood that had no doubt trailed behind him from his cabin. It was too late for any of the crew to still be up, wasn't it? He didn't want to wake anyone. Perhaps he could just clean it up himself.

Stepping gingerly towards the galley, he was about to walk inside and start rooting around for a bandage and a cloth, when he heard soft voices inside. He peered through the window: two people were standing at the other end of the galley.

The stewardesses. They're up late. He went to knock on the door, but something about their body language told him not to interrupt. He paused – not meaning to eavesdrop exactly, just . . . waiting for a good moment to announce his presence.

'I can't believe he came to the crew cabins – twice,' Johanna said. 'How did he even get in this afternoon – and again tonight? And . . . you don't think he was being serious?' Johanna's arms wrapped around her body. Her tone was urgent; nervous. The crew were always so calm and collected. It was unsettling, hearing them like this.

'I don't know – he must have got hold of a key card somehow – didn't Noah say he'd lost his? And no, maybe he wasn't being serious. But just . . . the way he said it, you know?' Michaela's voice was worried too, but tinged with anger.

'What are you going to do? Have you told the captain about him getting in our quarters?' Johanna asked.

Sam shifted on the spot, careful to stay out of sight behind the galley door. He knew he shouldn't be listening, but he felt trapped. If he walked into the galley now, they might realize he'd overheard them. Best to wait until they'd finished talking before he moved.

'Yeah, I've spoken to her again – she said I don't have to go back on guest duties for now. I'm sorry, Jo, it's not fair on you. But nothing this bad has ever happened to me on a charter before – a bit of drunken banter, yes, but coming to find me below deck . . .'

Johanna's response came more softly this time; Sam strained to pick up her words: 'Listen, maybe he was just messing around. And honestly, Mic, no one would actually *do* anything on a yacht full of people. He'd have to be crazy to even try.'

So they were talking about a man on board. Someone had said something that had frightened Michaela – threatened her, or made her uncomfortable, at least.

And Sam would bet his annual salary that he could guess who.

Another pause, then Johanna added: 'Try not to worry. I've got your back.'

Out of the corner of his eye, Sam caught something move in the shadows of the salon behind him. He turned around to look; it was dark, though, and he couldn't make anything out. Probably just the sea breeze shifting the awning.

He turned back and felt a flash of guilt. *What am I doing?*

This wasn't right; he should stop listening in. Whatever was going on, he wasn't going to get to the bottom of it like this, lurking in the shadows. He swayed slightly, the pain radiating from the sole of his right foot now making him wobble.

He had an idea: he'd walk back a bit, then pretend he'd just come up to the galley – he'd make it look like he hadn't been waiting there, listening to a conversation he knew was private. He took a couple of painful paces backwards, then stepped towards the galley door and pushed it open. 'Oh! Hello, you two. You're up late! All good?' His voice came out too bright, forced.

Michaela startled and took a step back from Johanna, who turned and flashed Sam a smooth smile. 'Is everything okay, Sam?' she said, with no trace of the worry in her voice that Sam had heard a moment ago. She sounded like the same Johanna that had been offering them drinks since they'd arrived back on board. 'Do you need anything?'

Sam swallowed; he glanced at Michaela, who had fixed a smile on her face too, but wasn't meeting Sam's eye. 'Ah, actually, I do,' he said, trying his best at nonchalance. He pointed to his bloody foot. 'This has started bleeding again, and I've managed to get a few smears on the stairs – I'm really sorry. Is there any chance you could find me a new bandage and clean it up?'

'Oh, goodness. Poor you. Of course.'

Johanna walked to a cupboard near the galley door, opened it and rifled through. She pulled out a fresh dressing and some antibiotic cream and handed it to Sam.

'Will you be okay dressing it yourself? We were both about to clock off, and I'll need to clean the floor before I go down . . .'

Sam frowned. Do it himself? Weren't these stewardesses supposed to be there to cater for their every whim, twenty-four seven? Then he caught himself: *Jesus, what's wrong with me? I sound like Rory. His condescending attitude is rubbing off on me.*

'Ah, sure, thanks,' he said with a shrug. 'I'll be fine, don't worry.'

As the two women walked past him and out of the galley, Michaela met Sam's gaze briefly, then looked away – but not before he caught a flicker of something in her eyes that made him turn cold.

He'd seen that flicker before – more than once. It was uncomfortably familiar. He'd seen it in his fifteen-year-old sister Anna's face, that morning she'd told him what happened with her sixth-form boyfriend the night before.

Sam had made the mistake of not acting fast enough on his sister's behalf, and the failure cost him dearly. He should have been watching more closely; he should have stepped in sooner.

When Anna had started seeing that boyfriend, Sam was ill at ease – and not just in an overprotective, big brother kind of way. The lad had been in the year below him, and despite Sam having left college to start his estate agency apprenticeship, he remembered him well. Jamie, his name was: good-looking, popular and charismatic – and with a reputation as a womanizing arsehole. Sam told Anna he didn't like the idea of her going out with him; that she could do better. Anna had responded by telling him, in no uncertain terms, to stay the fuck out of her business.

Sam did as she'd asked. He didn't push it. He could only

watch from a distance as Jamie reeled Anna in, made her think she was in love, plying her with Bacardi Breezers at house parties with men in their twenties. He hadn't intervened. He hadn't protected her. And then he'd had to listen to his mam weeping that Sunday over her breakfast after Jamie had got Anna hammered at a party the night before and his sister had woken up in nothing but her bra, bleeding. *He assaulted her, Sam. She was so drunk, she couldn't have said yes. She's fifteen years old . . . my precious girl.* He vowed he'd never get it so wrong again.

So when he'd seen the same expression again in his workmates' faces, years later, when they'd opened up after a few glasses of wine, he knew he'd have to do something. The first night it happened, he'd sat there, one hand gripping his pint, the other fiddling with a beer mat as he listened in open-mouthed shock. He remembered the way his colleague had been twirling the stem of her wine glass between her fingers, her mask dropping as she shared things that she'd never have revealed if she hadn't been three glasses in.

This is why it's so important to keep an eye on things. To stay close to the women around him, listen to their words, watch what their body language gave away without them meaning to. Because it didn't matter how strong they thought they were, how independent. There were times they needed someone else to step in.

So yes, he knew Michaela's expression well.

It was a look they all tried to hide, but Sam saw it just the same.

GENDARMERIE MARITIME DE POLYNÉSIE FRANÇAISE

CASE NUMBER: 247849

DATE: 11/06/2026

INTERVIEW EXCERPT TWO (TRANSLATED FROM FRENCH TO ENGLISH)

Interview subject: Kai Tehau, deckhand on board *Lusso di Mare* charter

Interview conducted by Chief of Police Henri Robert

M Robert: And you were on watch duty that second night, is that correct?

M Tehau: That's right, it was my turn on day two.

M Robert: And what does that entail, exactly? Your watch duty.

M Tehau: Well, on a passenger charter like this one where the guests are sleeping on board overnight, we have to do a few things on night watch. Security checks of the vessel – looking out for any fire or trip hazards. Making sure all our safety equipment and the tender are in the right place and functioning as they should. Then keeping lookout – checking for any other boats that might be approaching ours, in case of collision. And in the case of bad weather overnight, we might need to secure everything on the outer decks. That's about it, I think.

M Robert: And that night, on your checks, everything seemed normal? Everything was as it should be?

M Tehau: Ah – mostly it was, yes. Though I suppose I did see one thing – I didn't think too much of it at the time. Only now, looking back . . . <inaudible>

M Robert: What did you see? It's very important that you share any relevant details with me as part of our investigation into—

M Tehau: Of course, I know that, but it didn't seem like a big deal. It still might not be. But yeah, around two-fifteen, two-thirty a.m., I went to check the salon and the galley area. And I saw one of the guests hanging around outside the door to the galley.

M Robert: Which guest did you see?

M Tehau: Sam. It was Sam out there.

M Robert: I see. And why was that unusual?

M Tehau: Well, everyone had gone to bed a couple of hours earlier, so it was strange to see him up from his cabin. But it wasn't just that – sometimes, guests need something in the middle of the night, or go outside and look at the ocean if they can't sleep. That would have been pretty normal. But he wasn't doing that. He was . . . waiting – kind of hovering? Outside the galley. Michaela and Johanna were in there, talking. I don't know what about, but I think Michaela was upset. And he was outside, just . . . listening.

M Robert: I see. And what did you do, when you saw him there?

M Tehau: I stayed there for a minute, keeping an eye on him. I wanted to make sure he wasn't going to try anything inappropriate – I knew Michaela had been getting some hassle from the guys, and I didn't know which ones. But then he kind of stepped back, and walked forward really quickly straight into the galley so the stewardesses saw him. I think he was trying to pretend he'd just got there.

M Robert: And what did you make of it? What did you think about it at the time?

M Tehau: <pause> I guess I just thought it was kind of weird then. But now? After everything that's happened . . . <longer pause> It's hard not to think that it was all part of something bigger – something we just didn't know about yet.

[TRANSCRIPT ENDS]

LUCY

Lucy woke with the gnawing feeling that something wasn't right.

She leaned over to her bedside table where her phone was charging and checked the time: *1.37 a.m.* She'd only been asleep for a couple of hours. What had woken her?

She rolled over and realized Mark wasn't there. He must be in the loo – perhaps him getting up was what had disturbed her. She shifted back into her favourite sleeping position – on her side, arms wrapped around one of her pillows – and closed her eyes, hoping against hope that she'd be able to nod off again. Sleep had never come easily to her, and often when she woke in the middle of the night, she'd stay awake until her alarm forced her out of bed.

After five minutes or so of trying to relax enough to nod off again, she realized she'd not heard anything from the bathroom. *Is Mark okay in there?* He'd clearly drunk far too much last night, judging by that bizarre outburst at Rory; maybe he was feeling sick. As confused and irritated as she was by the evening's turn of events, she didn't like the thought of him being unwell. She should check on him.

With a groan, she lifted the duvet and swung her legs to the floor. She padded over to the bathroom and opened the door, noticing that the light was off. She turned it on and peered inside.

He wasn't there.

Lucy glanced back around the cabin, checking he hadn't gone to sleep on the sofa – or rolled off the bed and crashed out on the floor. She wouldn't have put it past him, the state he was in. But with the bathroom light illuminating the room, she could see perfectly well that he wasn't there.

Strange. Where's he gone at this time?

Maybe he's just popped to the galley to refill his water.

With a heavy sigh, she switched off the bathroom light, got back into bed and waited. She closed her eyes, tried to will herself back to sleep, but as the minutes ticked by, she became more and more uncomfortable. It shouldn't take this long to get a glass of water, surely?

She was just considering heading out of their cabin to search for him when she heard the click of the key card and saw Mark's tall, lean frame silhouetted in the door frame by the lights of the passageway. On impulse, she rolled back over and feigned sleep; wherever he'd been, she didn't have the energy to ask about it now.

A few hours later, as the dawn light began to creep into the cabin underneath the thick curtains, Lucy decided trying to get back to sleep was pointless. She reached to the bedside table, pulled the charging cable out of her phone, then unlocked the screen.

A calendar alert popped up: *Alfie and Mum: two years.*

The surge of emotion took Lucy's breath away. She hadn't forgotten, exactly – the date it happened was etched on her brain – but she'd been so distracted by work and this trip, and now Mark's weird behaviour, it must have slipped her mind somehow.

Seeing it there, the words on top of her screensaver – a holiday photo from when she was little, Mum giving Lucy's brother Alfie a big kiss on the cheek while Lucy grinned in rainbow-patterned sunglasses – a kaleidoscope of memories danced in front of her vision. Mum playing air guitar in the kitchen to some embarrassing eighties power ballads, making Lucy wheeze with laughter, Alfie flapping and spinning with joy. Taking Alfie to swimming for the first time, watching him come to life as he splashed in the water, creating huge waves. The table piled extravagantly high with cheap presents her mum couldn't afford for both of them on their birthdays.

Then the early, happy images morphed into the more recent ones: Alfie sitting motionless on the sofa, staring into space, eyes vacant and blank. And then, two years ago . . .

Tears settled behind her eyelids now, in the cabin of this luxury bloody superyacht. Some days, she coped well enough with the memories – when her brain was quiet, free of the terrible images. But sometimes – when something big happened, like going on holiday, or on birthdays, or on anniversaries like this – it was too overwhelming to bear.

She took a few quiet, steady breaths and tried to get a sense of the expression on her therapist's face, or the words she'd say. Things like: *You can cope with your own pain.* And: *If you focus on what's in front of you today, nothing can overwhelm you.* Or: *You're doing really well.*

These words were comforting; Lucy breathed more easily. As her chest began to relax, she let the grief and the pain settle into something else: grim, furious determination. She had come on this bonus trip for a reason – and she wouldn't leave here without getting what she needed. Her search yesterday in the master stateroom had been interrupted before she could get far enough, but she still had a couple of days left. She could try to find another moment to sneak back in there today, unnoticed this time . . .

'Morning.' Mark was awake; the light from her phone must have disturbed him. He was a light sleeper too – the pair of them often grumbling to each other in the morning about who was more tired than who, like some kind of depressing competition.

Lucy put her phone down and turned to look at him. He was bleary-eyed and pale.

'I feel rough as a monkey's arse.' He moved closer to her, wrapped his arms around her waist. She fought the urge to pull away. *Just let him. It'll make things easier.*

'It's badger. Rough as a badger's arse.'

Mark groaned. 'Whatever.' He studied her for a moment. 'I know you've been feeling seasick, but you're all right, aren't you? This is the trip of a lifetime,' he said. 'Honestly, Luce, I still keep pinching myself that we're here. We should be having the time of our lives, and you seem a bit . . . dunno. Flat?'

Lucy swallowed. 'I'm having a great time,' she said. 'It's lovely. Apart from the nausea.'

Mark edged his face closer towards Lucy's, pulled her towards him, and moved in for a kiss. She jerked her face away – but not before she caught the flash of hurt in his expression.

'Sorry,' she said flatly.

He sighed, leaning back on his pillow. 'For God's sake. Am I not allowed to show you some affection – here, on our own, in bed, on the most amazing holiday we've ever had?'

'Of course you are. It's just . . . I haven't slept,' she said, her eyes darting away from him and up to the ceiling.

'Okay,' said Mark, staring at the ceiling. 'You're tired, I understand that. But don't be weird with me for getting excited about spending some time together, just the two of us. It's not often I get you to myself, especially these last few months. I feel like I've barely even seen you . . .'

Lucy wanted to respond with the sarcastic retort on the tip of her tongue – *Well, maybe you should get out more then?* – but then thought better of it. Now wasn't the time. There were things to clear up, and she wouldn't get answers by antagonizing him. Instead, she shut him off with: 'Why did you do it?'

The question bubbled up from somewhere deep in her chest and came blurting out of her mouth, catching her off guard, before she could do anything to stop it.

Mark turned back to face her. 'Eh? Do what?'

'Rory. Last night. Why were you yelling at him – why were you right up in his face?'

Mark cupped his palms over his eyes. 'Oh – that. Lucy, I feel like shit. I've not drunk that much for years. Can we talk about this later, please?'

'No.' Lucy wasn't relenting. 'We are talking about it *now*.'

He sighed heavily. 'There's nothing to talk about, Luce. I just drank too many cocktails. It's not a big deal – the conversation got out of hand.'

'But *how* did it get out of hand? Why were you even talking to him one-on-one in the first place?'

'Jesus, I can't even remember – it's all a big blur, to be honest. He made some dickhead comment about journalists, I think. Thank fuck you dragged me away when you did before I made an even bigger tit of myself.'

Lucy sighed. 'Well, quite.'

'I'm sorry – I genuinely don't know how it spiralled that badly,' he went on. 'I promise, I didn't mean to embarrass you. I'd never want to do that.'

Lucy nodded; she appreciated the apology. But it wasn't the embarrassment that was bothering her. It was that she'd heard snippets of what Mark had said – and it definitely *wasn't* to do with Rory's opinions about journalists.

'All right,' she said. 'But what about disappearing in the middle of the night, then? Where did you go, for nearly half an hour, at half one in the morning?'

Mark frowned. 'What? I didn't go anywhere.'

Lucy exhaled sharply. 'Yes, you did. I woke up and you weren't here. You didn't come back for another twenty minutes.'

Mark screwed his face up in concentration. 'Oh. Hang on . . . I just remembered. I think I went to get something to eat,' he said. 'I was starving, and the booze was all sloshing about in my stomach. I've got vague memories of going into the galley and asking one of the stewardesses for a toastie . . .'

Lucy snorted, despite her gnawing unease. 'Well, I suppose that does sound like something you'd do.'

There was a long pause, and then: 'Are you all right, Lulu? Just tell me what you're thinking.' Mark's voice was all concern. It irritated her.

She looked away from him and picked up her phone again. She was still angry; she still felt he wasn't telling her everything.

And besides, it had become a habit now, dismissing him, pushing him away – protecting herself from his incessant concern, or trying to. 'I'm fine. Let's not talk about it any more.'

Mark said nothing for a moment, and a sick pang of guilt rose in her throat.

I'm sorry, she told him silently. *I don't want it to be like this either.*

'This is all pretty rich of you, you know,' Mark mumbled. Lucy put down her phone; her guilt evaporated in an instant, replaced with a cold wariness. *I bet I know where this is going.*

'What's rich of me?'

'Getting all suspicious about what I'm doing. I seem to remember it was only yesterday I caught you sneaking around in your boss's cabin.' Mark's eyes narrowed. 'I'd say that's a fuck of a lot shadier than me getting rat-arsed and saying some stupid shit.'

'I told you. I was looking for some paperwork. You can ask Rory about it if you want. He'll know what I was doing.' It was a bold suggestion; one that she knew Mark was unlikely to take her up on, especially after embarrassing himself last night.

'Maybe I will,' he replied.

'You do that.'

'Fine.'

'Fine!' Lucy half-shouted the last word, no longer able to keep her irritation under wraps. *Good God, we've reverted to monosyllabic adolescents.* She should apologize, for her tone if not the things she'd said. But she couldn't seem to force the words out of her mouth. She wasn't ready to close the gaping chasm between them yet; she couldn't, even if she wanted to.

'I just can't believe you're mistrusting me,' Mark said huffily. 'We've been together since sixth form. And I've been by your side through everything these last few years. Doesn't that count for anything?'

Lucy sighed. The irony of his irritation wasn't lost on her: for months, she'd been busy keeping secrets from him, telling him half-truths, and now here she was, indignant at him for one evening's odd behaviour. She wondered if this was how it had felt for him; if he'd been living with a constant nagging feeling that something wasn't right between them. It was a miserable experience. No wonder he'd been so keen to come on this trip with her, to try to make things feel okay again.

And after all, this was *her person*: the man who'd made her feel as a teenager, for the first time in her entire life, that she wasn't a total freak, a weirdo. He seemed to innately understand her in a way no one else – except perhaps her mum and Alfie – did. The man who not only *indulged* her info-dumping about random historical figures and obscure eighties punk bands, but seemed to actually *enjoy* it. The man who understood that, even though she came across as blunt and her small talk was abysmal, she never meant to be rude or standoffish. He was the only one who understood that she showed her care and empathy by trying to do something to help, rather than offering hugs or empty platitudes.

'Of course it counts,' she said finally. 'But being together since sixth form – even supporting me through a crisis – it doesn't mean you can act completely fucking *unhinged*, on holiday with my boss, and expect me to just . . . nod along and put up with it.'

Mark whipped the duvet off his legs and got out of bed.

He stood towering above her and looked down into Lucy's face, his eyes flashing.

Lucy stared back, an acidic taste on her tongue. 'What?' she snarled.

'Lucy, if anyone's acting unhinged in this relationship, it's sure as hell not me!'

Lucy gaped. 'And what on earth is that supposed to mean?' She couldn't hold back, even though she knew she should leave it now. This argument was getting worse by the second, and Mark's attention was turning uncomfortably close to her behaviour too.

'Oh, come on. You've been acting weird for months! You've been—'

Lucy had heard enough; this had to stop. 'I'm going for breakfast – come too, or stay here – do whatever you want,' she snapped, cutting him off.

She whirled out of bed, grabbed some clothes and stormed into the bathroom to change. She didn't especially want to leave her cabin and join the others – it was hard to put up with the continued tension and frostiness, especially from some of the other women – but at least with everyone else she'd have some protection from Mark's accusations: the invasive questions, delivered with his laser-eyed focus.

And at least, if she left her cabin, the opportunity might arise for her to sneak back into Rory's.

She gave Mark one last, withering look as she stomped out of the en-suite and towards the cabin door. He watched her go, an expression of hurt confusion crumpling his features. Then she closed the door behind her, tears of frustration threatening to spill.

If only I'd gone into work that day. If she'd been in the office, he wouldn't have seen the invitation, with its picture of the *Lusso di Mare*, pop up in her inbox when they'd both, unusually, been working from home.

If only she'd come up with a better excuse for why she was admiring an image of a superyacht.

If only he hadn't read the subject line, announcing the opportunity to bring a plus one, before she'd minimized her Outlook window.

If only he hadn't come here.

After all, she hadn't even wanted him on this yacht in the first place.

SAM

'No – stop!'

Sam's eyes shot open to a yell from one of the cabins close by. *What the fuck was that?* He sprang upright in his cabin's single bed – sleeping in the yacht's only twin room was a fun reminder that he was the odd one out on this trip, without a partner – and tuned in. It was quiet now – too quiet. A kind of dead silence, like the split second before a crash of thunder erupted.

He heard a door shutting – he couldn't be sure which one, all the guest and crew cabins were in such close proximity – and then swift footsteps, perhaps two sets, moving along the passageway and up the stairs to the main deck.

All fell silent again. He closed his eyes, tried to replay in his mind the voice he'd just heard, tried to work out who it might have belonged to, but the memory was too blurry, too caked in sleep. He forced his brain to trudge through a mental map of the cabins' layout, trying to remember which couple was in the room next to his. Then again, he couldn't be sure the sound had come from the nearest cabin – the corridor separating them was narrow, and both the shout and the door could easily have drifted from one of the rooms across the hallway.

Or there could have been no shout at all.

Maybe he'd imagined it. Was it just the remnants of his vivid, scattered dreams? That was the most likely explanation. He took a few deep breaths, became aware of the thuds of dull pain repeatedly assaulting his skull. He'd got too much sun yesterday. And he'd been drinking way more than he usually did on this trip – even last night, when the mood had been subdued and everyone had been in bed before midnight.

Another door along the passageway closed; hushed voices reached his ears, then footsteps starting up the spiral staircase. Sam leaned over to the cabin window near his bed and tugged the blackout curtains apart slightly; he caught a glimpse of the bay where they'd been anchored last night, but the sunlight was blinding so he closed them again.

What time is it, anyway? He scratched his neck – something had bitten him in the night, the fucker – then fumbled around for his phone. It wasn't on the bedside table; he reached a hand under his pillow and his fingers touched its cool surface. He'd been sleeping on it the whole night. He held it in front of his face and tapped the screen.

It was 9.47 a.m. *Shit – I hope it's not too late for breakfast.* Then he remembered: they literally had a private chef on board. Sam could just put in a request for anything, any time he wanted. He was pretty sure Leilani had all the ingredients for a Bloody Mary to go with his fry-up. That'd sort him out.

There was an unread text in his message inbox, from Rory. It had arrived an hour ago. He opened it: *Sam. I do hope everything is to your satisfaction so far.*

He groaned. *Fuck Rory and his pompous fucking tone.* His careful words that he could always explain away.

Well – apart from the ones he couldn't. Like what Sarah in marketing had overheard Rory say about her six months ago. His boss hadn't been able to explain *that*.

He remembered when Sarah had told him, that night in the pub. Sam had kept asking her more questions. He was just so shocked. His first reaction was that she'd got it wrong. People got confused or misremembered – or made up weird shit – all the time, didn't they? People lied; *she* was lying. He'd been sure: *Rory wouldn't do that*.

Sam had been with Ashworth for more than ten years by then – practically his whole career. He'd been in hundreds of meetings with his CEO, had chatted to him at dozens of parties and after-work drinks. Yes, Rory was politically incorrect; he was baffled by the communication styles and *workplace boundaries* of the Millennials and Gen Zs who worked for him. But he was good to work for; he treated people well. And just look at his wife, Sam had thought – an absolute stunner who Rory clearly adored. It'd be madness to risk losing her if shit like this ever got out.

But then, what possible reason would Sarah have to make it all up? She had fuck all to gain from telling Sam about it – and a hell of a lot to lose. He felt ashamed now that he'd wanted to write her off as full of shit – even though she was struggling to get the words out; even though she kept dismissing herself: *I might have got it wrong . . . there's no point in saying anything, no one would believe me anyway.*

He'd been in a daze the morning after when he'd left his flat, replaying the booze-soaked conversation over and over.

He'd walked to the wrong platform at Clapham Junction – then by the time he made it to the right one, he'd missed a train. When he finally arrived for his meeting at the Rosenberg office, he'd been so flustered, he'd fumbled the sales presentation. David Rosenberg had walked away from a development opportunity that would have been worth millions. He'd cocked it up – because of *Rory*. Sam's boss had been responsible for him losing almost everything good in his life: first, his career progression, and then later, something far worse. The love of his life.

Sam's head throbbed again; he clamped his eyes closed and tried to breathe through it. He must have some paracetamol somewhere; he'd taken some yesterday for the cut on his foot – which was feeling a bit better today, probably thanks to the cream Johanna had given him last night. He'd have a look when he managed to get out of bed. It was quiet again now – no more noises from the cabins around him. Just a couple more minutes in bed, and he'd get up and go in search of his cooked breakfast.

He lifted his phone in front of his face, moved a finger towards the apps on the home screen and tapped on Instagram, keen to check out how many views his story from yesterday evening had got. That selfie was gold: Sam grinning like a loon, posing near the hot tub on the upper deck, holding up a fat tumbler of whisky, a radiant pink and orange sunset behind him. He hoped Claire had seen it.

The app started to open, then stalled; it was having trouble loading. *Come on, come on.* He waited a few more seconds for anything except a blank page to appear, then flicked his eyes upwards to the top of the screen – *oh right, that'll be why.* There was no Wi-Fi: his phone was using the local 4G to try to connect, clearly without much luck. The satellite wireless must have gone down overnight – or maybe the crew had switched it off for some reason.

He sighed – *so much for scrolling* – and leaned his head further back into his pillow. He felt his eyelids start to droop, when a loud thud at his cabin's door forced him upright with a jolt.

'Sam? You alive in there?' It was Mark in his slow northern drawl. *What does he want?*

'Yeah, grand, just sleeping off my hangover – you all right, fella?' His voice was thick, groggy.

'I think we need you up in the salon – the captain wants a meeting with everyone.'

Sam groaned. 'No problem, mate,' he called. 'I'll just jump in the shower and head up. Be there in ten.'

'Ah, Sam – sorry, but I think it's pretty urgent,' Mark replied. 'She said we're all needed there straight away – everyone else is waiting for you.'

A knot twisted in Sam's gut. Had something happened while he'd been asleep? Maybe that would explain the shout he'd heard earlier – perhaps he hadn't dreamt it after all. And then a thud of panic: *What if someone's had an accident – or been injured?*

That thought was enough to make Sam lunge out of bed and drag on some shorts and a T-shirt. He stumbled towards the cabin door and yanked it open to see Mark standing in the doorway, hands shoved in the pockets of a pair of camo-printed shorts.

'What's going on?' he asked, searching Mark's face.

Mark shrugged. 'No idea, mate.'

* * *

'Oh good, we're all here,' said Captain Taylor, as Sam arrived in the salon, walked over to the dining table and took the empty chair next to Nick. The rest of the guests were already seated, coffees in hands, and Johanna and Brett stood either side of the captain.

Sam glanced around the table, looking for a sign that any of his fellow guests were responsible for the shout of pain he'd heard below deck. Eleni was holding Nick's hand, smiling and bright in a long-sleeved pink kaftan; Talia looked bored and disinterested, with Rory rolling his eyes and tutting impatiently beside her. Only Lucy looked pale and anxious, her chair shifted away from her boyfriend's; his mouth was turned down sulkily. *Maybe she's given Mark a bollocking about his drunken performance last night?*

'Thanks for joining me,' said the captain. 'I'm sorry for gathering you all here already this morning – I know some of you haven't eaten breakfast yet.' She paused to take a sip of water. 'Unfortunately, at around midnight, our satellite Wi-Fi went down – and with it, one of the communication links we have with ports and marinas in the area.'

The internet's gone down? Is that all? Sam breathed a sigh of relief. He'd worked that out already. It was annoying, sure, but they could survive without going online, couldn't they? This wasn't a big deal – not a big enough deal for a morning meeting, anyway.

'I've not been able to figure out what happened yet,' said Brett. 'Or how to fix it. And there aren't any specialist engineers here in Huahine, or none that we've managed to get a hold of anyway. We might need to wait until we get to Raiatea tomorrow to get it fixed.'

The captain nodded. 'We'll do our best to find someone tomorrow. But it's possible we may not get it back up and running until we arrive back in Tahiti, I'm afraid.' She paused. 'As I say, I'm sorry for the inconvenience.'

'I'm sure we can live without the internet for a day or two, can't we?' Talia said, her tone dismissive. 'I've barely even used it since we got here.'

Ha, that's bullshit. Talia had been surgically attached to her phone for the whole trip so far; even over dinner, Sam had caught her – trying to be subtle, but failing miserably – peering down into her handbag, then putting her hands inside and swiping and tapping with an urgent expression on her face. There was no way she'd not been rinsing the Wi-Fi since they'd been out here – and there was no need to lie about it. Sam had been using it too, to stay in touch with his sister and his mates – there was nothing wrong with that.

Rory shifted in his chair, clasped his fingers together and stretched his arms out in front of him: his classic gesture to say he was *about to get down to business*. 'Well, of course, doing without Wi-Fi for a while is no problem,' he agreed, giving Talia a paternal pat on the hand. 'But the captain also mentioned some issues with communications,' Rory went on. He turned towards Captain Taylor. 'How serious are these issues, Captain? Will we still be able to make contact if we need to during our sail tomorrow, for any reason – if we get into any trouble?' He said the last words with a laugh, but Sam caught the note of anxiety in his voice. 'We don't want anything going wrong.'

Captain Taylor offered him a tight smile. 'Well, first up, I'm not expecting us to get into any trouble. And second, it's only the satellite part of the comms that have gone down – our main method of communication, which is two-way radio, is still up and running as usual. So, no, this isn't a serious issue, and I'm not concerned. If we need to make contact, we've got other ways of doing that.'

'And I'm going to keep trying my best to resolve the issue,' added Brett. 'I've got a few more things to try.'

There was a pause as the room digested this.

'Well, that's good to know,' said Rory. 'In that case, I'm not sure what else there is to discuss – let's just get on with our day. Does everyone agree?'

'That's fine with me,' said Lucy firmly; Mark shrugged next to her.

'It's cool,' agreed Sam.

'Yeah, all good,' said Nick. 'Sure that'll be all right with you too, Els? You can stay off the family WhatsApp group for a bit, right?'

Eleni glanced at her husband, rolled her eyes and smiled. 'Yes, of course I can. Captain, that all sounds perfect.'

'Well, that's settled then,' said Captain Taylor, pushing her chair back and getting to her feet. 'I'll head to the control centre now and try to make contact with an on-shore engineer in Raiatea in advance of our arrival.'

'Sounds good,' said Nick. 'Hey, have we got a bit of time to play with those water toys today? I'm still dying to try out my skills on a jet ski.'

'Bloody marvellous idea!' Rory clapped with boyish excitement. 'What do you say – can Noah or one of your deck boys sort that out for us?'

Johanna nodded briskly. 'Of course. How many of you would like to use them? We have two jet skis, and two people can ride them at a time. Rory and Nick – anyone else?'

'Not me,' Eleni said, shaking her head with a laugh; Talia also murmured a *no thanks*.

'Me neither,' said Lucy. 'Water sports aren't really my thing. I think I'll go and enjoy the hot tub for a bit.'

Mark scowled. 'Not in the mood either,' he said sullenly. 'Probably need a bit more sleep – I'll see you all later.' He stood and stomped indoors, stroppy as a teenager. *Those two look like they're on the rocks . . .*

'Sam?' Nick turned to him. 'Up for it, mate? Come on – it'll be a laugh. Your foot's healed up all right now, hasn't it?'

Sam puffed the air out of his cheeks. His foot *was* feeling a bit better now, and he didn't want to miss out. He'd never been on a jet ski before, but it looked like good craic. And it might be just the thing to blow away the grog of cobwebs that still lingered in his brain this morning.

'Ah, sure, go on then. Johanna, lead the way.'

Out on the stern of the main deck, Noah and Kai released the jet skis from the garage behind the swim platform. As Kai prepared to launch them by lowering the platform, Noah handed the three of them safety helmets and life jackets.

'Okay, gents. We can take two of you at a time. Who's coming first?'

Rory frowned. 'Can't we all go? I thought the jet skis could fit two people each.'

'Yup, they can, but you'll need me and Kai to ride with you. You need a licence to ride a jet ski – unless any of you fellas have one?'

Sam shook his head. 'Nah, never been on one of these bad boys before.'

'Me neither,' said Nick.

'Well, we're in luck then – I did my training in the Caribbean,' said Rory, a smug grin lighting up his face. 'Drove all around the private island we hired.'

'You've got your watercraft proficiency?' Noah clarified.

'Oh, yes. I'm an expert water sportsman, I think you'll find. I'm sure I've got the paperwork somewhere in my emails . . .'

Sam rolled his eyes behind his sunglasses. Noah chewed on the side of his lip for a second, scanned the three of them, then nodded. 'No need, your word is enough for me. In that case, I'll ride with Sam. Rory and Nick, you two hop on together. Sound good?'

'Works for me,' said Nick.

Sam frowned. He'd really rather the crew had checked Rory's credentials. He wouldn't trust Rory behind the wheels of a kid's tricycle, let alone the aquatic version of a motorbike.

'You sure?' he asked Nick. 'I'm more than happy to sit this out, so you can go with Noah . . .'

'Ah, come on now, Sam,' said Rory, a mocking glint in his eye. 'Scared I'll go too fast for Nick, are you?'

Sam noticed a muscle twitch in Nick's jaw.

'Rory,' Nick said curtly. 'Trust me, you can go as fast as you like.'

Clambering aboard the jet ski, helmets and life jackets strapped on, Noah instructed Sam to hold onto the handles behind him. With a violent growl, the jet ski roared to life in the bosun's hands, and quickly picked up speed across the water.

Sam laughed – the wind whipping past his ears, the scattering of salt water onto his arms – this was exhilarating, exactly the kind of thing he'd come on this trip for.

He looked over at the other jet ski. Rory was driving much faster than Noah – and much more recklessly. Sam caught Nick's voice from across the water – yelling something Sam couldn't make out – his voice was drowned out as Rory's engine roared louder. It looked like Rory was revving up the acceleration and at the same time jerking the vessel in sharp, dizzying circles, whooping and shrieking as he went. Sam could see Nick's back bumping against the rear handlebars, his pelvis hitting the seat hard as they skimmed and thudded back down on the waves.

'Hey – slow down – Rory! SLOW DOWN!' Noah yelled across the water. It was pointless; Rory either couldn't hear him, or was pretending he couldn't. Rory steered sharply again to the right, the jet ski falling almost flat, making Nick dip precariously close to the surface of the water, his hands grasping to hold firm on the spray-covered handle behind him.

'That's too fast – it's too low – he's going to fall – STOP!' Sam was screaming at the top of his lungs now, Noah was slowing their jet ski and still yelling at Rory too, but their words blew away with the salt spray of the ocean; Rory was driving like a maniac, turning in opposing directions with nauseating speed.

At one more brutal twist of the jet ski, Sam watched helplessly as Nick's hands lost their grip and he lurched violently to the right, off the seat and into the air.

And then he was flying, flying, so fast, so far, and time was slowing down, it seemed to last for ever even though it could only have been milliseconds, because gravity couldn't hold him for long, and Nick began to fall, fall, fall . . .

Until he crashed face-first onto the surface of the sea.

GENDARMERIE MARITIME DE POLYNÉSIE FRANÇAISE

CASE NUMBER: 247849

POLICE EXHIBIT FOUR

Excerpt from log of Captain Sophie Taylor, 09/06/26

06:23: Alerted to on-board Wi-Fi disruption by First Officer on waking.

07:55: Crew morale appears low again this morning. Michaela continues to report to me privately that she wishes to end the charter early; that she has been subjected to inappropriate behaviour and harassment by a male guest. I plan to remove her from service involving guest interaction as far as possible and keep her on laundry/below deck duties. However, her report of a guest entering the crew quarters on two separate occasions is concerning.

10:06: Enquiries into Wi-Fi connectivity issues made ahead of sail to Raiatea. Guests satisfied that we are doing all we can to resolve issue.

11.24: Guest has fallen from jet ski during ride with primary. Deck crew report primary at helm, executing repeated tight turns at unsafe velocity. Urgent medical assistance requested to attend vessel.

11.36: Tension within guest group appears to be escalating. In light of rising potential for impact on guest and crew welfare, I am reassured that additional security measures have been put in place to safeguard all on board. I will continue monitoring closely.

ELENI

Eleni watched as they set off, the jet skis zipping quickly away from the *Lusso* – one of them much faster than the other. She squinted: it was Rory's jet ski, with Nick on the back, that was moving at the greater speed. Whoops and cheers drifted from the sea – clearly they were enjoying themselves, though it looked bumpy as hell from where she was sitting.

Little boys and their toys . . . She didn't see the appeal. Those things went thunderously fast – the idea scared her, to be honest. She laughed at herself. Wow, she'd changed as she got older – or maybe it was since becoming a mum. As a child, she'd been fearless: climbing skinny branches to the tops of high trees, begging her *badera* to take her on the scariest roller-coasters on their annual trips to Thorpe Park.

Now, though, she perceived danger everywhere: she'd see it in the tab at the top of an open drink can, or hear it in the squawk of a bird overhead. She saw future disaster unfold in the blink of an eye – for her kids, for herself – a horror movie playing on a reel inside her brain, leaving her grasping for an off-switch. It was exhausting.

Rory was starting to move in circles now, making sharp turns. Eleni cringed. *He's showing off.* He dipped the jet ski low to the left, then spun in another fast circle and dipped it back to the right. She gasped; it looked unsafe – Nick had been scarily close to the surface of the water on that last swerve.

Kai must have caught sight of Rory's reckless driving – he started towards them in the tender, waving his arms and shouting. But – *fucking hell!* – it was too late. Nick slipped, tried to grab hold of something but missed, then tumbled off the back of the jet ski, flew sideways and upwards and landed with a hard-hitting *smack* on the water.

'Nick!'

'*Slow your engines and return to the yacht immediately*!' yelled Kai into a megaphone, gesturing to the two drivers while he steered the tender with the other hand. Rory's jet ski slowed and headed back to the swim platform, as Kai raced to the spot where Nick was drifting on the surface of the sea, unmoving, his life jacket keeping him afloat.

Eleni turned and bolted down the stairs, yelling to Johanna who was setting the table for lunch: 'Nick's fallen off the jet ski – I think he's hurt!'

Johanna took off after her, following her down the spiral staircase to the main deck and the swim platform; by the time they got there, Kai had reached the edge of the stern in the tender and, with the help of the deckhands, lifted Nick from the boat and carried him over to a shaded sunbed next to the hot tub. He was horribly quiet and still.

Captain Taylor ran onto the deck, her radio crackling, Brett and Johanna close behind. The crew surrounded Nick, blocking Eleni's view – she tried to get nearer to see what kind of state he was in, but she couldn't get sight of him. *Oh my God. Is he . . . ?*

Nick started coughing violently – Eleni still couldn't see him, but there was no doubt. *He's alive.*

'Take it steady – deep breaths. You're all right,' Noah was saying. The coughs subsided. 'You gave us all a scare there, bro. You hit the water hard – that's why we get you wearing those helmets.' The relief was evident in his voice.

Eleni heard someone breathing heavily at her side; she turned to see Rory, looking dazed, shell-shocked.

'I don't know what the hell happened. I thought he was holding on. Let me see him – come on, out the way,' he barked to the crew. They stepped aside and Rory walked towards Nick; Eleni followed. She could see him clearly now: Nick was shaking, still taking short, wheezing breaths, but looked otherwise unharmed. She took his face in her hands, kissed his forehead. As Rory moved closer to them, Nick cringed backwards onto the sunbed.

'I . . . asked you . . . to slow . . . *down*,' he managed.

Eleni shook her head. *Jesus, Rory. What the hell were you playing at?*

'Damn it, I'm sorry,' said Rory. 'I didn't hear you over the engine. I thought you were having the time of your life.' He wiped a hand down his face then flung drops of sweat and salt water to the floor. 'He'll be all right, won't he, Captain? It was just a bit of water . . .'

The captain stared at Rory for a long, tense moment, then looked at Nick. 'I've called for a medic to check you over –

they're on their way. With these kinds of incidents, there's a small risk of concussion, so I want us to take every precaution. How are you feeling now?'

Nick nodded. 'I think I'll live.' He tried a smile. But watching him there, Eleni thought how fragile he looked; how scared. That was always there, wasn't it? Behind every man – no matter how successful, how strong, how powerful – was a frightened little boy who just wanted their mum.

'Is he okay?' Sam had appeared behind Eleni, placing a hand on her shoulder. She turned to him.

'I think so.'

Sam exhaled, shook his head, then leaned down and whispered in her ear. 'That was wild, the way Rory was driving. It looked like he was trying to knock Nick off.'

Eleni acknowledged him with a tilt of her head, and said nothing.

But the truth was, she'd been thinking exactly the same thing.

The table was quiet as Johanna served lunch. The group – minus Nick, who was seeing the doctor in the sky lounge – ate their chicken skewers with pineapple chilli sauce in silence. Lucy and Mark had reappeared separately just before lunch, and were barely looking at each other. Eleni remembered the scene last night vividly: Mark– all up in Rory's face – drunk, yes, but clearly furious. It was weird – the aggression had come out of nowhere.

Or had it? Eleni recalled the bruise she'd seen yesterday on Lucy's arm. A bruise that looked, to her eyes at least, as though it came from something other than a night-time stumble. She tugged absently at the sleeve of her kaftan, then glanced at her boss. Rory – who as far as Eleni knew, didn't get embarrassed by anything; didn't take the blame even for things that were his fault – looked shame-faced. None of it made any sense; Rory had no reason to want to harm Nick – unless . . .

No. Much more likely, Rory had been showing off and taken it too far. That would be typical: Rory could be an arrogant twat, yes. But he wouldn't want to hurt anyone, Eleni was sure of it. She just hoped he wouldn't feel guilty enough about this to start avoiding Eleni and Nick altogether. *Maybe I should try to talk to him later, reassure him there are no hard feelings.*

After they'd cleared their plates, the doctor returned to the main deck and got back into the tender for Kai to return him to shore. Eleni got to her feet. 'I'm going to see how Nick's doing.'

She headed upstairs and found him lying on a sofa in the sky lounge, remote in hand, flicking through channels on the flatscreen TV with the volume low. He looked listless; depressed. As Eleni approached, he switched off the TV and smiled at her.

'Hey,' she said, sitting at his feet. 'What did the doctor say?'

'Ah, I'll live, apparently.' Nick shrugged. 'No concussion. Just a sore head, not that I didn't have one of those already.'

Eleni rolled her eyes. 'What happened out there? It looked painful, that landing.'

Nick frowned. 'Rory was driving like a complete fucking maniac. I lost my grip.'

'He's an idiot. I'm sorry.' Eleni shifted her gaze towards the windows, watched the endless sea roll gently past the yacht.

'Are *you* okay?' Nick asked. He was watching her intently.

'Oh, I'm fine,' she said. 'Just a bit unsettled by what happened to you, I suppose. But everything's good, I promise. Listen, I'll let you get some rest this afternoon. I need you back on form in time for the James Bond party tonight.'

Eleni kissed him goodbye and checked the time on her phone as she made her way downstairs. Damn. She was desperate to see the boys' faces, and talk to her sister, but it was the middle of the night back home. Still, while she had a few moments alone, she could check in with a voice note. She'd go down to her cabin for some privacy.

As she approached the dim lower passageway at the bottom of the stairs, she shivered and tried to brush off the sudden, irrational sense of foreboding. *Stop it.* There was nothing amiss down here; nothing to provoke her senses into alarm. Everything was fine; normal. As it should be. *I'm upset by what happened to Nick. And it's dark and quiet down here. It's just the contrast with how bright and loud it is everywhere else.*

Still, she stepped cautiously into the corridor and breathed in relief as the sensors picked her up and the overhead lights flickered on. She unlocked the cabin door, stepped inside and let the door fall closed behind her with its soft, expensive *click*, and felt lighter.

I think I'm getting better at spending time on my own. She didn't mind that her day-to-day life involved so much time around other people: her children and her work were her sources of joy. She could spend days at a time with the kids in the summer holidays or over Christmas and somehow never end up feeling suffocated or smothered, in the way other mums described. She enjoyed being around them; preferred it, actually, to being alone.

It was different on this boat, though. The seven of them – plus the crew – all together in such close quarters; it was claustrophobic, even with the time they'd had off the *Lusso*. She needed these brief moments on her own to ground herself again. She could get some thinking time, try to make sure everything was moving forward with her ambitions to get closer to Rory and Talia. She'd not made enough progress yet, but there had been interruptions: the tension last night between Mark and Rory, Talia's continual snubbing of her, and now Nick's accident. She still had time, though. There would be more meals, more wine, more cocktails: plenty of time to let their inhibitions drop, to get closer to each other . . .

Eleni settled on the chair next to the dressing table, her eyes landing briefly on her laptop, which sat in its case on the floor near her feet. She shouldn't have brought it, really. She needed the break, and everything would be ticking along fine without her.

But the truth was, she loved her job. The treasure hunt for potential sites and the excitement when she discovered one; negotiations with landowners and investors, even tricky ones. Property and buildings were in her blood: her dad had been an architect, and her most precious memories as a child were accompanying him on site visits, wearing the miniature hard hat and safety glasses he'd bought her, holding his hand and gazing at the buildings in wonder.

Eleni took her phone out of her bag and opened WhatsApp, then scrolled down to find Mariana's latest chat. Her sister had just changed her profile picture on the app; Eleni clicked to enlarge it, and the faces of her sister and her two boys filled the screen, her mum's kitchen table with remnants of dinner and schoolbooks and toys scattered on its surface behind them. Her heart squeezed.

She closed the picture back down and tapped the microphone, then started speaking quietly into her phone.

'Hey, Maz. Love the new profile pic! How are you all? I'm missing the boys so much – and you and Mum, of course. I hope they've been all right and you're managing okay.' She paused to take a deep breath. 'And I was wondering whether . . . if everything *else* is going okay? Could you give me a quick update when you're awake?' Eleni dropped her voice lower. 'I know you keep saying not to worry, but I can't help it. It's impossible . . .' Tears filled Eleni's eyes; she blinked them away and sniffed. 'Sorry, you know what I'm like, too bloody emotional! But I'm fine. Everything's going okay here.'

She hit send, hoping there'd be enough 4G coverage for the message to make it through without Wi-Fi, then dropped her phone on the dressing table and sat back in the chair. It was a shame she hadn't managed to FaceTime when the boys were awake; when she'd actually get to see them. They'd be missing her – and Nick, too, no doubt. Lucas, in particular, adored his dad – especially his rough tickles, and the way Nick turned him upside down until he screamed with laughter and begged to be upright again. Eleni closed her eyes briefly at the memory: the sound of Lucas's giggles; the scent of freshly baked bread that seemed to cling to Theo's hair . . .

Feeling restless now, she stood and walked over to the bed – just as a familiar, cold sensation crawled down her spine; the tiny hairs on her arms rising up in unison . . .

I'm not alone.

The voice sounded so sure, so confident, in her mind. As

though she knew it with absolute certainty. *I'm not alone? Where did that even come from?* Irrationally, driven by pure instinct, Eleni whipped her head around the room and saw no one.

Then, feeling like a child checking for imaginary monsters in her wardrobe before she went to sleep, she got down on her hands and knees and looked under the bed: nothing. She stood up and walked to the cupboard facing the bed, took a deep breath and swung the doors open: just their clothes sitting neatly on hangers.

Still not satisfied, she stepped towards the closed door to the en-suite, turned the handle – her hands shaking slightly – and swung open the door.

Walk-in shower. Wet room floor. Double sink. Loo. The bathroom was empty.

I'm being ridiculous. She sat back on the bed. Still, that sensation though. Eyes on her. Either this cabin was haunted – an idea so preposterous, Eleni wouldn't give it credence; she didn't believe in ghosts any more than she believed in Father Christmas, no matter what she promised the boys every December – or someone was covertly keeping tabs on her, without her permission.

This gut feeling was all too familiar. She'd lived with it ever since her adolescent body had begun to develop. She'd spent decades being subjected to other people's gazes – men's, mostly. Yes, she was getting older, and she looked knackered most of the time – but still. Like most women, she couldn't walk down a busy street without being noticed; she couldn't relax alone at a bar for more than a few minutes before a stranger made his approach. Even at work – even in a boardroom full of architects and compliance officers – she felt their eyes linger too long when she'd finished speaking.

She held her breath now and listened. *What was that?* That buzzing again. Had she actually heard it, or was it in her head? She could hardly tell now, thanks to how loudly her heart was banging against her ribcage. She forced it to slow: all was quiet. All was still.

The feeling passed. *No one's watching me.* She shook her head, exasperated with herself, then picked her phone up from the dressing table to check the time. They'd soon be off for their tour of Huahine – exploring on e-bikes, if she remembered right. Perhaps she could still take a couple of minutes now, to just breathe. Breathe and remember what she was doing here, and why.

Her gaze drifted to the doorway, and her heart pumped more quickly again – that was one place she hadn't checked.

Is there someone on the other side, looking in?

She got up, walked over and lifted the rim of the peephole – where a pair of eyes were staring back at her.

GENDARMERIE MARITIME DE POLYNÉSIE FRANÇAISE

CASE NUMBER: 247849

DATE: 11/06/2026

INTERVIEW EXCERPT THREE

Interview subject: Noah Bailey, bosun on board *Lusso di Mare* charter

Interview conducted by Chief of Police Henri Robert

M Robert: You witnessed the incident that took place between Rory and Nick during their jet ski ride, is that correct?

M Bailey: <sniffs> Too right I did. Scared me half to death. We thought he'd end up with a head injury – or worse – for a sec there.

M Robert: Did anybody else see what happened, that you know of?

M Bailey: <pause> Ah, the deck crew. The captain and the first officer – they were watching from the bridge. Not many of the guests, I'd say. I'm pretty sure Eleni was watching. Not sure about Lucy and Mark – they might have been on the sun deck, or in the interior somewhere. I doubt Talia saw . . . even if she'd been on deck, she was probably too distracted to notice . . .

M Robert: What do you mean by that, Monsieur Bailey?

M Bailey: Uh . . . sorry. Shouldn't have said that. Probably not relevant. Listen, what does all this have to do with the murder?

This wasn't even—

M Robert: We'll get to that in good time, I assure you. Please tell me what you meant by your earlier comment – about Talia being distracted?

M Bailey: Ah, just that . . . she seemed worried. Anxious, maybe. She spent a lot of time below deck, away from the others, especially that day onwards, from what I remember.

M Robert: And why do you think she did that? Why was she distracted, in your opinion?

M Bailey: <sighs> I really don't know. I didn't speak to her that much, the whole trip. I didn't get to know her. Maybe she was just trying to get away from her husband. Can't blame her if she was, to be honest.

M Robert: I see. And what were your impressions of Talia's marriage at that time – how were she and Rory getting on?

M Bailey: Ah, Christ, it was pretty gross. He was all over her – touching her, kissing her, calling her his 'darling' all the time. She kinda . . . indulged him, I guess? But it felt over the top from him, you know? Insincere. <sigh> So yeah, I knew there was trouble brewing between everyone. I just didn't realize how much.

[TRANSCRIPT ENDS]

TALIA

'Goodness. Whatever's wrong with you?' Talia asked.

Eleni was peering from behind a crack in the door of her cabin, eyes wide, jaw tensed, as though she'd been expecting someone to be outside delivering terrible news. 'I was only going to knock on the door – I came to get you,' Talia said. 'We're ready for the cycling tour of the island – everyone's waiting for you.'

Eleni swallowed hard. 'God, of course. Sorry, I just got myself spooked in there on my own for some reason. Bloody overactive imagination . . .' She shook her head, looking embarrassed, the anxiety draining from her features but leaving a slight flush to her cheeks. Then she stood a little straighter, adjusted her garishly pink kaftan, and seemed to gather herself. 'Thank you so much for coming to get me, though.' She smiled warmly at Talia.

Talia narrowed her eyes. 'Well, it made sense. I had to come and get something from my cabin anyway.'

Eleni's shoulders dropped; she looked crestfallen for a

moment, then perked up again and plastered the ingratiating smile back across her face. 'Still – I appreciate it. Would you mind waiting for a moment while I gather my things together for the trip? Then we can go up together.'

'Ah – well, I should really get back . . .'

'Oh, I'll only be a second.' Eleni was already bustling around her cabin, opening cupboard doors and throwing things into a beach bag. Talia watched as Eleni opened the wardrobe to show neatly pressed and ironed shirts, skirts and dresses on hangers in a colour coordinated sweep – dark clothes on the left, bright in the middle, pale pastel on the right. The open-fronted shelves underneath held perfectly folded T-shirts, socks and underwear – again, meticulously colour-coded.

'It's all very tidy in there,' remarked Talia.

'Oh – yeah,' said Eleni, appearing back at the door, a touch breathless. 'Yes. It's just how Nick likes things, I suppose. Shall we go?'

They began to make their way along the corridor and upstairs.

'I love your earrings,' said Eleni as they walked. 'You have such great style.'

Talia's eyes flickered sideways. Why was she doing this again – insisting on paying Talia endless compliments? 'You're very kind.' *But please, stop.* The endless flattery wasn't endearing – it was irritating.

As they reached the top of the stairs, Eleni came to a sudden stop and turned her eyes upwards, fixing on something on the ceiling.

'You don't think they put cameras below deck too, do you?' she murmured.

Talia flinched. 'Pardon me?'

'God, I'm sorry. I didn't mean to say that out loud. It's just this feeling I keep having of being watched on the yacht – in my cabin, mostly. But maybe it makes sense – there's CCTV pretty much everywhere, isn't there?'

Eleni pointed up to a dome-shaped camera fixed above the entrance to the salon. From its position there, it would be able to capture the whole sweep of the room. Talia's stomach churned.

'I'm sure no one really watches it,' she murmured absently.

'I suppose not,' said Eleni, with a shrug. 'Just seems a bit pointless having it then, doesn't it?' She smiled at Talia, then strode ahead to join the others out on deck.

Talia sat next to Rory in the tender as Kai sailed the group – everyone except Nick – closer to shore, taking in the white sandy beach and vibrant corals of the bay near Fare village. The view anchored off Huahine was breathtaking. Of the islands they'd visited so far – Tahiti, Moorea, now here – this one might be her favourite. The sand on the beach was impossibly pale; the sea the most stunning, vibrant turquoise. And it was so peaceful, this bay – a true desert paradise.

With the tender docked at shore close to a yacht club, Kai helped everyone out of the boat and led them along the beach. From there, it was a short walk to the paved road of the village, lined with thick green foliage and dotted with low, cream-coloured houses and shops with brightly coloured fascias, some of them screaming brand names at passers-by.

After a few minutes on foot, they arrived at a bike shop, where seven bikes were lined up outside. Kai stepped inside and emerged a few moments later with a map for each of them, detailing the area surrounding Fare.

'Okay, everyone, you're going to be free shortly to explore the surrounding villages and hiking trails on your e-bikes – feel free to have your own adventures this afternoon!' said Kai. 'Some quick safety pointers for using your bikes in the area . . .'

Talia tuned out as he talked through the mechanisms of the e-bike, and took in the quiet buzz of the village around her. Four-by-fours tightly packed along the edges of the street, ferrying locals on their way to the supermarket. A handful of tourists strolling by, eyes fixed on the colourful store fronts, pointing and snapping photos with their phones.

'Enjoy yourselves, and make sure you're back here at this same spot at five o'clock to return to the boat. Everyone has a watch or a phone on them, yes?'

The group murmured their agreement, then began studying their maps.

Eleni was trying to catch Talia's eye. *She probably wants to ask if she can join the two of us – God forbid.* But Rory was already astride his bike, saying he didn't need directions. 'Shall we take a tour on our own, darling?' he called. She looked at him. The eagerness in his expression was almost too much to bear.

'Yes, of course. That will be nice,' she said. *And a blessed relief to get away from some of his colleagues.*

She put on her helmet, climbed on her bike and – with an excited squeal, she'd never ridden an electric one before and the way it glided forward with such minimal effort made her laugh with surprise – rode with her husband away from the others. Just Talia and Rory, alone.

* * *

After twenty minutes of riding, taking them away from the village centre and upwards on a small path that climbed into the nearby hills, Rory began to slow to a stop. 'Wow – just wow. Look at this view!'

They'd reached a clearing in the trees, and beyond it, the South Pacific stretched blue and still for miles. 'Shall we stop and sit in the shade for a few minutes, take it all in?'

She observed her husband: his cheeks were pink and sweat had turned his polo shirt into a sopping clump that clung stickily to his chest and shoulders. He was clearly struggling with the heat, but far too proud to admit it.

'Yes, of course,' she said. 'I could do with a bit of shade.'

Rory hopped off his bike and laid it down gently on the grass; Talia followed suit. They sat down, nestled their frames inside the curved roots of a nearby mape tree, its wide trunk solid against Talia's back. As the hum of their bikes faded, they were encased in the dense silence of the lush hillside, only gentle gusts of wind through leafy branches and the faint chatter of nearby birds reaching her ears now.

'This is glorious, isn't it, darling?' said Rory, taking hold of Talia's hand.

Talia looked at her husband – really looked at him. She saw the try-hard, eager-to-please boy behind the facade of the high-powered man. She saw the subtle eye-rolls in response to his poor jokes; the awkward ways he tried to ingratiate himself with people; his out-of-touch attempts to show his care for those he loved.

Shame and regret and the blood-curdling terror of exposure gnawed hotly in her stomach, curdling together in a vile, broiling mess, exactly as they had done every day for the past few months.

She dug her long nails into the palm of her hand, then gasped in pain: she looked down and saw pinpricks of blood.

Damn. She'd managed to cut herself. She stared at the oozing red drops in horror, then pressed a finger down onto her palm to stem the flow.

'You're bleeding, my love. What happened – did you cut yourself on one of these spiky roots?'

'Gosh – I think I must have done.' Talia blinked away her hot tears, felt a rush of gratitude for her thick sunglasses. *What the hell is wrong with me – what am I doing? Surely I don't want to hurt myself . . .*

But then again, she already was, wasn't she? Not in a way that would draw blood – she was hurting herself *inside*, and that was far worse. And she wasn't just doing it to herself. What she'd been doing all these months – what she was *still doing* – was harming other people too. Perhaps bleeding was her just reward.

'Do you want to go back into the town – see if we can't find you a plaster?' Rory asked.

Talia smiled, touched at his concern. 'You're sweet, darling, but no. I'll be fine – it's just a scratch.'

His kindness in moments like these only made her feel worse. If only she'd got out of the affair straight away – ended things before they'd started, told the other man it was a mistake, blocked his number, whatever it took – she could have avoided doing any serious damage. No one else would have got hurt, least of all herself. She wouldn't have been at risk of getting caught and losing everything.

But she hadn't got out of it. She'd done the opposite: she'd got deeper and deeper *in*.

'Phew. Well, I'm about ready to head back anyway, if you are? This heat is really quite something.'

'That's fine with me.'

Rory took her face in his palms and leaned in to kiss her. 'I do love you, darling, very much. You know that, don't you?'

Talia frowned; these moments of sentimentality were rare for her husband, and usually only happened after they'd had sex – a once-per-month occurrence these days, if that.

She smiled. 'Of course. And I love you too – very much.'

And it was true: she *did* still love Rory – perhaps more as a friend than a lover, but they'd been together for twenty-odd years – their days of heated passion had cooled to a companionship that was steady, warm, and in many ways fulfilling.

Until now, she'd always been honest, loyal and supportive to her husband, even when he'd embarrassed her with his outdated jokes; even when she'd cringed at his banter that reflected his position as a man of a certain era; a certain upbringing. Despite all that, she did care for him – and it left Talia baffled at exactly how she'd got to this point. At what exactly had happened that led to her starting an affair.

On their ride back downhill, Talia turned the past few months over in her mind. It wasn't like she'd been going out looking for something to happen – she'd been content with life; she had more than most. She had her husband, two beautiful daughters, a wonderful home, plenty of money, and good health. There was nothing missing – or nothing on the surface, at least.

But something in her changed after both girls left home last year – Nina into her own flat, Chloe away to Cambridge for university. Talia had given up her career as a solicitor after Nina was born: she'd devoted herself to raising her children, picking up some pro bono legal cases to stay busy when they were in school. Now that they were grown, and with only her part-time job at the charity – plus her weekly Pilates sessions and lunch with friends to keep her busy – she had become that cliché of an empty-nester: wandering around their Hampstead townhouse, finding things to clear up, decorating, pottering in the garden . . . All while feeling slightly flat; empty.

But that's no excuse. This isn't who I am. It can't be. She'd always been revolted by the thought of ending up like her dad, and her grandad before him, carrying on the cycles of infidelity that ran back through her family history like a generational curse. Dad, 'working away' most of the week; coming home with an extra spring in his step and the lingering reek of sickly floral perfume in his dirty laundry.

Her mother had turned a blind eye to it, but Talia was all too aware – by the time she hit her mid-teens, she could see her father for exactly who he was: a cheat and a liar, and not even a convincing one, at that. Her mother's wilful ignorance had come to a shattering end when, on Talia's eighteenth birthday, he'd confessed that he was in love with someone else – a younger woman, of course; how clichéd – and moved out the next day, leaving his family reeling.

She'd hated him for it. And yet here she was now. Sneaking around behind Rory's back, lying – and even worse: over time, she'd become good at it. Much better than her father had ever been.

Back on board the *Lusso*, Rory ushered Talia in Michaela's direction; the stewardess was tidying in the salon.

'My dear wife managed to get a cut to her finger while we

were on the island,' he said. 'See to it that it's cleaned and patched up, will you?'

As he walked away, Talia gave an exasperated groan. 'Michaela, there's really no need. It's just a scratch.'

Michaela smiled. 'Well, why don't you come into the galley with me anyway – I can have a look and grab the first aid kit if we need.'

'Fine,' said Talia, with a brisk nod. She followed the stewardess through the salon and into the galley. She'd not been inside the yacht's kitchen before, and took a moment to admire the gleaming silver surfaces. She sat on a barstool by the counter and held out her hand, as Michaela soaked cotton wool in antiseptic and dabbed it on Talia's palm.

Just then, the stewardess's crew radio crackled to life. 'Captain to First Officer, please confirm all CCTV is back up and running now that guests have re-embarked. Over.'

Then an almost immediate reply: 'Captain, this is Brett. All cameras now back up and running. Over.'

Talia's mouth went dry; she thought back to her conversation with Eleni about the cameras, just before the biking tour. She studied Michaela as she neatly cut a plaster to size and gently applied it to Talia's cut. 'Isn't it a little . . . excessive, to have CCTV running all the time we're on board?' she said, attempting levity.

Michaela looked up. 'It's just a precaution,' she said. 'In case anything goes wrong, and we need to look back to understand what happened.'

Talia nodded. 'And does it get recorded over, after a day or so?'

She shook her head. 'Usually not for thirty days. At least, until well after a charter is over.'

Talia pulled her hand away. 'And does anyone watch it otherwise? If nothing's gone wrong, I mean?'

Michaela's eyebrows knitted together. She glanced briefly at the galley door, as if to check no one was outside listening, then turned back to Talia.

'Talia,' she said quietly. 'I'm not sure exactly what you're asking. But, yes – sometimes, the crew watch the footage. And we . . . we *see* things on charters. Not just on CCTV.'

Talia took a deep breath. *Where is she going with this?* 'I don't know what you mean,' she said, examining the plaster on her hand, the dry flakes to the side of her nails.

'It's just – well, being so close to people, in such a tight space . . . it's hard not to pick up things about the people on board with us,' the stewardess said softly.

Then Michaela leaned closer to Talia; so close that as Talia looked up, she could make out the flecks of brown in her light green eyes. 'Of course, we try not to involve ourselves in guests' business. It's part of our job, to keep things to ourselves. But—'

Talia clattered off the stool and drew herself up to her full height. 'What are you trying to say, exactly?' she said.

The stewardess lowered her gaze. 'I – I'm sorry. I didn't mean to upset you. I'm just concerned.' She met Talia's eyes. 'I think you need to be more careful.'

ELENI

Stop staring at her. She's going to clock it any minute.

Eleni couldn't tear her eyes away from Talia. They were back on board the *Lusso* after their bike tour, stretched out on sunbeds near the hot tub, sipping cold champagne. Rory had requested a themed *Casino Royale*-style party for this evening, requiring them all to put on their finest black and white glad rags, but they still had an hour to relax before getting ready. There was more of a breeze this afternoon, and the wind kept rustling the pages of her magazine. But at least out here in the sun, Eleni had an excuse to keep her shades on.

From her nearby lounger, she watched as Talia pushed cubes of ice around her cocktail with a straw, occasionally looking up and staring into the distance, then back down at her glass. Her usually immaculate hair had formed frizzy curls at the edges – a product of the briny sea air, no doubt. And she'd clearly been picking at her hands – there was a plaster on her palm, and the edge of one of her nails was a throbbing red; it had scabbed over slightly, as if it had been bleeding.

Talia seemed to be quietly unravelling. For the past two days, she'd looked constantly on edge: startling when anyone brushed past her too closely; wincing at Rory's touch; spending more and more time between their meals and activities alone in the master stateroom. And she'd looked completely panicked for a second earlier, when Eleni pointed out the CCTV camera.

Eleni didn't want to make it too obvious she'd noticed; that she was dying to know what Talia was thinking and feeling. She realized she had developed a kind of fascination with the woman – her straight-backed Pilates posture, her elegant gestures, the clipped edges of her voice.

She looked away, finally, as Rory got hastily to his feet, lifting his phone in the air and waving it around. 'Damn poor signal – and no Wi-Fi! Can't even read my bloody emails. How am I supposed to get anything done?'

Talia reached up and touched his arm soothingly. 'Well, you're meant to be on holiday, darling. Maybe it's not the end of the world if you can't check your messages for a few days?'

'That's all well and good for you to say – you're not running a stock-listed company, are you? You've got no bloody idea!' Then he stomped up the stairs to the sun deck, muttering something about finding a better signal higher up.

'Wow,' said Sam. 'Somebody's not exactly in the holiday spirit.'

Too right – and he's not the only one. During the e-bike tour, Eleni had wanted to join Rory and Talia – but they'd been keen to take a trip alone, just the two of them. Disappointed, she'd ridden with Lucy, Mark and Sam while Nick rested up back on the yacht after his plunge into the water that morning. It was a strained few hours, the tension between

Lucy and Mark practically tangible – the couple barely said a word to each other.

'I think he just got a little hot on our bike ride today,' said Talia smoothly – though her voice caught as she spoke. Eleni could empathize – she wouldn't like her husband speaking to her so rudely in front of everyone, either.

'Are you okay?' she asked, offering Talia a sympathetic tilt of her head.

'I'm fine,' Talia snapped. 'But I think I've had rather enough company for now. I'm going to lie down before the party.' With that, she stood up and stalked across the deck to the salon's doors and disappeared inside.

'Whoops. What have I done wrong now?' murmured Eleni, half to herself. How was she *ever* going to get closer to Talia if she could barely say a word to the woman without inadvertently pissing her off? Maybe it was time to change tack; try to talk to Rory alone, instead. She turned to Nick, who was dozing next to her, then stretched and sat up.

'Hey, I've finished my magazine,' she said. 'I think I'll go and get my book from the cabin.'

'Another destination thriller thing?' he mumbled sleepily. 'You've always got one of those on the go . . .'

'Well, I *like* them,' she replied. Nick opened his eyes. *Oops*. She'd sounded snappy – she hadn't meant to; she was rattled by the tense atmosphere and having unintentionally annoyed Talia. 'But, you're right, I do literally inhale one book after the other. I promise, they're holiday reads only.' She laughed, gave him a kiss on the forehead and got to her feet.

'I'll come with you,' he said, sitting up.

Eleni frowned. 'Why? No need. I'll only be a sec.'

Just then, Johanna appeared at the top of the stairs. 'Can I get anyone another drink? Nick – a cold beer, perhaps?'

He lay back down. 'Actually, yeah. That sounds good.'

Eleni exhaled. 'See you in a minute, then.' She picked up her beach bag, walked downstairs and towards the salon door. Then, checking no one was watching, she quietly reversed her steps and climbed the stairs to the sun deck.

Her boss was stretched over the railings at the bow, holding his phone precariously high in the air above the sea. 'Rory?'

'What is it?' he barked, without turning to look.

'Be careful with that phone of yours.'

He dropped his mobile back down, turned and then, when he saw her, seemed to soften.

'Ah, Eleni – it's you. I'm sorry for letting my temper get the better of me down there.' He sighed, then took a few paces towards her. 'Is everything all right?'

She smiled. 'Don't worry, it's fine – it's pretty intense here. But now that I've got you, can we have a chat?'

'With my favourite land buyer? Of course.'

Rory moved towards the sofa at the bow, patting the seat next to him. 'Come and sit down.'

Eleni nodded and took a seat beside Rory. She could feel her cheeks starting to flush now; she wondered if there was a telltale sheen of sweat above her brow.

'So, what did you want to talk about?'

Eleni took a deep breath. 'Nick's . . . fall this morning from the jet ski. I want you to know, there's no hard feelings. I know you'd never do something like that on purpose. But – how did it happen, exactly?'

'Ah, yes. I did wonder if you'd bring that up.' Rory sighed. 'And I'm afraid the simple answer is: I was being an idiot. I wanted to show a strapping young fellow like your husband that I've still got it, I suppose. I'm sorry – really, I am.'

Eleni nodded. That did make sense; it was the kind of thing she could imagine him doing. 'It's okay – no harm done. Accidents happen, and Nick's fine.'

'Of course he is. With the size of the muscles on your policeman husband? It'd take a lot more than that to bring him down.' Rory laughed and nudged Eleni in the side. She offered him her most winning smile.

'He is quite the catch, isn't he?' she said. 'And not just because of the muscles. I'm very lucky.' She examined her fingernails. 'You are too, of course. Talia's wonderful.'

'Indeed,' said Rory, closing his eyes for a beat, almost in reverence. 'Some would say she's rather out of my league.'

'Not at all,' exclaimed Eleni. 'You're a perfect match. And it's great, the four of us spending time together, isn't it?' She paused; her racing heartbeat was painfully loud. Could Rory hear it? 'Actually, thinking about it, wouldn't it be nice if we—'

A soft thud sounded, close to the edge of the steps. Eleni glanced towards the stairwell to check whether someone was coming up. Maybe Nick was looking for her – she'd said she'd only be a minute. There was no one there.

At least, no one she could see. But still, the cold, creeping sensation crawled from the nape of Eleni's neck to the base of her spine, with horrible familiarity.

That feeling again. Someone's watching me – someone's watching both of us.

Her eyes darted around the deck; she turned her head and

peered around the bow. She craned her neck to get a clear view down towards the stern.

Did something just move over there? Is someone out there, halfway up the stairs – watching us, listening to us?

'Eleni?' said Rory, sounding baffled. 'Earth to Eleni! Whatever's the matter with you?'

Eleni forced her gaze away from the empty doorway and shook her head. 'Sorry – I thought . . . I just had this weird feeling. But no – it's nothing.' Eleni's throat had gone dry; her words emerged sounding cracked and rasping. 'Sorry – what was I saying?'

Rory frowned. 'Ah – something about how nice it is to all spend time together. And I couldn't agree more, by the way. You know, Nick reminds me a lot of myself when I was younger—'

But his words were cut short: Sam strode onto the sun deck. He saw the two of them and laughed. 'Thought you said you were going to get your book? Had to stop for a bit of a chinwag with the boss first, by the looks of it. Or maybe you're planning to coordinate your outfits for this evening! Anything I need to know about?'

Eleni blinked. His glib tone was so at odds with her current state of mind, it was jarring. *Has he been standing near the stairwell this whole time? Is that why I felt like someone was watching us?*

'Did you just come up here now?' she asked.

The grin disappeared from Sam's face. 'Er . . . yeah. Only walked up the stairs this minute.' He shrugged. 'Why?'

Is he lying? Nothing in his expression was giving anything away. But Sam had appeared like this before, hadn't he, loitering at the edges of their conversations? Happening to be nearby at exactly the right moment? *And the constant checking in: are you okay? Are you sure? Do you need anything?*

'Can I grab either of you a drink?' Sam asked, pointing to the bar on the deck. 'I've just started on some James Bond-themed cocktails, and even Lucy's got herself a Prosecco . . .'

Eleni felt suddenly ridiculous. *I'm being paranoid. He's a nice guy. He's not up to anything weird.*

'Not for me,' said Rory briskly. He got to his feet. 'I'll see if I can have any more luck getting a signal over at the stern. See you later, Eleni.' He gave her a paternal pat on the head and walked away.

'Well, I should *actually* go and get that book,' Eleni told Sam. She got up and started towards the stairs.

'Ah – actually, Eleni?'

She turned back. 'Yeah?' Sam was staring at her, his eyebrows drawing together.

'You're okay, Eleni, aren't you?'

She frowned. 'What do you mean?'

'I mean, is there anything that's worrying you – or has anything upset you?'

Eleni felt a flash of unexpected anxiety. She glanced around the sun deck to make sure they were still alone, then lowered her voice. 'I – well – I can't think of anything . . . nothing specific, anyway. I was a bit shocked by what happened to Nick on that jet ski, of course, but – sorry, why are you asking?'

Sam was still eyeing her closely. 'It might be nothing. It's just . . . this morning, I heard something in one of the cabins. I've not caught you alone since then, but I wanted to ask you about it.' He fixed her with that intense expression.

Eleni shook her head, confused. 'You wanted to ask me about what – what did you hear?'

He swallowed. 'Like a . . . shout? A cry? Someone yelling *stop it*! It would have been just before ten. I wouldn't mention it, but it kind of sounded like someone was – in pain, or scared, or something . . .'

In pain? Scared? Eleni swept back a strand of hair that had come loose from her ponytail – she saw Sam watching her, expectantly. 'I honestly don't know, but it couldn't have come from me. I came up to the salon for breakfast around nine, and I only popped back to our cabin once to get my sun cream . . .'

Sam nodded. 'Was anyone else downstairs, do you know?'

She thought for a moment. 'Gosh, now you're asking. I honestly can't remember – people were up and down all morning – coming up for breakfast, going up and down the stairs. I'm sorry.' She tried racked her brains for another plausible explanation. 'Are you sure it wasn't one of the crew? Their cabins are just down from ours, aren't they? Maybe one of them was just messing around . . .'

'Could have been, I suppose.' Sam paused. 'There is something else, though.' He looked out to sea for a moment, as if weighing up whether or not to go on.

'Well?' Eleni was hot, and didn't have long before she'd have to get ready for dinner. She'd have to get back to Nick soon, too – she'd said she'd only be a couple of minutes grabbing her book.

Sam sighed. 'I overheard Michaela and Johanna last night. Michaela was really worried about something. She said she was scared of someone here – one of the guests. One of the *men*.'

Eleni swallowed. *One of the men?* It was oddly specific – and yet not specific enough. 'What did she mean by that – she was scared of one of the men?' she asked. 'Did she mention who? And what they did to freak her out?'

Sam was shaking his head before Eleni had even finished speaking. 'She didn't say. All I know is that one of us men apparently approached her – intimidated her somehow – badly enough that Michaela didn't even want to finish the charter.'

The stewardess wants to leave because of one of the guests? Eleni thought for a moment. 'But who would have done that? We'd have noticed, wouldn't we, if someone had been hassling her? We're all in such a tight space! You can hardly turn around in this effing yacht without bumping into someone . . .'

She paused for breath. She was rambling now, in her anxiety, but she couldn't stop her words; they kept on tumbling out of her, as fast as the thoughts racing through her brain. 'And who do you think it was? Honestly? If you've got any ideas, just tell me.' She swallowed. 'I assume it couldn't have been . . . *you*?'

Sam looked shocked; he shook his head furiously. 'No way. I'd never . . . and I'd hardly mention it to you, if it was me, would I?' Then he waited a long moment, before he spoke again, more slowly: 'I don't know for sure which of us. But I have my suspicions.' He shrugged. 'I probably shouldn't say. I think it'll all come out soon enough.'

Eleni willed herself to keep her expression impassive; she only dipped her head slightly.

'I hope you know, Eleni, you can always talk to me, yeah?' Sam went on. His voice was soft, empathetic. 'Like, if you ever need to?'

Talk to him? About what? The memory struck her, suddenly, of Sam huddled up close with a woman from the sales department on a rare Thursday night work drink that she made it to – one on one, at the bar, away from the loud, boozy teams taking over the giant tables playing drinking games. Clearly this was something he did. It should warm her to him, but somehow – after what she'd just been thinking a moment ago about his sudden appearance here – it left her cold.

'I appreciate that and I'll bear it in mind,' she said. 'See you at dinner, yeah?'

Eleni turned and headed down the stairs, still feeling Sam's eyes on her. Once she had stepped inside the cabin and closed the door behind her, she leaned back against the wall, trying to breathe through the sudden swell of panic in her chest. Worse than Sam blowing the first chance she'd had to talk to Rory alone, now there was the threat of someone hassling the stewardess. And she still had the eerie feeling of being watched.

She was running out of people she could trust here.

GENDARMERIE MARITIME DE POLYNÉSIE FRANÇAISE

CASE NUMBER: 247849

POLICE EXHIBIT FIVE

Transcript of text messages between Noah Bailey and Brett Marchant, 09/06/26

18:14 Noah: Mate, can we chat when you get a minute? Below deck – maybe during dinner service? I want to keep this on the DL

18.18 Brett: Hey. I'm going on break over dinner. But we can text now. What's up?

18:19 Noah: All right. Something's up with the guests. It's getting weird. The jet ski this morning, all the weird side-eyes, the tension. And did Michaela tell you what happened in the crew quarters? I dunno, feels like some serious shit's about to hit the fan

18:22 Brett: Ha. It's always the same, especially after a few drinks. You're being paranoid. Just ignore it. Don't worry, Cap's on it with Michaela – she can stay off guest duty tonight

18:23 Noah: OK. But this feels different. I don't like it. We can all sense it – like something's about to go off. Should I talk to Cap?

18:25 Brett: No! Seriously, you're being dramatic. There's not long to go – let's just get the rest of the job done, and it'll all be over soon

18:27 Noah: OK. But don't say I didn't warn you. And if someone flips a table over at dinner, I'm not steam-cleaning that shit . . .

18:28 Brett: Oh, but you are mate. Ha!

18:35 Noah: Yeah yeah. But seriously, bro – this lot are ready to explode

[TRANSCRIPT ENDS]

TALIA

Alone in the safety of her cabin, Talia watched the daylight begin to fade, the sun dip on the horizon at the edge of the ocean. It was getting late; she wouldn't have long now before she'd need to get dressed for dinner, put her make-up on and keep up the appearance of a happily married wife on the holiday of a lifetime.

The tears she'd stifled in Rory's company earlier returned now, a storm of sobs that wracked her body. Lying on her side on the bed, she clenched a hand into a fist and stuffed it in her mouth to dull the sound. *What have I done? It's unforgivable. I'm unforgivable.*

Michaela's words played on repeat inside her skull: *You need to be more careful.* The stewardess was clearly trying to warn her, but why? About who? And after that anonymous note . . .

But even now, full of guilt and terror and regret, the memory of the first time she'd met him made her body tingle.

Talia wished she could turn back the clock, and not have agreed to go with Rory to the charity awards night earlier that year, when Ashworth had been shortlisted in the Property Innovation category. He'd invited her, along with several team leaders and their plus ones. He saw paying for three tables as an investment: a networking opportunity – as well as the chance to show everyone what a generous boss he was.

Talia understood why her husband had wanted her there, but God, she wished he hadn't. If she hadn't gone, life would have stayed the same as it had been for decades: comfortable; fine; good enough. Instead, she'd dropped a bomb on her life, and its effects were still rippling now. Because that night, she'd met *him*. He'd shown an interest in her, in a way few people had for years. She'd felt invisible in her middle age, in her role as wife and mother and homemaker and now a lonely empty-nester. Where Talia had once turned every head as she walked down a street, now not even builders on a construction site gave her so much as an admiring glance.

And then there she was, next this man who was really, truly *seeing* her. Something sparked to life as they chatted over champagne and smoked salmon blinis. He told her how lovely she looked, how wonderful it was that she was working for a charity, how admirable it was that she was putting her talent and experience to good use. He'd asked her how *she* felt about her work. He'd made her laugh with witty observations about the event. For a moment, she'd felt like the Talia she'd been in her twenties: wild, and free, and attractive, and full of possibility. The Talia she'd been before she met Rory.

But then her husband had joined them, and they'd all started talking about the venue and the naff entertainment and the fact that they'd been *robbed, absolutely robbed* not winning the award – and the spell was broken. She remembered, rightly, who she was: a fifty-five-year-old married woman. She'd never be desired by someone like him – and even if she were, she couldn't possibly do anything about it, could she?

Only, at the end of the night as she'd collected her coat from the cloakroom, he'd asked for her number. And she'd been so giddy and captivated, she couldn't turn him down.

By the time Talia stopped crying, she was exhausted, her nervous system drained of energy. But the release had helped; she felt a little better for it. She was clearer, too: *this has to stop*. When she got home, she'd block him on every channel. She'd never speak to him again; she'd never risk bumping into him. She'd put all this behind her. It was a mistake – a horrible, stupid, selfish mistake – but that was all. It didn't have to ruin her life, or anyone else's. She'd forget it happened and move on.

Talia stretched a hand out to the master light switch. The room had darkened, and she could hear doors opening and closing with a soft *click* as the other guests got ready for this evening's party. She needed to tidy herself up, change into the black silk evening dress she'd brought for tonight, put on her bravest smile, then head above deck.

Tap tap tap. She stopped on the way to the bathroom at a soft knock at the door. *Did Rory forget his key card? He must be coming down to change for dinner.* She walked quickly to the sink, splashed water on her face and rubbed at her mascara-stained cheeks with a cotton pad, then paced to the cabin door and flung it open.

'You haven't lost your key—' She'd started speaking before the door had fully opened, and when she saw who was standing there, her words tailed off. It wasn't Rory, after all.

'Eleni,' said Talia curtly. *What does she want?*

Eleni was radiant in a midnight-blue, floor-length satin gown with matching long gloves. Her hair was swept in a glamorous up-do, and sparkling silver drops hung from her ears; her skin was dewy and glowing – just like Talia's had been in her thirties. A rush of envy flooded Talia's body, so strong that she almost gasped.

'I'm sorry, I thought it was that husband of mine.' She attempted a laugh; it emerged hollow.

'No worries! So sorry to bother you in the middle of your preparations. I was just checking you were all right?'

Talia flinched; she wondered how obvious it was that she'd just been crying. 'And why wouldn't I be?'

A flash of hurt marred Eleni's warm brown eyes. 'I . . . well, it's just that you've been in your cabin for a while, and you seemed a bit upset after what Rory said to you earlier, on deck . . .' She tailed off.

'I appreciate your concern, Eleni, but really, I'm—'

'Actually, can I come in for a sec?'

Oh for goodness' sake. Talia was still in her day dress, her hair wasn't done, nor her make-up. The bed wasn't made after her crying session, and damp, scrunched-up tissues lay next to her pillow. 'I was in the middle of getting ready—'

Thankfully, she was rescued that very moment by her husband, stomping down the staircase and along the passageway. 'Ah – not ready yet, Mrs Ashworth? Hurry up, we're about to get started. Finally managed to get a bloody signal up there.' He turned to Eleni and made a soft whistle. 'And don't you look the business?'

Eleni laughed and gave Rory an extravagant twirl; Talia stifled an eye-roll.

'I'd better get dressed, then,' she muttered. She backed into the cabin, then to the bathroom to shower and dress and put on make-up that, no matter how long and hard she tried, would never make her look as effortlessly beautiful as Rory's young, fresh-faced colleagues.

The atmosphere was strained as Talia took her place for dinner under the awning, despite the elegant black-and-white decorations and blaring Bond theme tunes. Rory – at the head of the table, dapper now in his tuxedo and bow tie – was clearly on edge, checking his phone and muttering frustrated profanities about data usage limits amid the ongoing lack of on-board Wi-Fi. Opposite Talia, Lucy and Mark had shifted their chairs slightly apart; they wouldn't even meet each other's eyes.

'Wow,' said Eleni, smiling as Talia sat down across from her, in between Sam and Rory, accepting a cocktail from Johanna once she was settled. 'You look stunning.'

'You all do,' said Sam. 'And us gents have scrubbed up pretty well too.'

He was right – all four men looked astonishingly handsome. Sam's beard was neatly trimmed, Nick's muscular frame filled his fitted shirt almost to bursting; Mark had slicked his hair back with gel and left the top button on his collar undone. They were all – as Chloe would say – *hot as hell.*

'Hear, hear,' said Rory. 'Look at the lot of us – you've all made a real effort. Cheers to that!'

He raised his glass and the group clinked their martinis together. Talia took a long sip. It was strong; the gin and vermouth burned pleasantly down her throat as she swallowed.

Johanna reappeared with their starters – grilled shrimp with honeydew gazpacho – just as Sam asked Rory: 'Did you manage to get onto your emails in the end, then?'

'Yes, just about – managed to get on using 4G.' Rory paused, spoon already halfway to his mouth. 'And I'm glad I did. Someone thinks we might have a way to get back in with Rosenberg, but for the Southall site. It would be quite the boon, to get them locked in – potential for a lot of new sales.'

Eleni's cutlery clattered onto her side plate. 'Rosenberg?' She looked at Sam. 'Hang on a second. I thought we were already in with them. Didn't you—'

'No,' Sam said, with a shrug. 'It fell through.'

'Oh – I didn't realize. Not sure how I missed that. So then, how come you—?' Eleni stopped talking abruptly, and covered her mouth with her hand. Nick glanced at her sharply.

Sam's shoulders hunched almost to his ears. He put his spoon down too, took a sip of his drink. 'How come I what?'

Eleni shook her head. 'Sorry – I didn't mean . . . it's nothing.'

Sam dropped his shoulders back down. 'I can take a good guess at what you were about to say. How did I win the bonus trip if Rosenberg fell through – right?'

Eleni shrugged and said nothing; Sam turned to Rory. 'Would you like to explain to our colleagues why I still got a place here? You'll do a better job than me, I'm sure.' Sam stared at Rory, a challenge in his expression. Talia squirmed; Sam's daring tone was making her uncomfortable.

Rory swallowed his mouthful of gazpacho then began nodding emphatically. 'Well, as you'll all know, Sam is quite the standout employee – he's been working at Ashworth for more than ten years, and that sort of loyalty merits reward.' He was rambling; talking much too fast. *What's got him so rattled?* 'Besides, it's not always about bringing in the big accounts! I wanted to do something different this year – as we can see with my choice of winners.' Rory gestured towards Lucy as he spoke.

'What's that supposed to mean?' Mark interrupted. 'Was Lucy something different, then? A *special case*?'

Rory and Mark glared at each other for a moment, flashes of last night's tension still alive between them. *This is going to get out of hand*. 'Yes, I suppose she was,' said Rory. 'But only in the sense that I've never brought along a colleague from finance before – however, Lucy's work is so impressive, it wasn't a hard decision.'

A muscle twitched in Mark's jaw, but he stayed quiet.

'And I'm very glad I did,' Rory bumbled on, as Johanna cleared away their starters. 'Because look at you – the journalist and the data analyst, both keen-eyed and ambitious! Just the kind of people I like around me. A real power couple.'

Mark snorted. 'Hardly.' He lifted his martini glass to his mouth.

Lucy leaned closer to him. 'Please be quiet,' she hissed.

'What? I'm just pointing out, we're not exactly changing the world together, are we?' Mark glared at Rory again. 'How could we, when you spend more time with your boss than you do with me?'

Talia gasped; across the table, Eleni's martini glass wobbled in her hand and nearly spilled. Rory looked at Talia in panic; she reached a hand out to soothe him. He sighed. 'Ah, now, come on, Mark – let's save the lovers' tiff for the privacy of our own cabins, shall we?'

From the other side of Talia, Sam grunted his displeasure.

'What, like you did this afternoon?' he said. 'When you spoke to Talia like that, in front of everyone?'

Please don't bring me into this. 'Sam, really,' Talia interjected. 'That's quite enough.'

'No,' Sam said, 'I don't think it is.' Then more quietly, so only Talia could hear: 'You shouldn't have to put up with it.'

Across the table, Eleni started to cough violently. Talia glanced over; she'd gone bright red and was waving her hands in front of her face.

'Sorry,' she choked out. 'Drink went down the wrong hole.'

'Are you all right?' Nick turned to his wife and started patting her on the back. 'Take a deep breath, you're making it worse by trying to talk.'

Slowly Eleni began to breathe normally again, her cheeks returning to their usual colour. Behind Talia, Johanna wandered between them awkwardly, placing their main courses on the table.

'Christ, this has all turned a bit depressing,' said Rory, sawing vigorously at his steak. 'Let's lighten up, shall we? Johanna – let's open the red, please. Come on, folks, let's enjoy ourselves – remember why we're all here . . .'

'Oh, I remember,' murmured Lucy, half to herself. Talia shook her head. *What on earth is the matter with everyone?*

'Well, I think the honesty is great, actually,' said Sam. 'It's healthy. Everyone getting things out in the open. So – anyone else? Anything you'd like to share, while we're getting things off our chest? Lucy – Eleni?' He glanced around the table, then to his boss at its head. 'Rory?'

'That's quite enough, Sam,' said Rory, leaning back in his chair. The colour had drained from his face; his hands were shaking.

'Rory's right,' piped up Eleni. 'That's enough. There's no need for all the hostility. Look where we are – on the trip of a lifetime. We're all so lucky to be here.' Her voice sounded cheerful, and she took an enthusiastic bite of her steak once she'd finished speaking, but there was an unmistakeable note of fear in her eyes.

'Well,' said Nick, his eyes narrowing a touch. 'I'm lucky to be alive *at all* after Rory's stunt on the jet ski this morning.'

Rory's fork clattered onto his plate; his jaw dropped; his mouth opened and closed like a ventriloquist's doll. 'I . . . I told you, Nick. It was an accident. I thought you were holding on tightly—'

'Yeah, of course – an accident,' Nick said, waving a hand. 'It was my fault, wasn't it, I suppose?'

Eleni's eyes widened. 'Nick, please . . .'

But the quiet tension Rory had been keeping under wraps exploded then into quick, urgent rage. 'For God's sake, all of you!' he snarled. 'Of course it wasn't anyone's fault – it was just one of those things. And I'd appreciate less of these ridiculous accusations when I've brought you all on the trip of a bloody lifetime!'

Talia stood up, mute with shock, watching as Rory turned and stormed across the deck and inside the salon, main course half-eaten, swearing loudly. She too was flooded with rage.

The audacity of Rory's co-workers – these . . . these *children*, who stared at spreadsheets and went on jollies visiting old buildings and patches of land; who had no idea what it meant to build a business up from its roots; who couldn't possibly imagine what it had taken out of Rory – out of their entire family – to build the company and the life that he had;

to have done well enough that he could reward his colleagues every year with something as spectacular as this.

'You've all crossed the line,' Talia seethed. 'And I won't watch you three' – she gestured to Rory's colleagues – 'sit in silence while people accuse my husband – the man who's brought you here on a very expensive holiday, for God's sake – of . . . of . . . I don't even know what!'

'I'm sorry,' Lucy said. 'I'm sure no one meant to upset you, or make you cross. I'm very grateful to Rory for giving me a spot here.'

'Me too,' said Eleni. 'Truly, I'm so sorry. We all are.'

The heat of Talia's anger cooled; the women looked genuinely shame-faced. But the same couldn't be said for the men around the table.

'I don't need you apologizing on my behalf,' Nick told Eleni. 'I'm done here.' He stood abruptly, knocking the edge of the table.

Talia's newly filled glass of red wine wobbled and, before she could catch it, toppled over, spreading crimson liquid across the tablecloth, dripping over the edge and onto the floor.

She watched in horror as the white fabric turned blood-red, dread forming in the pit of her stomach. Staring at it, she had the unshakable feeling that a door leading somewhere awful had just opened tonight.

And that perhaps it was already too late to close it.

SAM

Tonight had well and truly exploded.

Talia turned and stormed inside.

Sam wanted to go and ask her if she was all right; he could try to comfort her maybe, offer her a shoulder to cry on. But she'd disappeared into the salon and he could hardly follow her there – it would look odd. It would be inappropriate. Besides, she'd presumably gone to find Rory after his dramatic exit.

Sam couldn't help it: he'd enjoyed seeing his boss pissed off; it was no more than he deserved. The image of him stomping across the deck struck Sam as faintly ludicrous: the CEO of a stock market-listed development firm having a strop on a luxury superyacht because of a few snarky comments from the lads. *Oh, Rory – it could get so much worse than that.*

Johanna stepped discreetly towards the speakers and switched off the music. Sam looked across the table to where Mark, Lucy and Eleni were sitting in silence, picking at the remains of their dinner.

'Fuck me,' Sam said. 'That went well.'

Mark grunted. 'Talk about a dinner party from hell.'

Eleni shook her head, her expression vacant; she looked dazed. *Not surprising after the way that just blew up.* 'I don't understand how it all got so . . . *toxic*,' she said. She sighed heavily.

'Are you all right?' asked Lucy, turning to her.

'I'll be fine. I'm just . . . not great with conflict. Arguments, people going at each other . . . I hate it, to be honest.' She took a sip of water. 'I'm usually the one trying to keep the peace – didn't do a very good job of that tonight, though.'

Lucy nodded. 'I'm the same – well, most of the time.' She glanced at Mark, who stared intently at his wine glass.

'Actually, I think I'll take my drink up to the sun deck,' he said, getting to his feet. 'See you later.'

Sam was left sitting opposite Eleni and Lucy, alone. He considered heading down to his cabin, getting an early night, but – he checked his watch – it was only just gone nine o'clock, and this was supposed to be a *party*.

Both his colleagues seemed to be in their own worlds – and not especially happy ones, either. Maybe this was his time to step up – to see if he could get closer to them both. To see if he could help. And things were escalating between everyone: Eleni was right – toxic was exactly the word. Some weird shit was going down – not just couple drama, but between *everyone*.

'Hey,' he said. 'We're still here, aren't we? The three lucky winners. We should make the most of the night – we didn't even get to have dessert.'

Eleni offered him a sad smile. 'Not sure I'm really in the party mood, after that.'

Lucy shrugged. 'Me neither.' She cocked her head to one side and appraised him. 'It's a shame, though, after everyone made such an effort. You really do look very smart in your outfit, Sam.'

Sam grinned. 'Ah, thanks. A shame my ex isn't here to see me in it.' *Oh, Jesus. Why did I just say that? Too many martinis . . .*

Eleni offered Sam a tight smile. 'You never told us what happened with her – why she ended up not coming along . . . Claire, is it?' she asked.

'Ah . . .' Sam faltered. 'Yeah, it was Claire. We broke up a couple of weeks ago.'

'Oh shit, sorry – I did know that.' Eleni rolled her eyes and swatted a palm to her forehead as if to say, *silly me*.

'Nah, it's fine. Would have been a bit awkward if I'd still brought her after she dumped me . . .' He tried to laugh, but it emerged as a sort of croak; something bitter had caught at the back of his throat. 'Why do you ask?'

Eleni shrugged. 'No reason. I'd just been wondering what happened, with you coming here by yourself.'

Sam stared at his hands. 'It's not exactly how I wanted things to go. Don't know what to do with myself here, sometimes, around all you couples.'

'Why did you break up then?' asked Lucy. The bluntness in her question took him aback for a second, and he noticed Eleni's eyes widen too – but then he laughed. 'Sorry,' said Lucy, turning pink. 'I don't mean to be rude. I can sound a bit short sometimes, or so I've been told.'

Sam didn't mind that kind of directness. At least it was honest. He knew where he stood with plain talking, and it made a refreshing change from the bullshit chit-chat he had to make when he was trying to sell luxury flats. He just wasn't sure how he was going to answer this particular question. He could hardly tell them the truth: *It's Rory's fault we broke up, and I'll never forgive him for it.*

He sighed. 'No, it's okay. But honestly, sometimes I don't even know the answer myself. Things were going so well. Better than any of my other relationships, truth be told.'

It was true. They had fun, and she was hot, and warm, and kind, and easy-going – about most things, anyway. And the sex had been . . . well, the best of his thirty-six years. He'd be picturing her – the way she looked him dead in the eyes as she went down on him, the way she laughed sometimes with pure joy as he fucked her – in bed for the rest of his life, most likely.

He'd asked her to move in with him after less than a year; she'd met his whole family over in Dublin. Anna had loved her, and his mam had too. This was big stuff, for him. He had high standards, and he wasn't willing to give up his comfortable solitude and the ease of casual sex and situationships for just anyone. But he'd wanted to do all that *for her*.

Love had made him a fool. He shouldn't have trusted her with the stuff he found out. He'd just been so sure she'd get it. She'd said she was a feminist – look at the way she was always on the side of women who revealed abuses of power: men were guilty at the first sniff of misconduct, that was her opinion. She'd stopped watching *What's for Tea, GB?* the same day a vague news report came out about one of its presenters inviting a junior production exec to his hotel room. Swore she'd never give him another second of her time.

Sam loved that fierceness about her. And he *agreed* with her – that was the whole point. He was trying to stand up for exactly the same kind of thing. Even if the way he'd had to go about it was a little . . . unorthodox.

'Sam?' Lucy prompted. He'd wandered off there for a minute, into his thoughts, and left them hanging. He had to say *something*.

'But, ah, you know. It just didn't work out.' He shrugged. 'We didn't see eye to eye on a few things. Turned out, those things were a deal-breaker for her.'

Eleni tilted her head to one side and made a sympathetic noise. The gesture made him think of his mam. He had a sudden pang for her – the feel of her soft belly when she wrapped him in a hug; the way she always smelled vaguely of lavender and banana bread. She'd been so proud of him, getting a place on this trip. He swallowed.

'I met her once, I think,' said Eleni. 'At the awards do earlier this year, maybe?'

It took Sam a second to work out they'd been talking about Claire – not his mam. He nodded. 'Yeah, sounds right. I brought her along.'

'She seemed lovely – I remember now, we were chatting about her little niece and how excited she was for her sixth birthday. She even indulged me by looking at pictures of my kids, bless her. I'm really sorry things didn't work out.'

'That sounds like Claire. She was . . . I mean, *is* lovely.' He caught himself. 'Got to remember to still talk about her in the present tense. Don't mean to make it sound like she's . . . like she's *dead*!'

He attempted a laugh, but the sound took him by surprise;

it came out all wrong – it was more of a sob. *Oh God*. To his horror, Sam realized his eyes had filled; he blinked rapidly. *I haven't let myself cry about her once. Why the fuck is this happening now, in front of people I work with?*

Maybe it was the way Eleni remembered Claire at that event. Or how kind she was being about her. Or even just the fact that someone had actually *asked* him about it, and said they were sorry, rather than dismissing it; rather than telling him he'd be fine, that there were plenty more fish in the sea. Because it wasn't true; there weren't. Not like Claire. Rory had destroyed the best thing that ever happened to him.

'Sorry,' he croaked. 'The salty air makes my eyes water, I think. And my throat is so dry.'

He reached for the jug of icy water garnished with cucumber and mint, poured a glass and downed it in three gulps. He was so *hot* in this stupid suit. He patted at his cheeks: they were boiling. He poured some more water in the glass, then splashed it onto his hands and used them to cool his face.

Lucy was watching him curiously. As he met her eyes, she pushed her chair back. 'Sorry this hasn't been the party we were hoping for. But all this drama has wiped me out – I'm going to get an early night.'

Perhaps she was desperate to get away from him now, after he'd revealed the pain of his heartbreak. It was weak, letting them both see him like that. It was embarrassing.

'Night,' said Eleni, waving her off. They both watched as Lucy stood and walked away and through the salon doors. Sam took another glug of wine; he was feeling it now.

'Bit weird, isn't it?' he murmured. The booze was making him bold.

Eleni met his eyes. 'What is?'

Sam shrugged. 'I don't want to sound like a dick. But just . . . Lucy.'

'You think Lucy's weird?'

'I don't mean *she's* weird, exactly. But just . . . the way Mark said she's, like, a special case. Not Rory's usual pick. I gotta admit, I was a bit surprised when I found out she was coming.'

Eleni sighed. 'Yeah. I was too, at first. But I get it now, sort of. It's like Rory said – he wanted to mix things up a bit. And she's good at her job, isn't she?' Eleni gave Sam a meaningful look.

'We all are,' he replied hastily. 'But with Lucy – you don't think . . . ah, no. Never mind.'

Eleni leaned forward, rested her elbows on the table. 'Think what?'

'That she's one of Rory's women.'

'His women?' Eleni was indignant. 'And who are they, exactly?'

I've gone too far. 'Forget I said anything. Honestly, it doesn't matter.'

'No, no. I want to know now – tell me, please. Who exactly are Rory's *women*?'

Sam fiddled with the stem of his wine glass for a moment, then dropped his voice low: 'You must have noticed. He's got his favourites – and it's usually the young, pretty, new joiners . . .'

Eleni snorted. 'I'm sorry, but . . . what are you suggesting exactly? That Lucy's – what, sleeping with Rory to get ahead in her career? That's ridiculous, Sam.'

'That's not what I meant. I just wouldn't be surprised if, you know, he'd approached her some time. Hit on her. Decided to reward her with special favours because he's taken a liking to her.'

'Oh,' said Eleni. She stared at her hands.

'Has he – has he ever done that to you? You can tell me, Eleni.'

Eleni got to her feet. 'No – he hasn't. And I think it's time I went to see where Nick's got to.'

'Ah, Eleni – don't go . . . I'm sorry if I upset you, I'm only trying to help . . .' But Sam's words were met with silence as Eleni walked off briskly, back inside and away from him.

Sam stayed at the dinner table, alone and contemplative. Clearly, he wasn't going to get anything more out of Eleni about Rory: to be fair, if she said too much, it could cause no end of drama between Nick and Rory on the rest of the charter – Sam had already seen a hint of that this evening.

Johanna stepped out of the salon and began clearing the table. 'Can I get you anything else?' she asked.

'I'm good, thanks.'

Johanna started stacking plates, turning away just as Sam thought of something. Eleni and Lucy hadn't opened up to him this evening; maybe, though, the same couldn't be said for the other people he was sharing this yacht with: the crew. Perhaps they might be a little more willing to get things out in the open. He could only try.

'Johanna?'

She turned back. 'Yes? What can I get you?'

'Oh – nothing. I just wanted to check you're all okay. I know Michaela hasn't been feeling well. Is she better now?'

'Yes, she's fine – thanks.'

Before Sam could say anything else, the stewardess walked briskly inside. *No luck there, either.*

But this trip wasn't over yet. He had another day to go, and he wouldn't give up: it was his duty to discover if any of these women were feeling unsafe; if they were facing danger of any kind.

Because Sam already had a good idea of what – or rather, *who* that danger could be.

He just hoped he wouldn't have to keep it to himself for much longer.

GENDARMERIE MARITIME DE POLYNÉSIE FRANÇAISE

CASE NUMBER: 247849

POLICE EXHIBIT SIX

Transcript of audio from CCTV footage, *Lusso di Mare* camera 3 (Main Deck awning), conversation between Michaela Stevens and Johanna Nebeker

09/06/26, 23:45

Johanna: They've all gone down. We can talk. Oh my God, Mic! Have we ever seen a dinner party crash and burn that fast before?

Michaela: <quiet laugh> I'm not sure we have. This tablecloth's not coming back from it, that's for sure. Here, pass me the other end . . .

Johanna: Poor Talia, though. She looked ready to burst into tears before she even sat down. I feel bad for her, to be honest. Imagine being married to that . . .

Michaela: I know. But I don't think her husband's the only thing worrying her.

Johanna: Fair point. And did you see the way Eleni jumped in, trying to diffuse everything, when they were all going in on Rory?

Michaela: And how it was the women, apologizing for the men's behaviour? Aaah. It grinds my gears . . .

Johanna: Me too! <quietly> Are you okay, though? After . . . you know.

Michaela: <pause> Yeah. Nothing's happened so far today. It's been a massive relief to stay away from guest duties, though – I'm just sorry you're having to pick so much up on service.

Johanna: No, honestly, it's fine – it's better this way. But if he so much as . . .

Michaela: He won't. Captain's keeping an eye on everything – I know she's got my back. Still, I feel . . . pretty uncomfortable.

Johanna: I don't know how you're staying so calm. I shit you not, I wanted to deck him tonight.

Michaela: Oh hon, I'd want to too, if I had to wait on him. But I'm not sure that'd do much to help with anything. Okay, I think we're about done here. I'm going to go down. And Jo?

Johanna: Mmm?

Michaela: Keep your radio close tonight – okay?

[TRANSCRIPT ENDS]

ELENI

10 JUNE

Eleni leaned across to the bedside table and checked the time on her phone. *10:36 a.m. How have I slept that long?*

She'd headed to bed when she'd finished talking to Sam last night after the fractious dinner party; she'd been rattled and edgy, but exhausted. When she got to their cabin, there was no sign of Nick – she hadn't seen him since he stormed off during dinner. She'd been so deeply asleep, she'd barely stirred when he crawled in next to her at some point, presumably in the early hours. She had a vague, dream-like memory of his arms scooping her body, whispering sweet words in her ear, pulling her close to him . . . and the pulsing that still throbbed between her thighs reminded her what had happened after.

Eleni looked at her phone again. Four new messages had made their way through the shaky 4G and appeared on the family WhatsApp group: photos of the boys' sports day yesterday, and a voice note from Mariana. She clicked on the images and zoomed in; her heart swelled. In one of them, Lucas was holding a bronze medal, his little round cheeks rosy with pride. She glanced at Nick; he was still fast asleep.

Careful not to wake him, she held the phone close to her ear and pressed play on Mariana's message; her eyes filled with tears – of relief, this time. It was so good to hear her sister's voice. Then she tapped a quick reply: *Thank you soooo much, Maz, I can't tell you how grateful I am. Can you show this to the boys? Wow, look at you two! Mummy is so proud. Miss you both so much. Not long till we're back home! Love you. Xoxo*

Breathing more easily now, she sat up slowly and placed her feet on the floor, managing not to make a sound. She rested there for a moment, noticing how still it all was – no motion of the water underneath the yacht; no gentle bobbing of the waves on the *Lusso*'s underbelly. They weren't sailing yet then. The realization struck her as odd: Eleni was sure they'd been due to cast off for Raiatea at first light for their final day, before starting their long journey home tomorrow. She felt a flash of anxiety.

It's got to happen today. It's my last chance.

She tiptoed to the window, edged back the blackout curtains and peered outside. They were still anchored in the same spot off Huahine; something must have happened to interfere with their scheduled itinerary. The sky was its usual cloudless, deep blue, and the sea was calmer than she'd seen it since they'd arrived: almost completely still, only the gentlest of waves lapping onto the nearby strip of sandy beach.

Her mind drifted back to dinner last night. How did it all end up such a fucking car crash? She'd hated every minute of it – the tension, the accusations, Nick's thinly veiled resentment towards Rory. She expected he'd regret it afterwards – but still, it was embarrassing, her husband getting so close to losing his rag like that in front of everyone. *I hope everyone was drunk enough not to remember.*

Then the awkward conversation afterwards with just the three of them left – and Sam's weird theory about Lucy being one of Rory's 'women'. Eleni knew what Rory was like – and yes, he did turn his attentions to young women when they first joined. She'd always sort of accepted it: it was just part and parcel of working for him. And he'd never made her feel truly uncomfortable; he'd never actually crossed a line with her.

But Sam's hushed rumour-mongering made her stomach turn – because of how he was going about it, more than anything. She didn't like the way Sam seemed to be lingering close by when she was alone, or when it was just women gathered together.

This morning, all of that and Eleni's own, more private fears curdled in the pit of her stomach as she looked out to sea. *I've got twenty-four hours left. Everyone's counting on me.*

Nick stirred in bed; she turned to look at him as he blinked groggily. 'Can't you close the curtain, babe? It's too bright . . .'

'Sorry,' she murmured, pulling the blinds back into place. 'I'm going to get dressed and go up. We should have set sail by now, and I want to know what the hold-up is.'

No response; after a few seconds, he was snoring again. She sighed, headed to the wardrobe and slipped off her silk cami and shorts, folding them neatly and placing them in the correct drawer. Then she dressed quickly in linen trousers and a vest and left the cabin, taking care not to make a sound as the door closed behind her.

* * *

Under the awning on the main deck, the other five guests were already sipping coffee around the dining table, their breakfast plates now empty, Rory's morning papers spread out in front of him, taking up half the table. She sat down next to Lucy, taking note of the frosty silence. *I'll have to try to cheer everyone up.*

'Morning, all,' she said in her chirpiest voice. 'I can't believe I stayed in bed so late – I think that's the longest I've slept in years.'

Lucy rewarded her small talk with a tight smile. 'Good for you,' she said. 'There's still some croissants and things left . . .' She gestured towards the centre of the table, where the usual array of dishes was on display.

'Good morning, Eleni,' said Johanna, appearing behind her. 'What would you like – eggs Benedict again today?'

'That would be lovely.' She waited for the stewardess to leave, then leaned in towards the others and whispered: 'I can't believe I'm thinking this, but I'll be happy to have a good old bowl of Shreddies for breakfast when I get home.'

'Ha,' said Sam. 'I know what you mean. I don't think I'll ever be able to hack another gourmet pineapple pudding in my life after this, either.'

There. I'm lightening the mood already. Relieving the tension: it was what she was good at; it was what she knew. She wished it was working for Talia too, but she still looked downcast this morning, glumly picking at a bowl of tropical fruit. Eleni added a couple of pastries to an empty plate, then filled a cup with filter coffee. She sat down, took a bite, then asked: 'Any idea why we're not moving? I thought we were casting off early this morning, and it must be gone eleven by now.'

Rory held his hands up. 'Ah, yes. That's my fault, I'm afraid.'

Eleni took a sip of orange juice. 'Oh? Why – what's happened?'

'The Wi-Fi still isn't fixed, and I need to get to my emails with some urgency today to pick up on this opportunity with Rosenberg.' Rory sipped his coffee. 'I've been using my data to get online, but it's slow – and costing me an arm and a leg. Once we're sailing, I won't even be able to access *that*. So I told the captain early this morning that under no circumstances are we leaving without it being fixed.' He winked at Eleni. 'It may have helped that I threatened her crew with no tip if it's not sorted. Ha!'

In the chair next to her, Eleni noticed Lucy's fist clench, then release again. She tried to catch her eye, but Lucy was staring at the table, unblinking.

'I see,' said Eleni. 'And is it going to get sorted soon?' She glanced at Talia, who was staring resolutely into her coffee cup. 'Sorry, Rory, but it's our last full day. It seems a shame to miss out on our time in Raiatea – we should be making the most of every minute now, all of us . . .' *And being stuck here on a stationary yacht with the atmosphere so tense isn't going to get us together the way I need . . .*

'That's what I said,' agreed Mark. He looked sullen this morning, arms folded across his chest, his chair turned away from Lucy's. 'Whatever it is, it can't be that urgent.'

'Yes, yes, you're both quite right, of course,' Rory said. 'The captain wasn't best pleased either – apparently there's a spot of rough weather along the way. If we don't leave soon, there's a bigger chance we'll run into it. But I'm sure it'll be working again any minute – we should miss the rough seas and still have plenty of time at our final stop.'

Eleni stifled an eye-roll. They *wouldn't* get plenty of time in Raiatea – it was a four-hour sail to get there. They wouldn't even drop anchor until mid-afternoon, at the earliest. And rough sailing conditions did *not* sound appealing. *So we're now going to miss most of the day there and probably hit a storm – all because of bloody Rory.*

In one swift movement, Talia shoved her chair back and stood up, picked up her phone from the table and stalked through the doors into the salon. Eleni watched her go.

'What's wrong with Talia?' asked Sam.

Rory stared at Sam darkly across the table for a moment, then returned to his newspaper. 'She's quite all right, I can assure you.'

'She didn't look all right,' Sam muttered.

Sam and Rory are still at odds this morning, then. The whole group is cracking at the seams . . .

Michaela returned with Eleni's breakfast. Eleni took a mouthful, then cleared her throat. 'Rory, why don't you go and check on her? It all got a bit . . . tense last night, didn't it? Maybe she could do with some cheering up?'

Rory frowned and shook the pages of his newspaper. 'Goodness, no. I expect she's enjoying some time alone.'

Eleni lowered her voice and leaned towards her boss. 'And you're sure everything's . . . all right between you two?'

Rory put the paper down and looked at Eleni. 'Of course. When you've been together for as long as Talia and I have, disagreements are simply part of the package – throw menopause into the mix and – well! But that doesn't mean we don't still . . .'

Abruptly, Lucy pushed back her chair with a screech,

interrupting Rory's monologue; Eleni managed to disguise her snort of laughter at Lucy's rudeness as a spluttering cough. 'I think I'll take the rest of my coffee up to the sun deck,' said Lucy. 'Mark, would you like to come too?'

Mark shrugged. 'Fine,' he said. 'Let's go.'

Eleni picked up her plate and coffee and moved to Talia's empty seat, next to Rory. She turned to him and placed a hand on his wrist. 'I'm sure Talia's fine – like you say.' From further down the table, she could feel Sam's eyes on her; she lowered her voice. 'I do wonder, though – have you ever thought that she might be—'

'The Wi-Fi's back up and running,' called Captain Taylor. 'Brett tried a harder system reboot, and it worked. No need to wait for an engineer.' Eleni turned to see her at the bottom of the stairs that led down from the upper deck. 'Now, I'll make our final preparations for casting off and we'll be on our way in the next few minutes.'

Rory erupted into enthusiastic cheers; Sam immediately got his phone out of his pocket and starting scrolling. Eleni was glad they were setting sail soon – they might get a few hours on Raiatea before it got dark – but she still had more to say to Rory, and their moment had been interrupted yet again.

Rory plucked his laptop out from underneath his newspaper. 'Just what I've been waiting for,' he said, brandishing the computer like a trophy. 'I'm off to work on that proposal.' He got to his feet.

Eleni's heart leapt; she sprang out of her chair. 'Oh, are you going down to your cabin? I was about to head back too – I'll come with you . . .'

'Eleni, were you listening to a word I said earlier?' Rory

rolled his eyes playfully. 'Come on, keep up. Talia enjoys some time by herself, and I'll work much better without my wife in the same room. I'm off to the sky lounge upstairs – and I'd appreciate not being disturbed, please.' He glanced at Sam, who glared back at him, then headed up the spiral staircase.

Eleni stepped away from the bow, made her way to the stern of the boat and stared out into the vast, endless ocean. Rory was gone; she'd missed yet another chance, and the yacht would be moving soon.

By tomorrow, it would all be over – one way or another.

Eleni clasped her palms together and breathed deeply. *This is it*. One last day.

Her final chance to do what she came for.

LUCY

Lucy couldn't avoid Mark any longer. After the disastrous dinner party last night, she'd fallen asleep before he returned to the cabin; today, she'd gone up for breakfast alone before he even woke up. Truth be told, they'd barely spoken since the morning after he'd drunkenly approached Rory. But she couldn't carry on like this – not with so much tension on board, not with everything she was carrying. She felt adrift and rudderless – Mark was her anchor, and she needed him.

They settled into the cushioned seats of the sun deck's bow; Lucy edged her bottom closer to Mark, and he wrapped his arm around her shoulder in response. This time, she didn't want to pull away.

'Nice to have a bit of space from everyone,' said Mark. 'If I had to listen to one more piece of patronizing advice coming from that sanctimonious prick . . . as if we've got anything to learn from someone that age, anyway. He's a fucking *dinosaur*.'

Lucy snorted. 'He's not *that* old. Only mid-fifties.'

Mark's eyes widened in surprise. 'Is he? I thought he was seventy-odd.'

She grimaced. 'Seventy! Jesus, why? He acts like a bloody teenager half the time.'

'Yeah. That prank with the jet ski was proper schoolboy, to be fair,' said Mark. 'No, it's more . . . I dunno. His sense of humour. The stuff he says about women. It's so outdated. Like, the sort of stupid jokes and comments my gramps used to make.'

Lucy picked at her fingernails. *As if that's the worst thing about him*. 'I know. It's pretty cringe, isn't it?'

'Like how he calls you all *girls* – and the thing about how Michaela is more than just a pretty face?'

Lucy wrinkled her nose in disgust. 'Gross. But that's Rory, isn't it? He's in his own little world of wealthy, white, male privilege. He doesn't think about how the stuff he says or does impacts anyone else. He's never had to. He gets away with whatever he wants.'

Mark stiffened; he lifted up his sunglasses and turned to stare at her. 'Like what?'

Shit. Had she gone too far? She needed to manage this carefully. 'Ah, I don't know . . . I didn't mean anything specific. Just that he's clueless about how most people live their lives, you – you know?'

Mark nodded and looked away; he stared out to sea for a moment, but the silence was loaded. 'Last night went off a bit, didn't it?' he said finally.

Lucy groaned. 'Tell me about it. What a disaster. I've got no idea what Sam's problem with Rory is.' She took a deep breath. 'And I thought it was pretty out of order, the way you spoke to Rory too – and to me. Accusing me of spending more time with my boss than I do with you . . . saying that in front of everyone. It wasn't cool.'

Mark scowled. 'I wasn't wrong, though, was I? You're obsessed with that place – obsessed with *him*.' Lucy opened her mouth to interject, but Mark raised a hand to quiet her. 'But fair enough. I shouldn't have said it in front of everyone. You're right – it wasn't okay.'

Lucy stared down at her hands. 'I'm not . . . *obsessed*,' she said quietly.

Mark scoffed. 'Oh, come on. Do you really not get where I'm coming from? Do you not think it's been hard for me, these last few months – you've been completely consumed by Ashworth. I've not seen you – you've barely even spoken to me!'

Lucy flushed hot with rage. 'Barely spoken to you? Don't be ridiculous, Mark. We live together, for God's sake. We talk to each other every *day*!' She was raising her voice now – shouting – she didn't even care if the other guests heard her.

'No' – Mark was shaking his head in frustration – 'that's not what I mean. Yes, we've talked about who's taking the bins out and whose turn it is to cover the online shop. But we haven't talked *properly*. And this whole time, it's felt like there's stuff to do with work – to do with Rory, especially – that you're keeping from me.' He stared at her now; the intensity in his gaze almost hurt, but Lucy couldn't bear to look away. 'Lucy . . . do you remember when you first went to the interview at Ashworth?'

Can't he just leave it? 'Yes,' she answered coldly. 'I mean, it was a few months ago, but I remember it. Why?' Oh, she remembered it. It was etched in her mind in permanent marker.

Mark frowned. 'You were so excited about it, weren't you?'

'Yes. And rightly so. I knew it was going to be the opportunity of a lifetime.'

'And remember when you came back after – you said you'd blown him away with the data analysis you did beforehand?'

Lucy closed her eyes at the memory; she'd been so proud of herself. Before the interview, she had printed out highlighted spreadsheets of an analysis she'd made of last year's annual report. She'd already found areas for the company to improve. Rory had been impressed by her initiative; he said she was the first and only candidate he'd seen who'd put that kind of effort in. 'Of course,' she said. 'He offered me the job on the spot.'

Rory's offer had come as a sweet relief: she was convinced she'd blown it, earlier in the interview. When she'd first stepped into his office, Rory had stared at her for a moment, in intense curiosity. 'You've interviewed for a role here at Ashworth before, have you?' he'd asked.

She'd been momentarily stumped. 'Ah – here? No. This is the first time I've ever been in the building.' Rory had looked baffled; he said he could have sworn he'd seen her before – that he had *a memory for faces*. She'd racked her brains, managed to come up with a plausible explanation about doing work experience at a nearby brokerage, and passing him on the street. He'd looked unconvinced – but, thankfully, he'd moved on.

Mark examined his fingernails. 'I've never seen you so determined about anything as you were to get that job. But you were doing okay at Baker Hartwell before, weren't you? You were happy enough. I still just don't understand why you wanted to move so badly, to Ashworth – to work with him. With Rory.'

Lucy's mouth went dry. 'Well, it was a decent pay rise,' she said carefully. 'We needed the cash – I've got so many outgoings, and we want to save up for a deposit, don't we? I'd love us to get on the property ladder one day. And Ashworth have excellent benefits – just look where we are.' She gestured towards the sea.

'So you're saying it was nothing to do with Rory? And him treating you like a *special fucking case* is just – what, because he's so interested in your career?'

Lucy swallowed. *Oh no. Mark's got this so, so wrong.* 'Hang on a minute . . . do you think there's something going on with me and Rory?' Mark watched her closely, but said nothing; only raised his eyebrows in subtle challenge. 'Do you – do you think I'm *sleeping* with him or something?'

Mark's eyebrows arched even higher. 'Well, are you?'

'Am I *what*?'

'*Are you sleeping with Rory*?'

Lucy's jaw dropped. The idea – the *image* of it in her mind – was so off-putting; so preposterous that she burst into horrified laughter.

'Jesus Christ, Mark, no! Of course not. I'd never cheat on you – ever. And if in some alternate universe I wanted to have an affair – please. Come on, I've got some standards, haven't I? He's old enough to be my dad, and he's . . . he's *Rory*. Is that really what you thought – is that why you've been acting like such a . . . such a *dick*?'

Mark lifted his hands to his face and rubbed his eyes. 'Oh, fucking hell, Lucy, I don't know. Maybe not – not really. And I've not been that much of a bellend, have I? I've probably been drinking too much – but like I said, it's been bothering me, how distant you've been since you started working there . . .

and the way you didn't even tell me about the trip! I only found out about it because I saw the email. Were you even going to invite me?'

Lucy's chest constricted at the hurt in his expression. Truthfully – no, she *wasn't* going to invite him. She didn't want him here, seeing what she was up to, interfering with things, distracting her. And she'd been right – he'd done exactly that. Walking in on her rifling through Rory's cabin on their second day, casting suspicious glances at her ever since, making it nearly impossible to hunt for evidence again. But she couldn't tell him that – at least, not yet. He wouldn't understand.

'Of course I was going to invite you,' she said, rolling her eyes. 'So this is why you've been so weird, then . . . is that why you got up in his face like that the other night? You thought I was cheating on you – with him?' It made a horrible, sad kind of sense. 'And is that where you went in the middle of the night afterwards – to confront him again?'

At that, Mark looked stunned. 'What? Of course not. I told you where I went, when you asked me the next morning. I woke up feeling sick, and I needed something to soak up the booze. I got Johanna to make me a toastie – ask her, I'm sure she'll remember. Jesus, what did you think I'd been doing? That I'd gone after Rory in his cabin in the dead of night?'

She stared back at him in silence, shame now starting to bloom in her chest. Her suspicion sounded ridiculous, now he'd explained it like that. *Oh God, what was I thinking? This is Mark – my Mark. When did I stop trusting him – with everything?*

'You're right. I'm sorry. I'm not thinking clearly – I don't think I've had my head straight for a while, to be honest . . .'

Mark's hand gave her shoulder a gentle squeeze. 'Thank God. Are you finally going to tell me? I've been waiting so bloody long. I've given you so many chances, Luce.'

A band of tightness squeezed across her chest. 'Chances? For what?'

'To tell me the truth.'

She flinched. 'The truth about *what*?'

'About why you wanted to work at Ashworth so badly. I know there's something else – something you've not been telling me. I know you better than anyone. You can't keep lying to me.'

His eyes were locked on hers; Lucy felt the heat crawling up her neck, her throat. She wrenched her gaze away, pulled her hand free and stumbled to her feet, moving away from the bow and towards the staircase.

'Lucy, don't. What are you going to do? Get on a tender and sail off into the South Pacific? You'll have to come back to the yacht sometime. You'll have to come back to *me*.'

She stood still. *He's right. I can't escape him. I can't escape any of it.* She turned back to look at him; his hands were shaking, and his expression was all heartache. Lucy's stomach churned. *This is why I didn't want to tell you.* She couldn't bear the hurt, the confusion, the anger. She couldn't bear him trying to help her, or protect her, by convincing her to change her mind.

But she also couldn't keep lying to him; holding him at such a lonely distance. He'd have worked it out eventually, anyway. This man, who'd earned himself a reputation as the reporter who missed nothing, who could sniff out the truth like a hound tracking blood. He probably even read the press release three years ago – maybe it was filed away in his memory just like it was in Lucy's:

APD is delighted to announce the acquisition of Willowbrook Lodge, a long-established residential care home in North London, with plans to redevelop the site into a collection of high-specification luxury apartments . . . The developer will work closely with local authorities and care providers to ensure all residents transition to alternative facilities that meet, and in many cases exceed, their current level of care . . . their wellbeing remains APD's absolute priority . . .

'Okay,' she said, and sat back down, close to him. 'If you want the truth, I'll tell you. None of this is about me having an affair. I'd never, ever do that to you.'

'Then what?' His eyes were pleading with her. She had to tell him; it was now or never. She'd already left it too long.

She exhaled and said: 'I joined Ashworth because of my brother. All this is because of Alfie.'

GENDARMERIE MARITIME DE POLYNÉSIE FRANÇAISE

CASE NUMBER: 247849

DATE: 11/06/2026

INTERVIEW EXCERPT FOUR

Interview subject: Leilani Bambridge, chef on board *Lusso di Mare* charter

Interview conducted by Chief of Police Henri Robert

M Robert: Leilani, how much do crew members know about the guests who come on board during a charter?

Mme Bambridge: Ah, well – we get a preference sheet for everyone. It tells us the kinds of things they like to eat, and anything they don't like. And they tell us in there about what they'd like to do on their trip. The captain also gets a bit of background information about the primaries – you know, what they do, where they come from, any special occasions taking place during their charter. That kind of thing.

M Robert: And the captain shares all this kind of information with you?

Mme Bambridge: Yes, monsieur. We have a meeting the day before the charter starts, usually, and we go over it all then.

M Robert: That was the case with this trip?

Mme Bambridge: That's right – there was nothing unusual. Nothing to worry about – no allergies or over-the-top requests.

M Robert: But you wouldn't learn things like whether any of the guests have a criminal record, for example? Or if they'd been arrested, suspected of crimes in the past – things like that?

Mme Bambridge: Oh, no. No, never. We don't ask about things like that, and we don't expect to find them out, either. If they're paying good money to be there, well then . . . how they live their lives when they're not on board the yacht is not our business.

M Robert: Yes, that's as I thought. So is it a surprise that we learned one of the guests on this particular charter had a previous arrest for assault on their background checks?

Mme Bambridge: No, honestly. I can believe it of some of those men.

M Robert: But it wasn't a man. It was one of your female guests. She was arrested for attacking a male victim. So, you can see why we need to investigate this more thoroughly . . .

Mme Bambridge: <audible intake of breath> Excuse me? One of the women has been arrested in the past? For assault, you said . . . <gentle murmuring>

M Robert: Leilani, you seem distressed. Are you all right? What's upset you?

Mme Bambridge: No . . . no – it's just – it's what you just said. It turned everything upside down – you see? Topsy-turvy? Just like a boat in a storm . . . I'm sorry, monsieur, I need some air. Please . . .

M Robert: Interview terminated at 19:19.

[TRANSCRIPT ENDS]

ELENI

Nick was just leaving their cabin as Eleni reached the bottom of the stairs below deck.

He stepped out into the corridor and lit up as he saw her; Eleni's stomach did its usual flip-flop. Even hungover, with dark circles under his eyes and messy hair and unbrushed teeth, he was the most beautiful man she'd ever laid eyes on.

'How are you feeling?' she asked. 'Are you heading up for some breakfast?'

'Yeah, and coffee. All the coffee.' He kissed the top of her head. 'You already been up?'

'Yep. I'm sorry – I was hungry, and I didn't want to wake you.'

'You going to stay here in the cabin while I eat?'

Eleni nodded. 'I think so. I can wait for you, then we'll decide what to do on the sail. See you in a bit?'

'Yeah.' He gazed at her for a moment. 'I'm sorry about last night. You know I love you, don't you?'

'Of course, Nick.'

'And?'

'And . . . I love you too.'

Back in the cabin alone, Eleni sat on the bed and tried to hold back the tears of frustration and fear that threatened to overwhelm her. How could this be their last day? How was she still floundering; missing every possible opportunity to bring her plans to fruition? She took her phone out of her bag and listened to her sister's message again, out loud this time.

'Try to stop worrying, sis. I know it's hard, but – everything's going fine. Not much longer to go – you can do this.'

Eleni let out a slow breath. And then, in the stillness that came right after the last of the air had left her lungs, she heard it: the soft, almost imperceptible whirring that lasted a second, perhaps less. Then, again, the unmistakeable, familiar feeling of eyes on her.

No. Come on – this is ridiculous. Maybe I'm losing the plot on this boat. I'm hearing things. I'm imagining things. It's all the stress . . . the claustrophobia . . .

There was another whirr.

'Right, I've had *enough*!' Eleni yelled out, to no one. She grabbed a bobble to sweep her hair out of her face into a bun, then jumped up and started moving her hands along the walls of the cabin, systematically, inch by inch. If someone had hidden something in here to watch her – a secret camera, or a spyhole somewhere disguised as something else – she was bloody well going to find it. She felt a rush of determination. Here was the old Eleni again: there was no stopping her when she'd made up her mind.

She strode to the wall opposite the bed, where the TV was mounted, running her fingers along its edges. *Nothing*. Then she headed to the wardrobe, ran her fingers through the immaculately organized clothes.

She sighed, then moved back to the bed, crouching to the ground and reaching underneath the bedframe to feel along its edges. Eleni realized she felt slightly ridiculous.

What the hell am I doing? This is absurd . . . it's pure paranoia. Of course there isn't a sodding spy camera . . .

She paused, picked up her phone from the bed and typed a quick search into Google, silently appreciating the return of the Wi-Fi. She scrolled through the first few hits for *secret camera* and saw nothing of interest. She tapped instead on images – and almost immediately something caught her eye. She inhaled sharply. Now that she'd seen that picture, it seemed obvious. *Why didn't I think of that before?*

Eleni put her phone down and started dragging the chair from the desk in the corner over to the centre of the room, glancing up at the ceiling as she went. She set the chair down directly underneath the smoke detector, then rolled up the bottoms of her trousers and climbed onto it. She looked up at the round, white detector above her head, blinking out its intermittent red flash.

She reached for it, then faltered. She had no idea what she was doing – she was no electrician; she'd barely even changed a lightbulb. *What am I going to do? Take the bloody thing apart?*

She thought back to the picture she'd just seen. It looked practically identical to the contraption screwed into the ceiling. She had to at least try. 'This is the last place I'm going to look,' she said aloud.

Eleni twisted the top of the detector, and it sprung loose with a *click*.

Inside was a tiny, black circular lens, and a small slot holding what looked like a SIM card. This wasn't a real smoke detector; it was a camera made to look like one.

I fucking knew it.

Eleni stared at it, at first triumphant, before a shadow of horror dawned over her. *Who the hell would do this to me?* Installing cameras in her private space – it was extreme, not to mention illegal. Furious, she removed the battery from inside the camera and placed it on the bedside table.

Then she narrowed her eyes.

I've got a feeling I know exactly who would do this.

And he isn't going to get away with it.

Her trousers still hitched up, random strands of her hair tumbling out of their messy bun, Eleni stormed out of her cabin into the passageway, then up the stairs to the salon. The person she was looking for wasn't there – and as far as she could see, he wasn't out on the main deck, either. The sky was darkening, with grey clouds now forming above the *Lusso*'s bow – perhaps her fellow guests had headed below deck. She went up another deck to do one last check, was about to enter the sky lounge, when she heard voices above her. People were gathered on the sun deck, then.

She took the stairs two at a time and burst onto the deck. What she saw there made her stop in her tracks: sitting in the cushioned area at the bow, Lucy was talking rapidly to Mark – with tears pouring down her cheeks. She was speaking so fast, and between such racking sobs, that Eleni couldn't make out most of what she was saying – but she did manage to catch two names: one that she didn't know, and one that she did.

Alfie. Rory.

'Oh – shit,' Eleni blurted. 'I'm so sorry. I was just looking for—'

'It's okay.' Lucy stopped talking and wiped the tears from her cheeks. She gave a wobbly smile, then frowned as her eyes scanned Eleni, no doubt taking in her red-faced, dishevelled appearance. 'Are you all right?'

Eleni knew her perfectly manufactured facade had started to drop; she was aware of how she must look right now, wide-eyed and sweating and unkempt and angry. But truth be told, she didn't give a flying fuck.

Mark looked between the two women for a second, then wrapped Lucy in a long, firm hug. He whispered something in his girlfriend's ear, then got to his feet.

'I'll leave you two to chat for a minute. I think the weather's going to turn soon, though – Luce, come back inside soon, yeah?'

Lucy waved him off and gestured to the empty space next to her. 'Do you want to sit down?'

Eleni was torn. She was on a mission to find the spy-cam perpetrator, there was still Rory and Talia to deal with . . . and she'd told Nick she'd stay in their cabin. She didn't even know Lucy that well; she certainly wouldn't trust her with any of her worries. But her colleague was clearly upset, and Eleni didn't like the idea of leaving her here alone and crying when she evidently wanted to talk. So she nodded, walked across the deck and sat next to Lucy.

There was a beat of silence, then: 'Who's Alfie?' Eleni asked.

'Sorry – I heard his name when you were talking to Mark just now. Is he why you're upset?'

Lucy looked startled. 'Ah, yes, I . . .' Lucy faltered. 'He's my brother.'

Her brother? Eleni frowned. 'Okay.' This wasn't what she'd been expecting. She assumed whatever they were upset about was to do with her and Mark – she'd joined the dots wrongly, and thought Alfie might be 'the other man'. But then, surely Mark wouldn't have hugged Lucy so fiercely if she'd just revealed an affair. No; clearly, this was a family thing. 'And . . . has something happened to him since you've been away? Why are you so upset about him?'

'Something *did* happen, yes. Not since we've been here, but . . . Alfie's got cerebral palsy, and autism, and learning disabilities,' said Lucy, looking away from Eleni and staring out to sea. 'He doesn't talk – he never will – and he needs a lot of help. A lot of care. It's been . . . hard, at times.' Lucy turned her eyes to Eleni warily, as if waiting for judgement or dismissal. But Eleni wasn't going to give Lucy either of those things.

'I'm sorry,' she said. 'That must be tough.' One of Eleni's younger cousins was autistic and had a lot of complex needs. The whole family adored her, but she knew the strain it had placed on her aunt and uncle, caring for her. She could imagine how hard it was, growing up with a sibling who needed so much support.

Lucy shifted her weight on the cushions. 'When Alfie's calm – when he's happy – he's the sweetest, kindest, most loving person you've ever met. He's so affectionate; he's like a big ball of cuddles.'

'Right . . . ' Eleni replied. *Where is this going?* She waited, trying to be patient. She was open to hearing what Lucy needed to say; she wasn't going to abandon her mid-conversation. But she still had no idea what this was about, and she was losing precious time.

Lucy sniffed. 'But when he's not happy – when he's dysregulated or distressed – he can't control himself, he does things he'd never *mean* to do. He'd never want to hurt anyone – especially not his family.' As she spoke, Lucy's hand moved to rub her upper arm, where the bruise that Eleni had noticed a couple of days earlier was now fading to a greenish yellow.

In an instant, Eleni understood. That bruise – and perhaps many more like it – hadn't come from clumsy wanderings in the middle of the night; they hadn't been anything to do with Mark, either. It was Lucy's brother who'd hurt her: the person she probably loved most in the world, and who undoubtedly loved her just as much back.

A lump formed in the back of Eleni's throat; she swallowed it down. She didn't know what it was like for Lucy, exactly – she didn't understand the finer details of her experiences with Alfie – but the realization that someone Lucy loved so much had been harming her, over and over, probably for years . . . it was almost too much for Eleni to bear.

She turned back to Lucy, a question still nagging at her. She didn't want to pry – but there was another name she'd overheard when she came up here, and she still didn't understand how the pieces joined together. 'But . . . what does Alfie – what does *all this* – have to do with Rory?'

Lucy's eyes widened in shock; she opened her mouth, looked as though she was about to reply – when an urgent call reached their ears.

'Lucy – Eleni – sorry to interrupt.' It was Johanna, calling to them from the spiral staircase. 'But you need to come indoors right away. It's not safe out here – any minute now, we're going to hit the squall.'

SAM

Sam stood at the bow of the main deck and stared darkly out to sea. Since he'd been hovering here, the sky had morphed from its usual electric blue into a dull, muted grey. He checked the time on his phone – it was only mid-afternoon, but he could barely see a few metres ahead.

At first, with the sea calm and the sky clear, he'd thought the captain was worrying about rough weather for nothing – she'd been pissed off about casting off late, though she'd bowed to Rory's pressure in the end, as people usually did. Now, as the clouds clustered into one dark mass, he realized she'd been right.

Sam could hear the others getting settled in the salon; he didn't want to join them. He was still feeling the after-effects of the night before: the dinner that had started like a scene from a glossy magazine with Bond music and martinis – and ended in drama and hostility.

He'd felt such a rush of smug pride at making Rory squirm when he'd asked him to explain – in front of everyone – why

Sam was here. The panic in Rory's eyes – the blustering explanation. That part felt good.

But he still stung with bitter disappointment too. At Talia's expression when Sam had spoken up for her: the flicker of irritation, as if he'd crossed a line. The irony of that made him wince; there was only one man around that table known for crossing lines, and it sure as hell wasn't Sam. All he'd done was tell the truth – Rory *shouldn't* have spoken to her like that; he *didn't* know why Talia put up with it.

Then, after the big blow-out, when it was just Sam and Eleni left and he'd tried to talk to her about Lucy – and about Rory's patterns, more generally. The way she'd just brushed him off – as if *Sam* was the problem; as if it was all in his head! He'd only been trying to help – to give these women a voice. And they'd shut him out in the cold. *Just typical*. People never saw what he was really trying to do – not Claire, and not the women on this yacht.

Sam rubbed his arms; the breeze had picked up. For the first time since they'd got here, he was cold. He should go inside, grab a hoodie, get himself warm. But everyone else was in there, on the sofas in the salon. He'd have to walk right past them, and the crew would no doubt make him sit down with them all. He *really* didn't feel like doing that. His mood fit much better out here, under the increasingly black skies.

The sea was turning choppy now too. The *Lusso* was bobbing higher and falling lower with each wave, forcing a watery nausea to rush up Sam's throat with each dip and swell. Through the thick clouds, he tried to catch sight of the horizon ahead to quell the sudden rush of seasickness – but as he leaned forward, a wave smashed so violently against the bow that it splashed upwards, drenching his face, making him yell out and step back from the edge of the deck.

As he rubbed the salt water out of his eyes and tried to dry his face with his T-shirt, Sam stepped further away from the bow. He caught the voices of the deck crew from further down the yacht, at the stern. They were calling out to each other as they collected loose items and equipment from the outer decks and stowed them in the garage.

He wandered closer. Kai and Noah were now securing everything left on deck with lanyards and thick ropes. They were toiling away at high speed, a different energy to their usual relaxed vibe. It felt almost surreal, like Sam was in a nautical TV drama – not a luxurious work trip with his colleagues.

In between their work, the two men were chatting casually. Sam thought he might approach them and ask to watch, maybe even join in the banter – maybe it would help lift his gloomy mood.

But then he caught some of their words:

'Nah, I'll be pleased to see the back of this lot, mate,' Noah was saying. 'Don't blame the girls for being pissed off. Only another day after today, and we're done.'

Sam froze. *They're talking about us*. He tucked himself out of sight between the yacht's superstructures and the bulwark lining the edge of the vessel, and listened.

'Thank God. I just hope no more shit goes down later,' said Kai. 'Did Michaela tell you how bad it got over dinner last night?'

'Oh yeah, she did, mate. What a fucking shitshow.'

'Yup. I'm telling you, we've all seen way too much for one charter. We're going to need therapy after this, I swear.'

'Ha,' Noah snorted. 'Nah, we'll never be able to breathe a word about it. Not even to a therapist. Captain will lose her mind if one of her charters ends up in the gossip columns.'

'Fair. But seriously, I'm going to need help,' Kai said. 'The accidents, the fights, the tears, those two messing around . . . we should be charging extra for emotional labour, bro.'

Messing around? A flicker of heat ran through Sam's body, as if someone had just lit a match inside his stomach. He leaned further against the railing and tried to tune in so he could hear their voices over the gathering wind.

'Tell me about it.' Noah was almost yelling now, trying to be audible over the increasingly violent waves. 'If their other halves find out what's going on, someone's going overboard before we drop anchor in Raiatea.'

'Keep your voice down, mate,' Kai warned.

'Yeah, I know, I know,' said Noah. 'They're all in the salon, though. We're good.' The yacht lurched violently to the left. Sam almost lost his grip on the railing; he scrambled to stay upright.

'Shit, dude, this is really picking up – come on, let's get this done and hole up in the crew mess,' shouted Noah.

The two men went quiet and focused on their tasks for a moment, then Noah picked up the thread: 'Still, two guests having an affair? Getting it on, right here on the yacht, when they think no one's watching? It's nuts. We've not had that on a charter before, have we?'

'Not that I can remember. But it's not just what's going on – it's who's doing it . . .' And then Kai said them: two names of his fellow passengers.

Sam's heart leapt into his mouth. For a moment he just

stood there, clinging to the railing, the wind buffeting his face, replaying what he'd heard.

He stayed frozen, thinking. What if they'd been caught in the act? His eyes flickered upwards to the centre of the superstructure, facing the awning and the bow of the main deck. *Yes – there it is. This could be the answer to everything.* There was CCTV everywhere on this boat. If the cameras had been facing the right direction . . . if there was footage of them on CCTV . . .

He could picture it in his mind: a grainy, late-night video of two figures moving towards each other, pulling each other into an embrace . . . Claire's face flashed in front of his eyes: the reason she left him. *You're not who I thought you were.* He flinched and forced the memory away, then tried to tune back into the voices of the deck crew – perhaps there was something else they'd found out on this charter that Sam needed to know about. But they'd headed inside the tender garage now; his time for eavesdropping was over.

'Sam – you shouldn't still be out here!' *Shit*. It was Johanna, shielding her eyes from the rain, calling out to him from near the bow. 'I've been looking for you everywhere. Come inside right away, please. We're on high alert because of the approaching squall – we need everyone inside now – in the salon, life jacket on.'

Sam stumbled towards her, being buffeted by the wind, holding onto the edges of the railings to stop himself from tumbling over as the main deck rose and lowered beneath his feet. He reached the door to the salon and stepped inside. Everyone else was sitting on the sofas in the area furthest from the exterior doors now, life jackets strapped around their waists and holding onto the edges of their seats. A selection of plastic bowls sat in the gaps between them.

Oh, for Christ's sake.

He turned to Johanna. 'Can't I just go down to my cabin?'

The stewardess answered him with a firm shake of her head. 'I'm afraid not. It's Captain's orders – we need to keep everyone together so we're got sight of you all. I'm sorry, but it's protocol.' She shrugged apologetically. 'Captain Taylor is expecting us to be through the squall in about the next twenty minutes, or maybe a little longer – so you should be able to go below deck soon. Here.'

She helped Sam towards a space at the end of the sofa next to Mark and Lucy – Lucy's head already dipped over a bowl. Sam held his arms out, feeling stupidly like a small child as Johanna reached the life jacket around his body and fastened it round his front.

Health and safety requirements met, Sam's eyes – still stinging and sore from the salt water – moved around the room to study his companions. On the sofa opposite him, Rory was sitting next to Talia; beside her was Nick, and Eleni sat next to her husband at the sofa's other end. Talia had turned her back to Rory; her eyes were fixed on the floor, her complexion grey.

Nick was drumming his fingers against the edge of the sofa, staring into space. Eleni's face was pale and she looked uncomfortable; she was twiddling strands of hair between her fingers. As Sam watched, she looked up and met his gaze: there was an open hostility in her expression that forced him to look away. *Christ, what's her problem?*

Next to Sam, Lucy glanced up and offered him something between a smile and a grimace. Mark had one arm draped around her shoulders; Lucy reached up to his hand and gave it a squeeze. Whatever had been causing tension between them, they'd clearly worked through it. Watching them, something dropped heavily in Sam's chest.

Jesus, what's wrong with me? He got his phone out of his pocket and scrolled down his WhatsApp messages. He wanted to read Claire's old texts – he still did that sometimes, though he wasn't sure why – it only made him feel worse. But then, he supposed, Claire was the reason he'd started all this. She was still the ghost that haunted him, forcing him to see his plans through. Forcing Sam to give his boss what he deserved for destroying his relationship – and all the other terrible things Rory had done.

A deep calm descended suddenly on the yacht – the crashing of the waves against the hull stopped, and the rocking underneath them stilled.

'Hold on tight,' said Johanna, from a seat at the furthest end of the salon, near the galley. 'I'm afraid things are about to get very bumpy.'

Sam tried to steel himself – and not just for the squall. He needed to think positive – and there was still plenty to be optimistic about, especially after what he'd just overhead.

He wasn't out of options – nowhere close. One way or another, he'd make use of the crew's eagle-eyed observations.

He glanced at Talia again across the salon; tried to catch her eye. Even pale and seasick, she was luminous.

Sam smiled to himself, the thrill of his secret making his chest puff outwards, making him sit up a little straighter.

After all, his mission was almost complete.

He could destroy Rory's entire life now, the minute he chose to.

GENDARMERIE MARITIME DE POLYNÉSIE FRANÇAISE

CASE NUMBER: 247849

POLICE EXHIBIT SEVEN

Transcript of call between Captain Taylor and operator at CROSS Papeete

10/06/2026 16:40

Operator: This is CROSS Papeete. Go ahead.

Caller: This is Captain Taylor on the *Lusso di Mare*, currently at sea, fifteen nautical miles east of Raiatea. We've sustained a passenger injury on board during a pretty rough squall. Can I request immediate medical assistance on arrival into Raiatea, please?

Operator: Location copied, *Lusso di Mare*. Can you please confirm the condition of your casualty?

Caller: Of course. A guest slipped on interior stairs while moving during some heavy rolling. Some bleeding to the right temple and right side of the face. The passenger is conscious and . . . <static> . . . but a little disorientated.

Operator: The line's a little patchy, Captain, but understood. Please keep the casualty lying flat, apply pressure to the wound, and monitor consciousness. And contact us immediately if there's any change. Are there any additional casualties at present?

Caller: No. All other <crackling sound> are secure in our <hissing static>

Operator: Captain? You're breaking up. We're alerting local emergency response at Raiatea Marina and medical team for dockside transfer. What's your ETA to port?

Operator: Captain?

Operator: *Lusso*? Captain Taylor? <rustling noise> Damn – I've lost her.

[TRANSCRIPT ENDS]

TALIA

Talia gripped the underside of the sofa beneath her thighs and braced herself. With an abrupt *thump*, the wind began to hammer at the doors leading out to the main deck. She glanced across the room and saw the rain hitting the windows sideways in thick, heavy sheets.

Just get through it. Only an hour and we'll be on land.

She was desperate to go below deck, close the door to her cabin and keep her distance from the others until they reached Raiatea. But now the weather had started to turn, and Johanna was insisting everyone stayed together in the salon. The timing couldn't be worse. Still shivering, she was sitting here, clutching on for dear life, trapped in the same room as the man she'd wanted so badly to escape from.

She held on more tightly as the yacht tilted to one side now; an electronic humming sound rose in volume from the engine room two decks beneath her. The *Lusso* sounded it like it was straining to stay upright. Through the panoramic windows, the normally flat horizon was rising and dipping again as the swells lifted the yacht's bow, then lowered it again, like a slow, graceful nod.

She studied her fellow guests. Sam kept glancing at her, then staring at his phone, typing and swiping. Lucy was clutching Mark's hand, which he'd wrapped around her shoulder; her other hand held the sick bowl close. Mark was watching his girlfriend closely; clearly, he was less affected by the rough seas than either Lucy or Talia herself. As she looked on, Mark's eyes drifted towards his phone. He moved his arm from around Lucy, wrapped his palms around the edge of the screen and began to scroll.

Talia's phone vibrated in the handbag on her lap. She yearned to check it, but there were too many eyes on her. *That bloody phone.* She'd never had such an intense relationship with an inanimate object in her life. The endless checking for WhatsApp messages; the Google searches on how to turn on read receipts and how to hide texts without deleting them. The countless occasions she'd turned the thing off, or locked it in a cabinet to try to stop herself from reading through her chat history again and again, her fingers itching to swipe and scroll.

Sometimes, she'd just sit and reread the texts she couldn't bring herself to delete, see the fake name she'd saved him under: *Amanda Tennis Club*, and feel the rush of dopamine flood her system. They sent each other photos – intimate ones: Talia finding a quiet hour in the day while Rory was at work to pick out her most flattering lingerie and take selfies that she deleted the moment they'd been opened. He'd return the favour by sending photos back of the impact she'd had on his body.

She could recall every detail in those images now – and, of course, in the picture he'd sent two months ago that had changed everything. The picture he'd sent that had shown her how wrong she'd got it all. How badly she'd messed up.

Talia remembered her surprise when the notification popped up with a photo attached, only hours after they'd seen each other. They never usually messaged right after meeting. As soon as they'd both come and she'd peeled herself away from him, the shame of what she'd done would hit her in a brutal, crushing wave. She'd spend the next twenty-four hours in a state of overwhelming guilt, trying to make up for her appalling betrayal by taking extra special care of Rory with smiles and home-made dinners and streams of ego-massaging compliments.

But that day, when Talia saw he'd sent a photo, she knew she had to open it. It was an image of a white and gold luxury yacht – the same yacht she was now sitting on, dipping and rolling in a South Pacific squall. Underneath it were the words: *Our first holiday?*

The audacity of him. *How dare he?* He should have turned the opportunity down, not even considered it. She'd tried to reason with him – she'd called him straight away to try to beg him, plead with him not to accept the invitation. When he hadn't picked up – because of course he hadn't; they had a rule never to call each other without planning the time in advance – she'd left him a voice note, saying it was too dangerous, that it was reckless for both of them. That he simply couldn't come on the trip.

Because what else could she have done? Getting him to change his mind had been her only option. Rory would never have accepted her not wanting to go – she'd shown so much enthusiasm about the trip already, and he knew she'd had the dates booked in for months by then. Equally, if she'd tried to talk to Rory about who he'd invited along – to get her husband to offer the place to someone else – he'd have been baffled, or worse, suspicious: it was none of her business who came on his bonus trips.

She'd got a response to her voice note five minutes later. *You're joking, right? Turn down the trip of a lifetime – and with you on board? No chance.* And then another: *Don't even try to talk me out of it. Nothing's going to stop me from coming.*

So she'd had no choice in the end. Going ahead with it was her only option. She'd had to come on the trip, with both her husband and her secret lover on board. She'd had to share the same living space as both men, breathe the same air.

She'd given in to just one electrifying, thrilling moment with him – right here in the salon on their second night here. And look what had happened! They'd been so stupid, right underneath the cameras; the crew had almost certainly seen it. That momentary slip could have cost her everything.

Ever since then, the tension within her had felt unbearable; and now, here in the salon with her husband and the man she'd been cheating on him with . . . she thought she might implode before all this was over.

She startled as Eleni let out a yell at a particularly aggressive roll of the waves – her scream audible even over the crashing and rumbling of the yacht.

'Are you all right?' Johanna called across to her. Eleni responded with a feeble nod. Talia studied her for a moment. Eleni was a beautiful woman, really quite lovely, even bare-faced and pale as she was now. She usually wore a lot of make-up – but not today. Without it, she looked years younger, and more vulnerable somehow. Talia noticed deep grey hollows beneath her eyes.

'Please don't be alarmed – we're used to this kind of weather, and the *Lusso* will have no problem getting through it,' Johanna reassured her. 'We can't be too far out from Raiatea now, anyway. I promise the captain has this under control.'

'Doesn't seem very under control to me,' mumbled Nick.

'Oh, poppycock,' Rory yelled right into Talia's ear; she instinctively cupped a hand over it to cover it. 'This is nothing – just a small squall. Don't know what all the fuss is about.'

Talia wanted him – all of them – to be quiet, to just bloody *shut up*. But a split second later, right after another of the boat's violent turns, an enormous wave – higher than the yacht itself, or at least that's how it looked to Talia – belted against the boat like a wall of concrete with a deep, thunderous crash. There was a piercing yell from the control room above them – then seconds later, the *Lusso*'s lights went out, leaving the salon and the deck outside, as far as Talia could see, in a murky, grey gloom.

A burst of hot fear slammed Talia's chest; for a second, it felt as though she couldn't breathe.

'What was that? What's happening?' It was Eleni; at the same time, Lucy spoke over her in fear: 'Why have the lights gone out?'

Johanna snapped into immediate action. 'Please don't panic. It'll just be a brief outage – most likely caused by that wave. A small amount of salt water might have infiltrated the engine room and touched the generator. It can happen in intense squalls like this one, but it'll be short-lived – the battery-operated back-ups should kick in as soon as we can get them started.'

The group visibly relaxed at her words. Talia tried to breathe too, to steady herself. This wasn't a disaster – like Johanna kept saying, everything was under control. The sun was still up, and the thick swirl of clouds directly above them wasn't able to block out all the daylight. The lights would be back before total darkness set in.

She tried out the sensation of Johanna's words in her head, thinking of her own life, the mess she was in. *This will be short-lived. Try not to panic. Everything's under control.* She only wished she could believe it.

'Well,' boomed Rory, startling her. 'This is quite the adventure, isn't it? Not sure any of us were prepared for a rendition of *The Tempest* on our summer holidays. Ha!'

His words fell flat. No one laughed; no one smiled. No one was in the mood for making light of their current situation, least of all Talia: she felt sick, and she was uncomfortable, and she felt guilty and afraid. But the lack of response riled him, and moments later, Rory started to huff and mutter next to her, writhing and twisting on the sofa.

'I'm afraid I've had about enough of this,' he said. 'I refuse to sit here in the gloom on a faulty yacht – with no damn Wi-Fi while I'm trying to send an email – and all because of a bit of bloody bad weather. I'm going to find the captain.' He stumbled to his feet, lurching and wobbling through the centre of the seating area, arms flailing then grabbing onto the railings around the stairwell.

'Rory, don't!' Talia called after him. 'You'll hurt yourself – please!' She tried to grab his hand as he walked away, but he flung it loose.

'Mr Ashworth, for your own safety, it's really best if you—' Johanna's words fell on deaf ears; Rory had already staggered past her and started up the stairs towards the bridge.

He can be such a reckless idiot. With Rory out of the room, Talia shifted on the sofa and edged further from Nick and Eleni. Turning her back on them both, she dug her phone out of her handbag. She read the text that had just come through, unblinking:

I need to see you. Come and find me below deck when this is over.

A nauseating thrill jolted her stomach, sloshing with the tonic water she'd been drinking to cope with the rough seas.

She stared at the text for a long moment, then closed her messages and shoved her phone back into her bag. *No*. She wouldn't go and find him when this was over – of course she wouldn't. It was too risky.

There was a loud thump from the deck above; then a muffled cry. Talia knew that voice. *Rory*. She leapt to her feet on instinct, but the roiling of the yacht threw her back onto her seat with force. She landed with a painful *thud* to the back of her hips. 'Ouch!'

'Are you all right?' Mark called across to her.

Tears stung at the back of Talia's eyes. No, she wasn't all right. Not by a long stretch. She was a maelstrom of fear and desire and regret and yearning. But now she had more immediate concerns. She shook her head. 'Did anyone else hear that? That thump. I think Rory might have fallen . . .'

Johanna's radio crackled to life, the captain's voice just audible through the static and the slamming of the waves. 'Johanna, Johanna. Assistance required in control room for the primary. Small amount of bleeding to facial area. Please bring your first aid kit.'

Frowning and shaking her head, Johanna got to her feet

with impressive steadiness. It amazed Talia that despite a violent squall, an electrical blackout and a guest injury, Johanna remained business as usual. She must be trained for it, but still. She took *keep calm and carry on* to a whole new level.

Johanna looked at Talia. 'It doesn't sound serious – I'm sure he'll be all right. Please stay in your seats. We'll be through the squall in a few more minutes.'

Talia closed her eyes. It was dangerous, trying to walk around the boat in these conditions – Rory had just made that clear. She'd stay put until they were free to move again, then head down to her cabin and keep her distance from everyone.

Soon, the worst of the battering wind started to quieten; the yacht's violent motions began to lessen until it became relatively still on the water again. *Thank God.* They must be through the worst of it.

A moment later, there were footsteps on the staircase: Johanna and Brett were making their way carefully down from the bridge, Rory supported between them. He looked at Talia and smiled sheepishly as he reached the salon. 'Managed to scrape my cheek on the side of the captain's desk. Johanna's bandaged it up for me. I'm sorry, darling – that'll teach me to ignore a woman's orders.'

Talia sighed with relief. 'I'm just glad you're all right. But yes, that wasn't your finest move.' She smiled at him and shook her head indulgently.

'We're going to settle Rory below deck on a massage bed in the treatment room – it's the closest thing we've got to a first aid room,' said Johanna. 'He should be fine after a bit of rest and some painkillers. Talia, please stay where you are for a little longer – when the sea is calmer, you can come down and check on him.'

Talia dipped her head and watched as they led Rory through the salon and towards the treatment room. A moment later, Brett reappeared.

'A quick update for you, folks,' he said. 'I'm sorry about the cut to our power. The captain can manage without me for now, so I'm heading down to the engine room to get the back-up generator started. It shouldn't take me too long, providing the seawater didn't get to it.'

Thank God.

Brett paused, then added: 'We, er, unfortunately got blown somewhat off course by the squall. So it's going to take us a little longer to reach Raiatea – another hour or two, still. You might not get much daylight there, but you'll still have the evening.' He shrugged apologetically, then made his way below deck.

Talia tried to focus on just breathing. *Everything is under control.* The lights would turn back on any minute; they'd anchor safely at Raiatea in only a couple of hours. They'd be close to shore well before it got dark, even if the back-up generator didn't kick in.

She touched the edges of her phone in her handbag. Perhaps, before she left, she *would* see her lover one last time – tell him her decision, face to face. That would be more appropriate, wouldn't it? That was the grown-up thing to do.

It was almost over. Soon she could fly home and leave all this chaos behind her.

LUCY

Through the flickering of the yacht's emergency lighting overhead, Lucy couldn't take her eyes off Rory's phone.

It had fallen out of his pocket when he'd stumbled off to go and find the captain. He'd been so unsteady on his feet, so rocked by the waves, he hadn't noticed when his phone slipped out, tumbled to the ground and slid across the slanting floor. It had landed underneath the sofa, right beneath where Nick and Eleni were sitting.

Lucy needed to get to that phone. If she could just grab it and tuck it away in her pocket, then she could hide it in her suitcase when she got below deck. Rory would just think he'd lost it somehow; that it had fallen overboard, even, in the chaos of the squall and the injury to his face.

I've got to get it right now. Perhaps if she could access it in the next couple of minutes, the lock screen might not have kicked in. That way, Lucy could bypass needing to know Rory's password. Yes: one way or another, getting her hands on Rory's phone right now was *everything*.

On it, there was almost certainly the evidence she desperately needed. On that phone, there would be emails or messages or archived files – *something* that proved Rory had rushed through the takeover of Willowbrook Lodge, the specialist residential care home where Alfie had been doing so well, where he'd been happy. Lucy and her mum had been able to take a deep breath; to sleep through the whole night; to focus on their own lives for those few precious years. And Alfie – he'd been thriving. Willowbrook had everything he could possibly need, and more. He'd made so much progress; he'd flourished there . . .

Right up until he'd been turfed out without a scrap of regard for his welfare. Alfie had nowhere to go when the care home was taken over by an ambitious property development firm, chomping at the bit to turn this imposing Victorian mansion into a set of soulless, luxury flats. *Ashworth Property Partners.*

Because of that deal, Lucy's brother lost his carers, his support, and the home he'd got so used to, overnight. None of the promises of *appropriate alternative accommodation* and *significant financial compensation* were ever realized. So when Alfie came back home to live with their mum, his state of mind deteriorated rapidly and his meltdowns escalated – they became bigger and more frightening for him than ever before. It was hardly surprising: he was confused. He was bereft. And he didn't have the language or the tools to express his feelings in any other way.

She should have seen it coming; it was little wonder things spiralled as badly as they did.

Lucy blinked away her tears and leaned into Mark's shoulder. She could trust him again, now that he knew everything. He'd said he was willing to do whatever he could to help with her plan while they were still here. He could start by helping her with *this*. So she moved her lips close to his ear and whispered, 'Shh – don't react. Rory dropped his phone. It's under the sofa, near Eleni.' Lucy couldn't see his face; she hoped it remained impassive. He gave the slightest nod; he understood. She murmured into his ear again: 'Do you think we can try to reach it somehow?'

Mark stared ahead thoughtfully. Lucy wondered if he was ruminating on the same unfortunate notion that she was: the squall was calming at the most inconvenient time. If the yacht had still been rolling and sliding on the water, either she or Mark could have feigned tumbling off the sofa and landing, sprawled out, on the floor near Eleni's feet. It would have been so easy to reach for the phone then, unnoticed.

But the worst of the weather was over: the motion of the waves was gentle – barely enough to make Lucy shift lightly up and down in her seat. Falling to the ground now would look suspicious, not to mention bizarre.

She'd have to try something else. Bobbing her head from side to side, raising her eyebrows like an overenthusiastic primary school teacher, Lucy tried to catch Eleni's eye; she was sitting almost directly above the phone. Maybe if she got Eleni's attention, she could try mouthing to her, gesture underneath the sofa and urge her colleague to pocket the phone.

But I still don't know if I can trust her. She's not my friend.

Eleni had been lukewarm towards Lucy all week: suspicious, as if she didn't understand what Lucy was even doing there. She hadn't expected them to become best friends on the few days of their holiday – she wasn't *that* naive. But she'd hoped they might at least get to know each other a little. It would be nice to have an ally at Ashworth; someone she could count on.

More than that, though, Rory *adored* Eleni – everyone knew that. He indulged her like a daddy doting on his precious firstborn. Lucy was aware that was why a part of her wanted to tell Eleni everything, up on the sun deck a moment ago. Even starting to tell her about Alfie felt like an embarrassing overshare now – what did she think Eleni was going to do? Suddenly become her staunchest ally?

This is why everything goes better when I plan my conversations thoroughly in advance.

At least she hadn't said any more – she'd been saved from that by the approaching squall. In any case, Lucy's attempts to get Eleni's attention were failing; her colleague was clearly distracted, anxious, even. She kept flickering nervous glances at Nick, then towards Sam, then back to Nick again. It was impossible to get her to look Lucy's way.

Mark turned his face towards hers and leaned in close. 'You just need to be patient,' he whispered. 'When the squall's over and everyone's left the room, we'll get it.'

Lucy sighed. He was right, of course. She was in too much of a rush to get to it before it locked, but trying to grab it now was risky. She reassured herself: even if it needed a password, she'd find a way in, if she had to. She'd never tried to break into a phone before, but it was the kind of thing her brain could work its way around in a few minutes of googling – she was sure of it.

Just then, the yacht gave a sudden lurch as a wave hit the hull; Lucy's back slammed into the sofa behind her while the three passengers on the sofa opposite were shunted forwards.

Rory's phone slid out from under the sofa, coming to a stop just in front of Eleni's feet. Lucy stared at it, her pulse racing now, then gave Mark a gentle nudge in the ribs. He looked at the floor, then turned to Lucy, eyes wide.

'We could say there's a phone on the floor – then I grab it, pass it to you, and we pretend we don't know whose it is,' he whispered.

She thought for a moment, then: 'Oh – what's that?' she said loudly, leaning forward and pointing to the phone.

'Looks like someone's mobile? Don't move, Luce – I can reach it,' said Mark. He crouched forward, stretched one long arm across the floor. His fingers reached for the phone and he swung back to his seat. 'Here,' he said, handing it to Lucy.

'Isn't that Rory's work phone?' *Damn.* Talia had noticed.

'Oh, is it?' Lucy paused. 'Well, in that case, maybe I could check his emails for him? I can look for this urgent work issue he was worrying about – try to sort it out myself, even.'

Talia gave her a disdainful look. 'You want to check Rory's emails.'

Lucy gave Talia what she hoped was a reassuring smile. 'Well, why not? It might help. He did say it was all very urgent – there's some big news he's waiting for, isn't there?'

'There may well be, but nothing will have come through about it without internet connection, will it? And besides, I'm sure he's quite capable of dealing with it himself,' said Talia.

'Even after his injury?' piped up Mark. 'Isn't it better to give him a bit of a break – let him rest up for a bit? We can tell him we've looked into it for him, so he doesn't worry.'

Sam shifted uncomfortably in the seat next to Lucy. 'I'm not sure he'd want you – or any of us, actually – going through his work emails,' he said. There was a note of anxiety in his voice; Lucy turned to look at him curiously.

'Why?' she asked. 'We'd be doing him a favour, especially now he's hurt.'

'I'm sure he'll be better soon. And he'll be none too pleased if he finds out you've looked through his phone,' Sam said. Then he sighed. 'Don't say I didn't warn you . . .'

In one smooth sweep, Talia stood up, reached over to pluck the phone from Lucy's outstretched hand, then stepped backward and sat down again.

Talia brushed a strand of hair from her face. 'I doubt he'll mind me doing it,' she said, glancing at the screen. 'I'll keep hold of it for now, thank you – perhaps I'll have a quick look.'

Lucy's heart sank. This had felt like the moment she'd been waiting for – a gift from the heavens. She'd felt so hopeful. Now, with Rory's phone firmly in his wife's hands, all the hope drained out of her, as if someone had just yanked out a plug somewhere deep in her heart.

'Oh – I think the screen's locked, unfortunately,' said Mark. 'Maybe I can just take the phone to Rory, and he can—'

'No, that's not a problem,' Talia interjected. 'I know Rory's password.'

'Ah, of course,' said Mark. He was fidgeting next to her; Lucy could feel his frustration and disappointment, matching her own. She reached for his hand and squeezed it; he leaned close and whispered, 'We'll find another way, love. We won't give up, for Alfie's sake.'

At the mention of her brother's name, Lucy had one last, desperate idea. 'Talia, maybe you should check his emails for something to do with a care home?' she said.

Talia looked up. 'A – I'm sorry? What care home? I've not heard him mention anything like that since we've been here.'

Lucy swallowed. *Idiot. This was a stupid idea.* 'Oh, I just thought . . . I'm sure I overheard Rory saying something earlier about the acquisition of a residential care home, if I remember correctly. A potential new development, perhaps?'

'A residential care home?' said Sam. 'Not Rory's usual thing, is it?'

'Never mind. Maybe I misheard,' mumbled Lucy.

Johanna came back into the salon then, just as Talia's finger landed on the phone's screen.

'Do you think we've seen off that rough weather now?' Sam asked her. 'It seems a bit calmer now. And I thought squalls only lasted a few minutes.'

Johanna nodded, without looking at him. 'It was on the longer side, that's for sure. But I'd say we're well through the worst of it.'

'Thank goodness for that,' murmured Eleni. Lucy was relieved too: she'd survived the worst of her nausea, but there was still a lingering queasiness at the back of her throat. Mark gave her hair a gentle stroke, then turned to Johanna.

'In that case, d'you think we'll be all right to head down to our cabins – if we take it slow and steady on the stairs?' he asked.

'Okay,' Johanna said. 'I think you should be fine to move. But make sure you hold onto the railings the whole way down. And when you get to your cabin, I'd ask you to stay seated or lying down, and in one place, just for the next ten minutes or so.' She smoothed down her polo shirt. 'I'm going to speak to Leilani about the plan for dinner now that the power's out.

Take care as you walk around.' Then she disappeared into the galley, the doors swinging open and closed behind her.

'Hear that, Luce?' said Mark. 'Shall we head below deck for a bit?'

Lucy nodded. *We might as well go. There's nothing more I can do about that phone.* 'Yes, but let's hold onto each other. The boat's still a bit wobbly, and the light's not the greatest over there . . .'

'I've got you.'

They stood and Mark helped Lucy take cautious paces to the top of the stairs. Just before she placed her foot on the first step, she glanced back at Talia. She was scrolling now, her cheeks an artificial white above the glow of the phone's screen.

As Lucy watched, Talia's eyes scanned from side to side in impatient disinterest – but then her expression changed. Confusion, and something else – disbelief, maybe.

'Talia – are you all right? What is it?' she asked.

Talia frowned, eyes still fixed on the screen. 'Nothing for you to worry about,' she snapped. Lucy turned back and followed Mark carefully down the staircase.

Nothing for you to worry about.

But Lucy knew what she'd just seen.

And whatever it was, it wasn't nothing.

TALIA

Talia tapped on the phone's lock screen and typed *Ashworth2007* into the password tab – chosen for the year Rory formed the company. Her husband had always been an open book – he'd happily let her log in and use his work computer several times over the years if hers was unavailable. He shared all his passwords with her. He trusted her not to look at anything confidential.

He trusts me far too much.

The phone unlocked. She moved her fingers to the Outlook icon and clicked to open his emails. Since the power outage had taken down the Wi-Fi again and so far from network range, no new emails could be downloaded – but she wasn't looking for those, anyway. It was the ones he'd already got that she was interested in – whatever it was that he'd been worrying about before the squall started.

There were a few recent emails with Rosenberg in the subject line. She glanced through those; it seemed like everything was under control. Rory had responded to one just before the squall started, setting up a time for a meeting when he got home.

She was about to put the phone away when she remembered what Lucy had said. *What was it she just mentioned – a care home?*

She typed *care home* into the search bar at the top and waited for the results to show. Nothing. She scanned down the folders in the sidebar, looking for a pertinent label – perhaps the right emails just weren't coming up in the main search for some reason.

Nothing seemed relevant, but then something else caught her eye: a folder labelled *INTERNAL DEALINGS – PRIVATE AND CONFIDENTIAL.*

She hesitated; she shouldn't really be looking at anything confidential, should she?

But the words had piqued her curiosity. And perhaps it would be helpful to Rory for Talia to be fully up to speed with any work matters, especially with an injury likely to set him back for a few days – maybe she could bring him some useful information when she went to see him. He'd appreciate that – and Lord knew, she needed to make things up to him somehow, even if he'd never know why.

She double-tapped to open the folder, and a series of emails filled the screen. Talia frowned. All of them were from the same sender, but they all had different subject lines. Some of them sounded innocuous – *Following up* and *Thanks for the meeting*. But some of them sounded . . . unusual.

One by one, pulse quickening now, she clicked on the emails and began to read.

A few minutes later, Talia dropped the phone into her lap and stared straight ahead, frozen in muted shock.

Audio recordings . . . Transcripts . . . Inappropriate behaviour . . . Harassment . . . Young women . . .

The words swam in front of her eyes in a swirling, nauseating mass. Accusations – shocking, disgusting claims – made against Rory by his colleagues, female colleagues specifically, all gathered in one revolting folder of emails and used as a way for someone to blackmail him. And worse: the blackmail attempts were working.

According to the emails, Rory had been crossing the line with his co-workers for months – possibly longer. He'd asked a gay colleague if she ever missed 'the ramming of a real dick', among other comments. He'd told a new starter he'd give her 'a good spanking' if she didn't fill in her timesheets properly. In another email, there was the claim that he'd repeatedly stared at a senior colleague's breasts in team meetings.

Tears collected in Talia's eyes. *How could he?*

And how will we ever move past this?

No; she knew it already, with horrible certainty: she'd never be able to forgive him. If it had just been a one-off, she might have found a way to work through it. They had decades of history – a family together. She could have urged him to make a public apology, perhaps, and go to therapy to work through some of his internalized misogyny. She was hardly the perfect spouse either; they'd both made mistakes. And she'd learned it from her mother: *you don't give up on a marriage*. You turn a blind eye or bury your head in the sand – you just do whatever it takes to stay together.

But this wasn't just one time. There were a number of incidents outlined in detail, and still more were hinted at. This was a pattern. There were attachments and links in the emails to further evidence – recordings and statements from the women involved. She couldn't access them now without the internet, or get onto the Ashworth network, but Talia didn't doubt her husband's guilt, not for a second.

Because if Rory hadn't done the things he was being accused of here, he wouldn't have given in to this despicable extortion so easily, would he? Her husband was clearly desperate enough to do pretty much *anything* to keep these accusations from getting out. If it were only unsubstantiated rumour, he wouldn't have been so scared by the threat of the recordings being leaked.

Talia picked the phone back up and forwarded each of the emails in the folder – attachments included – to her own email address. She would need this evidence for whatever legal battle was to come. The emails wouldn't be sent until the power came back on, but she had no intention of allowing Rory anywhere near this phone until well after that happened. She put it away again, feeling the tears dry on her cheeks, listening to the swell of the sea.

'Are you all right, Talia?' Eleni was leaning forward, looking at her from along the sofa; her eyes weren't the only ones she'd felt on her the entire time she'd been reading.

Talia got to her feet so quickly she felt a rush of dizziness, and stumbled towards the toilets adjoining the salon.

She stepped inside and locked the door behind her, catching sight of her reflection in the mirror. Clearly, she wouldn't have been able to hide her distress in the salon: streaks of mascara stained her cheeks, her eyes were red and her face blotchy.

She collapsed into heaving, breathless sobs. *My marriage is over.*

Perhaps, deep down, she'd already known that. Maybe that

was why she'd been drawn to another man. Not that she wanted to be with her lover now, either. She'd seen things, on this trip. He wasn't who she thought he was. No; perhaps she wouldn't be with *any* man. And maybe that wouldn't be so awful. Hadn't she only recently read a piece in the Sunday supplement about how women who lived alone tended to not only be healthier and happier, but were able to actually rewire their entire nervous systems for the better, because their brains and bodies could finally relax?

She picked up the hand towel and dabbed gently under her eyes. *I can survive this.* She'd manage without Rory's financial support if she had to. She had some savings of her own, and the inheritance from both her parents that she'd tucked away. Perhaps she wouldn't be able to keep up the lavish lifestyle she'd been accustomed to, but she'd be all right. She could ask for more days at work; cut back on some of her luxuries. She could start shopping at Sainsbury's rather than Waitrose. *See?* She still had her sense of humour. This wouldn't be the end of her . . .

She looked at herself in the mirror. *I've just got to get through the next few hours.* She could hide in the cabin, keeping her distance from both Rory and her lover, under the pretence of a migraine perhaps, until tomorrow. Then she could go home and start making plans for a formal separation.

Talia knew she needed to leave the bathroom. But he was still sitting out there – the man who'd been blackmailing Rory all these months.

It all made such horrible, perfect sense now. His hatred towards Rory; his keen interest in Talia – and now that she thought about it, his attempts to get closer to the other women here too.

The evil, scheming bastard.

Sam never really cared about Talia. He wasn't interested in protecting her from Rory's occasional harsh words and condescending comments. He didn't *really* think she deserved 'so much better' than the marriage she had.

All along, Sam had only wanted more evidence to keep blackmailing her husband.

GENDARMERIE MARITIME DE POLYNÉSIE FRANÇAISE

CASE NUMBER: 247849

POLICE EXHIBIT EIGHT

Emails recovered from guest laptops on board the *Lusso di Mare*

Date: 16 March 2026
Sender: Sam.Doherty@ashworth.com
Recipient: Rory.Ashworth@ashworth.com
Subject: Great meeting today

Rory,

Thanks for the meeting earlier – I thought it was very productive. I'll look forward to receiving confirmation of my space on this year's bonus trip.

Best,
Sam

•

Date: 23 March 2026
Sender: Sam.Doherty@ashworth.com
Recipient: Rory.Ashworth@ashworth.com
Subject: Following up

Rory,

I've still not had confirmation of my place on the sail around French Polynesia – and I've already got my suitcase out!

You do remember what we talked about, don't you? That

for me to keep this quiet, I'm going against my morals, for you – and for the company. It's quite a sacrifice to make. A sacrifice that deserves the reward you promised me.

I don't want to sound like I'm making a fuss over nothing. I'm very happy to show you exactly what I've been putting together.

I'll give you a week. It's your call.

•

Date: 30 March 2026
Sender: Sam.Doherty@ashworth.com
Recipient: Rory.Ashworth@ashworth.com
Subject: You left me no choice

Here's the link to the secure folder, with:

– Audio clips (the recorded conversations I told you about)

– Testimony notes from four employees who don't want their names used

– The details of my contact at The Mirror.

In my next email, I'll be pasting the transcript from those audio clips. Just to give you a gentle reminder of exactly what we're working with here.

If you want it done the easy way: the bonus trip will be confirmed by the end of tomorrow. The hard way? In just over a day, everyone at Ashworth – and in the press – will know exactly who their CEO is.

The folder goes live in 24 hours if this isn't resolved.

You've got one more day.

SAM

Sam watched Talia walk to the bathroom, unsteady on her feet, and lock the door behind her. He had a good idea what she'd seen on Rory's phone; why she'd been on the verge of tears after a few minutes of scrolling.

He had only ever meant well – at least, in the beginning. He'd meant to protect women who needed protecting; to be a voice for the voiceless, like he'd failed to do for Anna. He could hardly take all the blame for things spiralling out of control the way they did. And besides, the only person who was supposed to end up suffering was Rory – and if anyone deserved punishment, he did.

His concern for Sarah from marketing had been genuine. That night in the pub in January, three glasses of red in, when she'd told Sam how she'd overheard Rory in a meeting room where they were about to discuss tweaks to the digital comms plan. Rory was chatting to Tim, the chief financial officer – they clearly didn't realize she was right outside the room – when Sarah heard Rory say they'd 'better be careful' when she arrived, because 'everyone knows what those muff-divers are like' and she 'really just needed a good battering with a firm todger'.

Sam was horrified. He would never speak that way about his colleagues – about *any* women. It was vile; it was beyond unacceptable. Sarah had been so appalled, she'd cancelled the meeting and feigned sickness; she'd gone home and sobbed her way through a bottle of vodka on her girlfriend's shoulder. Then she'd come back to work the next day wearing a brave face and planning her resignation.

He had felt bad for her – and angry. It wasn't okay that Sarah felt forced to leave a job she'd only just started, and where she was doing well – through no fault of her own, but because of Rory's complete lack of workplace boundaries. And then Claire gave him some food for thought. She'd said these things were bound to be happening to other women – worse, maybe. Men like Rory had a pattern; it was who they *were*.

Sam mulled it over for a few days, then took up the mantle: it was his duty as a man to work out exactly who else Rory had made suffer. And to find that out, he had to get his colleagues to trust him enough to reveal it. So he turned up his nice guy charm; befriended everyone; took an interest in their lives, and their feelings about work and Ashworth. And it wasn't *all* an act – whatever Claire thought in the end.

But she'd got him wrong, when she said she hadn't known him at all – when she found out about his blackmail of Rory, and said he was behaving like a different person. This was always who Sam was.

Because Sam *did* care about the women around him.

But at the end of the day, he cared about himself more.

* * *

Sam got up and used the railings to help him walk to the toilets. He waited outside the door for a beat, then gave it a gentle rap with his knuckles.

There was a pause, then: 'Who's there?'

'It's just me. Sam.'

'Go away.' The reply was immediate, and hushed. So Sam was right. While she was looking at Rory's phone, Talia must have seen Sam's emails. Clearly she'd have nothing to say to him. She probably didn't want him near her ever again.

'Talia – what's wrong? I just came to check on you.' He tried to sound like his usual self, all ease and charm.

'To check on me?' she hissed through the door. 'Why – have you got the tape running, Sam? I know what both of you've been up to – both you and my husband,' she snarled. 'And I never want anything to do with either of you again. Now, *fuck off*.'

Sam exhaled slowly, taking his time. Then: 'No,' he said softly, 'I don't think I will. I need Rory to keep giving me what I want. So *you* need to keep this to yourself.'

Talia made a noise of disgust. 'You realize, Sam, that using a recording you've obtained without consent for the purpose of blackmail – you know that's illegal, don't you? You could be arrested the second you step back onto British soil.'

'Oh, I don't think so,' he replied. Sam had leverage now, after all. He could afford to be bold; he could take a gamble. 'Best if you keep this quiet, Talia. Or I'll tell Rory what you've been doing too – right here on the yacht.'

Talia said nothing.

'Oh yeah – I expect you didn't know,' he went on. 'There's some CCTV footage that's the talk of the crew. I'll make sure Rory sees it and finds out *exactly* what you've been up to – and knowing your husband, I'd imagine you won't do well out of your divorce settlement. You might not even get to see your daughters again.'

Sam let his words hang in the air for a moment. Then he turned and strolled back to the sofa, as casually as if he'd just been chatting to Talia about the weather.

The heaviest of the clouds had thinned, but with the power still out, it was darker than it had been at this time every other day of their trip. The gloomy sky was as depressing as his thoughts.

He was almost out of options now. He'd been holding out hope of getting Talia on side, but now she knew what Sam had been doing all these months, there was no way she'd trust him again; not enough to even talk to him, let alone reveal anything useful about Rory's misdemeanours.

And although Sam knew Talia was cheating, and had threatened her with exposure, he knew his words to her had been empty – he couldn't really do anything with that information. She wanted to leave Rory now, by the sounds of it – and who could blame her? Sam couldn't use the threat of destroying her marriage as leverage. He wasn't worried by her threats of the police. He was aware of the law; he knew an arrest or a record was unlikely. But he'd lose his job. His reputation would be fucked, and he'd struggle to get a new role – he'd never get a reference from Ashworth after this.

This is a fucking shitshow.

Tomorrow was their last day. Once they anchored at Raiatea, they'd stay on the *Lusso* one final night, then pack their things and start the long journey home. The trip was almost over, and Sam had barely made any progress. He had almost nothing new to help him keep blackmailing his boss.

He glanced at Eleni across the salon. There was no use trying again with her, or with Lucy. Even after last night's drama, they had given him *nothing* the entire trip – and not for lack of trying. Clearly, the pair of them were tight-lipped about something – and Lucy's thinly veiled resentment towards Rory was growing by the day – but neither of them had breathed a word about what it was. Getting close to them was like trying to wedge himself inside a bolted, cast-iron door.

He had to face it. All three women were useless to his plans.

But perhaps he still had one last bit of influence.

Nodding to himself, he got to his feet and started towards the stairs.

It was time to talk to Rory and finish this himself.

Rory lay pathetically on a massage bed in the treatment room below deck, a large blood-soaked dressing covering the right side of his face from temple to chin. Only his left eye was visible, and Sam watched as it bulged from its socket when he stepped into the room, the rest of his face turning a violent, crimson red.

'What the *hell* do you want?' Rory hissed, attempting to sit up. 'I have nothing to say to you – especially not while I'm lying here, injured.'

'Ah, come on now, Rory. No need for that,' said Sam. 'I thought I should update you. I'm afraid the terms of our arrangement have changed.'

'Our arrangement? How dare you bring this up here?' Rory spluttered. 'I gave you what you wanted, didn't I? This has to stop, Sam. My *wife* is here. Our colleagues!'

Sam licked his lips. 'Oh, I'm aware of that. All the more reason for you to give me that promotion when we get back.

We did say we'd talk again, didn't we? You can't have forgotten that conversation.'

Sam still remembered every word. It had all coincided with such seamless timing: he'd got three more colleagues to open up about Rory's misdemeanours – a new starter in the accounts team, a girl in HR and a comms exec – back in March. Over drinks in a quiet corner of the pub, he'd used his phone, sitting innocently on his lap, to record them. He'd had to do it without telling them, which he didn't feel great about, but they'd never have agreed to be taped – and then where would he be? It'd be unprovable gossip; Sam could have been accused of making it up. That wouldn't help anyone – the women included.

Then, the day after he'd spoken to the girl in comms, he found out he'd missed out on the promotion to UK Head of Sales Operations – the role he'd been waiting for, for two years. All because of that deal with Rosenberg falling through, the morning after Sam's trust in Rory had been blown apart. After that, chances of being in the running for the bonus trip were vanishingly slim too.

He *needed* that promotion, and the trip. He'd sworn to Claire that they were done deals. He shouldn't have said that – it was premature – but he'd wanted to impress her, to give her more of a reason to stick around. This was the first relationship he'd had where it felt like she was holding more of the cards than he was. Sam knew he'd always been more into her than she was into him. Claire liked him – he knew that – but she always let him know that she'd also be okay without him. Sam didn't want to give either of them the chance to prove that was true.

And then it came together. Sam needed a promotion and a flashy bonus trip he could take his girlfriend on. Rory was the one person who could give him those things – and Rory was *also* the person Sam had been gathering career-destroying evidence on for months. It was a gift from the heavens, that's how he'd seen it.

Sam would stop his CEO from humiliating any more women – at the same time as giving his career and his relationship a boost, in one gratifying swoop. He'd booked Rory for a meeting, sat down opposite him and, without saying a word, set his phone on the desk and hit play on his voice memos. It hadn't taken long for Sam to get exactly what he wanted.

Now his boss stayed silent, shrinking back on the massage bed. 'Surely you remember it, Rory?' Sam prodded. 'You remember that you still tried to brush it off as *hearsay nonsense* even after I'd played the recordings? And that it was only when I said I'd be uploading them onto our Slack channel and sending them to my buddy at the *Mirror* that you decided to take it more seriously? You thought it was best if we kept it under wraps – remember that?'

Sam dug his phone out of his pocket and waved it in Rory's face. 'This is the email I've drafted to Mike – my journalist friend. You can see all the files are attached, can't you?' The colour drained from Rory's cheeks; he looked like he was about to throw up. Sam smiled. 'I want a leadership role,' he said. And then: 'And a fifty per cent pay rise.'

Rory dropped his head, but said nothing. *For fuck's sake.* Sam strained to keep the frustration from his voice. 'All right. I'll just go ahead and hit send then, shall I? And upload the folder to the intranet while I'm at it. Then everyone else can decide whether it was all just men being men, or – what was it you said? – *hearsay nonsense*.'

'Well, you can't do that now,' spluttered Rory. 'The power's down, there's no Wi-Fi and we're in the middle of the bloody ocean with no signal! Where's my phone – where's my *damn phone* . . .' He started patting down his pockets, fingering the sides of the bed. 'I'm sure I had it before I . . .'

'I've thought about that. If I get everything ready to upload, it'll send as soon as we get the power back up – I'm sure it'll be any minute now. Oh, and don't panic. Talia's got your phone.'

Rory looked dazed for a moment. 'Talia . . .'

'We'll be within range of Raiatea soon. I'll have a couple of bars of signal – enough to send an email, anyway.'

Rory's mouth opened, closed, then opened again. 'Like I told you then, Sam, I'm not in a position to make promotions at random – and certainly not while we're in the middle of the South Pacific! You must understand, this all has to go through the board . . .' He groaned, lifted a hand to the wound on his face. If the gesture was supposed to invoke sympathy, it failed.

Come on, come on. Sam needed this to work now – like it had back in March. After Sam had played the recordings, Rory had agreed to the trip – but not the promotion. That had gone to someone else. But Rory was the CEO. He could up his pay cheque and create a new role for Sam with a wave of his hand.

He took a step towards Rory; his boss cowered back on the bed again. Sam smiled.

'All right, Rory – you know me. I'm not an unreasonable guy,' he said. 'I'll give you some time to think about it.'

He leaned over, hovered his face right above Rory's, the tips of their noses almost brushing.

'I'll give you an hour.'

LUCY

Lucy leaned into the pressure of Mark's hands on the small of her back as he led her into their cabin and towards the bed. It was dark below the deck – not pitch black, but gloomy without the sun's usual brightness through the floor-to-ceiling windows – so Mark used the torch on his phone to help them through the room.

'Ugh. I feel gross,' she groaned, leaning back onto the plush pillows of their bed, wincing at the brightness as Mark's phone flickered across her face. 'This seasickness is so bloody annoying. Now would have been the perfect time to—' *To try to get into Rory's cabin again.*

Mark seemed to read her thoughts; he shook his head. 'Luce . . . you've tried everything. Don't you think it's time to let this go?'

This was exactly why I didn't want to tell you. She wriggled around to face him. 'No, Mark, it's the worst possible moment to let it go. Now, when I'm so close – physically close – his room's right there. And after what he did!'

'I know,' said Mark, closing his eyes briefly. He looked pained.

Seeing the sadness in his expression, Lucy's own grief and hurt and the *injustice* of it all came alive again in her body. She didn't know how to bear it. She didn't know how she *had* borne it, all these months, being in the same building as that man.

Mark ran his fingers down her cheek. 'He's a bastard. I understand why you hate him. Truly, I do.'

But you still want me to drop it. 'We can't let him get away with it,' she tried. 'Not after everything I've done – all the effort I've put in.'

Lucy's eyes filled with tears. It had nearly destroyed her, making a career at Ashworth that was built on her secret; her lies. She'd never really wanted to work there; never seen a future there. She'd engineered her way into the company, reading everything she could find about Rory online, plotting and researching how to ace the interview. It had almost killed her, working for that man for months, helping him grow his morally dubious empire.

She'd gritted her teeth, smiled and made conversation with him every day, laughed at his terrible jokes, asked after his family when he'd been responsible for tearing hers apart.

And she'd done everything she could over the past few months to showcase her work in the best possible light, to dazzle him with her cash-saving numbers, in the hope that she'd end up exactly where she was right now – on their bonus trip; in such close proximity to him for a week that there would be the chance to observe him and gather evidence in a way she couldn't do in the office. All with a greater purpose: to shine a light on the shadowy dealings she suspected, and to potentially uncover even more.

'Yeah,' said Mark, 'I don't know how you've done it, to be honest. Got the job there, kept all this inside. I wish you'd told me. You didn't have to go through all this on your own.'

Lucy felt ashamed, now, that she'd hidden it from him. She was riddled with guilt that she'd kept the details of her new job, her new employer, vague and imprecise all these months. She'd had to withdraw from him, emotionally and physically, to be able to make it work. She'd spent so many nights staying out late – wandering from cafe to cafe or bookshop to bookshop, then taking the Tube a few extra stops before coming home at midnight and going to sleep on the sofa, 'so as not to wake' him.

Then, most weekends, she slipped away to see Mum and Alfie, telling Mark it would only stress her brother out if he joined her. She'd avoided her devoted, supportive partner all this time, because she was convinced that if he found out, he'd try to stop her. Lucy was sure he'd have been too worried about her, about the impact on her mental health. She was on a high dose of fluoxetine already since Mum's injury and Alfie's sectioning, when her anxiety had spiralled to terrible, crippling heights; Mark would surely have forced her to give up on her plan.

'I was here for you all along,' Mark said. 'I could have helped.' He swallowed. 'But – I'm sorry, Lulu. I don't think there's anything else you can do. We already tried the lawsuit.' It was true – they had, not long after the residents were evicted from Willowbrook. They'd got all the victims' families together, all the ones who wanted to sue, but even with the five families who wanted to take Ashworth to court, they could barely raise half the legal fees.

'And we tried going to the press – I used all my contacts,'

Mark went on. 'Every time we spoke to a reporter, someone's editor shut it down.'

'Yes, because Rory got to them,' said Lucy. 'He must have done – either him, or his lawyers.' She puffed the air from her cheeks. 'So you get it, then – why this was my last option? It's why I wanted to get on this trip – and to tell you the truth, it's why I didn't want you coming with me.'

A flash of hurt crossed Mark's expression. 'I'm sorry,' said Lucy. 'I wanted to find some hard evidence while we were here. I didn't want you working it out and trying to stop me.' She wiped a tear off her cheek. 'Like you're doing now.'

Mark sighed and pulled her close for a hug. 'I get it, Luce. But for your own sanity, your mental health – it's time to let it go. It's not good for you, holding onto all this anger. And Rory's a dick, but he's not stupid. He'll have been covering his tracks . . .'

Lucy let out a sigh. 'I know.'

Maybe he's right.

Maybe she should face it: her plan had failed. Her idea – not even a very good one in the first place – had come to nothing. And she was suffering, the bitterness eating her insides like poison. 'Do you think I've gone completely mad with all this?'

Mark chuckled. 'Honestly – maybe a bit? But it's okay. I get it. I love you, and Alfie.'

Lucy studied him. Now that her eyes had adjusted to the gloom, and with the pale grey light reaching through the windows, she observed the sharp profile of his nose, the soft curve of his mouth, the brightness of his hazel eyes. 'I know you do,' she said.

Lucy loved Mark too. But she adored Alfie. He was her little brother, and right now, today – like every other day for the past two years – he was under section in a grimy NHS psych ward surrounded by people who didn't understand him. This very minute, he would be lonely, and confused, and afraid.

I can't give up yet.

Just because this plan had failed, it didn't mean that there wasn't another way forward – a more drastic one. A more brutal one. She thought for a moment. *I could go and find Rory now. I just need to make sure no one sees me.*

She swallowed, then coughed loudly. 'Actually, my throat is really dry – do you think you could go up to the galley and ask someone for a fresh bottle of water?'

'Yeah, course.'

He kissed her forehead then got up and left the cabin, returning a moment later with two fresh bottles. He pushed the door closed with his foot, walked to the bed and handed her one. 'Here you go.'

Lucy unscrewed the top and took a sip, then: 'Anyone else about?' she asked, as casually as she could.

'I saw Sam in the passageway when I was coming back down. He was heading upstairs. Eleni and Nick are still sitting in the salon – Eleni said Talia was in the bathroom up there. Maybe she's feeling sick . . .'

Lucy nodded. *Rory's alone. With the power out, there's no CCTV. No one will see where I'm going.*

Now's my chance.

Lucy nodded, twisting her hands in her lap. 'You know, now that no one's around, I think I might go and read in the sky lounge for a bit. It'll be a bit brighter up there, won't it?'

Mark smiled. 'That sounds good. I'll come with you.'

She reached for his hand, squeezed it. She was grateful for him, for all his support. *He's one of the good ones – the best.* But still, for this she needed to be alone. 'I'm so happy things are okay between us, and everything's out in the open. I'll never shut you out again, I promise. I just . . . I think I need a bit of space, on my own, to clear my head.'

He shrugged. 'Fair enough. Just keep your phone with you – the corridor and salon are well lit, but I dunno about outside . . .'

He believed her.

And Lucy's poor, bruised heart squeezed again with guilt that she'd told him yet another lie.

GENDARMERIE MARITIME DE POLYNÉSIE FRANÇAISE

CASE NUMBER: 247849

POLICE EXHIBIT NINE

Excerpt from log of Captain Sophie Taylor, 10/06/26

16:13: Severe squall encountered during passage from Huahine to Raiatea. Winds recorded at 50–55 knots with heavy rain and low visibility. All guests instructed to remain in salon.

16:25: Main generator failed following seawater ingress to engine room. Vessel without power and lighting until First Officer can initiate back-up generator; deck crew to undertake engine room pumping. I will attend engine room at earliest opportunity to assist. External communications, wireless internet and CCTV network also temporarily unavailable.

16:34: Primary guest sustained laceration to left cheek after slipping near the bridge; he left his seat against crew advice. No loss of consciousness. Wound cleaned and dressed.

16:47: Weather conditions improving. All guests accounted for, but crew report general atmosphere on board as tense and defensive. All are on high alert for potential escalation.

While confined to the bridge, I must rely on my crew to be my eyes everywhere else on board.

ELENI

They were through the worst of the squall, but Eleni still felt sick to her stomach. She had the sense that danger – real, life-threatening danger – was lurking on the horizon. Partly, it was what still needed to happen before she went home. The stakes were high, and she was almost out of time. She wouldn't fail. She *couldn't*.

But she'd also been too knocked off balance by the squall to confront the person she suspected had planted the camera in her cabin yet. And seeing Lucy so upset as she spoke about Rory and her brother – with Talia in apparent shock while she scanned Rory's phone – Eleni's mind had been reeling the whole time she'd been confined to this bloody sofa.

Light footsteps came up the staircase from below deck; a few seconds later, Sam emerged. Without even looking at them, he darted straight past and to the next staircase up, towards the upper deck.

Next to her, Nick stretched and gave an exaggerated yawn. 'All this rocking and rolling has knackered me out,' he said, offering Eleni one of his lopsided smiles. Her heart flip-flopped in her chest. 'I think I might go and have a lie-down.'

Now's my chance. 'That sounds good. I'll pop in on Rory, then come and find you, if you like?'

'Ah, you know what – why don't you stay above deck for a bit? I just want to crash out for a while.'

Eleni twisted her hands together in her lap. 'I'll see you later, then. Be careful as you go – it's still a bit bumpy.' She tried to keep the tremble from her voice – he made no sign of having heard it. With a quick kiss to the top of her head, he stood and made his way down the stairs.

Just then, Talia emerged from the bathroom and started walking to the stairs below deck, making a concerted effort not to meet Eleni's eyes. Eleni jumped to her feet and called out to her.

'Talia – are you all right? You were in there for ages – what's the matter?'

Talia stopped at the top of the stairs, but said nothing.

'I can see you're upset,' Eleni went on softly. 'Do you want to talk?'

Eleni didn't feel close to Talia – she barely knew her, and she was hardly the type of person Eleni would usually be friends with. But she didn't like seeing anyone this upset. And – less selflessly – she *really* wanted to know what had made her so distressed.

To Eleni's relief, Talia turned, walked over to the sofa and sat down next to her. Eleni smiled at her reassuringly. 'It's okay,' she said. 'Whatever this is – whatever's happened, Talia, you can tell me. We can keep it just between us, if you like.'

Talia sniffed, her eyes welling up. 'Thank you,' she said.

'Yes, I'd prefer it if you didn't tell anyone else for now. Just until I work out what on earth I'm supposed to *do*.' Her voice caught on her last words, and she dissolved again into floods of tears.

Eleni patted Talia's arm, then reached into her beach bag and pulled out a small pack of tissues. There were bloody Paw Patrol stickers all over it. *Never off Mum duty* . . . She dug one out and handed it to Talia. But the gesture only seemed to upset her more; Talia unfolded the tissue, covered her eyes and nose with it, and sobbed.

'It's Sam,' she said eventually, through shaking breaths. 'He's been blackmailing Rory – and Rory's been giving into it – it's why he got a place on this trip. Sam had all these recordings, and – oh God, Eleni – it's just so awful . . .'

Sam's been blackmailing Rory? Eleni gaped at her. 'So that's what he's been doing all week,' she breathed. It made sense: she'd suspected it was him installing the hidden camera, but now she was sure of it. *And he's been trying to get close to me and Lucy; maybe he was trying to get something out of us to blackmail Rory with. That sneaky, conniving, son-of-a* . . . 'I *knew* there was something. But what was he blackmailing Rory *with* – what does he have on him?'

Talia hesitated. 'I – I don't know if I should say . . . but it's something to do with other women. Some of your colleagues at Ashworth. Some . . . inappropriateness.'

'Right,' Eleni said. This revelation wasn't a huge surprise: she'd seen glimpses of it over the years. Like in the meeting a few weeks ago, when he'd said something about Eleni making his company look so good. And then his gaze had moved – lowered – to the curve of her breasts, then back to her eyes – so quickly she couldn't be sure if it had really happened. Eleni had moved an arm instinctively across her chest, even as she was shaking the thought away. She'd told herself she'd imagined it – but of course she hadn't.

Why do we women always do that? The self-gaslighting; the waving away of micro-aggressions. Maybe it came from childhood – the messages girls get about being good and nice and compliant, and *not making a fuss*. Even Eleni's parents – wonderful as they were – expected Eleni to be the one to make peace when she and her brother argued. It didn't matter who'd started it; it was Eleni's job to apologize – and she did, no matter how much it grated on her. No wonder she grew up unsure how to trust her own instincts.

'Don't worry – you don't need to tell me the details. Whatever Rory's done – however bad it is – Sam can't keep getting away with this.' Then all the fury inside her settled into stony resolve. 'Talia, we have to take him down.'

Eleni found Sam alone in the sky lounge. She needed to make this quick: she *had* to go and find Rory, she knew that. In a little over fourteen hours, they'd be leaving the yacht.

But she needed to do this first.

'How're you holding up there, Eleni?' Sam asked as she entered. His tone was as pleasant as always. As if he hadn't been gathering evidence from women at work and using it to blackmail their boss. As if he hadn't put a fucking spy-cam in her cabin to watch her and her husband.

She took the seat opposite him. 'I know what you're doing, Sam. I know what you've *been* doing this whole time.'

Sam laughed. 'What, you mean, sitting here in the dark

trying not to shit myself? I thought I was doing a half-decent job of looking calm and collected.'

Eleni shook her head. 'Nope. That's not what I mean. I mean, what you've been doing since we got on the *Lusso*. And what you were doing for months at work before that.'

There was a long silence. In the greyish light, Sam's body shifted in his seat.

He's uncomfortable. He knows I'm onto him.

'You've lost me now, I'm afraid. Ha.' That uneasy laugh again. 'What am I missing? What is it I've been . . . *doing this whole time*?' His fingers made quote marks in the air. Was he mocking her? After he'd spent the trip – and probably longer than that – spying on her, collecting information? Gathering stories for his own fucked-up agenda? *How fucking dare he?*

Eleni took a steadying breath. She should get a handle on her frustration; it wouldn't serve her to rant and rage before he'd even admitted to anything. Better to go in gently – give him enough rope to hang himself with. She'd change tack; she could use her negotiating skills to get him to open up. What was it she'd learned on that training course recently? *Start with empathy, move to assertion.*

'Okay. Maybe I'm wrong,' she said carefully. 'But I've noticed that you seem very . . . *interested* in the women here. And at work, back in the office. What we're thinking, how we're feeling, whether we're worried about anything. Stuff like that. You're concerned about everyone's wellbeing, I suppose?'

'Well, yeah. Of course I'm interested. But not like . . . not in a weird way. Just, you know, I see you and Lucy every day, and I care about you, both of you. The same as I care about loads of the people I work with – we spend more time with each other than our own bloody *families*, don't we?'

Eleni felt a stab of guilt. It was true: she did spend more time with people at Ashworth – men like Sam and Rory – than with her own family. Her own *children*. She didn't want that to be true, but it was. *Come on – focus*. 'If you care about your colleagues so much, then that's a really nice thing. Of course it is. And people trust you, don't they? They open up to you. I know I have this week, once or twice.'

Sam sniffed. 'I'm not sure where you're going with this. Sure they do. I'm a good listener, aren't I?'

Still pretending you're the nice guy. But he hadn't fooled his girlfriend. He hadn't fooled Talia. And he wouldn't fool Eleni. She'd known too many men like him – men who made the world believe they were decent, and kind, and good. Then behind closed doors, or computer screens in dank basements, or footage buried in hidden cameras, or intimate videos recorded without consent – they quietly controlled – no, *destroyed* the women who trusted them.

'That's enough, Sam. Just fucking stop it.' Eleni didn't have time for this. 'I know what you've been doing. To the women at work. To me, and to Lucy, and to Talia too – no, *everyone*, here on the *Lusso*. Watching your co-workers like a hawk, inviting them for drinks, encouraging them to tell you things they probably never intended to say. And then, *dragging* their stories out of them somehow – stuff they might not have wanted to share with anyone, let alone you. Did they give you consent to record them? Or was it even true – maybe you lied about having their words on tape, to get what you wanted from Rory.'

A beat of silence, and then: 'Talia told you all this, I take it?' Sam's voice was low, menacing.

'How I found out is irrelevant. But you know what, Sam? I'm sure Rory's done some revolting, stupid things. He's offended and hurt a lot of women. I'm not saying that's okay – it's not. He should step down. I hope he leaves Ashworth and never holds a position of power again. But you know what's just as bad – maybe even worse? It's recording women – spying on them – without their consent, and then using what you've found out to blackmail your CEO into getting what you want.'

There was a sharp intake of breath from Sam, then silence. 'I . . . but . . .' He gasped and floundered. 'No,' he said, finding his voice, quiet but firm. 'I'm not as bad as Rory. What I did isn't even in the same fucking league. You've got it wrong. It – it wasn't like that.'

Eleni twisted her mouth into a grim smile. 'Oh. Explain it to me, then. What have I got wrong? What *was* it like?'

'I was trying to *help*. That's all. When I heard the sort of shit Rory was saying, and how upset it was making some of the girls, well – I had to do something, didn't I?' *Oh please.* 'They weren't going to do it themselves – they were too worried about their jobs and their reputations to tell anyone – but I'm a bloke, aren't I? I've got, you know, privilege that you don't have. I had to speak up on their behalf. It was the right thing.'

He broke off as a stronger swell than they'd had since the squall had calmed lashed at the yacht's underbelly; Sam lurched forward and almost fell off the sofa. He straightened himself up. 'And listen, Rory's stopped now,' he said. 'I've not heard any new complaints for weeks, and I've been watching him since we've been here. I've not seen him try anything that bad with you or Lucy, that's got to be an improvement —'

'Okay, but none of that justifies the blackmailing part, does it?' Eleni interjected. 'Say I believed you – that you, in your bubble of *privilege*, truly thought you were doing the right thing, recording those stories on the women's behalf. How do you explain threatening to expose Rory if he didn't give you a place on this trip? How does that help anyone except *you*?' Sam stared at the floor; he said nothing.

'And it's not just Rory you've been watching while we've been here, is it?' Eleni continued. 'You've been keeping close tabs on the rest of us too.'

'Ah – well, it's like I said before, with you and Luce anyway, it's because I care . . . not because I'm trying to gather any more information. Honest. I've just been trying to look out for you – all of you – with Rory around.'

Bullshit. He's still lying.

'Sam, *come on*. You replaced my smoke detector with a fucking spy-cam. You must have done it that day when you were here on the yacht by yourself – when you skipped the forest hike after you cut your foot.' She was riling him up now, no doubt, and she didn't care. 'What did you do, *blackmail* Michaela to let you in our cabin? Threaten her with something so you could snoop around everyone's private spaces – is that why she was scared of one of the men – *you*? And what were you trying to find out about us, exactly? What was *that* ever going to get you?'

Sam stuttered in protest. 'Eleni – what the fuck are you talking about? A *spy-cam*? That wasn't me! I'd never do that – I wouldn't even know how to. Come on. You have to believe me . . .'

'Oh, enough with your lies!' she yelled. 'Who else would put it there? You're the only person here that would want to spy on me and Nick. You've made that clear enough with your eavesdropping and recording without permission.'

Sam held up his hands in defence. 'Yes, all right, like I said – I did do that – and yeah, I was using what I found out from some of our co-workers to get Rory to give me what I was owed – the trip here, putting me forward for the UK head of sales role. But seriously, even if you think I'm a prick for doing that – and I get that, really I do – please believe me when I say that I didn't put a camera in your cabin. Because, I swear on my life, I didn't. I swear on my mam's life.'

Eleni observed him closely. He looked genuine enough. But he'd lied already; he'd lied so many times, even in this conversation. He was admitting to bits of truth – but not the whole thing. Men like him were good at that. They thought that if they gave you just enough honesty, you'd believe them about everything else.

This was *classic*. She shook her head in disgust.

'I'm finished now, aren't I?' Sam sounded miserable. 'You're going to tell the others, if you haven't already, and everyone at work will know what I did. I'll have to leave Ashworth – I'll have to start again somewhere else.' He ran a hand across his brow, then Eleni watched as he got to his feet, his movements stretching long, tapering shadows onto the wall behind him.

He stood still in front of her for a moment, watching her. Memories of his – and other men's – subtle abuses of power were alive now, pounding inside Eleni's brain, reverberating against her skull. Like the beat of those fire dance drums, taking on their own hypnotic rhythm, swirling and rising with the rocking of the yacht on the waves beneath her feet.

He's watching us. *Tap tap-tap tap.* He steals our stories. *Rat-a-tat-tat-a-tat*. They're all the same. *Dum-dum-da-dum*.

Eleni felt unsteady in her seat. *Come on. I need to finish this.* She looked up at Sam.

'What happens to you is not my problem. You've made this mess yourself,' she said.

'Maybe. Unless . . .' Sam turned his head from side to side, then glanced behind him. A cold drip of fear trickled down Eleni's spine.

'Unless what?' Her voice didn't betray her anxiety.

Another pause, then: 'Unless we can find a way to keep this between us.'

Sam took one slow step towards her.

LUCY

Lucy crept further along the passageway below deck, turned the handle to the treatment room's door and stepped inside.

The room was dark; she needed the torch on her phone to see Rory. He was lying on the massage bed with his eyes closed, a thick bandage covering one side of his face. As she closed the door behind her, Rory startled and lifted the torch next to him, flashing its beam in her eyes; she shielded them.

'Lucy.' He exhaled; he seemed relieved to see her. *Was he expecting someone else?* 'Come to check on your old boss, have you? I'd love a foot rub, if you'd be so kind.'

Lucy wrinkled her nose in disgust.

'I was silly, not listening to Johanna about staying on the sofa,' he went on. 'That'll teach me to ignore the fairer sex.' Rory gave her what Lucy assumed was an attempt at a winning smile, but it withered away as he saw her expression.

'Indeed,' Lucy said. She cleared her throat. 'I'm here because – actually, I wanted to talk to you about something – a work thing,' she began.

'Mmm? That sounds ominous . . . especially on our holiday. If it's work-related, we can just pick it up back in the office next week, surely?'

Lucy gave a stiff laugh. 'Not ominous. Just . . . I'm curious, I suppose. I was thinking about Ashworth's acquisition of that care home – Willowbrook Lodge – before I joined. It must have been a couple of years ago now. Do you remember it?'

In the darkness, Lucy sensed rather than saw Rory's body stiffen: his jaw clench, his shoulders hunch.

'Goodness,' he said. 'What on earth got you thinking about that while we're in the middle of the ocean on the other side of the world? That deal was done and dusted, what – two, three years ago? It was way before your time.'

Lucy paused. She wasn't ready to reveal the whole story yet. She'd already come up with another plausible explanation. 'I read something online earlier about a psychiatric hospital being converted into luxury flats – it reminded me that I'd seen something about the acquisition of Willowbrook when I was looking into some historic accounts.'

'Really? Where's that, then? Who's doing the development, did it say?'

Damn. She should have anticipated he'd ask that. 'Gosh, I can't remember – sorry . . .'

Rory made a huffing sound. 'I'll have to see if I can find the article.'

'Anyway,' Lucy continued, 'it got me thinking about what actually happens to all the people – the patients, I mean – somewhere like that, when they're bought out.'

There it was again: the rise of Rory's shoulders; the twitch at his jawline. He didn't want to talk about this deal, or be reminded of it.

Rory sighed. 'The residents are all moved somewhere else perfectly adequate for their needs, with financial compensation to boot. That's what happened at Willowbrook, and it's what will happen in whatever this latest deal is too.'

Lucy spoke slowly. 'And you're . . . sure about that? That all those people were . . . properly taken care of?'

Rory tutted. 'For goodness' sake, Lucy. Why on earth are you bringing this up *now*? Can't this wait? I've just taken quite a bump to the face, and I've got more than enough to be dealing with already . . .'

Lucy shook her head. 'No. I'm sorry, Rory. It can't wait.'

She put the phone right in his line of vision. Muttering something under his breath, Rory squeezed his eyes shut, then opened them again. 'If you insist on me looking at this now, you'll at least have to zoom in, Lucy. I'm afraid my eyesight isn't what it used to be, and I don't have my reading glasses with me.'

Suppressing an eye-roll, Lucy pinched the screen with her fingers to enlarge the picture, then held it back out towards him. She watched as his eyes took in the person in the photo; he flicked her a confused look. 'Ah . . . who's this?'

'It's my brother. His name is Alfie. He has severe disabilities and needs lifelong care.'

Rory licked his lips, then reached to the shelf near his bed for a bottle of water. He took a sip and swallowed, his beady eyes fixed on Lucy's the entire time.

'I see,' he said slowly. 'And does this – does *Alfie* – have something to do with Willowbrook?'

Oh, well done. Slow clap for you, Rory. 'Yes. Alfie was one of the residents. After your deal saw him turfed out with nowhere to go, he became so distressed he attacked my mum and injured himself to the point of being sectioned. He's still on a psychiatric ward.'

The memory of that Thursday was forever marked on Lucy's brain. She'd been at work – she knew how bad things were and should have moved back home with Mum, but she didn't want to, couldn't face it. She'd never forgive herself for that. Alfie was so distraught that afternoon: he was smashing things in the kitchen, and Mum couldn't calm him down. She called Lucy, who'd left work straight away, but by the time she got there, it was too late. There were already three ambulances outside.

When she stepped through the door to the kitchen, it looked like a murder scene. There was blood everywhere, on the walls and the floor and the worktops. Alfie had thrown a dining chair at Mum's head with all his strength – the bleeding inside her brain was so severe that she'd never recovered. It affected her like a stroke – she needed daily care at home. And Alfie . . . Alfie had been locked up ever since.

The colour drained from Rory's face. 'Well, that's – unfortunate,' he stuttered. 'I remember the attempted lawsuits, of course. And I was very sorry to hear any families had suffered. But of course, none of it was *my* fault. I can't be responsible for the welfare of every single person who—'

'But that's exactly what you were supposed to be,' Lucy interjected. 'Responsible for making sure all the residents found suitable new placements. And you didn't do that. You did the opposite – abandoned them, forced them to leave their home in the early hours one morning, with nowhere to go – after everything you promised them.'

Rory shook his head. 'I don't think you're quite understanding the *nuance* of these sorts of deals, Lucy.' *You patronizing piece of shit.* 'I did nothing wrong. It was all by the book, and I did my absolute best to get everyone into alternative placements – but towards the end, the investor was breathing down my neck, putting a great deal of pressure on me. I tried to—'

'Oh, you *tried*, did you? I'm sure all the devastated families of vulnerable residents will be *so pleased* to hear that.'

Rory looked shamefaced; he fell silent. He watched Lucy curiously for a moment – and then abruptly, his eyes darkened. 'Tell me, Lucy. When exactly did you become aware of Ashworth's involvement in this deal?' Realization dawned on his features. 'I knew it – I knew I recognized you at your interview! I saw you one day at Willowbrook, didn't I?'

Lucy shrugged, not wanting to give Rory the satisfaction of an answer. She remembered it well enough. Two days before Alfie was forced out, she'd been at Willowbrook with Mum – packing his things, explaining to him what was going to happen, trying to prepare him. Rory had been swanning around the building with the team of architects they'd hired for the job. He'd popped his head around the door to Alfie's room, then winced when he'd seen Alfie in there, rocking backwards and forwards in distress at the sound of unfamiliar voices. Lucy had hated him at first sight.

Rory's lip curled. 'I told you, I never forget a face. I hope you didn't join the company under false pretences, Lucy – that would be a case for immediate dismissal.'

Lucy laughed bitterly. 'Do you think I give a damn about my job at your rotten, corrupt company? Go ahead – fire me. No, I tell you what, I'll make it easy for you. Here you go: I quit.'

Rory frowned. 'I see,' he said. 'I'll be sorry to see you go, but if that's what you want.' He lifted his shoulders to his ears. 'I'm not sure what you were trying to achieve, though, telling me all this.'

Lucy narrowed her eyes. 'Isn't it obvious? I want money for Alfie's care – for a suitable residential home that matches Willowbrook's facilities, covered for the rest of his life. But that's not enough. I want all of the families' care costs covered. And I want you to go on the record, publicly, and admit you messed this up and let all the residents down. I want this to be a lesson to other developers, that they can't get away with this sort of behaviour. That they have to be held responsible for the damage they cause.'

Rory laughed; a short, cruel bark. 'Dear, oh dear. Now listen here, young lady. There's not a chance in hell I'll be agreeing to any of that. Any money for this deal is long gone, and I certainly won't be risking Ashworth's reputation for you, or anyone! I've said I'm sorry. I won't allow whatever happened to your . . . your . . . violent, mentally retarded brother to affect my reputation and my business!'

A red haze of rage blurred Lucy's vision. Her beautiful, gentle baby brother – reduced to ugly, shaming words in this ugly, shameful man's mouth.

'Alfie isn't violent,' she said, her voice trembling. 'And he's not *retarded*. He's disabled – and he's ten thousand times the man you'll ever be.'

Shaking with fury, her eyes landed on a pair of scissors on the table – Johanna must have been using them earlier to cut Rory's dressing. They were only a few inches away from her.

It would be so easy.

I could cut his throat. I could wipe him off the face of the earth.

I could reduce him to nothing, just like he did Alfie . . .

She reached over and clasped her fingers around the handles.

TALIA

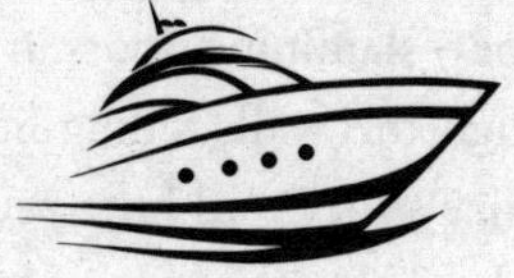

The knock at Talia's cabin door came sooner than she'd been expecting. She'd only arrived back in the master stateroom a couple of minutes ago after speaking to Eleni in the salon.

Talia met her eyes in the mirror above the dressing table as she stood and crossed the room, noting the mix of fear and determination in her own expression.

For one wild, risky moment, Talia had been about to blurt out the truth to Eleni: that she'd been cheating on Rory for the past four months, and Sam had found out about it. For a second, the pressure had felt too much; she felt she couldn't do it any more – hold it all inside, squash it down. She had to tell *someone*, and Eleni – well, she seemed kind and understanding, and she knew how it was to be married for years.

But she'd backed out the second Eleni offered her those tissues – a simple gesture, and a thoughtful one. Seeing the packet stopped her in her tracks: that blue sticker with cartoon dogs on, grey and grubby around the edges, imperfectly placed. Clearly her children had put it there. The memory booted Talia in the ribs: her girls had collected stickers like that too when they were little, whole albums of them.

My girls. She'd seen it all play out in a split second: the devastated expression on delicate, sensitive Nina's face when she learned of her mother's betrayal. Then Chloe – headstrong, stubborn, wilful Chloe – slamming doors in Talia's face, screaming profanities through the wall, telling her she'd never speak to her again. And Rory's fury and hurt pride – he'd make sure his lawyer would take Talia to town. Maybe, like Sam said, he'd even try to take their daughters away from her . . .

No. Telling Eleni – telling *anyone* – would mean bringing her hidden self in front of the harsh jury of the world, and Talia couldn't do that. And so she'd jumped, instead, on what she'd found out about Sam's blackmail. If Eleni had wondered whether Talia was hiding something else, she hadn't mentioned it.

Thank God I didn't tell her. At least now, she still had one last chance to get herself out of this mess without anyone else discovering it. 'You can do this,' she whispered to herself. 'You have to.'

Talia reached for the door, her hand shaking as she pulled it open slowly, inch by inch.

There he was – tall and solid, lips parted and eyes full of desire for her, leaning against the door frame, head cocked to one side. Heady with anticipation. Expectant.

'Nick,' she said.

Talia waited for him to speak, the man who'd been the sole focus of her thoughts, her feelings, these last few months. She couldn't bring herself to say what she needed to. But he wasn't talking, either. He was just staring at her, his pupils so large that his eyes were jet-black.

He stepped towards her, reached for her face with his hands, began to lean down to meet her lips with his, and it came rushing back, the desire, wanting it – wanting *him* – so desperately, so urgently, in that moment that she thought she might falter. *Perhaps just one last time. And then I'll end it, right after . . .*

No. 'No.' She put a hand to his chest and pushed him gently away from her. The firmness in both her voice and her gesture took them both aback. Nick jerked backwards and narrowed his eyes.

'What? Why not?' He came closer to her again. 'There's no one around – Eleni's upstairs, Rory's out of it . . . I was waiting for you to get back here, watching through the peephole in my cabin . . . we've got a few minutes to ourselves.' He reached for her again. 'Come here.'

Talia took a step back, putting more distance between their bodies – she couldn't trust her own not to respond if he stayed this close to her. But she had to hold firm, to stay strong.

'Nick, this has to stop. I can't – *we* can't do this any more.'

He frowned, gave a short bark of a laugh. 'What? Talia, you need to stop overthinking this. We're just two people with some insane chemistry enjoying each other's company. We're not doing any harm – no one's found out, have they? No one's getting hurt.'

Again, he moved towards her. Again, she stepped back.

'I mean it,' she said. 'I'm serious – I can't do it any more. And actually, someone *has* found out. I think the crew saw us, and Sam knows about us somehow – maybe he caught us that night in the salon. And we might not have hurt anyone else – yet – but this is hurting *me*!'

There was a tense pause. Talia watched Nick carefully, saw his expression darken – the desire in his eyes was gone suddenly, and replaced by something cold – something frightening.

'Hurting *you*?' When Nick finally spoke again, his voice was a low snarl, his lips pulled back into a cruel sneer. 'And how exactly did you come to that conclusion? I've given *you* – washed-up, lonely, menopausal *you* – the time of your life this year. I'm pretty sure I never heard you say a single word about how badly you were *hurting* when you were tearing my clothes off, or giving me some pretty average head.'

Talia's hand flew to her mouth; she thought she might throw up with the shock of his words. She'd never seen or heard him speak to her – speak to *anyone* – like this. What had happened to the admiring, affectionate man she'd given herself to these last months? This was someone cold; someone cruel. This was a completely different person.

'I didn't realize that's how you felt,' she said icily. Raising a trembling finger, she pointed to the door. 'But in that case, it all seems even clearer. This is finished, and you should leave now. It has all been a terrible mistake, and I'm sorry it ever started. Please – just go – back to your beautiful, lovely wife, who never deserved any of this – and let's forget it ever happened.'

As quickly as the callous version of him had appeared, it vanished again, replaced now by the Nick that Talia knew: tender, heartfelt, affectionate. 'Oh God, Talia. I shouldn't have said that – I didn't mean it. I'm so sorry.' He'd seemed to revert back to his usual self with as much ease as if he'd just slipped on a mask. Talia reeled, the switch was so fast, so unnerving. 'You just gave me a shock, that's all.' His voice was all softness again, all tenderness.

'Our time together – me and you – it's meant a lot to me. And listen, I know we always said—' He broke off for a second, his eyes damp and glistening. *Is he going to cry? Does he really feel that much for me?* 'I know we said we wouldn't get too attached – wouldn't let our feelings get involved. But I can't lie to you – I'm falling for you. I have been for a while, I think. I don't even love Eleni any more – things aren't good between us, honestly, not since last year.' He sighed heavily. 'There. I've said it. I'm in love with you, Talia. So, do you understand now why I didn't take you wanting to end things too well?'

He gave her a bashful smile; Talia looked away. 'I get it,' he continued. 'Sam finding out – that must have given you a scare. But don't worry, honestly. I can deal with him.'

She took another step backwards, then dropped down on the edge of the bed without thinking; all the fight had left her suddenly, so dizzying and confusing were Nick's abrupt changes in personality. 'Please,' she whispered. 'Please don't make this harder than it already is. I care about you, and our time together has been special to me too, but it has to end. Here – now. It's over, Nick. I'm sorry, but we're done. You can work things out with Eleni, I'm sure – you've got two young children, and she's a wonderful young woman . . .'

Her words fizzled out; Nick said nothing. He stood in front of her, staring at her for a long moment, his features shifting from sadness to anger to confusion to shock, then finally settling in the unpleasant snarl he'd showed her a moment ago.

A creeping sense of dread moved up Talia's spine, gripped

at her throat. She was alone in a cabin with this man, in the semi-darkness – this large, well-built, strong man – with the door closed and no one nearby; her husband incapacitated elsewhere. She'd been alone with Nick many times before, and she'd never been afraid of him. But how well did she know him, really? What if she'd got him wrong? If something happened here, now – if he tried to hurt her . . .

Why isn't he moving?

'You need to leave,' she tried again. Her voice emerged in a grating rasp, betraying her fear.

'I don't think so. Not until we've sorted this out.' He spoke softly, but his eyes were sharp shards of ice. 'I told you I was sorry. Didn't you hear me say that? I didn't mean what I said before. I don't want this to be over. And however scared you are, whatever you're saying now, I know you don't either.'

He took another step towards her, stood towering above her now as she sat frozen on the edge of the bed. Then, in one sleek, measured movement, he sat down next to her and pulled her towards him, gripping both sides of her face in his hands. The gesture was tender, and yet Talia's body pulsed with fear.

What will he do if I try to move away? She swallowed and stayed still.

'Do you want me to leave Eleni? Is that it?' One of Nick's hands moved lower as he spoke, down to her chin, then her neck. 'Is it seeing us together, here? Did it make you jealous? I'd do it, if that's what you want. I'd end my marriage. I don't love her.'

Talia opened her mouth and closed it again, her words forming and then sliding away out of reach. *He's bluffing. He can't be serious.*

'We could be together properly – you and me. Just say the word, and I'll tell Eleni – I'll tell her right now, and you can tell Rory. We'll say we're leaving them, and we want to be together. No need to worry about Sam then, either. We'll get it all out in the open, here on the yacht, and then we can start our new life when we get back.'

At that, Talia found her voice. '*No!*' She pulled away and jumped up to stand in front of him, a foot from where he sat on the bed. 'Oh my God, no. That's not what I want – it's never what I wanted. I want this to be over! Now, today. I don't want you to leave Eleni, I don't want anyone else to know. I want it to *stop*!'

In less time than it took for her to blink, Nick lunged up in front of her, the stone-cold expression back on his face. He grabbed her by the shoulders, pushing her back, and further back, until, with a slam that winded her and sent rockets of pain shooting from her skull down to her hips, she hit the blank space of wall between the bathroom and the cabin door.

She gave a sharp yell of pain, then fell silent as Nick's hands moved from her shoulders to her throat, and began to squeeze – now she could only make gasping, choking sounds as she fought desperately for mouthfuls of air.

'You don't get to decide when it's over,' Nick whispered. She grabbed at his hands, tried to scratch them, force them off her – but he was too strong, far stronger than her. There was a grim twist to his mouth as he gripped her throat harder and tighter, crushing the breath out of her – it was almost a smile. *He's enjoying this. He wants to see me suffer.*

There were stars in front of Talia's eyes now; the edges of her vision were turning dark and closing in. A rolling animation of images flickered through her mind like an old-fashioned movie reel, one, then the next, then the next. The soft, doughy smell of her mother's hugs; the girls' gap-tooth grins in their primary school photos; Rory's face lighting up, beaming, as she walked down the aisle on their wedding day.

And then her brain fast-forwarded, conjured visions of Rory finding her in here, dead; working out who'd killed her, and why; the girls at her funeral, sobbing . . .

From somewhere far away, a noise reached Talia's ears, her head pressed close to the wall. Vaguely, she remembered there was just a wall separating her from the passageway outside – that's where it was coming from.

Someone's coming downstairs.

Talia removed her hands from Nick's, curled them into fists and slammed them into the wall behind her – *thump*. She had no idea if it had been loud enough to attract attention, but the noise distracted him. His eyes flitted towards the door, for only a fraction of a second, but that was enough, enough for Talia to free one of her legs from the pressure of his body and use it to knee him in the groin with every ounce of force she had.

Nick groaned and loosened his grip around her throat. Talia dug her nails into the skin of his hands again and this time they loosened more – enough, finally, for her to take a deep breath. The inhale gave her a surge of strength, and she wrenched her body free of his grip, leaving him grasping at her hair – yanking out strands, making her howl – but at least he'd let go of her throat. She bolted towards the cabin door – *I've done it, I'm going to get away* – but no, *no*, he was already standing in the way, in her path – he was blocking her exit. *Where do I go?*

Without options, panicked, Talia darted instead into the

bathroom, closed the door behind her and moved her body in front of it, trying to stop him from shoving it open while she fumbled at the lock, taking in a few gasping, painful breaths.

She wasn't quick enough.

The door mustn't have closed fully – his fingers had jammed through the gap – and he was pushing now, yelling at her to '*Open the door, Talia, just fucking let me in*, *I'm sorry, I didn't mean to hurt you*', and she wasn't strong enough, she couldn't hold him back, he was going to get it open and, and . . . *oh God,* he was going to kill her now, wasn't he? She didn't believe that he was sorry – he'd hate that she'd got away once, it would only fuel his rage.

She did her best to keep her weight against the door, but he was pressing against it now, and it was too late – it was opening, and now Nick stood in the doorway, face purple with rage and indignation, watching with a snarl as Talia edged backwards, only able to put a few feet between them before her shoulders were wedged into the corner of the bathroom, and then she was trapped – there was nowhere else to go.

I'm going to die here.

Here, in the en-suite bathroom of her elegant cabin on this luxurious superyacht. All her wealth and beauty and privilege and success meant nothing at all in the face of a violent man who wasn't getting what he wanted from her.

He stood in front of her now. She closed her eyes as a rush of light-headedness washed over her, knowing she was powerless to stop him doing what he was about to do.

This is how it all ends.

GENDARMERIE MARITIME DE POLYNÉSIE FRANÇAISE

CASE NUMBER: 247849

POLICE EXHIBIT TEN

Transcript of text messages between Nick Michaelides and Talia Ashworth

08/06/2026

19:55 Nick: Meet me tonight? In the salon. Wait for me there, before you go to bed. Please?

19:58 Talia: I want to, but it's too risky. Someone might see us

19:59 Nick: Don't stress. We'll wait til everyone's gone to bed

20:03 Talia: Surely the crew could still catch us?

20:03 Nick: I doubt it. But even if they did, they'd never say anything. And they'll have seen way worse, I promise you

20:06 Talia: Maybe just for a few minutes then

20:07 Nick: I can't wait.

09/06/2026

01:13 Talia: I'm sorry we couldn't have longer . . . I kept thinking someone was going to come in

01:18 Talia: Nick?

01:21 Talia: I hope you're not too disappointed

10/06/2026

15:17 Nick: I'm going to come to you later, when the weather's cleared up. I have to see you.

16:41 Talia: OK. Come to my cabin soon. We need to talk.

[TRANSCRIPT ENDS]

ELENI

Eleni sat frozen on the sky lounge sofa. Was Sam threatening her? Was he going to try to force her to stay quiet? There was a coldness in his eyes that was painfully familiar.

With a burst of adrenaline, she leapt to her feet and ran away from him, out of the sky lounge, across the deck towards the control room, hoping to take refuge with the captain – but before she could reach the bridge, he was behind her, his feet almost scraping the back of her ankles.

'Eleni, stop – it's all right – I'm sorry, I didn't mean to scare you. I wasn't going to *hurt* you. I just wanted to see if we could come to some sort of . . . arrangement?'

She turned to him, braver now that she was within shouting distance of the captain. So *that's* what he'd meant. Of course it was; the man was utterly spineless. It was so predictable that in the end he only wanted to – Eleni didn't know what to call it, exactly – proposition her? Bribe her?

'If you keep this quiet,' he said, 'I'll put as many new acquisitions your way as I can – I'll share all my contacts with you, and when I hear about new land coming up, I'll tell you first – on the down-low. Come on – I know you're ambitious too. This can work out for both of us.'

Enraged, she rolled her eyes and stormed past him down the stairs to the salon and then towards the steps leading below deck. 'Fuck you, Sam. You're pathetic.' The *cheek* of him. She didn't need him to bring her contacts; she'd earned her place on this trip through her own hard work – she hadn't needed to blackmail anyone, unlike Sam. She was a genuine top performer – all her success was rightfully hers. Fair and square.

What a waste of precious time. This had been a pointless distraction – she had more important things to deal with.

Eleni started down the stairs towards the cabins. With no overhead lights, she had to rely on the emergency panels at the edge of each step. She clung to the railings and moved carefully. It was so dark, and so *creepy*, with these low-level lights. She lifted her phone and used its torch to guide her as she moved. It felt all wrong, this gloom. And it was so bloody *quiet*.

She took a deep breath – she had to get herself together before she went to find Rory. A thud sounded from one of the cabins when she was halfway down the stairs; she wasn't sure which room it had come from. Perhaps it was Mark and Lucy – they were back in their cabin now; they probably just dropped something.

She exhaled slowly to try to calm herself. Reaching the bottom of the stairs, she took a few steps along the passageway, but stopped abruptly at a more alarming sound – a moan or a cry, coming from somewhere close by. She lifted her torch, swung it down to the furthest edges of the corridor. There was no one else in the passageway.

Stop freaking out, Eleni. Mark and Lucy are probably just having an early evening shag. She took another deep breath. She was almost at her door now, was about to reach out with her key card, when she heard the sound again. But it wasn't coming from Mark and Lucy's cabin. It was coming from the one opposite: the master stateroom. Eleni stared at the door for a second.

Something's not right. She padded across the corridor, pressed her ear to the door and listened more closely. *What's happening in there?* This was the sound of someone crying; a set of horrible, choking sobs.

She rapped gently on the door, her legs unsteady beneath her.

'He – hello?' she stuttered. 'Talia? Is everything okay in there?'

A beat of silence, and then another awful choking sound.

Eleni tried the door handle without thinking, and to her surprise, it opened. *Of course – with the power out, the locks aren't working.* She held her phone out in front of her and followed the torch beam into the enormous, luxurious cabin. She couldn't see Talia – she couldn't see anyone, just the king-sized bed and a desk and a sofa, a suitcase neatly packed on a luggage rack in the corner furthest from her.

'Hello – Talia? Are you okay? Where are you?'

The muffled choke reached her ears again from somewhere towards the back of the room – she walked towards it, and realized the sound was coming from the en-suite bathroom.

Eleni took a deep breath and, hands trembling, swung the door wide open.

At first, looking straight ahead, she saw nothing.

And then the beam of her torch landed in the corner of the bathroom, where her husband was standing, looming above Talia, his shape casting a warped, giant shadow on the wall, his hands wrapped around Talia's neck.

Eleni stood frozen for a beat, mute and trembling. And in that instant, she pieced it all together, as a montage of memories and images flashed lightning-fast in front of her eyes. It was the story of her marriage, the story of the past decade of her life, whizzing through her brain in a split second: Nick, the handsome, sensitive police-officer-in-training making things exclusive with Eleni after only two dates. The long, wakeful nights he bared his soul to her, describing his harrowing upbringing with a violent, alcoholic father. The relentless calls to her at work when he couldn't get hold of her; the constant texts on her nights out with the girls that eventually made her give up her friendships altogether.

The first time he'd slapped her was the night of their wedding, when he said she'd embarrassed him by not laughing at the right places in his speech. Then the intermittent violence, woven between months – years, sometimes – of peace, and Eleni's desperate, futile hope that his remorse and his promises of it *never, ever happening again* would prove true.

And then the evening only last year, when he'd grabbed her by the neck, shoved her against the wall and, for the first time in her life, Eleni retaliated – and spent a night in police custody as a result.

It was the same thing, playing out again now, in real time, on this superyacht. Only this time, his violence was turned in someone else's direction.

I have to help her – now.

Eleni swiftly moved her phone behind her back before the glare of its beam alerted Nick that someone else was in the bathroom. She waited a second for her eyes to adjust to the dim light, then edged backwards and out of the bathroom as quietly as she could. On instinct, she lifted her phone again and used the torch to scan the master stateroom for something – anything – that she could use to protect Talia, to stop her husband. The wide bedside lamp, the miniature tree in its porcelain pot, the gold yacht-shaped ornament with its sharp pointed tip . . .

Its sharp pointed tip.

Without thinking, allowing the rushing blood pumping through her veins to propel her, she ran towards the desk next to the window, dropped her phone to the ground and picked up the sculpture with her free hand. It was heavier than it looked, but she could still lift it easily; she rushed back into the bathroom, and ran towards Nick.

The en-suite was gloomy, but Eleni's adrenaline seemed to have sharpened her senses and she could see – at least, well enough for what she needed to do. Talia was making awful choking, gasping sounds now, and with Nick's back to Eleni and his intent focus on what he was doing, he didn't realize she was behind him – he didn't hear her creep swiftly across the floor.

Don't let him see me, don't let him see me . . .

She walked softly closer, filling her lungs and holding in the air for fear he might hear her breathing. She'd stayed so quiet, she'd been imperceptible – but then, just as she was right behind him, the held breath in her throat caught with a soft wheeze.

Nick's shoulders froze. *Oh God, he's heard me – he knows I'm here.*

In the fraction of a second suspended in time as he began to swivel to face her, she saw it all: the woman she was before she met her husband, proud and bubbly and sparkling; then the small, scared life she'd had to carve out, existing every day in fear for herself and her children.

The impossible, awful strength it had taken her to do that was the same strength that came rushing back to her now.

Eleni lifted the sculpture upwards and plunged the sharp tip of the yacht's sail into the side of Nick's neck with all her strength.

It pierced his body near his spine, with a sickening wet sound; Eleni yanked the ornament back again and watched as her husband's hands dropped abruptly from Talia's throat, allowing the other woman to draw in ragged, gasping breaths.

Nick stumbled around to face her, dazed and stupefied, his hands clutching at his neck, blood dripping and coating his arms like thick crimson sleeves. When he saw who'd attacked him, he made a sound that was almost animal – and suddenly he was reaching towards her, flailing, grabbing for the sculpture. He grasped at Eleni's hands, tried to wrestle it from them – but Eleni held onto her weapon with every ounce of strength she had.

Nick's eyes began to roll back in his head; he was losing more blood, it was still streaming down the side of his neck, covering his shoulders and chest. He was losing strength too: Eleni could see him fading in front of her eyes.

Then he slithered noiselessly to the marble floor of the bathroom and fell still.

GENDARMERIE MARITIME DE POLYNÉSIE FRANÇAISE

CASE NUMBER: 247849

POLICE EXHIBIT ELEVEN

Arrest Summary Report obtained from Metropolitan Police Service, United Kingdom, via UK–France liaison officer

Date: 14/12/2025
Time: 23:42 hrs
Location: [address redacted], Oakwood, London N14
Officers: PC J. Andrews (7421), PC S. Patel (5563)
Incident Type: Domestic Disturbance/Common Assault (Domestic)

Officers attended the above residence following reports from neighbours of shouting and sounds of distress. On arrival, Nicholas Michaelides (37) stated he had been assaulted by his wife, Eleni Michaelides (34), during an argument. Victim displayed scratches to the face and neck and identified himself as a serving sergeant with the Metropolitan Police.

The perpetrator appeared visibly distressed but uninjured. Two children also present in the house, sleeping and unharmed. The property showed signs of disturbance but there was no significant damage. Due to the visible injuries on the male and conflicting accounts, officers had reasonable grounds to suspect an offence under Section 39 of the Criminal Justice Act 1988.

Eleni Michaelides was arrested at 00:12 hrs, 15/12/2025, cautioned, and conveyed to Edmonton Police Station custody suite for processing.

LUCY

The scissors clattered to the floor as Lucy backed out of the treatment room.

For seconds that felt suspended in time, she'd wanted to *kill* Rory – or at the very least, hurt him. She'd really thought she might: her rage and frustration . . . the *injustice* of it all was too overwhelming.

But she'd left him unharmed on the massage bed, except for the cut he already had. With the scissors in her hand, she'd stared at the bandaged wound on Rory's face – and she'd thought of Alfie, and her Mum, and all the blood on *their* faces that day.

On some telepathic level, she'd felt – no, more than that; she'd actually *known* – Alfie was telling her, in a voice she'd never heard anywhere outside of her own mind: *Don't do it, Lucy. I love you, and I need you. And you're better than this. He'll get what he deserves – and that's not violence or death at your hands.*

So she'd let the scissors fall to the floor. And as she did, she realized something else. That she didn't really want Rory dead – or even harmed, at least not physically. She wanted justice and she wanted peace, but hurting him wouldn't give her either of those things. Inflicting pain was never the answer: it would make her as bad as Rory, or even worse. *That's not who I am.*

I can't keep living like this. I need my life – my happiness – back. I can't let Rory steal it from me any longer.

Perhaps it really is time to let this go.

It was still gloomy as she headed out into the passageway below deck. *How is the power still not back up?* It must have been at least half an hour since the lights went out; she was sure Brett said the back-up generator would kick in soon. Maybe there was more damage to the engine than he'd thought.

Lucy hurried along the corridor, guided by the floor panels, keen to get back to Mark. He might have gone to the sky lounge to check on her by now – he would have realized she'd been lying. She'd tell him the truth: that she'd been to see Rory and tried to confront him. That she'd brought it all out in the open and ended up quitting her job; that her one last attempt to get justice for the people her boss had hurt had come to nothing. And that she knew now that Mark was right – it *was* time to let this go.

She reached their cabin door, pushed it open and peered inside: there was enough light in the room to see Mark sprawled on the bed, earbuds in, legs akimbo, fast asleep. She smiled at the sight and was about to go in and join him, when hushed voices caught her attention from across the corridor. Something in their tone – an urgent, anxious cadence – made her walk to the door opposite and press her ear against it.

She was right: the voices were coming from the master stateroom. She pushed against the door and it cracked open; it hadn't been closed properly. She crept into the suite and glanced around – there was no sign of anyone, but the voices were louder now, and Lucy could hear who was speaking: Eleni and Talia.

And what they were saying . . .

Lucy walked softly towards the bathroom, pausing for a second to allow her eyes to adjust to this shadowy area of the cabin, then pushed open the door to the en-suite – and stopped still in shock.

She stared at the marble floor, and saw the dark, almost black liquid – *blood*, so much blood – and the man lying in it, with some kind of ornament next to him, then clamped a hand over her mouth to dull the scream in her throat.

'Oh my God – Nick. What happened? Is he—?'

Both women started at the sound of Lucy's voice; then there was a heavy silence until Eleni said dully, 'He's dead.'

Lucy opened her mouth and closed it again, then managed: 'How did he . . . what the fuck happened? Eleni – Talia – tell me!'

There was no reply; it was difficult to see, but Lucy could hear Talia taking fast, laborious breaths. *That doesn't sound right*. Lucy switched on her phone's torch and shone it in Talia's direction – then gasped. There were reddish-purple marks criss-crossing her neck and throat.

'Talia – how did you . . . what happened?'

'Nick . . . did this to me,' said Talia.

What? 'I – I'm sorry,' Lucy stuttered, 'I don't understand.'

There was a pause, and then: 'Nick wasn't who you – everyone – thought he was,' Eleni said quietly. 'I mean, he was loving and generous and kind a lot of the time. But he could be cruel and controlling too – sometimes violent.'

No – Nick – police sergeant Nick? And Eleni – perfect, shiny Eleni – married to someone violent? I can't be hearing this.

'I thought . . . Nick . . . was going to kill me. She protected me,' croaked Talia. 'She stabbed him . . . with the statue. She . . . saved me from him – he was . . . a monster.'

Eleni's eyes flooded with tears. 'He wasn't always like that,' she whispered. 'It's hard to explain. He's the only man I've ever loved – the only man who's ever loved *me*.'

Talia shook her head. 'People who . . . love you . . . don't . . .'

Lucy could imagine what she was about to say: *People who love you don't hurt you like that*. But it wasn't that simple. This was a different situation, of course – Alfie never *meant* to hurt Lucy, to leave scratches and bruises on her arm. But still, Lucy knew how hard it was to let go of someone you loved, even if that person sometimes hurt you.

Eleni continued to sob quietly as she spoke. 'I know it's hard to understand. But by the time I saw who he really was, we were married. And he was always so horrified with himself afterwards. I kept thinking he could change – that it wasn't who he *really* was. That deep down, he was a good person; just wounded. Broken.'

She took an uneven breath. 'I know how naive that sounds. But I was able to manage him, most of the time. As long I did everything the way he liked, we got along fine – he smashed up the house a few times, and screamed at me pretty often, but I could handle that.'

Talia shook her head. 'Eleni, you shouldn't have had to handle that.'

'Oh Eleni,' Lucy managed finally, 'I'm so sorry. I had no idea – I thought you two were so . . . *perfect*. But why – why did he attack *Talia*?'

'Nick and I had been . . . we'd been involved,' Talia said. Lucy glanced at Eleni, who shrugged, her expression vacant. 'I wanted to end it, and I told him that tonight. It was as if a switch just flipped, and he—'

She moved her hands up to her throat. 'It was so fast. One second he was trying to sweet-talk me into keeping things going, the next he had me by the throat.'

A door closed somewhere nearby; Talia's expression darkened. 'Quickly – we need to work out what to say. We can't let you take the fall for this. You saved my life by coming in here and doing what you did, Eleni.'

Lucy thought for a second. 'We could go and tell the captain – and the police – the truth, all three of us. We could tell them Eleni was just trying to protect you, Talia, they'll understand. They'll let you go, Eleni – they'll have to!'

Eleni shook her head miserably. 'I don't know, Lucy. I've tried that before, and it . . . it didn't go well for me.'

Lucy frowned. 'What do you mean?'

Eleni sniffed. 'He had me arrested last year.'

Talia gave a soft gasp. 'He . . . what?'

'He tried to choke me, and I retaliated – the only time I've ever done that. I scratched his face, properly clawed him to get him off me. But our neighbours heard the screams through the wall and called the police.'

She paused. 'When they got there, Nick introduced himself

to the officers – he said he knew their sergeant. They looked at the bloody scratches on his face and listened to him explain how stressed and anxious I could get. He told them I didn't mean to hurt him, but I lashed out sometimes. I just let them put me in handcuffs and take me to the police station. They only let me off with a caution after Nick insisted they didn't press charges.'

'So he attacked you – nearly choked you to death – and you were arrested for it?' Lucy was aghast.

Eleni nodded. 'And with a police record, this won't look good for me . . . I might go to prison – I might never see my babies again . . .' She burst into heaving sobs.

Lucy frowned. 'Eleni . . . this is . . .' She ran out of words. *Come on, Lucy, think of something.*

Footsteps sounded in the corridor. 'Oh God – someone's going to hear us and come in.'

'Fuck. Please don't let it be Sam,' murmured Eleni.

They paused to listen, but the footsteps seemed to have moved away.

'I think whoever it was has gone,' Lucy said. 'But what do you mean – why would it be Sam?'

Eleni's face took on an expression of disgust. 'He's been watching us all like hawks this week, for his blackmail of Rory – he even put a camera in my cabin to spy on me.'

Lucy's jaw dropped. '*Blackmailing Rory?*' She looked at Talia.

'Oh yes,' Talia confirmed. 'Needless to say, our marriage is over.' She gestured at Eleni, who hurriedly related what Talia had found on Rory's phone.

'He's even worse than I thought,' Lucy said, shaking her head in revulsion.

'Has he . . . has he ever behaved inappropriately towards *you*, then, Lucy?' Talia asked.

'Oh, no, nothing like that,' she replied. 'I don't have time to tell you now, but in a nutshell, Ashworth destroyed my family.'

As Talia reached out a hand to Lucy in sympathy, a new voice piped up:

'Can I . . . can I help you?'

Lucy whirled around in horror to see Michaela hovering outside the bathroom door.

Shit. They hadn't noticed her come into the cabin – *what had she seen? What had she heard?*

'How long have you been there?' asked Eleni sharply.

Michaela stepped forward, took in the bloody scene on the bathroom floor and blanched. Then she exhaled. 'Long enough. I know what happened.'

Eleni got to her feet, began to approach Michaela. Lucy had no idea what she was about to do, but Michaela held a hand up to stop her, and said quickly, 'Please – I want to help, if you'll let me.'

Eleni paused. Lucy repeated: 'You want to . . .'

'I want to help you. After what I've seen this week – and after what Nick did to me . . .'

Eleni clapped a hand to her mouth. 'What did he do?'

Michaela swallowed, then glanced nervously between the three women. 'Since pretty much the first night, he was finding ways to get me alone and trying to . . . hit on me.' She looked at Eleni and mumbled, 'Sorry.'

Eleni waved her apology away. 'Go on.'

'I brushed it off at first – I'm used to it, to be honest, we get a lot of unwanted attention on charters. But then he got . . .

scary, I suppose. He got his hands on a crew key card somehow and tried to get into my cabin – thankfully Noah came down and scared him off, but he tried again later that night – I think he was drunk, and he backed out when he realized some of the other crew were nearby.'

'Jesus,' Eleni murmured.

Michaela went on, 'While he was there, he said he wasn't done with me yet. He said if I didn't give him what he wanted before the charter was over – or if I breathed a word about what he'd said and done – he'd—' Michaela's voice wobbled; she took a deep breath to steady herself. 'He said that with his police authority and his criminal contacts, he knew how to find my family back home. And that he'd find a way to make them suffer because of my stupid decisions.'

A guttural noise emerged from Eleni's throat, something between disgust and rage.

'He was trying to scare you,' she said. 'He wanted to get you under his control.' She took Michaela's hands in her own. 'I'm sorry. I'm so sorry.'

Michaela shook her head. 'No – don't say that. I understand. I saw what he was like . . . so, can I help?'

Lucy's mind raced. *Yes* – if this was all going to come together, they could use all the help they could get. *All hands on deck.*

'Okay. I think there's a way we can do this – but we need to work together, and we need to act quickly,' she said, her voice steely with determination. 'Here's what I need you to do.'

GENDARMERIE MARITIME DE POLYNÉSIE FRANÇAISE

CASE NUMBER: 247849

POLICE EXHIBIT TWELVE

Transcript of call from Maritime Rescue Coordination Centre to Chief of Police Henri Robert

10/06/2026 18:38

M Robert: This is Chief Robert.

Operator: Monsieur Robert, this is [NAME REDACTED], on the maritime distress emergency call response team.

M Robert: Go ahead, but be brief, please – we have a major incident unfolding here.

Operator: Copy that. This concerns the distress call made from the *Lusso di Mare* a few moments ago reporting a male passenger deceased on board.

M Robert: <intake of breath> Do you have information relating to the case?

Operator: Well, I'm not sure – maybe. But CROSS Papeete called into us about two hours ago reporting an injury to a male passenger on the same vessel.

M Robert: On the same . . . I see. And what were the circumstances?

Operator: This passenger fell during a patch of rough weather. They requested medical assistance.

M Robert: And this is the same yacht that just reported the deceased passenger on board? You're sure about that? And the same caller?

Operator: Correct, Chief. Same captain, same crew, same passenger list.

M Robert: Do we know if this was also the passenger – did Captain . . . ah . . . Taylor report the casualty's name to the coastguard?

Operator: Negative, sir.

M Robert: I see. Log the call as a priority notification. I want the full transcript too, please. <muttered voice> If they were already on high alert, how did they end up with someone dead?

[TRANSCRIPT ENDS]

SAM

'Oh, thank God – Sam – you're here!'

Sam couldn't make out the face behind the glare of a torch; its beam was ramming into his eyes and making him squint. But he recognized her voice straight away.

'Lucy?' he said, unable to disguise the irritation in his voice. 'What's going on?'

The squall had moved further off now. Through the fading light drifting through the sky lounge windows, Sam could just make out land on the horizon. There were only a few wisps of white cloud in the dull greyish-blue sky; the worst of the rain had stopped too, leaving only a light drizzle. They would soon approach Raiatea; it wouldn't be long until they saw the *Lusso* ease its way into the bay and drop anchor.

He'd been enjoying a last few moments of solitude on the sofa back up in the sky lounge: a much-needed beat of silence after the chaos of the squall earlier, and his unsettling conversation with Eleni. He was content biding his time alone –

waiting for the minutes to tick by until Rory's hour was up and he could return and force what he wanted out of him.

Sam felt a touch less sure of himself now Eleni had found out about the blackmail – but he was still hopeful he could work on her. Get her to see the mutual benefits of what he'd suggested – it could be career boosts all around, if she just saw sense.

'We need your help,' Lucy said, her voice trembling. 'Right now. Please, Sam – can you come with me below deck?'

Sam sighed. *What do they need me for?* 'Why? What's happened?'

Lucy moved the beam of her torch away and Sam's eyes adjusted in the dim light of the sky lounge to take in her features. Wide-eyed and breathing fast, she looked genuinely panicked.

'It's Nick,' she gasped. 'He just started going at Talia – attacking her, in her room. I can hear them in there, Sam – I think he's actually hurting her.'

Sam's jaw dropped. *What the fuck?* Nick, trying to hurt Talia? He didn't seem like the violent type. But then . . . was it that surprising, really? Nick was cheating on his wife, so clearly he wasn't a model husband. And he'd spoken to Rory so angrily last night at dinner.

In a flash, Sam remembered the shout of pain he'd heard in one of the cabins the other morning . . . his heart kicked against his ribcage. Is that what he'd heard – had it been *Nick* causing someone to yell out in pain, or fear? How could Sam have missed it? He'd been so focused on finding out what the women could tell him about Rory, he'd not bothered to think much about their own relationships – about the secrets that might be lurking there.

If only he *had* put a spy-cam in Nick and Eleni's cabin. He'd not even considered planting something in Rory's room, let alone anyone else's. But if he'd actually done it, then he'd have known what was really going on. And that could have been useful for him too.

'Sam – please,' Lucy said again. 'I can't find Mark, Rory's out of action, Eleni's too scared to help, and I'm not strong enough to fight him off on my own – if Talia's hurt, then she won't be able to defend herself.'

'What about the crew?' asked Sam. 'Shouldn't we go and get the captain, or one of the deckhands? They're strong lads, they'd be better at—'

'They're nowhere to be found!' Lucy interrupted, flailing her arms around desperately. 'I've looked everywhere. I think they must all be trying to fix the power failure in the engine room. We're running out of time . . .'

The crew – and Mark – nowhere to be found? That was weird – shoddy from the captain, right after a squall. But the urgent plea in Lucy's voice was stirring him. She clearly needed him – badly. This was a role he could step up to. Wasn't this who he'd always tried to be – wanted to be, if only his own selfish desires hadn't taken over? A protector of women; a hero; a saviour. Sam knew he'd never be able to take on a guy as built as Nick by himself – but with Lucy and maybe even Eleni to help, and if they could manage to find Mark or one of the deckhands on the way, well, they stood a fighting chance.

'All right – I'm coming,' he said. He got up from the sofa and followed Lucy's quick steps down the first staircase, then down again. She was right: it was like a ghost ship. There was no one to be seen.

As they descended, he caught a flash of colour somewhere close to Lucy's wrist – as if her hands had taken on a weird blue tinge. He shrugged it off – the strange effect of the emergency lighting was playing tricks with his mind, probably.

Just as they reached the passageway below deck and approached Rory and Talia's room, Lucy crouched to the ground for a moment near the doorway. It was an odd movement – as though she was reaching for something – but then she quickly stood again and pressed her ear to the door of the room. She was listening – and Sam did the same.

He heard nothing; the cabin was silent.

'Look, I think we can open the door ourselves – the locks are deactivated with the power out,' whispered Lucy.

As Sam turned the handle and began to ease the door open, Lucy thrust something into his other hand, something smooth and sharp. Sam ran his fingers all the way along it: a smooth, metallic surface, cool to the touch. This was a metal sculpture of some kind, with a sharp, pointed tip.

A weapon.

'Hang on – what's this – and where did it come from? Why do I need a—'

'Just take it, Sam – please. It's all I can find, and we don't know what he's capable of . . . I don't want you getting hurt. Now, go – Talia might be running out of time. We need you.'

At those words, as well as the frantic tone in Lucy's voice, Sam felt his chest expand. *They needed him*. Wasn't this proof of exactly what he'd been saying and doing all along? He was stronger than these women – than any woman. He was the one with the power now. And if he helped Eleni, no doubt he'd be able to use it later to his advantage in some way.

Clutching the metal sculpture in one hand, he pushed open the door to the cabin and stepped inside.

The room was almost completely in darkness; the curtains were closed and only a thin sliver of eerie red light from the passageway's emergency panels helped him make out the shape of the bed, the wardrobe, the door to the bathroom . . .

But there was no Nick. No Talia. There was no attack going on . . .

He turned back to the doorway, where Lucy stood, cowering slightly.

'They're not here,' Sam said. 'There's no one in the cabin.'

Lucy shook her head. 'The bathroom . . . Look, can't you see that?'

Sam peered through the doorway. Lucy was right, there *was* someone there: he could see the curve of shoulders and chest, the limbs splayed, head rolled to one side . . .

He took a deep breath. Heart pounding, he crept closer, the metal sculpture still clutched in his hand in case someone – Nick – jumped out at him in the dark.

He reached the bathroom door, stepped inside and knelt to the ground. Then he stretched out a slow, trembling hand; let out a whimper as his fingers touched the figure in front of him and came away wet and sticky . . .

This wasn't Talia.

It was Nick. And he was . . . 'What the fuck?'

The bathroom door slammed shut behind him; he turned towards it, yelled: 'Lucy – open up – I can't see properly—'

There was no reply.

Breathing heavily, Sam flailed as he tried to stand up. In his panic, he slipped on the wet, sticky marble and fell back down, dropping the sculpture to the floor.

Then with hideously uncanny timing, the lights came back

on. Sam's vision was flooded with a sight more horrifying than anything he could have imagined.

Nick, stabbed and lying in a deep pool of blood, his eyes rolled back in his head. *Dead*.

Now Sam was alone here, in the master stateroom's en-suite bathroom, next to a sharp object and a bleeding dead body.

And then, before he'd even had time to think what to do, the door burst open.

GENDARMERIE MARITIME DE POLYNÉSIE FRANÇAISE

CASE NUMBER: 247849

DATE: 11/06/2026

INTERVIEW EXCERPT FIVE

Interview subject: Michaela Stevens, chief stewardess on board *Lusso di Mare* charter

Interview conducted by Chief of Police Henri Robert

M Robert: Mademoiselle Stevens, do you have any idea whose fingerprints we were able to detect on the sculpture that was used in the murder last night?

Mlle Stevens: <sigh> I mean, I could take a guess. The suspect's, obviously. And you'd have found Talia's and Rory's, perhaps – it was in their room, so they could have touched it. You could have found mine too, or Johanna's. We might have picked it up when cleaning.

M Robert: I see. And, yes – that's what we'd have expected. But we found no trace of any fingerprints on the sculpture at all, except for Sam's. It was as though the object had been meticulously cleaned before he used it.

Mlle Stevens: <brief pause> Actually, that makes sense. We sterilize all the objects in every cabin before a new charter, using alcohol wipes. And it's completely possible that Talia and Rory never actually touched it.

M Robert: Of course. <long exhale> Can you tell me anything about your relationship with the deceased?

Mlle Stevens: I didn't have a relationship with him.

M Robert: Of course – let me put this another way. We have learned, through footage retrieved from the *Lusso* as well as your own personal text exchanges, that you had some involvement with Nick Michaelides. What was your opinion of him based on this, if you can say?

Mlle Stevens:<sighs> He wasn't . . . I suppose there's no point in lying to you. I didn't like him. He'd harassed me since the first day of the charter. He kept trying to get me alone – he even got into the crew cabins. So, yeah – it was annoying. I just did my best to avoid him, as much as I could.

M Robert: Understandably. That sounds very difficult. With all of your frustration and distress, you must have become angry – and afraid. I understand you were so upset that you didn't feel able to work one morning. That sounds more than just . . . annoying.

Mlle Stevens: Chief, I'm not sure what you're trying to say. Do you think – are you suggesting I had something to do with his death? The murderer was literally caught in the act, by all of us – we found him right next to Nick's body. I don't understand why you're even—

M Robert: Well, despite the overwhelming evidence, the suspect is repeatedly proclaiming his innocence. And even if we accept things on . . . face value, there is still the question of motive. Why would Sam want Nick dead? Is that something you can help me with?

Mlle Stevens: <pause; heavy breathing> I'm not sure I . . . why are you asking me this?

M Robert: I'm just asking questions, mademoiselle – it's my job to investigate every possibility. There are no implications – yet. But not everything in this story makes sense to me. And I'm afraid none of you are leaving here until it does.

LUCY

Lucy pulled the bathroom door closed behind her, whipped off her blue plastic gloves and bundled them into a ball that she clenched in one fist. She clung on to the door handle – any second now, Sam would start trying to get out – and inhaled until her lungs felt ready to burst.

Just then, with timing so perfect Lucy couldn't have engineered it better herself, there was a humming sound and the lights above her head flickered to life. It was so bright she closed her eyes on instinct; when she blinked them open again, she knew she had no time to lose.

In one exhausting, terror-filled scream, she yelled: 'HELP! Somebody stop Sam – please!'

On cue, Talia burst through the door of the master stateroom, an elegant silk scarf wrapped loosely at her throat, and joined Lucy in pulling at the bathroom door handle, using all her strength to keep it closed. Sam was banging on the other side of the door now, raging and screaming, yanking at his own door handle.

Eleni raced into the room from her cabin, caught Lucy's

eye and gave her a brief nod, then turned and ran along the passageway, yelling down the steps leading to the engine room: 'Michaela – Captain Taylor – we need help! Please come now!'

There was the sound of thundering footsteps, and then Mark came into the cabin, froze on the spot and stared at Lucy, wide-eyed in panic and confusion.

'Lucy? What's happened – are you okay? Why are you holding the bathroom door?'

Lucy's pulse was racing; she tried to breathe through the panic that was knotting up her stomach. *This has to work, it has to work . . .*

'It's Sam – he's in there with Nick – he had a weapon! Please, help me keep this door closed – we need to keep him trapped inside . . .'

'What?' Mark lunged forward, pushed Lucy out of the way. It looked like he was about to swing open the door, when heavy footsteps pounded along the passageway and a calm, authoritative voice rang through the dim shadows of the master stateroom.

'I'll take it from here, please. Mark, Lucy – I need you to stand back.' It was the captain, flanked by Michaela and the first officer, Brett.

Unnoticed in the chaos, Lucy stepped back towards Michaela, opened her fist and waited for the stewardess to take the scrunched-up gloves from her hand. In one smooth movement they were gone, ready for Michaela to bag along with her own pair, and the cloth she'd used to meticulously clean the sculpture with ethanol fluid, removing any trace of Eleni's prints before placing it outside the master stateroom door for Lucy to give to Sam.

Now Michaela would slip away to the galley, put something heavy in the bag to weight it down – a saucepan, a cooking utensil, *anything* – then drop it all into the waste disposal hatch that led straight down into the churning waters of the ocean.

Lucy breathed a sigh of relief – and then Captain Taylor stepped in front of her and flung open the door.

The bathroom ahead of them was a tableau of horror. Under the glare of the ceiling lights, Lucy took in the blood that spread across the floor, where Nick lay sprawled, head lolling to one side, eyes staring vacantly ahead, a puddle of crimson pooled around his neck and shoulders.

Sam was kneeling facing the door, staring up into all their faces, the sculpture next to his feet, his face a picture of shock and terror.

For a heartbeat there was only silence – and then: 'Oh my God – Nick!' Eleni burst into racking, heaving sobs. 'What have you done to him?'

She pushed her way into the bathroom, then dropped to the floor beside her husband. She reached over and touched his face, just as Brett yelled: 'Are you trained in first aid? Is he breathing? We need to start CPR—'

Brett and the captain rushed into the en-suite, elbowing Eleni to the side as they grabbed Nick's wrist to check for a pulse they wouldn't find, barking instructions at each other.

'Can we do anything to stem the bleeding?'

'Yeah, but I can't find a pulse . . . Captain – I think he's—'

'We need to at least try . . . We need to activate the radio distress signal. Get the defibrillator, quick – and Brett, radio for Kai and Noah to come up here immediately in case we need to stop anyone from leaving.'

'You mean me?' cried Sam. Lucy stood still, watching as he waved his hands in bewildered protest. 'But I just found him like this,' he said, his voice full of horror. 'Lucy told me to come in here – she closed the door – I didn't touch him. You have to believe me!'

No one was listening. Brett was now shouting into his radio for Kai and Noah to come to the master stateroom urgently. The captain was holding down a red button on hers, yelling *mayday, mayday* and a series of panicked updates to the coastguard's emergency operator. One phrase was clearly audible: 'It's too late – the passenger is deceased.'

Eleni's cries grew louder, while Talia took a step back, trembling, murmuring 'oh God' over and over again.

'She set me up!' Sam was yelling, pointing at Lucy. 'She made me come down here – just now, she came and got me from the sky lounge – she said I had to help Talia! She gave me that ornament – she put in in my hand!'

'What? No, I didn't,' Lucy piped up, her explanation ready. 'I've been with Eleni and Talia in Eleni's cabin for the past fifteen minutes at least – we were talking about Sam, and how oddly he's been behaving all week!'

'That's right,' said Talia. 'We've all been worried about Sam spying on us – and taking a very close interest in me, especially.'

'It's true,' Michaela piped up, already back from her swift trip to the galley and the waste chute. 'I went in to check on them only about five minutes ago, to see if anyone needed anything – right before I came to see how things were going in the engine room.'

Lucy exhaled in relief. *Well done, both of you.*

'And Nick wouldn't have been *attacking* anyone,' added

Eleni tearfully. 'Why would he do that? We've been so happy, especially since we've been here – we were doing so well! I loved him so much—'

'That's bullshit!' said Sam. 'He's been sleeping with Talia, here on the yacht – right under your nose, for fuck's sake.'

Eleni blinked, then looked in hurt confusion at Talia. *God, she's good*. 'Nick would never do that to me,' she sobbed. 'How dare you – how could you even *say* something like that?'

'And more to the point, why are we even *having* this conversation?' shouted Talia furiously. 'We've just walked in and found Sam shut in here with a murder weapon, next to Nick's dead body!'

'Then *why*?' spluttered Sam. 'Why would I kill him? You've got this all figured out, I see, so fucking tell me that?'

'Well, that's obvious,' spat Lucy. 'You've just admitted that you have some crazy theory that Nick and Talia were having an affair. And you've been practically *stalking* Talia – we've all seen it! The way you've been hovering around her all week, telling her she's too good for her husband. You were jealous and obsessed – plain and simple.'

'And she's not the only one you've been stalking,' added Eleni. She turned to the captain. 'He even got into my room somehow and put a hidden camera in there.'

'But I didn't!' Sam was apoplectic with rage.

'You *did*, Sam. Captain Taylor, it's in my cabin, sitting on the bedside table. I can show you, if you like.'

The captain looked up from Nick's body and gave Eleni the briefest nod.

'Sam's been creeping around you all week – the crew noticed it too.' It was Michaela, now with Johanna at her side. Kai and Noah stood in the doorway, like two bodyguards, ready to restrain Sam if he tried to make a run for it. Michaela looked at Sam. 'You're always wherever the *women* are.'

'That's so true,' murmured Johanna.

The captain put down her radio. 'The authorities have instructed me to keep Sam safely confined, away from Nick's body.' She waved the deckhands over, then turned to Sam. 'Will you come with Noah and Kai to my quarters willingly, or do we need to restrain you?'

Sam's shoulders dropped; he seemed to wilt under her gaze. *He knows there's no way out of this.* 'Fine. I'll come,' he said.

Then, watched by his audience of crew and guests, Sam was led out of the cabin and away above deck.

'I can't believe this . . . what the fuck just happened? I was only asleep for half an hour, wasn't I?' Mark was rambling, pale with shock. They'd grabbed a brief moment of refuge in their cabin; the captain had instructed everyone to wait under the awning on the main deck for the police to arrive, and any minute they'd have to join the others.

He looked at Lucy, dazed. 'Sam . . . killing Nick? I just . . . I can't get my head around it.'

Lucy took a deep breath. *I promised him: no more lies.* She wanted to be honest with him. But how would he ever understand? Mark, as good and decent as he was, was still a man. He could never truly get what it was like to suffer, as a woman, in the ways that Eleni and Talia both had at Nick's hands. *No*; she had to keep this one last secret from him.

'It's unbelievable,' she agreed. 'I'm in shock too. But it's not the only thing Sam's done this week.' She relayed everything

Eleni had told her about Sam's blackmail of their boss. 'If it gets out, Rory will never come back from it. This is the best leverage I could ever have hoped to get – and I didn't even have to get it myself. Talia's going to send all the evidence to me. And I'm going to use it to get justice for Alfie, for Mum – for all the families.'

Mark stared at her, a mixture of shock and something that looked like pride in his eyes. Then he shook his head slowly. 'I can't say I like the idea of you using something like this. But I get it – and I've got your back, with everything. Always.'

'Thank you,' Lucy breathed. She moved towards him and let him wrap his arms around her; she melted into them. *Cuddling – remember this?*

'I love you,' she said. 'I'm sorry. I should have told you everything. I shouldn't have kept all this from you. And sorry for being all . . . weird and secretive.'

'It's all right, love. Really – it's forgiven.'

A relief as warm and heavy as a weighted blanket enveloped her, and she sobbed – all the tears she'd held back every day as she got on the Tube in the morning and crunched numbers in front of a screen at Ashworth. Everything she'd done; all the ways she and Mark had suffered. Everything she'd been through to try to make things right for her family. It would all be worth it now. For the first time in more than two years, the power was in her hands.

ELENI

Eleni's heart drummed a marching beat in her chest as the gendarmerie boarded the boat just off Uturoa, Raiatea's main port.

Keep calm. They think it was Sam.

There's nothing to arouse suspicion – at least, not of me.

They were gathered under the awning – even Rory, still nursing the wound to his face, had been forced to leave the treatment room and join them. There they all sat, pale with shock and speechless, as the four uniformed officers swept across the main deck.

'Captain, please confirm the vessel is seaworthy before we proceed to the interior?' one of them barked.

'Yes, you're safe to proceed,' she replied.

He responded with a brisk nod. 'Everyone must remain here on this deck please, together and in one place, while we recover the body. Captain, can you confirm the deceased's location?'

'Yes, it's below the deck – the first cabin on the right-hand side,' she said.

'And the suspect?'

'He's locked inside my quarters next to the control room, one deck up from here – you can see the entrance to it, look.' She pointed to the bridge, then handed him her key.

The officer gave her a curt nod. 'Please be aware, everyone, that the whole vessel is being treated as a major crime scene, and we will be securing it as such. I'd ask you all not to return indoors and risk further contaminating any potential evidence. As soon as the body is recovered and the suspect has been restrained, we will escort you by tender to Raiatea – from there, you'll be required to travel to Papeete immediately to meet with our chief of police.'

With that, the officers marched through to the door to the salon.

Eleni swallowed down the lump at the back of her throat. This odd mixture of feelings was familiar somehow. She realized: *it reminds me of Dad*.

When her father had finally passed away, after months of a gruelling battle with cancer, she'd been struck by a strange sensation. A terrible, aching grief – the pain of knowing she'd lost a man she'd loved for so long – and at the same time, a deep, all-encompassing sense of being *released*. His release, yes, but hers too. She'd no longer have to suffer through the misery of his decline. She'd be free of it.

It was this same complicated blend that began to seep through her shock now. She'd loved this man; she'd married him, built a life with him; he'd given her two beautiful, perfect children. But God – *oh God* – she was so fucking glad he was dead.

'Well, this is all a dreadful shock,' murmured Rory. 'I can't quite believe it. Sam – a murderer! And your husband, the victim – and all because of Sam's bizarre infatuation with you. Eleni, I'm very sorry for your loss.' Eleni dipped her head. They'd agreed, the three women, that Rory didn't need to know the truth of Nick's character; that there was no need for him to learn about Talia's affair.

Talia sniffed. Rory reached a hand towards her; she pulled away.

'No – Rory, no. Please don't,' she said. 'I don't want you to touch me. Ever again!'

'What? You're in shock, Talia, darling. You don't mean that. You've just witnessed something horrendous – you're not thinking straight.'

'Oh, but I do mean it. Just before this happened, I saw the emails – *Sam's* emails!' Talia's voice shook with fury. 'I know all about what you've been doing to your co-workers – your *young, female* co-workers,' she hissed. 'I'll never trust you again. We are *finished*.'

Rory gaped at her for a long moment, his expression morphing from shock, to confusion, then despair – and finally, defeat. He sagged in his chair, shoulders low, head dropping downwards. 'I see,' he said softly.

He glanced at Eleni, then Lucy and Mark. 'I don't suppose there's any chance of the rest of you keeping this quiet, is there?' he murmured.

Lucy sat up straight in her chair. 'Well,' she said. 'That depends.'

Rory rubbed at his temples. 'Depends on what, Lucy?'

'I'm sure you remember the conversation we were having earlier. I still want justice for my family, and everyone who suffered after the takeover of Willowbrook. If you can make amends for that—'

'And resign from Ashworth,' Talia interrupted. 'So as not to risk any inappropriate behaviour towards women there again . . .'

Lucy picked up her thread: 'Then I think we'll all be willing to let this go. No one else needs to find out about what you've done.'

Eleni nodded in confirmation. 'Agreed,' she said.

Rory gaped at the group. 'But . . .' he spluttered. 'It's my company! I built it up from nothing. You can't just expect me to abandon it, for God's sake.' He gave an exasperated huff, then stared out to sea for a moment. 'Although – well, I suppose I could step back a little. Give up the CEO role and take another position on the board. I'd have to speak to the other executives first, of course – tell them I plan to retire and see what they're willing to offer me . . .'

'And what about Willowbrook?' asked Lucy.

He scowled at her. 'I will make sure you're properly compensated. You'll have the money you need for your brother's care, for the rest of his life. I suppose I could throw in some severance pay – perhaps your three months' notice – for you too.'

A slow smile crept across Lucy's face. 'Good,' she said. 'You're doing the right thing – finally.'

'But hang on – what about the other families?' asked Mark. 'Will you compensate them too?' Rory sighed, lifted a hand to his brow, but said nothing. 'Come on, Rory,' Mark went on. 'How much could you sell your shares in the company for? A few hundred mill? You can afford to give at least half of that away . . .'

'Half?' Rory spluttered. 'Come on, now! I mean . . . ah, Lucy – Mark – I'm sure we can come to some sort of agreement that all parties are happy with.'

'I'll send you a list of everyone who was affected by the deal,' said Lucy. 'You can give all the other families exactly what you're giving mine.'

'Fine,' Rory mumbled. 'I'll get my lawyer onto it when we get home. You have my word.'

Lucy glanced at Mark, who gave her the slightest nod. She looked back at Rory. 'Then we accept,' she said.

Rory gave a weary sigh. 'And may I have your word too?' He stared at Lucy and Mark for a moment, then shifted his gaze to Eleni. 'That knowledge of my previous . . . ah . . . indiscretions will not leave this boat?'

Eleni murmured her agreement, and Rory turned back to Talia. 'And you're sure – quite sure, darling – that there's no future for us?' His lip wobbled; his eyes were damp. *God, he really does love her, doesn't he?*

Talia looked away from him and stared out to sea. 'I'm sure,' she murmured.

Just then, the officers appeared back on deck, carrying a stretcher with Nick's corpse, wrapped in a black plastic body bag. Eleni clutched a hand to her mouth as she watched them; next to her, Talia began to cry quietly.

She closed her eyes for a moment and saw, behind her lids, the final seconds of Nick's life: the blood pouring from the artery in his neck, the terror and pain on his face. A wash of horror flooded her system. Eleni had killed him – she'd ended his life. And *Sam* was going to take the rap for it.

There was a scuffling sound from the staircase. Sam was

yelling in protest as two police officers brought him down to the main deck, in handcuffs.

'They set me up!' he was shouting. 'I didn't do it – it was the three of them – those fucking *women*!'

Oh, Sam. You messed with the wrong people. He was an idiot for thinking he could outsmart the three of them; for believing he could use them to his advantage. He'd misjudged Eleni – he'd misjudged them all.

Nick had misjudged Eleni too. He might have believed he was in control – and for a long time, he was. But the balance of power had shifted two months ago, when Eleni worked out that her husband was sleeping with Talia.

He must have thought Eleni was so stupid. That she wouldn't notice the evenings he came back, supposedly from work, smelling of sex and sweat and another woman's bedsheets. She already knew that part of his pattern of abuse was infidelity – and Talia was by no means the first.

Eleni always had to keep a close eye on Nick in her attempts to stay safe: to not trigger his anger; to not upset him or make him jealous. She was hyper-vigilant to his every word, his every mood. To protect herself and her boys, she had to see *everything* – it was the only means of control she still had left.

So of course she'd noticed the night Nick and Talia met; the way Nick devoted his attention to her at the awards night, turned all his charm in her direction. She'd even seen him type his number into Talia's phone that evening – right in front of her, for God's sake.

Nick changed his phone passcode regularly, but only ever by one digit. Once, a few years back, he'd told her an old version of it when he was drunk. It was an attempt to show his wife she could trust him – *see, you can look at my phone; just take it, read every fucking message if you want*. She'd done exactly that – but of course, he'd been sly enough to delete anything incriminating beforehand.

Ever since, she guessed his new passcodes and did a subtle check when she suspected something. For someone so desperate to stay in control, he'd become careless this time. Maybe he thought he held the cards firmly enough, or that he'd got away with it so many times before, that he was safe from suspicion. *More fool him.*

One day in April, he left his phone in the bedroom while he went for a shower. The boys were quiet in front of their tablets. Eleni grabbed the phone, only needing a couple of guesses at the passcode, then as fast as she could, she trawled through his messages. He'd muted and archived the ones from Talia, of course, and saved her under a different name – *Tom Gym Buddy*; how laughable, how clichéd – but it was obvious who they were from. The profile picture of Talia and Rory. The messages mentioning their spouses by name.

The photos . . . Though she'd known what was coming, seeing the explicit images turned Eleni's stomach. She might have hated the way he treated her, but a part of her still loved him. She'd even tried, over the years, to make things better between them in bed. She'd given in to his pressure for sex even when she was exhausted, or ill, or simply didn't want to – even here, on the yacht, when she knew what he was doing with Talia, she'd gone along with his desires last night. It was just easier that way.

With the women before Talia, he'd actually managed to convince Eleni it was her fault. But her boss's wife was a bridge too far. This was it: the final, *final* straw. No more wishing and hoping and waiting for him to change. No more believing that they could have their happily ever after. No more trusting him when he said it would *never, ever happen again*. This man didn't love her. If you loved someone, you didn't hurt them over and over. She was leaving him, and taking the boys with her. She just needed a proper plan this time.

And then there was the issue of the bonus trip. When Eleni had discovered Nick and Talia's texts, she'd wanted to back straight out of it. Knowingly giving her husband the chance to spend a week in paradise with the other woman he was fucking – with their spouses *right there* – was too much humiliation to bear.

But then she wondered: what if this was the perfect opportunity to expose them? If Rory discovered the affair while they were on the superyacht, there was no way Nick wouldn't react: he'd lose his shit. He'd get nasty. Nick would be revealed, publicly, as a cheater and an aggressive man; people would get a glimpse of who he really was. Even his friends on the force couldn't fob her off again, if someone as powerful as Rory was a character witness. Nick might even leave Eleni, or she'd come away with the support and the vindication she needed to finally leave him. Which was exactly what she wanted.

So she'd arranged for her mum and sister to help her and the boys move out, in anticipation. And she'd started planting seeds in Rory's mind, even before the trip. She'd commented on how attractive Talia was, mentioned how well she and Nick had seemed to get on at the event; asking whether Rory had, perhaps, noticed that too? And so wouldn't it be lovely for them all to get together on holiday?

Once they'd got here, she'd tried her best to bring her plans to fruition. She'd tried to find any opportunity she could to spend time together, the four of them, hoping the two lovers would slip up and expose their relationship. She'd tried to anticipate when Nick and Talia might be meeting up in secret, so she could send Rory to stumble across them.

None of that had worked; instead, the cheating couple had arranged a get-together that turned violent and deadly. Her stomach twisted with guilt; she'd never wanted Talia to get hurt. She'd tried to warn her on the first night of the trip, with that hastily scribbled note shoved in Talia's handbag. *What more could I have done?*

Eleni hadn't anticipated that Nick's violence would explode so quickly with another woman. She'd thought he only showed the worst of his cruelty to her – his wife. She'd thought abusing Eleni satisfied him, seeing as it was happening almost daily these last few months. Even here on the yacht, only yesterday morning, he'd squeezed her arm so tight when she accidentally woke him that she'd cried out in pain – the cry Sam had overheard, no doubt. She hadn't thought he'd unleash his true nature with the woman he was having an affair with. That was stupid – she saw that now. If Nick spent enough time with Talia – or any other woman – his patterns would always have emerged in exactly the same way.

Eleni watched Sam struggle off the *Lusso* and into the police tender, his hands bound behind him. Soon it would be their turn: they'd make their way back to Papeete and, no doubt, be questioned in detail about what exactly had happened, and how.

She briefly locked eyes with Lucy, then Talia. They'd been

so careful; they had their story straight. There was too much evidence against Sam for anyone but him to fully take the fall.

Eleni breathed in the fresh, salty air. Four days ago, she could never have imagined Nick would end up dead here; that she'd end up *killing* him – but in truth, this outcome was far better for her than exposing his affair. If they'd just split up, he'd always have been there, lurking, probably trying to get custody of the boys. She'd read stories of ex-partners of abusive police officers who'd spent years living under surveillance, followed by unmarked cars and spied on in their own home. She might never have been free of him – or at least, not free enough.

But now, she *was* free.

She had been granted a new life. A different life; a peaceful one.

A cycle broken.

A future of love and safety and joy – for herself and for her children.

GENDARMERIE MARITIME DE POLYNÉSIE FRANÇAISE

CASE NUMBER: 247849

DATE: 11/06/2026

INTERVIEW EXCERPT SIX

Interview subject: Captain Sophie Taylor, Captain on board *Lusso di Mare* charter

Interview conducted by Chief of Police Henri Robert

M Robert: Captain Taylor, I understand Michaela Stevens alerted you to the incident in the master stateroom while you were in the engine room attempting to start the back-up generator, is that correct?

Capt Taylor: Yes, Chief, that's correct. It was taking us some time, and it took the four of us – me, my first officer and the deck crew – to get it up and running. We were down there for close to an hour, perhaps even longer.

M Robert: I see. So your guests were left unattended for some time?

Capt Taylor: Not really, no. The stews were still there, and our chef, if they needed anything. And the power failure was the most urgent priority, after we'd come through the squall.

M Robert: I understand. As you may be aware, we're hearing conflicting accounts of what happened in the moments before Mr Michaelides' body was found. The suspect insists that he was led below deck by Lucy, and that she handed him the weapon which had already been used in the murder – that Nick was already dead. Who do you believe? What do you think happened to the victim? Give me your take on events, please, in as much detail as possible.

Capt Taylor: <long exhale> Well, I believe what I saw, and what the four passengers and my interior team have told me. That Sam got access to the master stateroom during the squall when the rooms all became unlocked. That he told Talia to leave the cabin, and after she'd left, he murdered Nick Michaelides with a nautical sculpture that he found nearby. I think Sam had become obsessed with Talia, and I believe he had quite the history of surveilling women, as part of his attempts to blackmail Rory Ashworth – including placing a camera in Eleni and Nick's cabin.

M Robert: And what evidence do you have to support this version of events?

Capt Taylor: Well, I don't have anything on tape, if that's what you mean. There's no CCTV below the deck, and all our cameras above deck were down during the power outage. So I can't give you anything concrete. But I have no reason to doubt the testimony of my crew and passengers – or what I saw myself: Sam alone in Nick's cabin, next to his body, holding the implement that was used to kill him.

M Robert: Indeed. Thank you, Captain. All of this does align, as you say, with several accounts we've heard and the evidence we've found so far. And are you quite confident that none of the female guests, or crew members, had any involvement in Nick's murder?

Capt Taylor: Absolutely confident. My guests all have quite clear alibis placing them elsewhere during the attack. As for my crew – they would have no reason to do something like this. My chief stewardess was irritated by Nick's unwanted advances, yes – but it's hardly unusual for her to receive this kind of attention from male guests. My crew acted with all their usual professionalism and care during this charter, doing everything they could to keep the guests safe at all times. None of us can be held responsible for the things people do to each other when we're not there to stop them . . .

M Robert: Thank you, Captain. I can't deny it concerns me that – as you yourself say – on the same vessel, the same day, there were two separate calls to the emergency services – one for Rory's injury, and the other a murder. However, I see that you've followed protocol, and it appears that your version of events is supported by everything else we've found out. There's no evidence to suggest that you or your crew were involved. I have no further questions for you at this time. You and your crew are all free to leave.

[TRANSCRIPT ENDS]

SOPHIE

EPILOGUE

The captain sits alone on the bridge. She is back in Papeete, and the crew have been dismissed. The police have finished their investigations, taken away what they needed as evidence. The *Lusso* is her boat again. She no longer has to play the role of captain; she can simply be herself. She can simply be *Sophie*.

She is glad this charter is over, and feels no sadness over Nick's death, though she is devastated that her guests will leave with memories of violence and lingering trauma. She doesn't want that for anyone. Especially the women who, like her, have been on the receiving end of male cruelty for far longer than the few days of this trip.

The police spent a day interviewing her and the rest of the crew. The guests were all released from custody too – all except Sam, of course. The evidence against him was far too compelling for Chief Robert to consider any alternative version of events.

Sophie has also finished sending investigators the CCTV footage from the yacht – not that they'd have found anything useful there. There are no cameras inside the crew areas or the cabins – that is, except for the fake smoke detector she planted in Nick and Eleni's ceiling on the very first night of the charter.

Sophie has an eye for abusers – she knows from first-hand experience the subtle ways they exert control. She'd been suspicious of Nick immediately and concerned for his wife. From day one, his easy charm and watchful eyes reminded Sophie far too much of her husband, Daniel. As for Nick's affair with Talia – Sophie had picked that up on camera on only the second day of the charter.

She'd seen enough of both the yacht's CCTV and her own secret footage to confirm exactly the type of man Nick was. She didn't need to see any more. Though she's glad Eleni left the camera in the cabin, albeit deactivated, and that the women blamed Sam for its presence – it would have caused Sophie untold problems if they'd traced its installation back to her. Her secrets are still safe.

More importantly, Nick's death means there is one less abusive man alive and walking the planet since this charter. The squall and subsequent blackout presented themselves at just the right moment, creating the perfect conditions for chaos below the deck.

The exact circumstances of his murder are still somewhat murky in Sophie's mind. Sam was caught, red-handed, next to Nick's body in a dark bathroom, with the weapon used to murder Nick at his feet. That makes it all seem like an open and shut case. And yet somehow, it doesn't add up. From everything Sophie observed, Eleni and Talia had far more motive to kill Nick than Sam did; and Sam had been adamant that it was the women who framed him.

And then there is her intuition that Michaela was lying to her. Sophie can't put her finger on it, but something about her insistence on the course of events and how the women couldn't possibly have been involved – well, it doesn't quite sit right.

Sophie is curious about all of that. She has a suspicion – perhaps more than that – that the female guests and her own chief stewardess were the ones who brought about Nick's demise. And that they somehow conspired to set Sam up to take the blame.

But she has no desire to investigate further. The police have concluded their interviews, Sam has been charged, and all of these women have suffered enough. If Eleni and perhaps Talia did end Nick's life, as Sophie suspects – well, then she feels only admiration for them. She is glad to watch Eleni go home and start her new future, safe and free, with her children. A fresh start, the chance to grab life with both hands again – just like Sophie herself has had.

This is the last time she will captain the *Lusso di Mare* – after everything that's happened, she no longer feels safe here. It is time to move on – to a new yacht in the Solomon Islands, perhaps, or Fiji. Witnessing Nick's cruelty has brought back too many memories for her, of her own marriage – a marriage Sophie was able to escape more than a decade ago. It's mind-blowing to Sophie how similar they all are, these cruel men. As though they've all read the same instruction manual: *How to Destroy Your Wife.*

At least Nick never made it as far as the final chapter.

Sophie checks the control centre and her quarters one last time. Satisfied that she's left nothing behind, she picks up her suitcase and walks down the superyacht's gangway to the solid ground of the marina.

With one last look back at the boat, she walks away from the harbour and towards the bustle of town.

She touches the tip of her tongue to the salty sea air that has settled on her lips, and smiles; it tastes like freedom.

ACKNOWLEDGEMENTS

Thank you Katie Allen-East: my sister and the lighthouse in my own stormy seas. Now director of a refugee charity, previously a champion for women survivors of war; forever the person who quietly champions the vulnerable. Your unwavering belief that every human being deserves safety and a better future is my inspiration and the source of my characters' courage.

Thank you to my favourite humans; my anchors; my crew: Stefani Ross-Steen, Amy Durden, Annmarie Carvalho, Bella Blissett, Tara Byrne, Janice Kate Fisher and of course my beloved John. And to the fellow authors who've been there for me through every brainstorm and every 'I can't write another book!' panic, especially Natasha Boydell, Anna Brook-Mitchell and Sara Ochs. I am forever in your debt.

Thank you to my wonderful editor, Raphaella Demetris, and to Rosa Watmough, Becky Lushey, Emelie Gerdin and Rosie Friis at Pan Macmillan for shaping this story and helping me bring it to readers. You are truly a dream team and I'm so grateful to be working with you all.

To Kate Burke, Sian Ellis-Martin, Isobel Dixon and the whole team at Blake Friedmann. Thank you from the bottom of my heart for your unwavering support!

And finally, a huge, massive thank you to the readers who read and enjoyed *The Hideaway*, and who I hope will enjoy this book just as much. You are the reason I write!

If you enjoyed *Below the Deck*, read on for an exclusive extract from Nikki Allen's pulse-pounding debut thriller, *The Hideaway* . . .

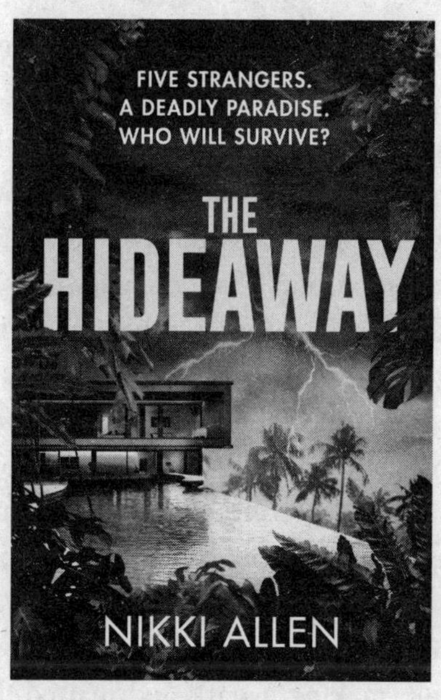

PROLOGUE

Beneath the canopy of the rainforest, the ground is alive. Leaves move seemingly of their own accord as the mammals of the tropical wilderness – spiny rats and coatis and agoutis – shuffle across the forest floor. Armies of ants march with purpose, swarms of beetles scuttle over the fallen branches and rotting vines.

Today, they are unified: they move as one, with a single mission, each organism compelled like a zombie army in the same direction. They advance towards the motionless figure lying under a hasty scattering of leaves and mulchy earth, a body so broken that it seems beyond all repair. The foliage beneath her head is gradually turning a deeper shade of crimson as the blood oozes through the back of her scalp, soaking through her hair, making it dark and matted, before it seeps into the damp earth.

Her hands unfurl from the tight fists they have been curled into, revealing a crumpled photograph inside them. A deep crease runs through its middle, and the face of the person in the picture is slightly faded, as though fingertips have caressed its outline, tracing the image over and over until the colours have begun to wear away.

The jungle's creatures are curious; greedy, now that they have found her. Their steps are careful at first. But soon they will rush in with wildness, with abandon. After that, a wake of vultures will begin to form, circling overhead. When they have waited long enough for her, when they are ready to devour her, they will swoop down, one after the other, over and over, leaving nothing but a heap of bones scoured clean by fast beaks.

Her eyes loll open, glassy, unfocused. But she is not dead; not yet – she is hanging to life by a scrawny strand.

I want to live, her desperate eyes tell the animals and vegetation around her, attempting to communicate her anguish in the silence.

Her eyelids flutter closed, open again, each movement laboured. Her breaths are shallow; they are becoming slower.

A croak emerges from her throat – a last, desperate call for help; a cry to the rainforest, to the creatures surrounding her. To anyone who happens to be out here in this wilderness with her.

But there is no one; not any more.

And even if there were, it is too late.

They can do nothing for her now.

FEBRUARY 2024

[Hannah looks to camera, smiling.]

Hello, my amazing spiritual seeking community – all ten million of you! How did that happen, right? Thank you so much for following me!

Now listen up, y'all, because the day has finally come. I am so excited to let you know that after two years of getting this incredible space ready for you, The Hideaway, my beautiful wellness lodge in the heart of the Costa Rican rainforest, will be launching in-person retreats in the next few months! Hold tight, because I'll be taking you on a virtual tour of the space in my next reel.

But first, I have some exciting news and my heart is bursting to share this with you! To celebrate The Hideaway opening up, I want to offer an exclusive group of you beautiful people the chance to come and experience the healing transformation that this luxurious eco-retreat, nestled amidst hundreds of acres of rainforest, can give you!

A select number of you will get to spend a week here at the end of April with me, healing and rejuvenating on a tailored, personalized wellness retreat – for free! You'll get to stay in my stunning ecolodge for a week, getting gorgeous pampering and bespoke treatments. I'll spend the first twenty-four hours getting to know each of you on a deep, intimate level, so that I can then create a customized programme of healing just for you, designed to give you the transformation you've been seeking. For the lucky few who win a place, all of your flights, transfers and taxis will be paid for – though be warned, this place is a little off the beaten track, so prepare yourselves for a bumpy ride!

[Hannah pauses; her expression turns sombre, and her voice becomes serious.]

Now, I want to make sure I'm offering this experience to those of you who will benefit from it the most. So, to be eligible, you must be genuinely ready for spiritual growth, to going inward, and to getting vulnerable – even if it's hard. You must be willing to take part in rituals and activities that push you beyond what feels safe.

Y'all, this is not just a relaxation retreat, but an opportunity to dive fully into what's holding you back in your life so that it can be released! That's why I can only offer this experience to such a special, limited group – because we are going DEEP and you'll be working with me one-on-one! You must be prepared to leave here completely transformed. And if you're not ready for that at this stage in your journey, then sadly this retreat is not for you.

[Hannah smiles, her tone of voice becomes upbeat again.]

All right, I'm almost out of time, I'd better wrap this up! To be in with a chance to win this amazing opportunity, DM me a three-minute video telling me all about yourself and why you want to come and experience The Hideaway with me. And open up! Share what comes into your mind and heart, talk truthfully about who you are, your struggles, and the transformation you truly desire for yourself.

I can't wait to see all your faces, and to host my first little group of y'all here!

Until then, peace and love, spiritual seekers.

[Camera fades to black.]

MIRA

'*Mierda!*'

Mira startled at the driver's exclamation as the jeep rocked wildly on the uneven track, tracing a path through gigantic trees, splashing through puddles the size of small ponds.

Is this even a road? She wound her window down and poked her head out, looked upwards, took in the lush forest that rose so high it seemed to touch the lowering sun, the tops of the trees barely visible. Above them, grey-black clouds were starting to gather and swirl – the approaching storm that she'd heard murmurings of at the airport.

Without the buffer of the window, she heard a cacophony of squawks and chirps. On her left, almost buried by the lush greenery, she caught sight of a smart wooden sign with *The Hideaway* painted in a beautiful cursive script, then a second sign underneath: *PRIVATE PROPERTY: GUESTS ONLY.*

Mira exhaled a shaky breath, tried to quell the nauseating mix of excitement and nerves that were curdling in her stomach. There had been brief moments on her journey here when she had questioned her sanity in accepting this invitation; seconds of wondering what she was doing here.

Back in London, she'd felt confident that she could handle the physical aspects of this trip – the weather, the activities. It had been true, mostly, on the health and safety form that Hannah had asked her to fill in, when she'd said she was well enough to travel; to exercise.

But already, the reality of the sweltering Costa Rican climate was a shock. Within minutes of getting off the artificially cool plane – first, the eleven-hour flight from Heathrow with the smell of *challah* still clinging to her maxi skirt, then the quick internal hop from San José to Puerto Jiménez – she was uncomfortable. Barely out of the airport terminal and she was swatting at insects keen to feast on her pale flesh. Then on the drive here, sweat from her thighs had soaked the ripped leather seat of the four-by-four taxi as it took her high into the hills of the Osa Peninsula, further from the sparkling turquoise sea lined with palm trees and white sand. A hot dampness itched at her scalp as they wove deeper into the jungle, further from the towns and beach resorts buzzing with ecotourists.

But then the doubts released her again, and her excitement returned, especially now that she was actually, finally, *here*. The same buzz of anticipation she'd felt the day she saw Hannah's video swept through her now. As soon as Mira had heard about this retreat – the way Hannah had *guaranteed that everyone who came here would leave totally transformed* – she knew it was the sign she'd been looking for. She was going, and no one – not even her husband – would stop her.

Mira drew in a breath as the taxi pulled into a clearing – a sudden reprieve from the thick canopy – and slowed as a large, open-sided wooden pavilion with a triangular, thatched roof and polished floorboards came into view a few metres ahead.

Two huge fans dangled from its ceiling, their silent blades stirring the humid air; thick wooden benches piled with fat white cushions lined the structure – and a tall, curvaceous woman in her mid-twenties stood at its centre, dressed in immaculate white trousers and tunic, and holding a platter of exotic fruit.

This wasn't Hannah. Mira recalled the numerous photos and videos she'd seen of the glowing thirty-something: long, dirty-blonde plaits, bronzed from head to toe, face full of piercings and often sitting in the lotus position. Quite different from this statuesque brunette, her dark hair pulled back in a high, smooth ponytail, a pair of bronze hoops dangling from her earlobes.

'*Gracias*.' Mira stepped out of the taxi, waited for the driver to lift her suitcase out of the boot and wheel it towards her. She took it from him, felt it sag into the soft earth. The humidity clutched at her throat, so fierce it almost knocked her petite frame to the ground. She sucked in a breath, steadied herself, and said a quiet prayer of thanks that she was here; that she wasn't at home, muted by the safety of her comfortable but stifling semi-detached house in Golders Green, the salty sting of brisket in her mouth; her mother-in-law, uninvited, at the kitchen table gossiping about the neighbours.

Mira climbed the three polished steps to the pavilion and was enveloped in a rush of enthusiastic chatter in heavily accented English. The woman smiled at her as she spoke, full lips parting to show neat white teeth in perfect rows.

'Welcome to Hannah's Hideaway. I am so happy you are here!' she said. 'I am Luisa – I am the assistant to our main housekeeper, and will be helping to make sure you have everything you need during your stay. You would like some passionfruit?' She held out the plate towards Mira. 'Or a glass of iced water, perhaps?'

Mira smiled at her warmth, her enthusiasm. 'Thank you,' she said. 'I'm Mira. And yes, I'd love both.' She put her luggage down, resisted the overwhelming urge to scratch at her scalp, then reached for the plate of green and yellow fruits. She took a glass of water from the side table next and glugged half of it down before digging her thumb into a ripe passionfruit. She devoured its soft, sweet flesh; it was delicious.

'Mira, yes, we are expecting you. Please, take a seat,' said Luisa. She gestured to the bench at the edge of the pavilion; Mira walked over and sat down. The fingers of her right hand began tapping on the wood at her side, knocking out some long-forgotten melody; her pianist's fingers now slower, but still practised. She could play almost anything she'd heard just once: it was her party trick, her one special gift.

She surveyed the empty space. *Where are the other guests – and our host?* 'Am I the first to arrive?' she said. 'And what about Hannah – I thought she'd be here to greet everyone?'

Something passed across Luisa's expression, a brief darkening of her striking features – but it was fleeting. Her beaming smile returned.

'Ah, yes,' said Luisa. 'You are here first, but the others will arrive soon. And Hannah will be here any minute – Paola will be here in a moment too. When she arrives, I will ask her, she will know everything . . .'

Paola, Paola . . . Mira recognized the name; Hannah had mentioned her in the welcome email, perhaps. *She must be Luisa's boss – the housekeeper.* She opened her mouth to check, but Luisa interrupted her before she could speak.

'Look, someone else comes now!' she said, pointing, that gleaming smile lighting up her face again. Another four-by-four taxi was lurching its way down the track, its brakes squealing softly as it came to a halt by the pavilion. A buzz of excitement grew in Mira's stomach, spread upwards to her chest. *Perhaps Hannah is in there? Am I really about to meet her?*

Or it could be one of the other guests. In her emails, Hannah had said she'd tried to arrange for them all to come in the same taxi from the airport, but it turned out they were all arriving at different times, so she'd asked them to make their own way to the retreat today.

Mira got to her feet, walked back towards the steps and shaded her eyes from the lowering sun as she watched two men climb out. The first was a thirty-ish, muscular, handsome blond in smooth linen trousers; the word *jock* sprang to mind, quite unexpectedly – though it did seem to suit. The other man was one of the tallest people she'd ever seen. He looked about her age – early forties – attractive, greying, with a warm, kind-looking face, and wearing a baseball cap, T-shirt and shorts that looked slightly too small. Watching him almost bump his head on the taxi door as he got out, she felt a rush of affection for him.

'G'day,' said the tall man, lumbering up the steps, ducking to avoid hitting his head again on the pavilion roof. 'Name's Scott. Good to meet you.' For someone so large, his voice was surprisingly gentle. Mira warmed to him a little more.

'And I'm Ben,' said the blond man in a thick southern drawl, staring at Mira. She caught him eyeing her hair with obvious curiosity before he seemed to realize his rudeness and abruptly averted his gaze. She smiled, shook his outstretched hand. 'Good to meet you.'

'So, are you Australian?' said Mira, turning to Scott, after Luisa had rushed towards the men, handing over slices of fruit and tumblers of water.

Scott nodded. 'Yeah, I'm born and bred in Melbourne,' he said. 'We're heading into winter over there soon, so this temperature's a bit of a shock. How about you? Or maybe I can take a guess from the accent – are you British?'

'Yes – I'm from London. And my name's Mira, by the way.' She paused to take him in, realized she was craning her neck just to look up at his face and, embarrassingly, standing on tiptoes – she'd not even realized she was doing it. She lowered her feet, but not before Scott noticed.

'It's OK – I get that a lot,' he said, smiling, bending down towards her a little. 'One of the hazards of being six foot six, I guess.'

'Are you really? Wow. Well, I'm five foot nothing, so we can be this retreat's little and large,' said Mira. Both men laughed; she knew it hadn't been that funny, but she appreciated the kindness. 'Did you two travel here together?' she said.

'Only from the top of the track there,' said Ben, pointing behind him. 'It was a stroke of luck – Scott was just coming down the pathway when we turned in.'

'I hiked most of the way here from Playa Blanca,' said Scott. 'I wanted to see as much of the area as I could before we start the retreat. I'm so happy to finally be here, though – I can't wait to see the place, and to meet Hannah, of course.' He was practically vibrating with excitement: bobbing up and down on the balls of his feet, eyes darting around, as he said: 'She's changed my life.'

'Yeah, Hannah's the best,' said Ben, nodding rapidly. 'I literally cannot wait to see her either.' He looked around the pavilion. 'Where is she, anyway? I thought she'd be here to meet us.'

'Hannah will be here any moment,' said Luisa. 'She is so excited to meet you too.'

'I hope she's not been caught up in the storm somewhere,' said Scott. 'The driver just said the rain has already hit the other side of the peninsula and it's causing all kinds of havoc to the traffic.' He paused to grab another thick slice of mango from the plate in Luisa's hand.

'Any more of those mangoes?' came a new voice with a Welsh lilt from behind them. Mira turned to see a tall, athletic-looking redhead in skintight leggings and a matching vest jog up the stairs, her high ponytail swishing as she moved, one side of her mouth turned upwards, teasingly. 'Hey, everyone,' she said. 'I'm Carly.' She moved around the group, shaking hands, smiling.

'Welcome!' said Luisa. 'Of course, Carly, we are so happy you are here!'

'Me too – and just in time,' she said, smiling. 'I was dying to get here before it got dark and the rain kicked in.' She raised her eyes heavenwards. 'It's starting to look pretty bleak, isn't it?'

Luisa looked up, nodded. 'I think the storm will come soon,' she said. 'I'll get Paola, and we will go to the house, OK?' But just as Luisa turned to leave, Mira heard something. A soft, swift *ding*: a text message. She rooted through the pockets of her backpack, found her phone. As she reached to swipe the screen, a series of similar *dings* echoed around the pavilion.

'Did we all just get a message at the same time?' asked Mira. 'Maybe it's . . .' She swiped at the screen, tapped the green icon, opened the text. It was a message from a number she didn't have saved, starting with the digits 506 – *is that the Costa Rican dial code?* – but next to it was a little icon with a picture of a smiling blonde woman she recognized. *Hannah.*

'Yes, it's her – did you all get one too?' The three of them nodded; Luisa turned back to the group to listen as Scott read the message out loud, Mira's eyes following the words on her own screen at the same time:

'Hey, everyone! Welcome to The Hideaway. I'm so happy you're here, but I'm sorry I'm not there right now. Earlier today, I took a boat to Golfito to pick us up some special supplies for our retreat. Now the weather has taken a turn for the worse and none of the boats will take me back! But I'll be with you just as soon as I can – the second the storm passes and these boats start up again, I'm out of here. In the meantime, enjoy a gorgeous evening of pampering at my Costa Rican home! I'll see you very soon – I can't wait! Love, Hannah.'

Scott finished reading and looked up at the group, his eyebrows drawn slightly together. Just then, Mira caught a flash of movement along the track, where a dark green jeep was jerking its way along the uneven ground. *I wonder who this is?* She peered over, tried to make out the features of the person inside before it came to a halt.

'Ah, Paola is here,' said Luisa.

She muttered something in Spanish, then jogged down the steps towards the jeep, calling, 'Paola, Paola!' She opened the driver's door, leaned over and spoke rapidly. A slight, grey-haired woman who looked to be in her late fifties, with narrow features and a pinched look to her face, wearing faded jeans and a T-shirt, stepped out of the jeep and walked towards the pavilion.

At the top of the steps, Paola offered each of them in turn a brief smile and a nod. '*Hola*, welcome to you all, our guests. I am Paola, The Hideaway's housekeeper – I look after Hannah's *casa*, and I will look after you all,' she said. 'I am sorry I was not here to greet you – I wanted to get to the store in the village for some fresh milk before the storm, but I was too late – it looks like the track will flood quickly in this rain.' She turned to Luisa, spoke in Spanish; Mira caught mention of Hannah's name, but not much else.

'Luisa has told me about your message from Hannah,' she said. 'She has taken the boat to Golfito, yes? She must have needed some extra things for our retreat – we were just with her this morning, weren't we, Luisa?' Luisa dipped her head in agreement. 'She was so excited to meet you all. I will call her now, to check what time she'll be here.'

Mira and the others watched as Paola pulled a mobile from her pocket and called Hannah on speaker for everyone to hear. But Hannah's phone was switched off; it went straight to voicemail, Hannah's chirpy Texan drawl asking the caller to leave a message.

Paola shrugged and hung up. 'OK, never mind,' she said. 'The weather sometimes affects cell service out here, and the storm is already starting further down the peninsula. She'll be back soon, I am sure.' She slipped the phone back into her pocket, looked around at the group, properly, for the first time.

Then she seemed to register something; her eyes roamed around the four of them, back and forth. They widened a touch, then narrowed. 'Wait a moment – there is a problem,' she said. 'There—'

But whatever Paola's problem was, they didn't get to hear

it: a crack of thunder erupted, so loud it was as if the sky above Mira's head was being ripped in two. Seconds later, fat droplets of rain began to plummet from the sky, lashing through the open sides of the pavilion into their faces. Mira had never been in a tropical storm before, and the mixture of heat and rain was strange. A bit like being in a warm shower, but out in the open air. She felt irrationally naked, exposed; she moved a hand quickly to her hair, held onto the top of her head. It was OK, everything was still in place.

Luisa fired some more rapid Spanish at Paola, who hesitated, looked at the group again, then glanced at the rain. She nodded, said: '*Sí, sí*. Everybody, let's get to the house – we can work this out when we get into the dry.'

Mira tugged her jacket out of her suitcase and threw it on, then lifted it onto its wheels and followed Paola and the others down the stairs of the pavilion, shielding her face with her hood.

She shivered and tried to shake off a prickle of unease. It was probably just her body reacting to the sudden rain, the violence of the storm, the darkening of the clouds. She pushed away the thought that her disquiet was because of something else. Like the expression she'd seen pass across Paola's face as she looked around the group of people gathered here.

She'd looked confused, thought Mira.

Understandably so, perhaps – it sounded like she'd not expected Hannah to take a last-minute boat trip just before the storm.

But it was more than that. She'd looked *afraid*.